Lisette lowered her arms and slid them around ~~his body~~, intending to explore his broad, muscled back, and encountered satiny feathers.

She broke the kiss, surprised, and lowered her heels to the ground. She had forgotten for a moment. . . .

"Lisette?"

She glanced up.

The need in his golden eyes turned her insides to liquid fire.

"Is it . . . is it okay to touch them?" she asked, unsure.

The beautiful wings disappeared.

"Touch *me*," he pleaded.

And any barrier that struggled to hold her back crumbled. Giving him a small smile, she nodded. Touch him? She could do that.

Lisette slid her arms around his waist and flattened her palms on his back.

She had been so distracted by his wings in the past that she hadn't noticed how ripped he was. Rising onto her toes, she brushed her lips against his. He responded hungrily as she explored his warm flesh with her fingers.

She had always appreciated strength. And Zach had it in spades. All muscle and sinew.

"You taste even better than I imagined," he murmured, sending a warm spiral of pleasure darting through her.

"So do you." And felt magnificent, too. Unable to resist, she drew her hands down and cupped his tight, leather-clad ass.

Also by Dianne Duvall

DARKNESS DAWNS

NIGHT REIGNS

PHANTOM SHADOWS

PREDATORY
(with Alexandra Ivy, Nina Bangs, and Hannah Jayne)

DARKNESS RISES

Published by Kensington Publishing Corporation

NIGHT UNBOUND

IMMORTAL GUARDIANS

Dianne Duvall

ZEBRA BOOKS
KENSINGTON PUBLISHING CORP.
http://www.kensingtonbooks.com

ZEBRA BOOKS are published by

Kensington Publishing Corp.
119 West 40th Street
New York, NY 10018

All Kensington titles, imprints and distributed lines are available at special quantity discounts for bulk purchases for sales promotion, premiums, fund raising, educational or institutional use.

Special book excerpts or customized printings can also be created to fit specific needs. For details, write or phone the office of the Kensington Special Sales Manager. Kensington Publishing Corp., 119 West 40th Street, New York, NY 10018. Attn.: Special Sales Department. Phone: 1-800-221-2647.

Zebra and the Z logo Reg. U.S. Pat. & TM Off.

First Mass-Market Paperback Printing: September 2014
ISBN-13: 978-1-4201-2980-9
ISBN-10: 1-4201-2980-5

First Electronic Edition: September 2014
eISBN-13: 978-1-4201-2981-6
eISBN-10: 1-4201-2981-3

10 9 8 7 6 5 4 3 2 1

Printed in the United States of America

For my family

Prologue

Bathed in the light of a full moon, Zach listened to the activity in the two-story house below him.

Gargoyle duty. Wasn't that what Seth had called Zach's propensity to perch upon rooftops and eavesdrop on or observe whatever happened beneath him?

He glanced around. Aside from the trees that towered over him and surrounded the house, his only companions were the shingles beneath his feet, the solar panels that reflected the moon like a tranquil pond, and an opossum trudging across the back lawn.

What the hell was he doing here? He had visited this particular house so often, he thought wryly, that his ass would soon leave a permanent imprint in the roof.

What drew him here?

The answer opened the front door and, offering her Second, or human guard, a "see you later," crossed to the motorcycle parked in the circular drive.

Lisette d'Alençon, a very rare female Immortal Guardian.

As silent as the faint breeze, Zach flexed his wings and took to the sky, seeking refuge behind one of the thick evergreens.

Lisette donned her helmet and lifted her chin to fasten the

strap. Her gaze, as it always did, went to the roof, wandering across the peak as though she expected to find something there.

Or someone.

Did she hope to find *him* there?

No. Of course not. He had only spoken to her twice. And one of those times had been when she and a couple of her fellow immortals had ambushed him, chained him up, and interrogated him.

She knew Seth, the leader of the Immortal Guardians, didn't trust him.

And yet, Zach almost convinced himself that he saw disappointment in her pretty brown eyes before she climbed onto the back of her sleek black Hayabusa and took off.

He might as well be a kite connected to her with a string. That increasingly familiar compulsion to follow her sent him sailing through the night above her.

Wings spread, Zach rode the breeze, swooping and twirling as he raced the motorcycle that ate up the asphalt below.

The slender figure guiding it nearly scraped her knee on the pavement as she leaned into a curve, taking it far too fast. Her long, midnight braid flapped and danced in the wind, bouncing off the sheathed shoto swords strapped to her back. Garbed all in black, she didn't wear her long coat tonight and, no doubt, would generate a great deal of attention if any other drivers on the road could keep up with her long enough to notice the multitude of weapons she bore.

And she knew how to use those weapons. He had seen her in action. Hunting insane vampires was a violent, bloody business. One made all the more so recently when mercenaries had gained knowledge of immortals, vampires, and the virus that infected them both.

Zach shook his head. Mankind was so predictable. Getting rich always triumphed over doing good. The mercenaries had seen the virus as a means of creating an army of supersoldiers they could hire out to the highest bidder. And their determination to understand why vampires were driven insane by the virus and immortals weren't had nearly led to Lisette's capture.

Slowing, the lovely immortal in question turned onto a private drive and stopped before a tall security gate.

Zach's gaze lingered on her long legs, outlined nicely by fitted cargo pants, as she straddled the bike and typed in the code.

When the gate swung open, she shot forward once more.

Zach swept his wings down, propelling himself forward and following her progress through the breaks in the trees that formed a canopy between them. She headed for the home of David, the second oldest Immortal Guardian on the planet. Zach had first developed his fascination with Lisette by spending time perched upon the roof of *this* house, which he often thought of as the hub of the Immortal Guardians' world here in the United States. David treated immortals, their Seconds, and the other humans who assisted them as family and welcomed any and all to visit whenever they wished to.

Any and all save Zach, who wasn't part of their world.

Completely distracted, Zach nearly crashed into a large owl. Feathers flew as the owl panicked. Talons threatened. Zach banked, reversed, dodged, and lost sight of Lisette. By the time he caught up with her, she had stowed her helmet away and was striding up the walk to David's front door.

Damn, he loved to watch her walk, loved those long, confident strides.

And damned if he didn't envy those inside who were about to share her company.

He waited until she entered, then spread his wings and gently floated down to the rooftop.

A heavy weight slammed into his middle, knocking the

breath from him, breaking several ribs, and lifting him from the roof.

North Carolina vanished, replaced by icy tundra being swept clean by a blizzard.

Zach grunted in pain as his back slammed down onto a glacial surface as hard as stone. Several bones in the wings he hadn't had time to retract broke, snapping like twigs. Ice pellets peppered him, stinging like needles and abrading skin left bare save for his usual leather pants.

Squinting against the white, he focused on the figure kneeling above him, face dark with fury, eyes glowing gold.

Seth, the eldest and most powerful Immortal Guardian in existence. The only Immortal Guardian who could match Zach, who had seen millennia, in age. Give or take a century.

Loyal leader. Fierce protector.

Seth had scorned the path Zach and the Others had chosen so long ago. He had chosen a far different path.

It wasn't until recently that Zach had begun to question which path was the right one.

"What—?"

"Did you think I wouldn't know?" Seth bellowed over the howling winds. "Did you think I wouldn't figure it out?" His large hand closed around Zach's throat and held him down.

Zach tried to teleport and couldn't. Seth must be doing something to block or hamper Zach's gifts.

"I warned you," Seth said. "I warned you I've been exercising and growing my powers while you and the Others sat on your asses. Did you think I lied?"

When Zach opened his mouth to respond, Seth lifted him and slammed him against the ice again, breaking more bones in Zach's wings.

"Just tell me why!"

"Why what?" Zach growled as agony overwhelmed him.

Lightning streaked through the sky and struck the glacier a few yards away.

He had never seen Seth so enraged.

"Don't fuck with me! Why did you restore Donald's and Nelson's memories? Why did you help them prey upon my Immortal Guardians?"

Donald and Nelson. Leaders of the mercenary group that had *twice* hunted immortals and twice been defeated in epic battles.

Seth and David had buried the two humans' memories of immortals and vampires after the first "final battle." And, once Seth and David had buried those memories, no mortal would have been able to resurrect them. Such could only have been accomplished by . . .

Zach shook his head, unable to speak past the fingers clutching his throat.

Roaring, Seth rose to his feet and waved an arm in a circle.

The wind ceased blowing. The snow it had been carrying fluttered down to the ground, settling upon Zach and decorating his eyelashes as silence engulfed them.

Shit. Seth could control the weather? None of the Others, himself included, could do that.

Zach started to rise, but found he couldn't.

Seth held Zach in place telekinetically, his power a frightening and tangible force. "Only you or an Immortal Guardian could have done it. And my immortals wouldn't betray me. Just tell me *why* you did it."

Zach shook his head. "Your problem, Seth," he gasped, "has always been . . . that you think yourself . . . invulnerable. Is it . . . so hard for you to believe . . . that one of your precious . . . Immortal Guardians might have betrayed you?"

"You deny it was you?"

"I deny nothing," Zach snarled, his own fury now matching Seth's.

"So be it."

The blizzard resumed, wind whipping Seth's long hair.

So quickly that he appeared to vanish for a moment, Seth drew a dagger and—kneeling—plunged the blade into Zach's chest an inch from his heart.

Pain shrieked through him.

Seth leaned in close and turned the blade, heightening Zach's suffering. "Listen closely, Cousin. This is but a tiny fraction of the power I wield. Betray me again, endanger my Immortal Guardian family again, and I *will* destroy you. If the Others don't like it and choose to confront me, I assure you they will meet the same fate."

He rose while Zach struggled for breath.

"Stay away from Ami. Stay away from Lisette. Stay away from *all* of us." Seth shook his head, his face full of scorn as his glowing gaze raked Zach. "What a fucking disappointment."

He vanished.

The pressure holding Zach in place fell away.

Raising a hand that shook, Zach grasped the handle of the dagger and slowly pulled it from his chest.

It fell to the ground, staining the ice red.

He tried to teleport and found he couldn't. Seth had done something to drain his powers.

Gritting his teeth, Zach sat up with a growl of agony and dragged his wings with him.

A shiver shook him.

He glanced around at the frozen landscape.

No structure or shelter in sight.

For the next several hours, until his broken wings healed enough to carry him home, Zach's only company would be the anger festering inside him.

That and the satisfaction of knowing he *wasn't* the one who had betrayed Seth.

Apparently, somewhere out there, an Immortal Guardian was plotting to take down his or her *illustrious* leader.

And Zach would watch it all with a smile.

Through the curtain of snow whipping past him, Zach caught movement.

He rose, muscles stiff with cold and strain. Gravity pulled at his broken wings, increasing the pain.

If Seth had decided to return, Zach would meet him on his feet.

He squinted against the stinging snow and ice.

A shadowy figure separated itself from the dark backdrop of night. Tall. As tall as Zach, who was only a couple of inches short of seven feet. His body bracketed by wings.

A second figure joined him. Similar height. Similar wings.

Then a third. And a fourth.

Nearly a dozen in all.

How had they—?

Shit. Seth. Of course.

After the first time Zach had strayed . . . to help Seth, the ungrateful bastard . . . and been punished, Zach had learned to hide his presence from the Others, to shield his movements and elude detection. The Others had had no idea how far he had deviated from their chosen path in recent months.

Until now. Until Seth had destroyed Zach's ability to evade their scrutiny and led them right to him.

The powerful men surrounded him.

"It appears you haven't learned your lesson," one pronounced.

Oh, but I have, Zach thought.

"We'll have to be more diligent this time in our efforts to impress upon you the importance of not deviating from the path."

He was certain they would be very diligent indeed.

Bitterness welled within him, nearly choking him in its intensity.

Little did they know their punishment, lesson, whatever

they wished to call the torture they intended for him, wasn't necessary.

Twice Zach had intervened to aid Seth and his Immortal Guardians. And all it had gotten him was a knife in the chest.

He wouldn't make the same mistake again.

If he survived what was in store for him.

Chapter One

Lisette prowled the University of North Carolina's campus in Greensboro. Though the fall semester had only recently begun, parties abounded. Freshmen, thrilled to have left the nest and escaped their parents' rule, got drunk off their asses and lured vampires like sugar lured ants. Male. Female. It didn't matter. Easy prey was easy prey. And vampires tended to be lazy that way. Even when the brain damage the virus caused in humans progressed enough to drive them insane, sheer habit—she supposed—prompted the vampires to return to college campuses.

Lisette headed toward the frat houses.

Everything else might suck, but at least she wouldn't descend into madness. *Gifted ones*—men and women like Lisette who had been born with extremely advanced DNA (the origins of which remained unknown)—were protected from the more corrosive aspects of the virus. They also possessed various and assorted gifts that humans and vampires didn't. Like the telepathy that let her hear the revolting thoughts of the vampires stalking a young couple deep in their cups.

Two vamps. Two potential human victims who had no idea

they were about to be fed upon by creatures who delighted in inflicting pain.

Immortal Guardians had recently taken an unprecedented step and begun attempting to recruit vampires who had not yet succumbed to the madness.

These guys didn't fall into that category. Bad news for them. Good news for her. She really wasn't in the mood for conversation.

Lisette raced forward so fast she blurred, little more than a breeze humans couldn't follow with their eyes. Zipping past the young couple, she barreled into the vampires like the athletes she so loved to watch in the NFL and drove them back behind the nearest building.

The vampires hit the ground hard as she released them.

Out of sight of the humans, she drew her shoto swords.

The vamps' eyes lit up like candles, glowing blue and green.

Her own, she knew, glowed a vibrant amber.

"Immortal Guardian," one vampire sneered, making the title an insult.

She saluted him with a sword as the vamps drew bowie knives longer than her damned forearm.

One good thing about vampires: Most were college students who had been turned after spending most of their leisure time lounging on their asses, gaming, texting, and surfing the Internet. Few had any real skill with weapons.

Unlike Lisette, who had trained with a master swordsman.

The vampires attacked simultaneously. Shoto swords met bowie knives, swept them aside, and struck flesh. Howls of pain pierced the night. The pungent aroma of wild fury mixed with fear suffused the air, accompanied by the metallic scent of blood.

One vampire circled around behind her.

Lisette merely turned to the side and continued to swing her swords, striking metal, metal, flesh, metal, flesh, flesh,

flesh. The more blood she drew, the more careless they became, at last allowing her to strike major arteries.

They dropped to their knees, spewing epithets and slavering like rabid dogs as they bled out faster than the virus that infected them could repair the damage. Weak and furious, they continued to cut the air with their weapons.

Lisette took a couple of steps backward and waited as they collapsed and drew their last breaths. It would've been a hard thing to watch had she not heard their twisted plans for the inebriated couple.

A moment passed.

Their bodies began to shrivel up like mummies as the virus devoured them from the inside out in a desperate bid to continue living. Dr. Melanie Lipton had told Lisette this virus behaved like no other on the planet, and the proof lay—disintegrating on the ground—before her.

She glanced around to ensure no humans loitered nearby.

"Don't do it," she counseled herself softly as a compulsion grew within her.

Yet again, the words didn't stop her.

Sighing, she looked up and searched the rooftops around her, waiting to see if a dark, winged figure would separate itself from the shadows.

It didn't.

"You knew he wouldn't be there," she muttered with disgust, and bent to retrieve the bowie knives.

"Who wouldn't?" a deep voice queried softly.

Gasping, she straightened and spun around. "You."

Just as she had imagined a thousand times, a tall figure emerged from the darkness and slowly approached her. Damned near seven feet tall, he towered over her five-foot six-inch form. Dark leather pants. No shirt. Just a leanly muscled form bereft of hair except for the raven tresses that adorned his head and fell beneath his shoulders.

Behind him spread beautiful wings that would span

twelve or fourteen feet when fully extended. Nearly translucent, the feathers that graced them were the same tan as his skin at the wings' base and darkened to black at their tips. Her fingers curled as she remembered touching them. Just once. So soft. Like the hair on a newborn baby's head.

"Zach," she breathed. The last time she had seen him he had saved her life.

Stopping several feet away, he closed his eyes for a moment. "You remember my name."

"Of course I do," she said, heart racing. "It's only been four months."

His eyes opened, so dark a brown they were nearly black. "Is that how long it's been? Four months?"

She nodded.

"Who were you looking for?" he asked.

"You," she admitted, though she knew she shouldn't.

A month ago, when curiosity and no recent sightings had driven her to ask about this intriguing, yet formidable immortal, Seth had not reacted well. Face dark with rage, he had instructed her to forget Zach and to stay away from him.

Zach tilted his head to one side. "Why?"

"I . . ." *Can't stop thinking about you.* "I wanted to apologize."

"For what?"

Was that moisture forming on his forehead? Even immortals *her* age could regulate their body's temperature without thinking about it. Though the night was unusually warm, his body should be cool.

"For what?" he asked again.

She swallowed hard, wishing now she had thought of another answer. This man possessed almost as much power as Seth. Pissing him off probably wasn't a very good idea.

He glanced to the side, as though he heard something she couldn't. "I don't have much time," he murmured, and returned his attention to her.

"I wanted to apologize because . . . I think I said something that made Seth angry at you."

His eyes flashed golden. "What?"

Thunder rumbled overhead, drawing her wary gaze. "After we fought Donald's mercenaries that last time, I asked Seth why he didn't just do what you did when you came to my rescue and kill all of our enemies with a thought instead of letting us risk our existence in battle with them." She shook her head. "The question seemed to anger him." An understatement. "But that anger seemed to be directed at . . . you."

A shadow formed on Zach's chest.

No. Not a shadow. A large bruise. Another darkened the area around one eye.

"I thought . . ."

A long gash, like that cut by a whip, streaked across his chest, parting the bruise.

What the hell?

Her gaze darted all around them, seeking but finding no assailant. "I thought," she stuttered, "that might be why I haven't seen you around." More gashes opened on his flesh as he stared at her, his handsome face expressionless. "I thought Seth might have told you to stay away." An ugly abrasion formed on his temple. Blood trailed down to the edge of his strong jaw and drip, drip, dripped onto his broad shoulder. She took a step forward. "Zach, what's happening to you?"

In what seemed like seconds, bleeding lash marks striped his arms, shoulders, chest, and abdomen. His jaw clenched as, beneath her horrified gaze, bones in his wings began to break.

Swearing, she raced to his side, swords raised to combat . . . whoever the hell was doing this to him.

Feathers fluttered to the ground at his feet as he staggered.

Those still attached to his wings began to glisten with crimson liquid as wound after wound appeared.

"Who's doing this?" she shouted, panic threatening. Who could move so fast that even *she* couldn't see them?

"I can't stay," he whispered, blood painting his teeth and staining his lips.

"Who's doing this to you?" she repeated urgently. "How can I help you?"

He shook his head. "You can't. I can't believe you would even want to, knowing . . ."

"Knowing what?"

He grunted as another bone snapped.

"Zach!"

His eyes rolled back as his knees bent.

Lisette dropped her swords and thrust her arms out to catch him as he sank toward the ground.

A warm breeze washed over her as he vanished inches before they touched.

Shaken, she stared down at her empty arms. "Zach?"

Turning in a circle, she waited for whatever unseen force had attacked him to turn its attention on *her* and begin inflicting wounds.

It didn't.

"Zach!" Lisette jerked awake, her frantic gaze taking in her surroundings. Heart racing, she sat up and reached over to turn on the lamp beside the bed. Though she could see clearly in darkness, she had never managed to abandon the comfort light had given her as a mortal and appreciated the dim glow that now illuminated the familiar basement bedroom of her two-story home.

A dream. It had all been a dream?

"So real," she whispered. Looking down, she discovered that her hands shook.

What had just happened? It *had* been a dream, but . . .

The fact that she had been fighting vampires didn't surprise her. When one hunted and slew vampires every night for two hundred years, one tended to dream of little else. But Zach's presence . . .

She frowned. Elder telepathic immortals like Seth and David maintained complete control over their gift and didn't hear other people's thoughts unless they chose to. Younger telepathic immortals like Lisette and her brother Étienne, who had only lived roughly two hundred and thirty years, had far less control over their gift and automatically heard the thoughts of everyone around them unless the telepaths consciously blocked them. Since she lost that ability once she fell asleep, Lisette often found herself pulled into the dreams of those with whom she was in close proximity. As did Étienne, who had *walked* into her dreams countless times over the centuries. She had learned very quickly to discern who was a natural part of her dream and who wasn't. When Étienne *walked* into her dreams, she knew it.

Only Lisette and Tracy, her mortal Second, slumbered in the house. And Tracy sure as hell wasn't dreaming of Zach. Tracy didn't even know Zach existed. No, a quick peek told Lisette Tracy dreamed of swimming in a lake near her childhood home.

"The dream was mine," Lisette said, trying to understand. But Zach had not been indigenous to it.

He must have *walked* into her dream.

Which meant he was nearby.

Excitement flared. Tossing back the covers, she sped upstairs, disabled the security system, and dashed out the front door.

Sunlight seared her.

Spewing French epithets, she darted into the heavy shade of the nearest tree.

How could she have forgotten it was morning?

Her skin pinkened with a sunburn as she wished for the

millionth time that she possessed elder immortals' stronger tolerance for the sun.

Turning around, she looked up at the roof, expecting to see Zach perched atop it as he had so often perched atop David's.

Nothing.

Clinging to shadows, she circled around to the back, again looked up, and found nothing.

Disappointment snuffed out excitement as she glanced around.

No need to worry about neighbors seeing her in her nightgown. Chris Reordon, head of the East Coast division of the human network that aided immortals, had built her house upon a nice, large tract of land so no one could live close enough to her for her to hear their thoughts or experience their dreams.

Thoroughly confused, she took the most shaded route back to the house, darted inside, and locked out the daylight.

"Are you mental?"

Lisette jumped at the question.

Tracy squinted at her through eyes puffy from sleep, her blond hair a tangled mess. Matching Lisette in height and slender of build, the Second wore only a large man's T-shirt that didn't quite reach mid-thigh and clutched two 9mm's. "What the hell were you doing out there?"

Lisette shrugged, feeling foolish. "I thought I heard something."

"Well, next time send *me* out to investigate. That's what I'm here for." Almost every Immortal Guardian was assigned a human Second for just that purpose: so they could do the things immortals couldn't (or shouldn't) do during daylight hours because of their photosensitivity.

Flicking on the safeties, Tracy headed into the kitchen. "Let me get you some blood to heal those burns."

Lisette listened as Tracy set her weapons down, opened the refrigerator door, and delved into the special compartment that contained bags of blood.

Zach had *walked* into her dream. She was sure of it. But, if he weren't here, how had he accomplished it? And what had caused those wounds to open up on him like that? She had never seen that before, either in a dream or in reality.

Finding no answers, she followed Tracy into the kitchen and took the bag of blood she offered. "Thank you."

Tracy yawned.

"Go back to bed," Lisette told her. "I'm sorry I woke you."

Nodding, her Second collected her weapons, then shuffled out of the kitchen and down the hallway.

Lisette let her fangs descend and sank them into the bag, siphoning the blood directly into her veins. Her skin ceased burning. Blisters swiftly healed. Pink faded.

Tossing the empty bag in the trash, she returned to her bed.

But she found no more sleep that day.

Zach struggled to hold on to the image of Lisette—racing to his side, swords drawn, ready to defend him from his attackers. He saw again her drop those swords and, face stricken, hold out her arms to catch him as he fell.

He could have felt those slender arms wrap around him, hold him close, then ease him down to the ground . . . as he had once done for her.

But the pain had finally gotten the better of him.

Too many blows to count had sealed his left eye shut. Sweat and blood stung his right eye as he cracked it open and peered around the dimly lit cavern. So cliché.

"Decided to join us again, have you?" a voice drawled.

"I told you he couldn't block us forever," another murmured.

If only . . . Zach thought bitterly.

"Resume," the first voice commanded.

Agony sliced through Zach as another bone in his right wing snapped. Though he made no sound, he jerked involuntarily. The thick chains that cut into his wrists and dangled him from the cavern's ceiling jingled as he swung slightly. Needles pricked every inch of his arms. Or at least, that was what it felt like. He had been hanging thusly for a very long time, his arms supporting all of his weight.

More feathers fluttered down from his broken wings, disappearing into the darkness that consumed the floor far beneath him. A whip opened his flesh again. And again. Blood seeped from wounds and trailed down his body in tiny tributaries that merged at his ankles before slithering down to cascade over his toes.

He had long since lost all track of time. Lisette had said she hadn't seen him in four months. His confrontation with Seth had transpired shortly after Zach's last encounter with her. Had he really been here that long? Or had those few seconds with Lisette merely been a fantasy?

"Where do you go when you do that?"

Zach ignored the question. Just as he had ignored all of those that had preceded it.

Another bone in his wing broke.

Bastards.

"He doesn't go anywhere."

"Are you so sure? He doesn't respond. Doesn't seem to feel pain. Mentally he seems to be elsewhere. Do you not think we should know where?"

Zach snorted before he could stop himself. They could do whatever they wished to him. He would never lead them to Lisette. He might be broken physically, but his mind remained sharp. His mental barriers held strong. And his fantasies . . .

Well, those enabled him to endure this.

Another bone broke.

Fuckers.

"Where do you go?" Lamech demanded.

"I've not left this cavern," Zach responded just to irritate them, "as you well know, since you guard me twenty-four-seven."

He supposed it should please him that they felt the need to.

They did, of course. Need to guard him, that was. Ever since Seth had first mentioned growing his powers a couple of years ago, Zach had been working to strengthen his own.

"He doesn't go anywhere. He meditates, like that guy in *Tribes*," Jared said.

Zach had always thought it odd that Jared was such a film and television hound. Zach and the rest of the Others paid little attention to the stories concocted by Hollywood. After all, what could possibly top what they had seen in the thousands of years they had lived? Mankind would freak if they knew some of the things that hadn't made it into the history books.

"The better question," Jared added, "is whom does he imagine he's with?"

Zach wasn't so sure he had imagined this last encounter with Lisette. Usually, when he fantasized about her, he controlled her every action, determined what she would say . . .

This time had been different. He hadn't chosen *where* they had met, *how* they had met, or *what* they had said. Had it been real? Or as real as it could be with his physical body trapped in this damned cavern? Had he managed to tap into her dreams?

He struggled to keep his heart from beating faster at the notion.

"Were you with Seth?" Lamech asked.

That rat bastard? *Hell no.*

"Why did you meet with Seth in the Arctic?" Jared demanded, taking the whip.

"Coincidence," Zach replied through cracked lips.

The whip tore into Zach's chest.

"What is your interest in Seth?" Lamech asked.

"What's yours?" Zach countered.

"What it has always been," Jared said. "If we don't keep Seth and his little Immortal Guardians in check—"

Zach laughed, then nearly wept at the pain it inspired. "When have we *ever* kept them in check?"

Another crack of the whip.

More feathers fluttered down into the void.

Lisette. Just think of Lisette.

If he had infiltrated her dream, then he must finally be regaining strength.

Not physically. Physically he had never been weaker.

But perhaps all of those fantasies he had been weaving around the fierce female immortal had accomplished two goals: distracting him from the pain *and* strengthening his mental gifts.

Mind over matter.

He found a smile.

Who would've thought that shit actually worked?

The dream haunted Lisette for the next two weeks. She had seen no sign of Zach since, neither awake nor when ensconced in slumber.

Each night she doggedly continued to hunt and slay vampires too insane to recruit.

Honestly, she didn't know why they weren't just killing them all. Humans infected with the virus had no hope. They would become vampire. They would lose themselves to madness. And they would prey upon humans, killing and often ruthlessly torturing them. Melanie had found no cure for the virus. Nor had she and the other researchers at the network found a treatment that would prevent or reverse the progressive brain damage the virus caused in humans.

Wasn't simply killing them the kindest thing immortals could do? Spare them those painful moments of realizing they had suffered a psychotic break and done something unspeakable? Spare them that slow descent into insanity? Spare them those last few lucid moments when they knew they were losing everything they once had been and were becoming monsters?

Yet, Seth had ordered them to continue to keep an eye out for vampires who weren't too far gone.

Lisette sighed. At least she didn't have to converse with the vamps the way other Immortal Guardians did. She could hear every depraved thought in the vampires' heads. Which also made it easier to kill them.

Every damned night without fail.

Then, as dawn approached, she would return home and seek her bed with an eagerness that disgusted her, hoping she would once more encounter Zach in Morpheus's realm.

Why was she so obsessed with the mysterious elder?

Why were he and Seth at odds?

Hell, if Bastien—who had thought himself vampire, loathed the Immortal Guardians for two hundred years, and pitted a vampire army against them—could turn around and join the Immortal Guardians, what the hell held Zach back? What bad blood existed between him and Seth? And how bad *was* it?

Lisette trusted Seth implicitly. Always had. So why should she doubt his judgment now? Because Zach had saved her life?

Well, that *had* been pretty big. The mercenaries who had cornered her and drugged her would have captured her and dissected her if Zach hadn't killed them. He could have just let her fall. Why save her instead if he were such a bad guy?

She released a sigh full of frustration.

And *why* could she not stop thinking about him? Had she not learned her lesson? Had she not already suffered at the hands of a so-called *bad boy?* She was immortal today because she had fallen in love with a man who had skated the edge. A rake. A reprobate. A charming, yet evil scoundrel who had nearly killed her by trying to turn her against her will.

How stupid would she be to make the same damned mistake twice?

"You look pissed," Tracy commented.

Lisette tried to erase her frown as she took the weapons her Second offered and prepared for the night's hunt. "I haven't been sleeping well."

A moment of silence passed.

"Do you want me to stay at David's for a couple of days?" Tracy asked.

Lisette smiled. "No. It isn't you. Or your dreams. It's . . ." She shook her head. If she told Tracy she was pining for a man who appeared to be Seth's enemy, Tracy would be unable to keep the knowledge from Étienne, David, and Seth should they read her thoughts. "It's nothing."

"Bullshit. You've been restless and moody for weeks. Months, actually."

Lisette hadn't realized Tracy was that attuned to her.

"Is it time to move on?" her Second asked.

"Move on?"

"Ask Seth for a transfer? Things have quieted down around here. I don't think he'd refuse, if you told him you were homesick and wanted to spend some time in France or that you needed a change and wanted to go . . . I don't know . . . anywhere but here."

"You'd be okay with that?" Lisette asked curiously.

"Sure. You know I'd follow you anywhere. And, when you weren't hunting vampires, you could introduce me to some hot European men."

She smiled. "I believe your true motivation has come to light."

"You know it." Though Tracy grinned, her eyes remained watchful. She handed Lisette a pair of shoto swords. "Just think about it. And, if the wild and wicked dreams I keep having about the guy with all the tattoos at the home-improvement store get to be too much for you, don't hesitate to boot me out." She winked. "If I dream about him at David's, maybe I'll accidentally suck Étienne into the dream and give him an eyeful."

Lisette laughed.

Maybe it *was* time for a change, she thought later as she walked the pathways of a quiet UNCG campus. Perhaps she only obsessed over Zach because she was lonely.

She snorted.

Hell, she had been lonely for decades. She was used to it. Resigned to it. Had thought it simply the way it would always be and accepted it . . . until her brother Richart had fallen in love with Jenna. And Étienne had fallen in love with Krysta.

Both brothers' finding happiness after so many years of the solitary, violent existence to which she had surrendered them had lifted a weight from her shoulders. Finally, the recriminations to which she had subjected herself nightly had faded to whispers.

But their marriages had rendered her the fifth wheel, enhancing the emptiness within her.

Kidneythieves' "Before I'm Dead" broke the night's silence.

Pulling her cell phone from her back pocket, Lisette glanced down to see who was calling and shook her head. Speak of the devil.

Or rather one of them.

"Oui?" she answered.

Richart appeared beside her.

Six foot one with broad shoulders, a leanly muscled body, short dark hair, and piercing brown eyes, he had always been a handsome rascal. Mortal women had never ceased fawning over him and striving to gain his favor. The fact that he had an identical twin had only titillated them more. But now . . .

Lisette had to admit happiness agreed with him. He looked good; his lips often curled up in a smile. She envied him. And felt petty and small for doing so.

He smiled down at her and raised his eyebrows.

Grinning, she shook her head. "You look just like you used to when you were a boy about to embark upon some mischief or other that would end with Étienne's being punished for your misdeed."

He laughed. "I'm very fortunate to have such a forgiving brother."

"Yes, you are," she agreed wryly. "So what has led you to grace me with your presence tonight? Shouldn't you be home, begging Jenna to make love with you or something?"

His eyes sparkled with amusement. "I don't have to beg. And she's with Ami tonight."

Lisette frowned. "Is Ami all right?"

Her brother nodded. "There was a brief scare this afternoon. Ami began to have contractions, but Melanie and Dr. Kimiko said the baby's lungs aren't developed enough yet for her to be safely born, so Seth and David had to stop Ami's labor."

"Are you sure she's all right?"

"Seth, David, and Melanie all insist she is."

"And Marcus?"

"He's fine whenever he's around Ami and a wreck otherwise."

She nodded, knowing there was nothing they could do for him.

"And you?" Richart asked suddenly.

She arched a brow. "Me?"

"You haven't been visiting David's very often of late. You used to haunt it nearly nightly. Now . . . *pfft* . . . we almost never see you. Even Seth and David have remarked upon it."

An unnerving thought, the last. She offered a nonchalant shrug. "The place is packed. It makes it difficult to sleep." Not a lie. Just not the reason she had been spending more time at home.

Thinking of Zach.

Inwardly, she sighed. Which was why she couldn't be around Seth and David. They'd read it in her thoughts. And if they believed even for a moment that Zach had come to her in a dream . . .

"Are you sure that's all it is?" he asked.

"What else would it be?"

Richart shrugged and perused the campus around them in a blatant attempt to avoid her gaze.

Lisette rolled her eyes. She had known him for almost two and a half centuries. Did he really think he could hide something from her?

In true sibling form, she didn't bother to ask his permission before she mentally barged in and listened to his thoughts, but all she could hear was him singing a nineteenth-century tavern song.

"You're hiding something from me," she said.

He snorted. *"C'est ridicule!"*

"You always sing drinking songs when you don't want me to read your thoughts. What are you hiding?"

"Nothing. By the way, Jenna asked me to invite you to breakfast."

"You're changing the subject. And thank you, but no. You're newlyweds. You need your privacy."

He laughed. "The world's most mischievous Second resides beneath our roof, along with Jenna's son. Privacy isn't a possibility. *And* we aren't newlyweds any longer."

"Pish posh. You're immortal. The two of you will be newly-weds for at least a century."

His brow furrowed. "You aren't avoiding us because—"

She held up a hand and turned her head, listening.

Richart glanced around, face alert. His mental singing ceased. *What is it?* Though he wasn't telepathic himself and couldn't speak directly into others' minds the way she could, he knew she would pick up on his thoughts.

She shook her head. *Vampires. But . . . something is off. What?*

Four are your typical vampire fare, thoughts a maelstrom of violence and glee over their most recent kills.

And the fifth?

Both could smell them now.

The fifth vamp feigns insanity, but is lucid.

Did he band together with the others for safety's sake?

She shook her head. *He wants something from them.*

What?

I don't know. But he intends to kill the others once he obtains it.

The vampires were almost upon them now.

Keep listening, Richart said. *See what you can learn from the poser.*

Should we try to recruit him?

Let's see what his game is first. For all we know, he may be another Bastien or Dennis, looking to raise a damned vampire army to eradicate us.

Just what we need.

This late on a weeknight, few moved about UNCG. Campus security performed occasional sweeps. But professors had long since left. Every once in a while a stray student, driven by either insomnia or stress, walked the campus grounds. But those were few and far between.

Nevertheless, Lisette and Richart waited to confront the vampires until they were in a relatively isolated area, distanced from student housing, in order to reduce the chances of mortals getting caught in the crossfire . . . or witnessing the battle and posting video on the Internet.

I see what you mean, Richart thought. *It's the large one who's built like a lumberjack, right?*

Yes.

The other vampires were a slovenly mess, no longer concerned with personal hygiene. Garbed in jeans and T-shirts with various and assorted smart-ass quips splashed across the fronts, the vampires could easily pass for students if one disregarded the bloodstains on their clothing, as well as the fangs and glowing eyes. The latter gave away the vamps' recent kill as much as the stains and their thoughts did.

Any heightened emotion—anger, excitement, lust, jealousy—made the eyes of both vampires and immortals glow. Which was one of the many reasons immortals had to be careful when they took mortal lovers. Glowing eyes weren't easy to hide.

Of course, that wouldn't be a problem with Zach. His own eyes glowed a beautiful gold, so if she took *him* as a—

She swore.

Why the hell couldn't she stop thinking about him?

What about the others? Richart queried mentally. *Do we take time to chat, or shall we simply attack?*

Attack. They aren't worth saving. The thoughts of those turned her stomach, the screams of their victims still echoing through their minds like a favorite tune.

The lost causes walked in pairs. Two swaggered in front, wondering aloud if they should seek new victims to torment. The other two scuffed along behind them and agreed, eager for another kill. The fifth brought up the rear.

The gaze that one directed at the others whenever they weren't looking held contempt. He thought them beneath him. Lesser creatures to be used and discarded.

Richart might be right. This might be the next vampire

who intended to declare himself king. (*Thank you, Bastien, for putting the idea of such uprisings into their heads.*) Perhaps, like Dennis, this one intended to make lowlives like these his whipping boys.

While Bastien had ruled his vampire army with an iron thumb, he had only used violence to keep the maddest of them in line when they'd strayed and had earned the devotion of his followers by giving them hope. Dennis, Bastien's successor of sorts, had used violence . . . just because. The vampires who had followed him had done so not because they thought he could help them and cure them, but because they had feared he would rip them to shreds if they didn't.

Again Lisette's gaze went to the fifth vampire.

Yes, this one reminded her strongly of Dennis. Already, he imagined tearing his companions apart.

She nodded to her brother.

Richart vanished and reappeared directly behind the first two vamps.

How she envied him his ability to teleport.

With a flash of his long daggers, he decapitated the vamps in front before those behind him could even utter yelps of surprise.

Lisette darted forward at preternatural speed, arriving just as Richart spun around and severed the carotid arteries of the next two.

They stumbled back, grasping their throats as blood spurted and they began to bleed out faster than the virus could save them.

Only the fifth remained.

Just as Lisette arrived, that one delivered a roundhouse kick to her brother's chest. Richart flew backward, hitting the side of a nearby building hard enough to crack the bricks. Dust and mortar exploded around him as he fell to the ground.

Merde! Lisette ducked the right hook the vamp aimed at her, dodged the upper cut that followed half a second later, and swung her shoto swords. He was so fast!

The lumberjack vamp spun out of reach of her weapons and drew his own: two sais, as long and sleek and well cared for as those Roland carried. And, unlike most vampires, the lumberjack vamp knew how to wield them.

He swung the sais.

Shock rippled through Lisette as she met his every strike. This vampire had been trained. And the bastard was tall, with arms that seemed as long as a gorilla's. But her longer shoto swords made up for her shorter reach.

She swore as one of his blades caught her across the cheek.

Richart? she called mentally, unable to take her gaze from her opponent long enough to check on him. *Are you all right?*

A slew of French expletives filled her mind, grumbled in her brother's familiar voice.

Relief made her smile. So did scoring a deep cut across the vamp's right arm.

Fury mottled his rough-hewn features. His moves grew more careless. His thoughts filled with such hate and violence that it was hard to read any one thought in particular, but she did manage to discern that he had believed he would easily overpower her because she was a girl.

Dumb ass.

She swept the sai from his right hand.

He curled his empty fingers into a fist and slammed it into her jaw.

Pain exploded through her head as bone cracked. Her fingers tightened around the grips of her swords as her feet left the ground and she flew backward the way her brother had. She didn't know what she hit, but stars burst into being around her, lighting up her vision and muddying it at the same time.

Richart roared over the ringing in her ears. *Lisette!* he shouted mentally as the sounds of fighting resumed.

I'm fine.

Dragging herself to her feet, she staggered a couple of steps until she could regain her balance. Bastard had *punched* her! When was the last time a vampire had caught her off guard or gotten close enough to strike her with his bare hands?

She didn't wait for her fuzzy vision to clear, just dove back into the battle. Racing to her brother's side, she added her blades to his. This vampire might be far more skilled with weapons than those they normally fought, but he couldn't best two of them at once.

They defeated him in short order, cutting his carotid, brachial, and femoral arteries.

Richart looked at her as the vamp fell over onto his side. "What the hell was *that?*"

She shook her head. *Some dumb ass must have turned a martial arts expert,* she told him telepathically. Speaking hurt her cracked jaw too much.

"Brilliant," her brother complained.

Too bad he wasn't a gifted one, she told him with a shake of her head. *With those skills, he would've made an excellent immortal.*

Richart's look turned uneasy. "You don't think . . . He *wasn't* immortal, was he?"

Nausea took her. Bastien had been immortal, but had lived as a vampire for two centuries. Hastily sheathing her weapons, she removed her cell phone from a back pocket and knelt to snap several pictures of the vamp's face before he could deteriorate beyond recognition.

When she rose, Richart was dialing his own.

"Yes?" the Immortal Guardians' leader said over the line.

"Seth," Richart said. "We need you. Now. It's important."

Seth appeared beside them.

Before he could speak a word, Richart pointed to the fifth vamp. "Do you know him?"

Seth frowned down at the vamp. "No."

"Are you sure?" Lisette pressed without moving her jaw.

He cut her a glance, then knelt beside the vamp and rolled him onto his back. A few seconds passed. "I'm sure."

Both she and her brother sighed with relief.

Seth rose. "What's going on?"

She fell silent as Richart told him.

His scowl deepening, Seth crossed to Lisette and gently cupped her face in his large hands. A comforting heat suffused her where they touched. The pain in her jaw disappeared as bone healed and swelling receded.

Smiling, she clasped his wrists and gave them a squeeze. "Thank you."

He nodded and dropped his hands. Turning around, he stared down at the vampire. "It happens every once in a while."

Richart raised his eyebrows. "Vamps turning someone who can actually challenge us in a fight?"

He nodded. "Ask Roland about the time a vampire turned a master swordsman in the fourteenth century. Roland was so caught off guard he nearly lost an arm."

Lisette smiled. "I would think turning a human who was better skilled in fighting would backfire on a vampire."

Seth laughed. "It did. The swordsman killed his maker as soon as he completed the transformation. I'm sure this one did, too."

Lisette eyed the pile of clothes, all that remained of their fierce opponent. "I think he intended to pull a Dennis and raise an army. He seemed to despise his companions and intended to kill them when they no longer proved useful to him."

Seth eyed her speculatively. "You gleaned that from his thoughts?"

She nodded.

He motioned to her phone. "Did you take pictures of him?"

"Yes."

"Send them to Chris. Let's see if his techno geeks can identify him."

Chapter Two

Large warm hands slipped beneath the hem of Lisette's sleep shirt. Tracing a path over her hips and up to skim the sides of her breasts, they eased the shirt over her head and tossed it aside. She hummed in pleasure as those hands returned to her breasts, stroking and teasing. Then lips tasted her, drawing a hardened nipple into a hot mouth to be tormented by her lover's tongue.

She had hoped she would dream about Zach again, but hadn't expected *this*.

A muscled thigh slipped between hers and pressed against the heart of her, sparking heat and need. Smiling, eyes still closed, Lisette buried her hands in Zach's hair, combed her fingers through his . . . short locks?

Her eyes flew open. Stiffening, she glanced down at the chiseled body atop hers, the hand at her breast. . . .

That wasn't Zach's body.

And those weren't her breasts.

Groaning, she realized she'd been drawn into Tracy's dream about her home-improvement hunk.

Lisette separated herself from Tracy in a blink and stood

beside the bed. Turning to leave, she glanced back at the writhing duo . . . and felt her mouth fall open.

"What?" she blurted.

Tracy's eyes, closed in ecstasy, opened and met hers. Her lover raised his head and looked toward the door.

"Holy—" Lisette awoke in her pitch-black bedroom. She heard Tracy curse upstairs. The sound of a door being yanked open followed.

Shocked beyond belief, Lisette sat up.

Bare feet thumped down the stairs with quick steps and padded down the hallway.

A pause ensconced the house in silence. Lisette's door slowly inched open, flooding the room with light from the hallway as Tracy peeked inside.

"Damn it!" Upon seeing Lisette's no doubt wide eyes, Tracy shoved the door the rest of the way open and entered. She wore a different sleep shirt than the one in her dream. Both it and her hair were rumpled, her face full of dread. "It was you, wasn't it? You were there?"

"Yes."

"You saw . . . ?"

"Everything."

Her Second flushed a bright red as she covered her face with both hands and groaned.

"I thought you said you were dreaming about a guy at the home-improvement store."

"This is *so* embarrassing," Tracy wailed, staggering forward a few steps and collapsing into Lisette's favorite reading chair.

"You're sleeping with *Sheldon?*"

"No!" Tracy nearly shouted, and dropped her hands. Pure misery hid among the red in her face. "No, I'm not. It's just . . . dreams."

"Erotic dreams. More than one. About Sheldon." The youngest Second in the area. Possibly in the country. Chris

Reordon rarely recruited men or women under the age of twenty-five, claiming he wanted to make sure they were past the party-their-asses-off-now-that-they-were-no-longer-under-their-parents'-roof stage and could be counted on twenty-four hours a day to take care of business.

Sheldon had been a teenager when he had begun to serve, at Richart's request. Apparently Sheldon was the descendant of Richart's first Second. Lisette hadn't even realized until then that her brother had been keeping track of his friend's bloodline.

"Sheldon," Lisette repeated, trying to wrap her mind around it.

Sheldon was twenty-one or -two now, she thought. And *so* green. He was the kid brother everyone picked on and teased. The screwup. The prankster.

He wasn't the no-shit, tough-as-nails kind of guy who usually attracted Tracy.

"Are you . . . interested in him?" Lisette asked hesitantly.

"No," Tracy insisted. "No, of course not." She chewed a thumbnail, brows drawn down in a troubled V. "I mean, that would be crazy, right?"

Certifiable. "Well . . ." Lisette wasn't sure what to say. "He *is* handsome. If he looks as good without clothes in real life as he did in your dream, I can see the physical appeal."

"He does," Tracy admitted grudgingly. "I accidentally saw him naked once when I was at Richart's."

"How did you manage that?"

Tracy rolled her eyes. "He was changing with his damned door open, and I walked past. The boy goes commando under those tight black pants and has no shame."

"The boy is built," Lisette pointed out, oddly surprised by the knowledge. It was going to be strange to see him in person again after seeing him naked and aroused in Tracy's dream.

And feeling his hands on her.

She suppressed a shudder.

"But he's just *that*," Tracy responded. "He's a boy. He's so . . ."

"Young?"

"Yes. He's like a puppy. All exuberance and energy and mischief."

"All qualities that might not be so bad in a lover."

Tracy laughed. "And inexperience?"

"With a body like that, I'm pretty sure that's not something you'd have to worry about."

"Maybe not with sex, but with everything else."

"I don't know," Lisette murmured. "Now that I think about it, he's come a long way in the past couple of years. He kicked ass when he backed up Richart and Étienne at Krysta's house that time. And apparently did so again when we stormed the mercenaries' compound."

"I know. I was with him at the compound." Tracy shook her head, her lips tilting up in a faint smile. "He was fierce. And freaking funny. I never would have thought I could laugh while so many people were trying to kill me, but damned if he didn't say the most outrageous things."

Hmm. Tracy said it with what sounded like affection. "I don't think he's made any other big blunders since he landed Marcus and Ami in trouble shortly after Ami became Marcus's Second. Maybe he *isn't* so inexperienced."

"But he's still young."

"So are you."

Tracy rolled her eyes. "Compared to you, who isn't?"

Lisette laughed. It was true. All mortals seemed young to her. Even octogenarians. "So there's a *minuscule* age gap."

"I'm nine years older than he is." Tracy frowned. "Wait. Are you trying to talk me into starting something with him?"

"Many more dreams like the one I saw," Lisette offered dryly, "and you'll talk yourself into it."

Tracy sat quietly for a moment. *(Was she actually*

considering it?) Then she shook her head. "No. No way. It's *Sheldon,* for crap's sake." Rising, she headed for the doorway. "You won't tell anyone, will you?"

"Of course not. You know me better than that."

She smiled. "You rock."

"So do you."

Tracy returned to her bedroom, climbed back into bed, and soon found sleep again.

Lisette lay back and stared up at the ceiling.

Why couldn't that have been *her* dream and featured Zach?

And why oh *why* could she not banish him from her thoughts?

Jealousy seared Zach. He had attempted to lose himself in fantasies of Lisette again and instead had stumbled into one of her own. One of her making love with Sheldon, a young, strapping Second.

How could she want that . . . *boy?*

For days, weeks, he didn't know how long, he dwelled on the image of her in bed with that man-child, writhing beneath him, a sensual smile tilting her full\ lips. Fury rose, irrational in the extreme, yet a very effective distraction.

He gritted his teeth as the whip opened new welts across his chest.

How long had it been since he had stumbled into Lisette's dreams for the first time?

And how long did the Others intend to continue this shit?

Desperate for solace, for relief, for escape, he ignored the pain of the lash (Wasn't that fucker's arm tired yet?) and focused once more on Lisette. Deep breaths in, despite his cracked and broken ribs. Deep breaths out, ignoring the pull of cuts and the ache of bruises.

Lisette.

The cavern around him fell away, replaced by Stygian forest. The light of a full moon filtered down through tree branches and dappled his bare chest and leather pants. A cool breeze ruffled his hair, carrying with it the scent he craved.

Zach strode forward, following it to a slender figure who stood, silhouetted, before a break in the trees. Beyond lay David's sprawling one-story home.

She didn't hear his silent approach.

Zach stopped a breath away from her back. Tendrils of hair escaped her long braid and floated on the wind, tickling his chest. She smelled so good.

"Waiting for someone?" he murmured.

Gasping, Lisette spun around and tilted her head back to look up at him. Her pretty brown eyes lit with pleasure as her heartbeat picked up. "Zach," she breathed.

The sound of his name on her lips should *not* affect him so strongly.

"What are you doing here?" she asked, her gaze dropping to his chest.

Backing away, he leaned against a tree. "What are *you* doing here? Are you waiting for someone?" He crossed his arms. "Sheldon, perhaps?"

Her brow furrowed. "Why would I be waiting for Sheldon? He's Richart's Second, not mine."

"Don't you *want* him to be yours? In every sense of the word?" he drawled, trying to keep the jealousy he felt from his voice.

She stared up at him for a long moment.

He knew the instant she realized he had seen them together.

Color exploded in her face. "You saw that?" she asked, shifting her weight from one foot to the other. "The dream?"

"Yes."

She shook her head. "That wasn't my dream, Zach."

"You were the woman I saw writhing on the bed with Sheldon."

"Well, you should have stuck around," she countered. "If you had, you would have seen me separate myself from the woman on the bed and leave the room."

He frowned. "What?"

"I'm telepathic."

"I know."

"Well, do you remember me mentioning—the night Roland, Sarah, and I, ah, questioned you—that I have no control over the ability when I fall asleep? That I'm often sucked into other people's dreams?"

Relief flooded him. "*Tracy* was dreaming about Sheldon."

"Yes. And I was sucked in." She grimaced. "I don't know how I'm ever going to be able to look Sheldon in the eye again."

He smiled, pleased that the young Second didn't interest Lisette. "I'm sure you'll manage." He nodded to the house. "So what are you doing out here?"

"I don't know," she admitted. "Habit perhaps. I've watched over Ami for so long, it's hard to stop. Or maybe . . ."

He arched a brow. "Maybe?"

"Maybe I was looking for you."

Heat swept through his body. "Me?" He straightened away from the tree.

"I was worried about you." She gave him a long, thorough once-over. "The last time I saw you, you were wounded. And, I have to tell you, you still aren't looking so good. Are you okay?"

He glanced down and swore when he saw the slashes that marred his form. "Don't worry about that."

"Zach—"

"I'm all right," he interrupted before she could protest further.

After a moment, she nodded, face pensive. How she tempted him. The sight of her in black pants that hugged full hips and long, slender legs. Full breasts stretching the cotton of her long-sleeved shirt. Moonlight flirting with her pale skin and plump, pink lips. Weapons adorning her like jewelry, an ever-present reminder that she was a warrior and could kick ass.

All beckoned him, daring him to do something reckless.

He moved a step closer.

She didn't back away.

He took another step.

She held her ground.

Barely a breath separated them.

"I want to try something," he proposed.

Her heartbeat increased. "Okay."

Lowering his head, Zach pressed his lips to hers. His pulse jumped at the warm contact, racing to match hers.

Her breath caught.

Tilting his head, he increased the pressure, deepened the contact, and drew his tongue across those soft lips. She tasted incredible. Made him want to devour her. And yet . . .

Frowning, he broke the sweet contact. "You didn't pull away."

Her eyes now bore a faint amber glow. "What?"

"You didn't pull away."

"Why would I pull away?" she asked, voice husky.

Because I'm me, he almost said.

Disappointment seared him. The pain of his injuries increased.

Just to be sure . . .

"I'm going to try something else now."

Her lips quirked up as she arched a brow. "Okay."
Raising a hand, he cupped her breast.
The amber glow in her eyes flashed brighter.

Lisette's heart slammed against her ribs.

Zach molded his large, warm hand to her breast as he watched her warily. His eyes shone with a faint golden light. His fingers squeezed gently before he drew his thumb across the taut peak that strained against the cotton of her shirt.

Lust whipped through her, weakening her knees and making her fingers curl with the need to touch him, to stroke him, to explore every muscled inch of him.

Swearing, he withdrew his hand and took a step back.

"What's wrong?" she asked, embarrassed by how breathless she sounded.

"You didn't hit me."

She stared up at him. "I'm sorry, what?"

"You didn't hit me," he said, and actually sounded angry. "I don't . . ."

Turning, he paced away several steps. "I thought this was a dream. I thought I had made it into another of your dreams. But I touched your breast and you didn't hit me, so this must just be another fantasy of mine."

Lisette bit her lip when she saw his back. He bore no wings. An oddity. She had never seen him without them.

No, tonight his back boasted only bloody stripes that had clearly been carved by a whip.

"You fantasize about me?" she murmured.

He glanced at her over his shoulder. "I've done little else since I met you."

Just thinking about it turned her insides to mush and upped her desire another notch. "Zach, this isn't a fantasy. This is a dream. It's *my* dream."

He faced her, his expression uncertain. "It is?"

"Yes."

"Then why didn't you . . . ?"

"Hit you?" she asked, amused by his confusion despite her concern for him.

He nodded.

"Because I *wanted* you to touch me." Emboldened by his uncertainty, she closed the distance between them. "And I fantasize about you, too." Raising a hand, she caressed his strong jaw.

He closed his eyes. Turning into her touch, he covered her hand with one of his own and held it to his cheek.

Minutes passed.

"Zach?" she asked at last.

His lashes lifted. "I'm going to try something else now," he whispered.

Her body went liquid as she wondered what he would touch next. "Okay."

He brought her palm to his lips for a kiss . . . then vanished.

Lisette turned in a circle. "Zach?"

Nothing.

"Zach!" she shouted.

It didn't matter if the immortals in David's house heard her. This was a dream. Whatever they—

Crash!

Lisette jerked awake at the sound of . . .

What the hell was *that?* It had sounded like a wrecking ball hitting the roof.

Sitting up, she reached over and flicked on the lamp beside the bed.

A loud rumbling above drew her eyes to the ceiling.

Tossing back the covers, she grabbed her shoto swords and hit the floor running. Out of the room and up the stairs she flew as whatever or whoever the hell was up there either rolled, leaped, or fell off the roof.

No daylight shone through the curtains in the living room as she sped toward the front door. Good. Still night.

No heartbeat echoed hers, so Tracy must have elected to stay at David's.

Lisette didn't even take the time to look out a front window. She just shut off the alarm, threw open the front door, and barreled outside, intent on taking out whoever the hell had dared to disturb her rest and trespass on her property.

Silence met her. Utter stillness.

Adrenaline racing through her veins, she spun in a circle on the front lawn—sharp eyes taking in every untrampled blade of grass, every undisturbed leaf—and found no interloper.

Yet someone was there. She could feel it. She just couldn't see him. A friend of the fifth vampire perhaps? A minion of a new king?

Tilting her head back, she drew in a deep breath, seeking her prey's scent.

Fresh blood.

Fury filling her—damned vampires tainting her sanctuary with their presence!—she raced around to the back of the house and jerked to a halt.

Shock seized her.

A long, muscled male, garbed only in black leather pants, sprawled facedown on the ground where he had tumbled from the roof. Once beautiful wings lay crumpled atop him, broken and twisted and bloodied.

"Zach!"

In a flash, she knelt by his side. He looked far worse than he had in either of the dreams. And these weren't the kinds of wounds one would sustain in battle. He had been tortured. She could almost see the bones in his wrists where they had been cut by whatever restraints had been used to incapacitate him. His flesh had been laid open by whip and blade in too many places to count.

Dropping her shoto swords, she gently covered the bloodied hand closest to her with one of her own, then brushed his tangled raven locks back from his face with the other. "Zach?"

No response.

"Zach, can you hear me? It's Lisette."

One of his eyelids twitched, then opened. The other was so swollen his lashes barely lifted.

Lisette lowered her head to the ground beside his so he could see her.

Brown eyes, so dark they appeared black, met hers and struggled to focus.

His hand moved under hers, turning so he could curl his fingers around hers.

"This had better not be another fucking fantasy," he muttered.

She smiled, despite her worry. "It isn't."

His eyes closed. His grip on her fingers slackened.

Sitting back on her heels, Lisette glanced around.

Only typical night sounds met her sensitive ears. And Zach's scent, including the blood that coated him, was the only one out of place.

Tilting her head back, she looked up. He couldn't have flown here with his wings as messed up as they were. He must have teleported to the roof and collapsed.

She studied his large, battered form once more. Though he was six foot ten and boasted over two hundred pounds of muscle, lifting him wouldn't be a problem. (Preternatural strength came in handy at times like this.) The problem lay with his wings, what to do with them while she carried him inside.

They were huge. And so damaged. She would have to

secure them with something to keep them from dangling and dragging on the ground.

Grabbing one of her discarded shoto swords, she pressed it into Zach's hand and curled his fingers around it. "I'll be right back," she promised. Taking the other, she zipped around to enter through the front door. It took only seconds to lock it behind her, drop the shoto, grab a blanket from the hall closet, and exit through the back door.

Zach didn't move when she approached.

Lifting his shoulders, she unrolled the blanket under him, then carefully wrapped it around his wings and tucked the ends in the front. It alarmed her that he didn't moan or evince any other sign of suffering at her touch.

Hoisting him over her shoulder, she rose and headed for the back deck. She didn't rush this time, but took slow, steady steps that jostled him as little as possible. Once inside, she locked the door, reset the alarm system, and headed down to the basement.

Her queen-sized bed seemed small when she lowered Zach onto it, facedown to protect his wings. Several of those soft, nearly translucent feathers floated down to the floor when she unwrapped and removed the blanket.

Lisette tossed it in a corner.

Listening to his labored breathing, she wondered what she should do. She had never learned all of the intricacies of first aid, because she had always had a Second to patch her up and had, fortunately, never had to patch up one of her Seconds.

She couldn't bring Tracy into this, because her Second's mind would be an open book to any telepath in the area. Seth would know instantly what had happened and . . . Lisette feared what Seth might do to Zach if he learned Zach's whereabouts. Or what Seth might do to Lisette if he learned she had disobeyed him and aided the immortal.

She ran down a quick checklist of the other immortals in

the area, trying to think of any who might be an ally to her in this situation. Picking up the phone, she dialed Ethan's number.

"Yeah?" he answered.

"I need you," she told him.

"I'm on my way."

Ethan was great that way.

Lisette exchanged her nightgown for hunting clothes and sat by the bed until she heard Ethan's motorcycle approach.

Heading upstairs, she disabled the alarm system and opened the door just as he leaned against the doorjamb.

He stood about six feet four inches tall with short, wavy black hair, a strong jaw, and the piercing brown eyes common amongst immortals. Broad shoulders tested the seams of a black T-shirt. Nicely developed pecs and biceps flexed as he combed a hand through his hair, leaving it slightly tousled. "I am *so* glad you called," he said, flashing her a boyish grin. "I *really* need to get laid tonight."

Rolling her eyes, Lisette stepped back and waited for him to enter. "When I said I needed you, I meant I needed your help." Closing the door, she locked it, but didn't bother to reset the alarm.

His face fell. "Ah, hell. You mean this wasn't a butt call?"

"Booty call, Ethan. I believe the term is booty call. Honestly, I'm a hundred and thirty years older than you and from France. How can I be more familiar with American slang than you are? You were *born* here."

He shrugged. "I don't watch a lot of television and my Second is going on sixty. Neither one of us keeps up with whatever the hip kids are saying these days."

"First, I don't think anyone says *hip* anymore. And second, Ed is going on sixty?"

"Yeah."

"Damn. He looks like he's in his late thirties." He was actually pretty hot.

"I know, right? He dates more than I do." Ethan propped

his hands on his black jean-clad hips. "This really wasn't a booty call?"

"No." Ethan was an American immortal born a century or so ago. Until recently, he had been the youngest immortal in the area.

He had also been Lisette's protégé.

Shortly after vampires had turned Ethan against his will, Seth had deposited him on Lisette's doorstep and assigned her to train and mentor him. Ethan had been handsome and charming and utterly smitten with her. Lisette had been lonely and flattered and physically attracted to him. So, for years, the two of them had carried on a clandestine affair that she didn't think even Seth and David knew about. The relationship had ended amicably. Lisette had begun to fear Ethan might be falling in love with her. (He was something of an anomaly in that his mind was almost impossible to read, even by the elders.) Unable to return the affection, she had reluctantly ended the affair.

But afterward, they had transitioned into what Americans called *friends with benefits*. When the loneliness grew too burdensome or whenever they simply desired a little physical contact, they gave each other a call. A comfortable and convenient arrangement.

Ethan pursed his lips. "Could we turn it into a booty call after I help you with whatever you need me to help you with?"

She smiled. "I don't think so."

"Damn." He loosed a half-sigh, half-groan that went on so long it nearly made her laugh. "All right. I'm over it. What do you need?"

She hesitated. "It's . . . delicate."

His face lit with curiosity. "Okay."

"And could potentially be dangerous." How the hell was she going to explain this?

"Okay."

"By dangerous, I mean it will likely piss off Seth if he finds out," she clarified.

A moment passed. "Okay."

That was it. Just okay.

It was a damned shame she didn't love him. At least not the way she still suspected he loved her. He would do anything for her.

"Come with me." She headed for the hallway and the door to the basement.

"Where's Tracy?" he asked.

"At David's. She'll be spending the day there."

"At your request?"

"No."

"Does she know about whatever is going on?"

"No."

"Okay." He said nothing more until they reached her bedroom.

Lisette stood quietly beside him, fighting the urge to chew a thumbnail, as he stared down at Zach for several long minutes.

"Where's the shovel?" he asked.

"The shovel?" she repeated, confused.

"Yeah. You want me to bury him, right?"

Her eyebrows flew up. "What? No. He isn't dead."

"He isn't? I don't hear a heartbeat."

"It's there. The pauses between are just very long."

"Oh. Right. There it is. I just heard one." Another moment passed. "So, who is he?"

Lisette frowned up at Ethan. "Wait. What exactly did you think had happened here?"

He shrugged. "I figured you must have brought a mortal home, gotten carried away, and accidentally killed him."

"During sex?" she asked incredulously.

"He *is* half naked," he pointed out. "And you said Seth would be pissed. You know how protective Seth is of mortals. He does *not* react well when an immortal inadvertently kills one."

"When have you *ever* known me to engage in rough sex?"

"Quebec. 1985."

She opened her mouth, paused, thought about it, then nodded. "Okay. You're forgiven."

He sent her a sly glance from the corner of his eye. "For 1985?"

She unsuccessfully fought a smile. "No."

He laughed. "Then for what?"

"For drawing the freakiest conclusion you could draw from this situation."

Still grinning, he shrugged. "It was inevitable. I have sex on the brain tonight."

"So I noticed." After another minute, she nudged him with her shoulder. "I can't believe you were just going to grab a shovel and bury the body, no questions asked."

Again he shrugged. "You know I'd do anything for you. What's this guy's story, anyway? What do you want me to do?"

"Patch him up?" she asked hopefully.

"Why would that piss off Seth? Like I said, he loves mortals."

Lisette motioned to Zach. "He isn't mortal, Ethan. Did you fail to notice his wings?"

"Those are real?"

"Yes."

"Then he's immortal. Why would patching him up anger Seth? Seth is even more protective of *us* than he is of humans."

She bit her lip. "Seth isn't terribly fond of him."

"Meaning . . ."

"All evidence points to him being on Seth's shit list."

Ethan whistled. "So you thought you'd try living dangerously for a while."

Now *she* shrugged.

His look turned discerning. "Like him a bit, do you?"

Sometimes she thought Ethan knew her even better than her brothers did.

Her gaze shifted to Zach as she debated whether or not she should speak the truth, then back to Ethan. "I don't know. I'm . . . drawn to him. I don't know why."

Had she not been paying such close attention, she would have missed the tiny muscle that flexed in Ethan's jaw.

His gaze slid to Zach. "Lucky bastard."

"Ethan—"

"Let me see what Tracy has in her medic bag." Spinning on his heel, he left the room.

Perhaps this hadn't been such a good idea.

Returning, Ethan sat on the edge of the bed and started digging through Tracy's first-aid bag.

It was actually a diaper bag. *Diaper bags have all kinds of little compartments and pockets that are good for organizing crap*, Tracy had said when asked about it. *They even have pockets that will keep blood cool if I have to bring you some.*

"So?" Lisette asked as the minutes stretched and Ethan continued to rummage through the bag.

"So," he responded, "it belatedly occurs to me that I don't know what half of this shit is for."

She groaned. "You've never had to patch up a Second?"

He shook his head. "I've only had three. The first retired without ever having suffered a major injury. The second bled to death before I could reach him. And Ed is tough as nails. Any time he's injured he just stoically sews himself up."

"You don't help him?"

He glanced up at her, his expression sheepish. "I'm a little squeamish around needles."

She stared at him. "Seriously?"

"Yes."

"You slice and dice and decapitate vampires every night."

"And you'll notice that I don't try to sew them back together again afterward." He set the bag aside and rose.

It appeared she was back to square one. "What should I do?"

He took in the patient once more and pursed his lips. "I think you're going to have to call in the big guns."

"I told you, Seth doesn't like him. If he—"

"Not Seth. Seth isn't the big guns. Seth is the fucking hydrogen bomb."

"Ethan."

"Bastien. I meant Bastien."

She blinked. "Bastien is the big guns?"

"Yeah," he said with a distinct *Duh* inflection. "The man raised and commanded an army of psychotic vampires. Not one or two or ten. An *army* of them. He actually lived with the crazy bastards and kept them in line. Mostly. Can you imagine the kind of balls that must have taken?"

She didn't have to. She had peeked into Bastien's thoughts enough to know just how much power and authority he had wielded. Even though Bastien was young for an immortal—roughly her own age—he really *could* be deemed the big guns.

"You're right. But what's to stop Seth from seeing this in Bastien's thoughts?"

"I don't think Seth spends much time in Bastien's head these days. One, Seth is too busy worrying about Ami. And two, Melanie is keeping Bastien in line, so Seth no longer has to."

"Hmm." Retrieving her cell phone, Lisette dialed Bastien's number.

"What?" he answered, his deep voice curt and unwelcoming.

"Bastien, it's Lisette."

"Oh."

Awkward silence.

Yeah. Bastien wasn't exactly a people person.

"Are you busy?" she asked hesitantly. She hadn't realized

until that moment just how rarely she had spoken with him since Seth had brought him into the fold.

"Not really. Why?"

"I have a . . . situation that I could use your help with."

"Okay."

Ethan's eyebrows rose.

She gave Bastien her address, then ended the call.

"I didn't think it would be that easy," Ethan said.

"I didn't either."

When the British immortal arrived, Lisette met him at the front door and led him down to her bedroom.

Bastien nodded to Ethan, then stared down at Zach. After a few moments, he looked around. "Where's the shovel?"

Ethan coughed to cover a laugh.

"I didn't kill him!" Lisette nearly shouted.

Bastien shifted his gaze to Ethan.

Ethan held up his hands. "Don't look at me. I didn't kill him."

"He isn't dead," Lisette snapped. "And I'm not into rough sex!"

Bastien stared at her. "Ooookay."

She frowned. "Isn't that what you thought had happened? That I had killed him during sex?"

"No. I just assumed he had pissed you off."

"Oh." Her face heated with a blush.

Bastien's lips twitched.

And Ethan was enjoying this way too much, damn him.

She counted to ten. "Why would the two of you think I would call you over here to bury him? It's not like I don't have the strength to lift him and do it myself."

Ethan shrugged. "You're a girl."

Lisette glared at them both. "And, what, you think I don't want to get my pretty little hands dirty?"

No response.

"You do know I kill vampires for a living, right?"

Bastien pointed at Ethan. "He said it, not me."

"But you were thinking it."

He scowled. "Are you reading my thoughts again, telepath?"

"I didn't have to. It was all over your face. Besides, I stopped peeking into your head a long time ago because all you ever think about is Melanie naked and your vampire friends."

Ethan's eyebrows shot up. "He thinks about Melanie naked with his vampire friends?"

Bastien popped him on the back of the head.

"Ow! Shit!"

Lisette pinched the bridge of her nose. "Let us return to the subject at hand, shall we? Yes, I'm a girl," she pointed out needlessly. "A girl who can kick your ass, Ethan."

"I know," he acknowledged with a grin as he rubbed the back of his smarting head.

"Bastien, my *guest* here," she said, refraining from mentioning Zach by name, "is immortal. I was hoping you might know how to tend his wounds. Neither Ethan nor I knows much about first aid."

"Why don't you just give him blood?"

"No fangs."

"You don't need his fangs to descend. You can transfuse him with your own."

She hesitated, unwilling to tell them what she suspected.

"What?" Ethan asked, picking up on her unease.

"He has wings," she said.

"Those are real?" Bastien asked.

"Yes."

He studied her stoically. "And—what—you think . . . ?"

Ethan frowned. "You don't think he's an angel, do you? Like a fallen angel?"

Some kind of angel. She hadn't thought about whether or not he had fallen.

"I don't know what he is," she hedged.

The two men shared a look.

At least they didn't laugh at her or mock her.

"He's probably just a shape-shifter," Ethan suggested.

Possibly, but . . .

"You don't want to give him blood," Bastien said.

She shook her head.

"All right. I'll tend his wounds."

"There's something you should know first," she cautioned.

"I'm listening."

"Seth isn't terribly fond of him."

Ethan crossed his arms. "Translation: He's on Seth's shit list. If Seth finds out we helped him, we will likely join him on that list."

A dark smile slid across Bastien's handsome face. "When has pissing Seth off ever stopped me from doing something?"

There were definite perks to having a black sheep in the Immortal Guardian family.

Bastien ended up being a remarkably capable medic. He seemed to know the use of everything in Tracy's substantial first-aid kit and used a hell of a lot of it to close Zach's wounds.

"Where did you learn to do all this?" Lisette asked, watching him stitch up a deep gash on Zach's arm.

"I commanded an army of vampires prone to psychotic breaks and a dozen or so human wannabe minions with violent tendencies. Severe wounds were a nightly occurrence, and Tanner and I were the only ones around who were guaranteed to be focused enough to take care of them. Hold his wings while I roll him onto his side."

Approaching the bed, she leaned down to grasp Zach's wings. They were so large. And so mangled. Broken in countless places. Feathers bent and torn. "Ethan, will you help me?"

They each took a wing and kept it as immobile as possible while Bastien turned Zach onto his side. Again Lisette marveled over how soft the feathers were. Softer than rabbit's fur.

"I've set countless broken bones in the past," Bastien murmured, "but broken wings . . . ? This is a first."

"I appreciate your trying."

He glanced at her as he worked. "Any particular reason you didn't ask Melanie to help?"

Bastien's wife, Dr. Melanie Lipton, was a now-immortal doctor who worked at the human network, searching for a cure for the virus. Either that or a way to prevent or reverse the brain damage it caused in humans. She was also doing everything she could to carry Ami safely through her pregnancy.

Lisette sighed. "I didn't want to get her in trouble."

His lips quirked as he manipulated one of the wings. "But you didn't mind getting *me* in trouble?"

Ethan snorted. "When are you *not* in trouble?"

Bastien laughed. "True. I'm going to need something I can use as splints."

Bastien slowly and methodically tended the many injuries that marred Zach's lean form. When he finished, Lisette walked Bastien upstairs and followed him out the front door.

"Will you have time to get home before sunrise?" she asked, eyeing the gray that preceded dawn.

"The way I drive? Yes." He paused on his way to a Chevy Volt and turned to study her.

Lisette shifted, uncomfortable beneath his silent scrutiny.

"Are you sure you're ready for this?" he asked at last.

"Ready for what?"

"Being on Seth's shit list."

Hell no. The thought of facing Seth's wrath made her quake in her boots. "You survived it," she replied coolly, but feared she didn't fool him.

He shook his head. "Only because Seth believed himself responsible. It's why he still tolerates my bullshit. And why he won't hold my helping you against me. He feels guilty about overlooking me and leaving me to fend for myself for two centuries."

Whenever a *gifted one* was transformed into an immortal, Seth sensed it, made his way to his (or very rarely her) side, and aided him in the transition into his new life. Seth then either trained the new Immortal Guardian himself, or saw to it that the newbie was trained by another and received the guidance all new immortals needed.

But Bastien had escaped his notice. So Bastien had mistakenly believed himself a vampire and had lived among those monsters for two hundred years.

All knew his violent, troubled past haunted their leader.

"Do *you* hold him responsible?" she asked.

"No," he said, his voice devoid of rancor. "And I'm sure he's seen as much in my thoughts. But the guilt nevertheless lingers and pretty much gives me a permanent get-out-of-jail-free card. *You*, on the other hand, don't have that protection."

No, she didn't.

"I learned very quickly," he went on, "that Immortal Guardians have a pack mentality." Three years with them, and Bastien still didn't consider himself one of them. "If Seth turns on you," he warned, "the others will, too."

She swallowed hard. "My brothers—"

"Have wives to think of. And, in Richart's case, a stepson."

"I know." She didn't have a problem with no longer coming first in her brothers' affections. It just felt a little scary to know they wouldn't always have her back now.

"Is he worth it—your fallen angel?" Bastien asked. Again, no scorn or mockery infused his voice.

She honestly didn't know the answer to that and settled for saying, "He saved my life. I can't forget that."

"That's a hard debt to forget." Turning, he continued on to the car. "You have my number."

"Thank you, Bastien."

He opened the driver's door. "Ethan's jealous as hell, you know."

Her eyes widened.

"Asshole!" Ethan called from inside.

Bastien laughed. "I guess this means you two are on the outs."

"You knew?" she asked, stunned.

How had he known about the affair when no one else had guessed?

He sank into the driver's seat. "I may not get along well with others, but I *am* a keen observer of them." The words seemed to carry a warning. "And I can feel your emotions every time I brush against you."

Considering how many times she had barged into his thoughts in the past, she decided she wouldn't let that bother her. "Give Melanie my love."

He winked. "I'll be too busy giving her mine." Closing the door, he started the engine and sped away.

Chuckling, Lisette stared after him. What an enigma.

Ethan exited the house and stepped up beside her. "That guy is so weird."

"You didn't tell him?" she asked.

"About us? No."

"Do you think he'll say anything to anyone?"

"Nah. Who would he tell, other than Melanie? And she isn't one to gossip."

"I don't want to end up in the betting books, Ethan."

Immortal Guardians, their Seconds, and the mortal members of the network would gamble on just about anything. She didn't want them to complicate matters between her and Ethan by betting on whether or not the two of them would get back together.

"If word gets out about your beau in there," he said, jerking a thumb back at the house, "they'll be betting on whether or not Seth will let you live."

A chilling thought.

What the hell was she doing?

Chapter Three

Ethan left shortly after Bastien did, still grumbling over the non-butt call.

Zach didn't so much as twitch all day. His breathing didn't deepen. His heartbeat didn't increase in frequency. His eyes didn't open.

Lisette eschewed sleep, preferring to watch over him instead and wonder about . . . so many things.

Immortals tended to sleep more deeply when healing from serious wounds, so his lack of response when she called his name didn't concern her *too* much. Particularly since his bruises faded. Cuts and gashes closed by Bastien's handiwork began to heal, angry red lightening to pink, edges smoothing, scars forming.

It took longer than she would've expected for an immortal his age. There must have been extensive internal damage. And there had been a *lot* of broken bones in his wings. One wing had nearly been completely detached. Bastien had had a hell of a time setting it and binding it. Those might take another day or two to heal.

Who had done this to him? And why?

She didn't think Seth had. When Seth punished an immortal, everyone and his or her brother heard about it. Although, as far as she knew, only she, Roland, Sarah, and Ami even knew Zach existed.

Lisette sighed as the sun set, no closer to finding answers. She touched Zach's hair. "Zach? Can you hear me?"

Nothing.

"You can answer me mentally if you can't speak." Though the gifts they possessed varied from immortal to immortal, Zach clearly was telepathic. Otherwise, he would not have been able to enter her dreams.

Silence.

"I have to leave for the night's hunt." She rose, her fingers already missing his silky locks. "I'll keep my Second away for the night and return as soon as I can."

She just had to think of something to tell Tracy.

Opening the wardrobe, she drew out a change of clothing and headed into the adjoining bathroom to shower.

The wardrobe actually served dual purposes, just as those in David's home did. Behind the curtain of black vampire hunting clothing lay a panel that concealed an escape tunnel that led deep into the surrounding forest, allowing her a safe exit beneath evergreens year-round should the need to flee during daylight hours ever arise.

She hadn't thought such necessary until Roland, Marcus, and Sarah had been attacked during the day, Roland's house set aflame with them inside it.

Lisette didn't linger in the shower. The sooner she left, the sooner she could take out a few vampires and return home. Surely Zach would awaken tonight. She just hoped, if he awoke while she was gone, that he would linger until she returned.

Upstairs, she packed on her favorite weapons—shoto swords, daggers, and a pair of silencer-equipped Glock 18's with thirty-round clips.

Grabbing her helmet, she headed outside and straddled her Hayabusa.

"Before I'm Dead" floated on the night.

Lisette drew out her phone.

"Did you get a good night's sleep?" Tracy asked as soon as Lisette answered.

"I did," Lisette lied. "Where are you?"

"I'm still at David's."

Which meant every immortal on the premises would hear both sides of their conversation.

Instead of responding verbally, Lisette texted her: Can you spend another night and day there?

Sure. What's up?

Will tell you later.

OK.

Seconds later, Lisette sped down a deserted North Carolina road, her thoughts consumed with the dark immortal in her bed.

Ethan prowled Duke's campus, full of restless energy. He hadn't encountered a single vampire all night. Not one!

Muttering beneath his breath, he slid a dagger from its sheath and began to toss it up in the air and catch it by the blade. It had taken him a while to learn how to do that without cutting himself, but he did it now absently as his eyes perused the shadows.

He was spoiling for a fight, damn it, and couldn't find one.

He'd been spoiling for a fight ever since he had seen that big-ass immortal sprawled in Lisette's bed. Sure the guy had been bloody and banged up. But he had been in her bed. Her *bed*.

And she had been willing to risk her ass to help him. Willing to risk *Ethan's* ass, too.

He scowled. And damned if he hadn't risked it for her. Or rather for *him*, whoever the bastard was.

What the hell was Lisette thinking, falling for someone on Seth's shit list? Was she crazy?

No, he answered his own question. *She isn't crazy. She's fucking smitten.*

Which was why he really, *really* needed to hit something right now.

Because *he* was still smitten with Lisette.

He had begun to fear he might always be, that he might end up like Marcus. Or like Marcus had been before Ami had come along. Marcus had pined after a woman he couldn't have for eight centuries and had been miserable.

Ethan did *not* want to follow his example.

Three human women approached. College students returning from a kegger by the looks of them. Giggles abounded as they chattered and staggered up the sidewalk in tiny steps made awkward by ridiculously high heels.

Lisette wouldn't be caught dead in those shoes. He loved that about her. She had had to conform to the binding, pinching, uncomfortable clothes of her time when she was mortal and said she would never do it again. Combat boots now dominated her nights, while bare feet were her preference by day.

Even her damned feet appealed to him.

Sheathing the knife, he swore and turned his head away so the women wouldn't see his eyes glow with frustration.

"Yum," one of them purred as they passed.

"He's so hot," another whispered.

"I'd totally do him."

A nice stroke of the old ego, but he couldn't care less about the trio . . . until dark figures slithered from the shadows and began to follow them.

Finally! Four vampires. A challenge for an immortal his age, but he was up to it.

Smiling, Ethan strode onward for a few more steps, then hung a U-ey and began to stalk the predators.

He gave a silent whistle. Two of them were about his size. Six foot four. Broad-shouldered. Packed with as much muscle as Ethan. The other two were lanky and looked as if they had never lifted a weight in their lives. Five-eight and five-ten. Twitchy. Reeking of old blood and unwashed bodies. They must have been infected longer than the other two. The other two wore freshly laundered clothing and had bathed recently.

The vampires made no attempt to silence their footsteps.

The students looked over their shoulders with flirty smiles, perhaps expecting Ethan. Those smiles vanished as they took in the menacing foursome tailing them. Exchanging uneasy glances, they huddled closer to each other and picked up their pace.

The two slovenly vampires produced rusty chuckles and walked faster so the coeds would know they were being hunted. The muscled vampires looked side to side and followed.

Fairly typical. Newer vamps tended to tag along with older vamps. And older vamps liked to toy with their victims, as enthralled by mortals' fear as moths were by flames. They wanted the women to tremble. Wanted the women's minds to conjure images of all the horrific things that would happen to them if they didn't elude their pursuers. Wanted the women to imagine the unimaginable. Then wanted to restrain them and elicit screams.

Without breaking stride, Ethan bent and scooped up a couple of the acorns that littered the path and crunched under the vampires' boots.

"Call campus security," one of the students hissed.

"I don't know the number."

"Then call 911 and tell them we're being followed!"

One of the vamps laughed. "You'll be dead before they get here."

The women looked over their shoulders.

"Oh shit. His eyes," one whimpered.

Student housing loomed in front of them. A few more yards and they would be safely through the doors, not that the vampires would let them make it that far.

Ethan drew back his arm and launched the acorns.

Thrown with preternatural speed, they would feel like bullets when they struck.

The two lanky vamps both stumbled forward and howled in pain as the acorns slammed into the backs of their heads.

"Ow!"

"What the fuck?"

Stopping, the women gaped at them.

Ethan waved a hand to get their attention, then motioned for them to get their asses inside.

The women spun around and ran (if you could call it that), their heels clickety-clacking on the pavement as their big-ass purses rustled and bounced on their hips.

Eyes flashing a brilliant blue, the vampires whirled to face Ethan as the students clambered up the steps and dove through the doors of the dorm.

The muscled vamps followed the crazy ones' gazes and turned to confront Ethan.

This would either be fun or painful.

Ethan backed away, luring them around the corner and out of sight of the women peering through the windows.

"Immortal Guardian," the skinny vamp in the gray T-shirt spat, he and the others matching him step for step.

"Well, aren't you bright?" Ethan said. Drawing two gleaming sais, he struck before they could respond.

The vamp in the gray shirt didn't even have time to re-trieve whatever blade he'd tucked into the sheath belted to his pants. As the vampire's fingers curled around the shiny wooden handle, Ethan swept forward and cut his carotid artery.

The muscled vampires circled around behind Ethan while the other lanky vamp whipped out a machete and brandished it. (How the hell had he hid that thing in his pants?)

Ethan gave the lanky vamp his back and spun to face the muscled duo.

Just in the nick of time.

He ducked a kick that would have cracked his jaw at the very least and lashed out with a sai. Astonishment gripped him when he missed.

He never missed!

Another kick nearly connected with his head. Ethan ducked and swept the vampire's feet out from under him. The vamp hit the ground hard. Ethan swung. The vamp rolled and leapt up. Sparks danced as Ethan's blade hit pavement.

He didn't know where the lanky vampire was, but saw the second muscled vamp circle around to attack him from behind again.

Ethan zipped around and placed the first muscled vamp between them, fighting for all he was worth. This man had been turned recently. Nothing ruffled him. And he had skills. He had been trained by a master in martial arts and weaponry.

But Ethan had trained with a master as well. Lisette kicked ass and had drilled him relentlessly to ensure Ethan could, too.

The vampire in the gray shirt, clutching the throat Ethan had laid open, staggered away a couple of steps and fell to his hands and knees. Blood poured down his front and pooled on the sidewalk. The other lanky vampire bobbed and bounced on his toes like a boxer, spewing slurs and curses. Muscled Vamp 2 again found his way to Ethan's back.

Hell. This was not going well.

Out of nowhere, a slender figure raced forward, leaped onto the back of the vampire who was down on his hands and knees, pushed off, flipped ass over elbow in the air, and landed behind the other lanky vampire. The vamp jerked around to attack her. Red handles gleamed as Lisette swung both shoto swords.

The vampire's head fell from his shoulders.

She offered Ethan a wink.

He grinned. How many times had she saved his ass like this in the early years of his immortality?

Muscled Vamp 1's dagger slid across Ethan's left arm, narrowly missing his brachial artery.

"Pay attention!" Lisette reprimanded as she dodged a kick by Muscled Vamp 2 and landed one of her own.

Two vampires. Two immortals. An even playing field now.

Disturbingly even. Ethan had to fight as though he were sparring with an elder just to hold his own with this prick. In all of his existence, he had *never* fought a vampire who possessed such skill.

From the corner of his eye, he saw Lisette's opponent land a fist to her jaw. She stumbled backward, French swear words pouring from her lips.

A dagger struck Ethan's side, slipping between two ribs and piercing a lung.

Hissing in pain, he cursed his own inattention.

Lisette looked his way, brow furrowed with concern.

A cut opened along her jaw as Muscled Vamp 2 took advantage of her distraction and tried to slit her throat.

"I'm fine," he gritted. "Just kill the fucker!"

Ethan saw her swing her shoto swords and returned his attention to Muscled Vamp 1.

Grunts and hisses of pain filled the air as blades drew blood and kicks and punches connected.

He heard Lisette swear again and swung his sai, ridding the vampire of one of his daggers. Before Ethan could swing again, the vampire jerked and dropped his other weapon. Gasping, the vamp gripped his chest. His face filled with fear. His wide blue eyes fastened on Ethan as he staggered back a step.

Ethan frowned and held his weapons at the ready, risking a glance at Lisette.

Falling still, she stared at the second vamp as his weapons clattered to the ground. The fingers that had loosed them clutched his chest.

Warm blood splattered Ethan's face as something bounced off his shoulder and fell to the ground.

Grimacing, he returned his attention to his foe . . . and gaped.

"*Ho*-ly shit!" he barked.

The vamp's heart had just burst from his chest.

The vampire collapsed.

Ethan turned back to Lisette as Muscled Vamp 2's heart burst from his chest, flew over Lisette's shoulder, and catapulted to the ground behind her.

The body that had formerly housed it collapsed.

Lisette stared down at the vamps, heart racing, body aching from the beating she had just taken, cuts stinging. *What the hell?*

"Okay," Ethan said, breath coming in gasps. "I'm not going to lie to you. That is the freakiest shit I've ever seen." He looked from one vampire to the other, his blood-splattered face stunned. "And I've seen some freaky shit."

She nodded. As had she.

"What the hell just happened?"

"I don't know," she murmured.

Their hearts had just . . . burst from their chests.

"Have you ever seen anything like that before?" he asked.

She started to shake her head, then froze.

"What?" Ethan prodded. "What is it?"

Zach. Zach had once instantly and simultaneously killed over a dozen mortal men, who would have captured her otherwise, by giving them ruptured brain aneurisms.

She looked around.

"Lisette?" Ethan raised his weapons. He probably thought she had heard something or that more vampires lurked nearby.

But Lisette sought someone far more dangerous . . .

She sucked in a sharp breath as her gaze landed upon him.

There. Leaning against the corner of the building, a shadow among shadows, the darkness broken only by the bright white bandages that covered his many wounds.

"Zach," she breathed.

Ethan's head snapped around. His brows drew down. "What?"

Sheathing her weapons, she strode forward.

Ethan's boots pounded the pavement behind her, then crunched in the dry grass as she left the path.

Zach didn't straighten as they approached. Lisette wondered if he even could. He looked no better than he had when she had left him earlier tonight.

Tilting her head back, she met his gaze. "What are you doing here?" she asked softly.

Perspiration dotted his brow. "I sensed you were in danger."

"I'm fine. I fight vampires every night."

He lifted a hand and brushed his index finger down her bruised cheek, sending tingles of excitement dancing through her. "He hurt you."

Beside her, Ethan raised an eyebrow. "And so you telekinetically ripped his heart from his chest?"

Lowering his hand, Zach looked at Ethan. "Yes."

Ethan sighed. "Okay. I'm liking you a little more now," he grudgingly admitted.

Zach's expression didn't change as he studied the younger immortal.

"You should be home, Zach," Lisette admonished gently. "You haven't healed. You should be resting."

He abandoned his scrutiny of Ethan and fastened those penetrating brown eyes on her. "*Your* home?" A golden spark entered his gaze. "Your bed? That's where I was when I awoke, wasn't it? Your bed? It carried your scent."

For some reason, heat rushed to her face. "Yes."

"How did I get there?"

"You don't remember?" She avoided looking at Ethan, who drank in every word, every nuance in tone.

"No."

"I'll tell you later," she promised, unwilling to say too much in front of their avid audience. She glanced over Zach's shoulder at the wings Bastien had splinted and bandaged so carefully. "How did you get here? You couldn't have flown."

"I teleported."

The fact that he had retained the strength to do so despite his severe injuries indicated just how powerful this immortal was.

"Then teleport back. To my home, I mean. Go back to bed. Get some rest. I'll be there shortly."

"It isn't safe."

"Yes, it is," she assured him. "My Second is staying at David's home and won't return until I call her. No one else will be there."

"I meant it isn't safe for you. If the Others come looking for me—"

"What others?" Ethan interrupted.

Irritation flickered across Zach's handsome face.

Lisette hastened to speak up. "Do you mean the ones who did this to you?"

"Yes."

"Wouldn't they have already found you if they could?"

"I've only been gone a couple of hours. Given a little more time, they should—"

"Zach," she corrected gently, "you've been at my place for almost twenty-four hours."

He stared at her. "What?"

"It's been twenty-four hours, give or take a couple. If they're as powerful as *you* are, wouldn't they have found you by now?"

His brows drew down in a frown. "Perhaps it's become second nature," he murmured.

"What has?"

"Eluding them."

Ethan leaned forward. "You still haven't told us who *them* is."

"Nor do I intend to," Zach responded darkly.

He didn't intend to tell Ethan? Or he didn't intend to tell either of them?

Lisette decided she would react to that later. "As I said, my place is safe. Ethan, Bastien, and I are the only ones who know you're there. Why don't you go get some rest and give your wings time to finish healing? I'll—"

"Bastien—the immortal black sheep—knows?"

"Yes."

"I'll have to locate him and erase his memory of me first."

"Erase?" Ethan spoke up, his voice reflecting the alarm she felt herself. "Or bury?"

"Erase." Something odd flickered in Zach's eyes. "Buried memories tend to resurface when you least expect them to."

Merde. Seth had said he and David usually opted to bury memories instead of erasing them because erasing them could cause brain damage.

"Please, don't do that," she said. "Bastien is the one who

bandaged your wounds and set your broken bones. I didn't know how to do it myself and asked him to tend your wounds as a favor to me."

Zach looked to Ethan. "What about you? What did *you* do?"

"Ate a sandwich and cracked some jokes."

"No, he didn't," Lisette hastened to deny.

Ethan raised an eyebrow.

"Okay, he did have a sandwich, but not until most of your wounds had been tended and he'd helped Bastien with your wings."

"And cracked some jokes," Ethan repeated.

Lisette resisted the urge to strangle him. Was he *trying* to antagonize Zach?

"Seth will read all this in their thoughts and turn his wrath upon you for helping me. I can't allow that."

"The chances of that are slimmer than you think. Seth rarely intrudes upon Bastien's thoughts anymore because Melanie is keeping him in line. And Ethan is very hard to read."

Zach stared at Ethan.

"What?" Ethan asked. A few seconds later, his face contorted with pain. "Ahh!" Dropping his weapons, he clutched his head and staggered to one side.

Lisette gripped his shoulder to steady him. "Ethan?"

A trickle of blood emerged from one nostril and trailed down over his lips and chin.

"Zach, stop!" she cried as she realized he was trying to scan Ethan's thoughts.

A sigh escaped Ethan. His face smoothed out.

"You're right," Zach said. "He *is* hard to read."

"Asshole," Ethan growled as he wiped the blood from under his nose. "What the hell was that? What did you just do to me?"

"Tried to access your memories."

"My memories are none of your fucking business."

And would reveal much about Ethan's relationship with Lisette.

Stomach twisting in knots, she forced herself to meet Zach's gaze. "Were you able to see anything?"

"No," he conceded after a long silence. "I thought you might object to the pain it would cause him if I dug deeper."

"Asshole," Ethan repeated.

Lisette didn't protest. It *had* been kind of an asshole-ish thing to do. "So now you see why Seth and David don't read his mind?"

"They wouldn't have to if either man volunteered the information."

"Bastien won't tell anyone, Zach. Neither will Ethan. Right?"

Ethan scowled. "I hadn't intended to. But if he pulls that shit again, all bets are off."

At last, Zach nodded. A muscle in his jaw jumped as he straightened and offered her his hand. "Come with me."

"I can't." She motioned to the disintegrating forms behind them. "I need to clean up our mess. I'll be home soon, though."

Zach gave her a curt nod, then vanished.

Drawing a deep breath, Lisette reluctantly faced Ethan. "Don't say it."

"Don't say what?"

"What you're thinking."

"That you're in over your head? *Way* over your head? That you're out of your fucking mind?"

"Ethan—"

"He was willing to give me brain damage to erase my memories, Lisette! Bastien, too. And he exhibited *no* regret over causing me pain when he tried to read my mind. Hell, the only reason he didn't damage my brain *then,* trying to dig deeper, was because he thought it would upset you!"

She couldn't deny it, and didn't like it any more than Ethan did. She hoped like hell Zach had done it out of a genuine desire to protect her.

"Do you even know who this guy is?" Ethan demanded.

"Yes. Sort of."

His look screamed that she had lost it. "Lisette, *Zach*"—the name dripped with scorn—"is bad news. *Zach* is Bastien times a thousand. He's Bastien with David's power. And you're risking Seth's wrath and, for all we know, severe punishment—if not execution—to help him. *Why,* for fuck's sake? Because he's easy on the eyes?"

"Because he saved my life!" she blurted, then cursed herself silently. Damned if she wasn't about to betray Seth again.

Ethan stilled. "What?"

She paced away from him.

"Lisette?"

"I'm not supposed to talk about it. Seth told me not to tell anyone."

"And Seth will never know."

"He will if he reads my mind."

He snorted. "What do you think will piss him off more if he reads your mind—that you told me whatever it is you're hiding, or that you welcomed Zach into your home and gave him safe harbor?"

"I know. You're right." The marks against her were really adding up. She turned to Ethan with a sigh. "Remember the night I planted the tracking device on that mercenary?"

"Yeah. That was kick-ass."

"Well, I didn't do it. Zach did."

He tilted his head to one side. "What do you mean? What happened?"

"I had just defeated some vampires—five or so, I forget how many—when a tranquilizer dart struck me. I barely had time to give myself the antidote before a couple dozen mercenaries closed in."

"Shit!"

"I held my own against them at first."

"Why the hell didn't you just run?"

"You know how badly we needed to tag one with a tracking device. We had no idea who we were fighting, who our enemy was. And every night we spent guessing, the threat grew."

He shook his head. "You could've been captured."

"I *would* have been captured," she corrected him, "had Zach not intervened."

"What was he doing there?"

She shrugged. "I didn't have a chance to ask. I did a good job of picking the mercenaries off, but took a lot of bullets in the process. Blood loss slowed me down and weakened me. I had nearly killed them all when the second wave moved in."

Ethan swore. Another trickle of blood emerged from his nose.

Reaching into her back pocket, Lisette withdrew a handkerchief and approached him. "There was no way I could've stood against those numbers. And I was too weak to outrun them." She took his stubbled chin in one hand and drew the soft white material across it, then dabbed beneath his nose. "I would have been captured, Ethan. I was bracing myself for it, intending to kill as many as I could before they took me, when Zach appeared and killed them all with a thought."

"He's that powerful?"

She nodded. "You saw what he did with the vampires' hearts."

"Did he do that with the mercenaries?" A spark of malicious pleasure glinted in Ethan's eyes at the notion. The mercenaries had been vicious men who had committed numerous atrocities, unconcerned by the innocents they killed in their quest to obtain the virus.

"No. He gave them all ruptured aneurisms. All but one of them."

Ethan whistled beneath the handkerchief.

"That one he tagged for me. Then he summoned Seth. He was gone when Seth arrived, but Seth saw all that had happened in my thoughts. He told me not to mention Zach to anyone and later told me to stay away from him, but didn't say why or even how he knew Zach."

Brushing the handkerchief aside, Ethan drew her close and locked his strong arms around her in a tight hug. "I can't believe I came so close to losing you and didn't even know it."

She hugged him back.

"Don't ever do anything that stupid again," he admonished, burying his face in her hair.

They held each other for a long moment. "Do you understand now?" she asked.

Withdrawing with some reluctance, he stared down at her. "Why you're helping Zach?"

She nodded.

"Yes, damn it," he grumbled, the battle he waged within obvious. "At least you aren't doing it because you think he has a nice ass."

Lisette laughed and headed over to the area in which the vampires had fallen. Only their clothing, weapons, dental fillings, and watches remained. "I'm sorry he hurt you."

Ethan grunted. "At the time, I thought he was just being a dick. But, after what you just told me, I think he might have actually been watching out for you, making sure Seth wouldn't find out about all of this." He picked up a nice-looking dagger, wiped it on one of the empty shirts, and tucked it into an inner pocket of his coat. "Why do you suppose Seth dislikes him so much?"

"I don't know." Lisette claimed the other dagger. "Zach

mentioned once that they had chosen different paths a long time ago and disagreed over which was the right one."

"What, like *path of life* kind of paths?"

"I don't know." She picked up a bloody pair of pants and started checking the pockets. "How's your head?"

"Better. Is my nose still bleeding?"

She looked up. "No."

"What are you doing anyway?"

"Trying to find some clue as to who the muscled vamps were. We're going to have to call Chris about this."

"I thought you didn't want anyone to know." He picked up another pair of pants and searched the pockets.

"Not about Zach. We'll have to leave that part out of it."

"No humans saw us. The mess is quick and easy to clean up. Toss the clothes in a Dumpster. Confiscate the weapons. Let the sprinkler system wash away the blood. No big deal. Why call at all?"

"Because Richart and I encountered a vampire like the big ones a couple of weeks ago."

"You did? He could fight like these two?"

"Yes. I thought it a fluke at the time. You know how it goes. Not *every* vampire led a sedentary life before he was turned. Some actually trained in martial arts or boxed. But those are rare. To encounter three who matched us in skill in such a short time . . ."

"Is no accident," he finished for her, brow furrowing. "Do you think another Bastien is raising a vampire army?"

Much to her surprise, Lisette found she disliked the comparison.

Sure Bastien had once been a villain. But he had redeemed himself since Seth had pretty much forced him into the fold. He had fought by their sides countless times. He had always been kind to Ami. Hell, he had even tested on *himself* the antidote Melanie had concocted to counteract the mercenaries' sedative to ensure no other immortal would be harmed if it went really wrong. Without that antidote, the Immortal Guardians would have been screwed many times over.

And he had done Lisette a *huge* favor last night.

"Not another Bastien," she corrected. "Bastien's on our side now."

Ethan sent her a crooked smile. "Won you over last night, did he?"

"He was already on his way to doing that before. I was just being stubborn because I liked Ewen." The Scottish immortal Bastien had slain so long ago had been a friend to all.

"You said yourself that Ewen attacked him."

She nodded. "I saw as much in Bastien's thoughts. But I also saw Ewen die."

"That sucks."

She collected the lanky vampires' flashy bowie knives. "Anyway, we may have another *Dennis* on our hands."

"Great. Just what we need: another self-proclaimed vampire king, raising and training an army of vampires and pitting them against us in a crazy-ass quest for world domination."

"This one isn't crazy yet. He can't be if he's creating vampires so well-trained and disciplined."

"And things were just returning to normal." Ethan dropped the pants and picked up a shirt. "I'm not finding anything. Are you?"

"No. Let's call Chris and see if his cleanup crew can discover something useful."

Chapter Four

Bastien sprawled in his favorite chair in Melanie's office at the network, indulging in his favorite pastime: watching his wife mutter to herself as she poured over test results and whatever other medical mumbo jumbo consumed her tonight. When she bent over her desk to search for a missing file, he tilted his head to one side and admired the trim thighs encased in formfitting faded blue jeans, followed them up to her tempting, shapely ass.

She straightened, file in hand, and began to flip through it. Her mind on the mysterious pages within, she absently reached up and tucked her hair behind one ear, exposing her profile.

Gorgeous.

His gaze slid along her jaw, down her slender throat, and caressed the full breasts below.

"Your eyes are glowing," she murmured, a smile in her voice.

"How do you know?" he countered. "You aren't even looking at me."

"I don't have to. The temperature in here just rose several degrees."

He smiled. "You've only your own tempting self to blame."

Closing the file, she turned to him with a smile. "You know I have work to do."

But work was *all* she seemed to do lately. She needed to relax. Grab a few light moments. Allow herself a release from the stress that had been weighing her down of late. He didn't like the furrow that now seemed a permanent fixture upon her brow.

Bastien sat up and leaned forward. Hooking a finger in one of her belt loops, he drew her toward him until she stood between his splayed knees. "Don't worry. What I have in mind doesn't have to take long. We are, after all, immortals . . . with preternatural speed."

She set the file on the table beside him. Her eyes acquired an amber glow as he pressed a kiss to the cleavage exposed by her V-necked T-shirt. "The vampires will hear us," she protested softly, leaning into him and combing her fingers through his hair.

Heat coursed through him, turning him rock hard, and she had barely touched him. "What happens at the network, stays at the network." He nudged the neckline of her shirt lower with his chin, dropped a few more kisses, stroked her breast along the edge of her skimpy bra with his tongue.

Her breath caught as he cupped the other breast in one hand and kneaded it.

"Um," Cliff, a former vampire follower of Bastien, said in his apartment across the hall, "that doesn't mean we *want* to hear it. It'd be too much like listening to our brother and sister do it."

"Dude, speak for yourself," Stuart, the vampire who lived next door to him, said. "They won't let me subscribe to the porn channels here."

Melanie's face flushed.

Bastien sighed. "And I believe that's Chris and Seth striding up the hallway, so . . ."

Eyes widening, Melanie tugged the neckline of her shirt up, grabbed the folder, and zipped over to her desk.

When Chris Reordon and Seth entered, she appeared to be studiously pouring over her notes . . . if one failed to notice the pink in her cheeks and her rapid pulse.

Seth glanced at Melanie, turned his attention to Bastien, and raised one eyebrow.

Bastien shrugged and nodded to Chris. "You need to add a quiet room down here."

If possible, Melanie's face grew even rosier.

"Why?" Chris asked. "For interrogation purposes?"

"Okay," Bastien said. It was as good a reason as any.

Chris frowned and glanced at Melanie just as she peeked at them over her shoulder. He turned back to Bastien. "Oh, hell no. I am *not* spending tens of thousands of dollars to soundproof a room down here so you two can have sex without the vampires hearing you."

Melanie covered her face with the file folder.

Seth crossed his arms over his chest, unable to suppress a smile.

Bastien quirked a brow at the irate human. "You *want* the vampires to hear us?"

"No," Chris sputtered. "I mean, I don't want you having sex! Not while you're both on the clock. Melanie is supposed to be working—"

"She is," Bastien defended her. "*Long* hours."

"And *you* are supposed to be serving as guard. Seven vampires live across the hallway. What are you going to do if a couple of them have psychotic breaks and try to escape while you two are having a quickie?"

"Chase them down bare-ass naked and give the human guards an eyeful."

"I don't know about you," one of the new vamps said in his room, "but I'm pretty sure even total mind-fuck madness wouldn't make me risk that guy chasing me down and tackling me while he's naked and has a hard-on."

Bastien and Seth both laughed.

"What?" Chris asked, unable to hear the vamps.

Bastien rose. "Nothing. Forget I mentioned it." At least the banter had given him a moment to get his body under control. He looked to Seth. "Ready?"

Seth nodded.

Bastien pulled the file away from his wife's red face and leaned down to brush her lips with a kiss. "I'll see you later."

She nodded. "Be careful."

Picking up the duffel bag beside his chair, he followed Seth across the hall to Cliff's apartment.

Reordon headed back to the elevator.

Bastien gave the door a perfunctory knock, then waited for Seth to wave a hand over the key-code pad.

A clunk sounded.

Seth pushed the door—as thick and heavy as that of a bank vault—open and motioned for Bastien to step inside.

Cliff slid off a bar stool, leaving behind a plate with sandwich crumbs, and smiled as Bastien entered. "Melanie is so going to kick your ass when you get home tonight."

He chuckled. "Not if I'm busy *kissing* hers."

"Damn it, Bastien!" she said from across the hallway.

Cliff laughed . . . until he saw Seth enter the apartment behind Bastien.

All of the vampires were uneasy around the powerful immortal leader, but Cliff, who had been infected the longest, was the most uncomfortable. Bastien suspected it stemmed from Cliff's knowing Seth could look into his mind and see every manic thought Cliff fought to hold at bay as the brain damage the virus spawned progressed.

"Hey," he greeted Seth.

Seth nodded. "Good evening, Cliff. How are you?"

"Fine, I guess." His brown eyes met Bastien's. "What's up?"

"Feel like taking a trip?"

He swallowed. "Now?"

Bastien nodded.

"Aren't you on guard duty?"

"Sean is on his way over to take my place. He'll be here in a few."

"Oh. Okay." Cliff's dreadlocks slid forward and hid his features as he bent down, retrieved a pair of sneakers from beneath the sofa, and donned them. Straightening, he wiped his palms on his jeans. "Can I say good-bye to Melanie first?"

"Bye, Cliff!" Melanie called merrily.

Cliff said nothing. He just stood there, looking as if he were about to walk the plank.

"Shall we?" Seth asked. Touching their shoulders, he teleported the three of them to the field that had once supported Bastien's vampire lair.

No structure remained. Only lumpy, uneven ground covered by grasses and weeds that swayed and rustled in the breeze.

As Cliff looked around, his expression lightened. "I never thought I'd see this place again." He drew in a deep breath. "Or smell it. Damn, it smells good out here."

Guilt pricked Bastien. Cliff had been cooped up at the network for so long. Perhaps if Bastien had worked harder to integrate himself into the Immortal Guardian family, he could have earned Seth's trust and done this sooner.

Cliff stared at the ground upon which Bastien's home had rested. "The old place is gone, huh?"

"Yes, as are the caverns we constructed beneath it."

"Wow. All that work . . ."

"I know." Smiling, Bastien tossed him the duffel bag. "This is for you."

Cliff caught it easily and unzipped it.

Inside lay hunting clothes and a nice assortment of weapons. Bastien had taken great care when he had chosen them, wanting his friend to have only the best. Cliff had been with him a long time. He was the last survivor of Bastien's vampire army. While three had surrendered during the final battle they had fought against the immortals, the other two had succumbed to the madness and . . .

Bastien mentally shook his head. He didn't want to think about that right now. Or about the fact that the young man before him would soon meet the same fate.

Cliff looked from the contents of the bag to Bastien. "What's this?"

Bastien clapped him on the back. "You're going hunting with me tonight." He had thought the young vampire would be as excited by the news as a child presented with a huge pile of presents on Christmas morning, but the smile Bastien expected never arose. "I thought you'd be pleased."

"He thinks we've brought him here to execute him," Seth said softly.

Bastien lost his smile. *"What?"* He waited for Cliff to deny it.

Cliff just stared at him, his hands clenched tightly in the material of the bag.

"Why the hell would you think that?"

Cliff glanced at Seth.

Seth looked to Bastien. "Because the violent thoughts are growing louder and harder to ignore, and he knows I can hear them."

Bastien's stomach sank like a stone. How much longer did they have until the psychotic breaks began? How much longer until Cliff asked Bastien to end it for him? "Why would I give you a bag full of hunting clothes and weapons if I intended to kill you?"

Cliff shrugged. "I thought maybe it was like people getting

their dog all excited about going for a ride in the car so he wouldn't realize they were taking him to the vet to have him put down."

Bastien stared at him. "That's fucked up."

"Yeah."

"Cliff, when the time comes, I'll either take care of it myself like I did with Vince, or Melanie will sedate you and drain you as she did with Joe. Either way, it will be on *your* terms."

"And," Seth added, "the hope remains that Melanie will discover a treatment before it comes to that."

Swallowing hard, the young vampire nodded and looked down at his bag of goodies. "So . . . this is real?" His eyes met Bastien's with a first flare of excitement. "You're really taking me hunting with you?"

Bastien forced a smile. "Yes."

Cliff glanced at Seth. "And you're okay with this?"

Seth nodded. "You've proven yourself to be a valuable member of our family. We could use another good hunter."

Cliff's face lit with a grin. "This is so cool!"

Seth smiled. "I'll leave you to it then. Enjoy your hunt."

As soon as the Immortal Guardians' leader vanished, Cliff stripped down to his skivvies and donned the traditional black hunting garb of Seconds and immortals. Black pants. Black shirt. Black coat outfitted with numerous pockets and sheaths.

"Will the coat be a hindrance to you?" Bastien asked. "You aren't accustomed to fighting in one."

Cliff picked up a couple of daggers and flipped them end over end, catching them with a flourish, then performed several experimental swings, kicks, twirls, and thrusts at preternatural speed. "No. I'm good with it."

He was also very good with weapons. The human members of the network would probably crap their pants if they knew Bastien hadn't just been sitting on his ass, playing video games when he visited Cliff. He had been training him. Cliff was almost as good a fighter as Bastien was. Had he possessed Bastien's age and the added strength and speed that came with it, he would've been capable of defeating immortals as young as Ethan.

"Shall we go then?"

Cliff nodded eagerly. "Where to?"

"I thought we would see what's happening at UNCG tonight." The campus was nearer network headquarters than the others. Seth had thought it best that they stick pretty close to home . . . at least on their initial forays.

"Wanna race?" Cliff asked.

Bastien shook his head. "Let's save that for the end of the night if you still have the energy. I've got a car parked through there."

Cliff followed him through the trees to the Chevy Volt and folded his thin frame into the passenger seat. He smiled. "It smells like Melanie in here."

Bastien nodded. "It's her car." Since he and Melanie were rarely apart, he hadn't seen a need to procure one of his own.

Cliff raised an eyebrow. "It also smells like sex."

His acute sense of smell *would* pick that up. "Yyyyeah. Melanie and I sometimes . . ."

"Go at it like teenagers?"

Bastien laughed. "Yes. Just don't tell her I told you that."

The drive was short. Cliff peered through the windshield, eagerly devouring the sight of the countryside he hadn't seen for so long. "I'm glad you two found each other," he commented as Bastien parked the car.

"Me too." Bastien kept his eyes and ears peeled for vampire activity as they strolled onto the quiet campus.

"Do you still feel like you don't deserve her?"

"All the time." And he had admitted as much often in the early days of their relationship.

"Well, you do," Cliff said. "Deserve her, I mean. You're a good guy, Bastien. I wish you could see that."

Bastien looked at him askance. "You aren't going to get maudlin on me, are you?"

Cliff laughed. "No, I just wanted to put that out there in case I don't have a chance to say it later. I really appreciate everything you've done for me. You've been a good friend."

It almost sounded like a good-bye. Alarm bells rang. Bastien stopped. "Cliff, if you're thinking of running, I've been ordered to—"

"I'm not," Cliff assured him. "I don't want to hurt anyone. I don't want to torture and kill innocents the way other vampires do."

"Joe didn't either when he surrendered and sought the network's help. But he wouldn't have hesitated to run if I had taken him hunting with me."

"I'm not suffering the paranoia that struck Joe." Near the end, Joe had become convinced that the immortals had tricked him and were his enemy, that they were actually *causing* his madness instead of trying to cure it. "I just have . . . violent thoughts. Really ugly, violent thoughts." His look turned pensive. "It's getting harder and harder to not act upon them when I'm around Dr. Whetsman."

Bastien snorted. "Hell, *I* have violent thoughts when I'm around Dr. Whetsman." The sniveling weasel was Bastien's least favorite colleague of Melanie's. "Even *Chris* has violent thoughts around Whetsman. He's a total prick." An incredibly intelligent prick, but a prick just the same. Chris had once admitted he would've fired Whetsman a long time ago if his input weren't so crucial.

Cliff's brow cleared. A smile dawned. "I still laugh when I think about the time you got all up in his grill about talking down to Melanie and giving her a hard time. I thought for sure he was going to wet his pants."

Bastien grimaced. "I almost wish he would've. Whetsman doesn't wet himself when he gets nervous. He farts."

Cliff laughed. "I know. Melanie has a hell of a time keeping a straight face when he's around us vampires. You know we terrify him."

Bastien laughed.

A cool breeze ruffled his hair.

"Wow, you smell that?" Cliff asked, tilting his head back and drawing in a deep breath. "The three B's: bad breath, B.O., and blood. Ahhhhh. It's like we're back in your lair again."

Bastien shook his head. He might have succeeded in forcing his vampire followers to eat foods he had hoped would slow the progression of the madness, but he had never succeeded in improving their personal hygiene. "Let's go check it out."

"Wait." Cliff stopped him with a hand on his arm. "What's my role here? When you said I could hunt with you . . ."

"I meant you could help me locate and kick some vampire ass."

Cliff offered him a huge grin. "Seriously? I get to join the fight and everything?"

"Absolutely."

"Awesome! Let's go!"

Bastien had only hunted with two others as an Immortal Guardian. Richart, when Seth had insisted Bastien have a babysitter to keep him out of trouble. And Melanie, when Seth had ordered her to monitor Bastien after he had dosed himself with the experimental antidote. Richart had been a pain in the ass, yet tolerable. Melanie had been deliciously distracting.

Cliff . . .

Hunting with Cliff was like hunting with a brother. After Melanie, he was Bastien's best friend. Being around him was comfortable and stress-free, with none of the constant need to prove himself or stay on guard to fend off the verbal blows other immortals slung.

In short, it was fun.

They found two vampires feeding on a couple of female students in the shadows between two buildings. Letting Cliff take the lead, Bastien held back and observed from several yards away, ready to intervene if necessary.

"Hey," Cliff greeted them, stopping only a foot or two away from the vamps. "What's up?"

They raised their heads and looked around, eyes glowing, fangs crimson and dripping.

Good. Had Cliff just yanked one of the vampires away from his victim, the vamp could have torn her carotid artery.

The blond vampire hissed like a cat.

Cliff burst into laughter. "Dude! Seriously?"

Frowning, the blond released the woman.

Eyes bleary and unfocused, she staggered a couple of steps backward, then slid down the wall to sit on the ground.

The vampire's brunet companion shoved his victim toward the other woman and faced Cliff. "Who the fuck are you?"

"I'm Cliff," he answered with a genial smile.

The two vampires looked at each other, bloody faces blank with confusion.

"What did you *think* I would say?" Cliff inquired. "That I'm your worst nightmare?" He drew two long daggers and displayed them in a series of showy swirls and flips and tosses. "I probably *am*, but thought it would be rude to say so."

The blond drew a bowie knife. "You're an Immortal Guardian?"

"Sadly, no," Cliff said, grin still in place. "But I *do* still plan to kick your ass."

The second the words left his lips, his eyes flashed bright amber, his fangs descended, and he attacked.

Swearing, the vampires scrambled to fight him off and avoid his blades.

Cliff struck with vicious intensity, his smile gone.

Bastien looked around to see if anyone dallied nearby when the vampires began to scream. He didn't know if it was pent-up energy, pent-up aggression, pent-up frustration, or a first display of the madness formerly held at bay, but . . . Cliff tore those vamps to shreds.

Had Bastien not done the same to the mercenaries who had shot Melanie, he would've been disturbed by it.

One vampire collapsed to the ground, already starting to shrivel up.

Cliff grabbed the other by the hair, yanked his head to one side, and started to sink his fangs into the dying vamp's neck.

Bastien shot forward and stopped him before he could. "Don't."

Cliff glared up at him.

Bastien could hear Cliff's heart racing, pumping adrenaline through his veins.

Cliff tried to shove him away.

Bastien didn't budge. "Don't."

"Why? They were draining those women. Why not give them a taste of their own medicine?"

"Because Melanie is worried that drinking the blood of another vampire will increase your viral load." He frowned. "Or is it viral count?" He shook his head. "I can't remember. I just know she's afraid that it will make the brain damage and madness progress faster."

Either Bastien's calm tone or the science jargon reached Cliff.

Dragging in a deep breath, Cliff calmed and dropped the vampire. "He'll be dead soon anyway."

Bastien clapped him on the back. "Good. How do you feel?"

Cliff thought about it as the vampire at their feet drew

his last breath and began to deteriorate. "Juiced. Relaxed. Relieved that I didn't lose it completely and try to bail on you or something."

"I knew you'd keep it together."

"Yeah, but I *really* wanted to bite that guy. I mean, I wanted to rip his throat out."

"Don't let it disturb you. I feel the same thing every night. I'm not exactly what one would call even-tempered."

At last, Cliff laughed. "I think you would bore Melanie if you were."

Bastien knelt before the women.

Brow creased with concern, Cliff joined him. "Are they going to be okay?"

Both females had lost consciousness during the battle, but a quick listen to their pulse told Bastien they'd survive. Neither, thankfully, would remember the vampires' attack. With the first bite, the glands that had formed above the fangs of vampires during their transformation would've delivered a chemical that acted like GHB in the system.

"They'll be fine." Bastien drew his cell phone out and dialed the network.

"Reordon."

"It's Bastien. Cliff and I found a couple of vampires feeding on two human women. Can you send a cleanup crew out here to see them home?"

"Sure. Where are you?"

Bastien gave him their location.

"How do you like hunting, Cliff?" Chris asked, knowing the young vampire could hear both ends of the conversation.

Cliff's eyebrows flew up. "It's weird."

Chris laughed. "I know, right? Jack will be there in ten to take care of the women."

The line went dead.

"That was weird, too," Cliff said as Bastien tucked away his phone.

"What was?"

"Reordon's asking me what I thought about hunting instead of asking you if I'd lost my shit."

Bastien shrugged. Both questions would have accomplished the same goal—letting Chris know if Cliff had lost it during the fight—but this way Chris had left Cliff's dignity intact. "I can't believe I'm saying this, but I think I'm actually starting to like that asshole."

"Chris?"

"Yes."

"Reordon's a good guy," Cliff said slowly. "He's been really nice to me ever since the mercenaries got their hands on me."

"Good. He should be. You saved a lot of lives that night."

Cliff smiled.

"So," Bastien said, "once the cleanup crew arrives, do you want to call it a night? Or are you up for more hunting?"

"More hunting," Cliff chose with amusing enthusiasm.

Zach perched on Lisette's roof, waiting for her to return home.

A long sigh escaped him. The shingles beneath him were beginning to acquire a shine only wear could deliver. He would have to find a new place to sit soon or his ass would end up going through the roof.

Gargoyle duty.

The description fit. He really *did* feel like a gargoyle tonight. Probably resembled one, too. He hadn't taken the time to look in a mirror before he had teleported to Lisette's side and ended her battle with the unusually powerful vampires.

He shifted, unable to get comfortable. Most of the wounds on his body had healed. His wings would need more time, though. The immortal black sheep had done a good job of splinting them. Zach supposed he would have to find a way to repay him. *If* Bastien didn't betray Lisette to Seth.

A raccoon the size of a beagle waddled across the lawn below him.

Zach's thoughts wandered to the scene that had greeted him when he had sensed Lisette was in danger and tele-ported to her, fearing the Others had found her.

Something about the vampires she and the younger im-mortal had fought hadn't been right. Not the lanky ones who had already fallen by the time he'd arrived, but the other two.

Mentally he replayed the scene over and over again. Two immortals working together should have had no difficulty defeating two vampires. He had seen Lisette drop five in one skirmish. Two shouldn't have even made her sweat.

Zach had given the vampires a quick scan, wondering at first if the two weren't immortals who, like Bastien, had been overlooked by Seth. No advanced DNA had inhabited their forms. Zach *had*, however, found blank spots in their minds. While the vampiric virus *did* cause brain damage that resulted in blank spots, the ones he had found in the muscled vamps' minds had been different. *Their* blank spots could only have been caused by one of two things: either memo-ries had been buried so deeply that they would never rise again or memories had been completely erased.

Someone with strong telepathic abilities must have buried or erased those memories.

Someone *other* than Zach.

Over the shuffling steps of the raccoon and the multitude of croaking frogs that lingered in a nearby stream, he heard the low rumble of Lisette's Hayabusa.

After Seth's unjust accusation—and the torture Zach had endured as a result of Seth's stealing his powers and planting a *Come and Get 'im, Boys* sign on Zach's head for the Others—Zach had thought it would be fun to watch some unknown immortal with aspirations of grandeur try to destroy his or her leader and usurp his command.

The betrayal would tear Seth up inside.

Watching his Immortal Guardians suffer on his behalf would kill him.

Revenge would be so sweet.

Unfortunately, Zach had neglected to consider that Lisette would be caught in the crossfire. That she could suffer or be destroyed, too.

His pulse picked up as she turned onto her drive and headed toward the house.

The thought of offering Seth aid—look what the hell it had gotten Zach in the past—really chapped his ass. But Lisette . . .

A low sound rife with frustration vibrated his chest.

Damn it, he was going to have to say something. Either that or watch over her twenty-four hours a day until whatever happened happened. He wouldn't let her come to harm. And Seth could go fuck himself if he didn't like it.

Silently, Zach watched as she parked the Busa. Removing her helmet, she stowed it away, tilted her head back, and looked right at him. "What are you doing up there?"

He would've shrugged if his wings hadn't been aching so much. "Waiting for you."

"Why didn't you wait inside? You should be resting."

"I *am* resting."

She pursed her lips.

"Being in your home when you were gone felt . . . wrong," he admitted. Being in her home *at all* had felt wrong. Her home was warm and comfortable and welcoming. He could practically hear all of the laughter she and her brothers and their Seconds had shared beneath this roof.

That was foreign to him.

She waved him down. "Well, I'm home now, so let's go inside."

A strange fluttery feeling invaded his stomach and chest.

Zach teleported to the ground, appearing a few feet away from her.

"You're scowling," she said.

Was that why her pulse had picked up? Did she fear him?

Zach endeavored to smooth his brow.

A tentative smile curled her full lips. "Better." She motioned toward the steps that led up to the front porch. "Shall we?"

Still he hesitated.

Following her through that front door would be tantamount to giving up any plans for revenge. He couldn't involve himself further in Lisette's life *and* sit back and watch Seth fall. Lisette would gladly die trying to protect her leader.

The silence stretched.

Stepping closer to him, she reached out and took his hand.

Zach's heart began to slam against his ribs as Lisette twined her slender fingers through his.

Her hand was so small and delicate within his. Her touch warm.

Giving his hand a light squeeze, she offered him a shy smile, turned, and led him into her home.

Chapter Five

Lisette wondered at her daring.

She could hear Zach's heart pounding in his chest, nearly drowned out by her own heart's attempts to burst from her breast. Did he feel the same thing she did? That sort of nervous, yet delicious excitement that she hadn't felt since she was a girl embroiled in her first infatuation? It had been so long, she had almost forgotten how wonderful it was. How alive it made her feel. How . . . happy?

Zach was so much older. So powerful. He had no doubt seen and done things she couldn't even imagine. Why would her touch make *his* pulse race?

Fatigue and weakness must surely be the cause.

"Have you eaten?" she asked him, trying hard to sound nonchalant.

"No."

She glanced down at her bloody clothing, stiff and crusty in places where the wind had dried it on her way home. "Give me a minute, then I'll fix us both something tasty."

His fingers tightened around hers momentarily. Then, releasing her hand, he nodded.

"Make yourself at home." Dashing downstairs, she entered her bedroom, tugged off her clothes, then slipped into the shower. Hot water sluiced down over her, rinsing the blood from her body. As steam rose around her, she tugged the tie from the end of her braid and unwound it.

She heard no movement above. Was Zach so quiet that even *her* sensitive ears couldn't detect him?

Hell, for all she knew, he could be in her bedroom right now, peeking into the bathroom.

Spinning around, she rubbed the foggy condensation from the shower door and peered through the glass.

No tall, dark form blocked the doorway.

Grabbing the soap and washcloth, she gave her body a quick scrubbing.

Seconds later, the hot water rinsed the frothy lather from her skin and left her clean once more. A quick towel dry, followed by a frustrating competition between her comb and the tangles in her long, wet hair, and Lisette found herself standing before her open wardrobe, vacillating over what she should wear.

Something pretty? Or the usual combat-ready clothing?

Sighing, she chose the latter. She was already feeling oddly unsure of herself. Why wear something that might not inspire the response she wanted and would make things worse?

She refused to contemplate exactly what response she was hoping for and donned clean hunting togs. Black pants that rode low on her hips. A black T-shirt. She even added the socks and boots.

Looking at herself in the mirror, she shook her head. As a mortal and the daughter of a French aristocrat, she had worn corsets and layer upon layer of clothing, had stuffed her feet into fashionable shoes that had pinched and mangled her toes, had spent hours styling her hair since she had lacked the easy-to-use styling products available today, and more. It had been miserable. It had been ridiculously time-consuming. And she had looked lovely.

Now this. Most nights she didn't mind dressing like a man, which was what wearing pants had been considered in those days. It was a hell of a lot more comfortable and far less trouble. But every once in a while, she missed feeling pretty and feminine.

Turning away from her reflection, she left the bedroom.

Upstairs she found Zach in the same place she had left him. While only a few minutes had passed, she had nevertheless expected him to at least seat himself in the living room.

"When I said make yourself at home," she said, striding toward him, "I meant for you to have a seat in the living room and make yourself comfortable."

He glanced at the living room. "Oh."

She waited for more.

Nothing came.

He reminded her a bit of Roland in that moment. Maybe he was antisocial, too. Or, for whatever reason, simply wasn't comfortable in social situations. He wouldn't be the first shy immortal she had met. Alleck, the German immortal who visited the network periodically at Seth's request to compare notes with Melanie, was about as shy as they came, and he was hundreds of years old. "Do you have a taste for anything in particular?" she asked as she headed into the large kitchen. She had a feeling if she hadn't asked the question, he would have continued to stand near the front door.

Slowly, he followed. "No."

She paused, fingers curled around the refrigerator door handle. "Do you need blood? I'm sorry I didn't think to ask earlier."

"No, thank you." He frowned. "Did you give me blood while I was unconscious?"

"No. Should I have?" she asked, unable to abandon the suspicion that he wasn't an immortal. Not like her and the rest of the Immortal Guardians anyway.

"No." He had the most deliciously smooth, deep voice. "I'm an elder. I don't need blood to heal."

Which told her nothing. Seth didn't need blood to heal either. She tried to recall if she had ever seen David infuse himself with blood and couldn't.

Opening the door, she considered the packed-from-top-to-bottom refrigerator's contents. (Tracy always kept it full enough to feed at least half a dozen.) Her brothers were big men, but weren't big meat eaters. Étienne had once complained that he could eat a whole cow and still be hungry afterward. So they preferred vegetables and fruits that were more filling. Lisette was a carbohydrate fiend. She simply could *not* get enough pastas, breads, potatoes, etcetera. And fighting vampires burned a lot of energy.

"Would pasta be okay?" she asked. "Tracy just made a huge pot of chunky veggie pasta sauce, so it'll be a quick and easy fix."

Zach didn't respond.

Glancing over her shoulder, she found him staring at her. "Zach?"

"I shouldn't be here."

She couldn't place his accent. It was similar to Seth's, which neither she nor her siblings had ever been able to identify. Eastern European? Egyptian? South African? Russian? She just couldn't tell.

But Zach's was a little softer, almost British.

"I thought we had already covered that," she said.

"The Others will be looking for me."

She drew the big pot of sauce from the fridge and set it on the stove. "Are you going to tell me who the others are?"

"No."

"Because you're the big, strong, silent type?" Common traits found in immortal males.

"Because they'll kill you if they find out you know."

A sobering thought. She turned on the burner.

"They'll likely kill you if they find out you aided me as well."

Well, hell. She had just thought he didn't share because he liked his privacy.

"I shouldn't have come here. I don't even remember how I got here last night."

"I'm not sure how you did either. I was asleep and only heard it." She began filling a second pot with filtered water. "It sounded like you fell out of the sky, hit the roof hard, then rolled off onto the ground. I don't know how you could have flown with your wings as damaged as they were, so maybe you teleported and miscalculated." Richart had done that several times when he was sorely wounded and couldn't think straight. Not that long ago, when drugged by Dennis, her brother had accidentally teleported to his mortal girlfriend's apartment instead of David's house and outed himself as an immortal.

"I should go," Zach announced.

Denial gripped her. "Can't you just—I don't know—block them or keep them from finding you?"

"Yes."

"Are you doing it now?"

"Yes."

"Then I don't see any reason for concern. If they were going to find you, they would've done it while you were unconscious and would have already come and gone, wouldn't they?" And slain them both, judging by his grim expression.

"I would've thought so, yes."

"Then relax." Lisette gestured to the table in the breakfast nook. "Have a seat. This won't take long to prepare. And you must still be weary." Shutting off the water, she set the pot on the stove and turned on the burner beneath it. Next she took down a big box of uncooked rigatoni from an upper cabinet.

"Why are you doing this?" Confusion colored Zach's voice.

Lisette set the pasta down and gave him her full attention. "Doing what?"

He hesitated. "Helping me. Being . . . kind to me."

Why indeed? She kept getting deeper and deeper and deeper into this . . . whatever this was. "You saved my life."

His lips tilted up in a faint smile that seemed to reflect cynicism, relief, and disappointment all at once. "Ah. You feel obligated. I understand now."

"Not obligated," she corrected. "Grateful. And . . ."

"And?" he prompted.

"Don't you know?" she asked curiously. "Haven't you looked into my thoughts?"

"No."

Interesting. Seth and David seemed to lack any reservations when it came to reading the minds of their charges. And, if she were honest, she and Étienne intruded on their friends' thoughts far more often than they should. One would think Zach, perhaps the antithesis of Seth, would possess even fewer scruples.

Or did he lie?

Could he be testing her to see if she would tell him the truth?

Hell, what did she have to lose at this point?

Crossing the kitchen, she stopped a foot away from Zach and tilted her head back to look up at him.

"Ask me again," she ordered softly.

"Why are you doing this?" he murmured.

"Because I'm drawn to you, Zach."

His heart began to beat faster.

As did hers. "I'm drawn to you in a way that makes me want to risk everything just for the chance to know more of you."

His eyes lit with a mild golden glow. "Why?"

She gave her head a slow shake. "I don't know. But I suspect . . . I *hope* . . . that it's the same for you, that that's why you came here—to me—when you were so badly injured and needed help."

He raised one of his hands and, almost as though she were a bird he feared he might frighten away, captured a damp strand of hair that dangled in front of her ear, testing its texture with his fingers. "I came to you because you were all I could think of while I was being tortured." He drew the lock closer to his face and breathed in the citrus scent of her shampoo. "I came to you because you were all that enabled me to endure it."

I am in so much trouble here, Lisette thought. Reaching up, she caressed his face, delighting in the rasp of his stubble against her fingertips and palm.

He stiffened.

"Is this okay?" she asked, wondering if he had gone so still because she was hurting him.

"I'm not accustomed to being touched," he whispered.

That surprised her . . . and didn't. Zach was so incredibly handsome. One would think women would throw themselves at him everywhere he went.

At the same time, though, he really did remind her of Roland. So untrusting. So solitary. So apart from everything and everyone. Who knew *how* long Roland had gone without a woman's touch before Sarah had come into his life. Perhaps it had been the same for Zach.

"I touched you in my dream," she said.

"That was different."

"How so?"

"It wasn't real."

In the dream, he had reached up and held her hand to his cheek. He had kissed her. Touched her breast. Set her body aflame.

He did none of that now, though he looked as though he wanted to.

"Should I stop?" she asked, filled with uncertainty. She didn't *want* to stop.

He nodded.

Hurt pricked her. Did he not like her touch?

"The water is boiling," he said, never taking his eyes from hers.

Oh. She hadn't even noticed.

Lowering her hand, she turned and headed back to the stove. Her long hair trailed through his fingers, then slipped free.

"Have a seat," she encouraged once more, trying to get her pulse back under control.

Finally, Zach relaxed enough to sit down.

Lisette didn't hear him move. She just glanced over and found him sitting sideways in a chair at the table, one arm resting on the chair back and the other on the table, the tips of his wings brushing the floor behind him.

"How are your wings?"

Zach watched Lisette move around the kitchen as she prepared their meal. "Better." He flexed his wings the tiniest bit. Pain arced through him like an electric current, but he bore it in silence. "They'll be healed soon."

"Good."

His heart still raced from her nearness.

Her hand had been small and warm against his jaw, her touch tender. So many feelings had inundated him, all new and unfamiliar, that it had been a struggle to speak.

"Is tea all right?" She removed a large pitcher from the refrigerator.

He nodded.

His skin still tingled. His thoughts raced.

No wonder, an inner voice spoke with awe. *No wonder Seth left us. No wonder he abandoned the cold, sterile existence of the Others and sought the companionship of humans.*

When Seth had first seen the human woman he had taken as his wife thousands of years ago, had he—like Zach—been instantly fascinated? Had his life changed course that very day? Or had Seth, like Zach, spent weeks or months watching her until he became willing to risk all just to speak to her? Hiding his fixation from the Others. Shielding his actions and whereabouts so none of them would guess.

And *none* of them had guessed. Zach had been as shocked as the rest of them.

Lisette approached—he loved to watch her move—and set a tall glass of tea on the table beside him.

Zach curled his fingers around the cold glass to keep himself from reaching for her. "Thank you."

She smiled.

Trebly rock music filled the kitchen.

Zach cursed whoever was calling when Lisette backed away and drew her cell phone from a back pocket.

"Excuse me, please. *Oui?*"

"Hi. It's me," he heard her Second say.

Lisette glanced at Zach. "Hi. Are you still at David's?"

"Yeah. How'd tonight's hunt go?"

"It went well. Ethan joined me, and we took out four vamps."

"Cool. I'm pretty bushed from training with Darnell. Is it okay if I bunk here again today?"

"Sure."

"Okay. Call me if you need anything."

"I will. Sleep well."

"You too."

Lisette ended the call and returned the phone to her pocket. Turning away, she drew a metal colander from a lower cabinet, placed it in the sink, and drained the water from the pasta. "Don't worry. She knows I want some time alone, but she doesn't know anything about this, so Seth and David won't see you in her thoughts."

He watched Lisette heap two plates full of pasta and top it with the aromatic sauce. "Doesn't she mind your keeping secrets from her?"

"Probably. But she understands the necessity of it. She's been around telepaths long enough to know that any secret I want to keep from Étienne, I must keep from her. Once his curiosity is aroused, he'll peek into any brain he has to, to find the information he wants."

"I would've thought an Immortal Guardian would suffer twinges of conscience over breeching another's privacy in such a way." Weren't Immortal Guardians supposed to be the boy scouts of the preternatural world?

She sent him a sheepish grin. "I'm just as bad." Picking up the plates, she carried them to the table. "If you weren't so much older than I am, I probably would have examined every nook and cranny of your mind by now."

Then he was fortunate she couldn't do so. There were some very dark days in his past.

Dark days and dark deeds he didn't want her to see.

She set one plate in front of him and one in front of the chair catty-corner to him.

Zach's view of her shapely bottom, as she turned away, was blocked by her long hair. He had never seen it loose before. The ends had begun to dry and curled every which way. The rest rippled with soft waves.

She returned, carrying a second glass of tea and a plate of bread.

Zach rose and drew her chair out for her.

Surprise and pleasure lit her light brown eyes as she sat and let him scoot the chair forward a bit.

He was a little surprised himself. It was yet another first for him.

Zach retook his seat and turned a bit so he could face the table more. Pain shot through his wings again when he accidentally jostled them.

"You didn't have wings in the dream," she mentioned, "when we were outside David's place."

He forced his muscles to unbunch and relax. He had kissed her in that dream, had touched her full breast. How he wished he could do the same now. Instead he picked up his fork and tucked into his meal. "I can retract them if I wish and make them—for all intents and purposes—disappear."

"Oh."

"I would do so now, but I can't until they're healed."

Her brow furrowed as she chewed.

She even did that beautifully, he thought with an inward shake of his head, following the motion of her pale, elegant throat as she swallowed.

"Does Seth have wings?"

Unease crept through him. He didn't know how he should respond to questions about Seth. "Seth is a shape-shifter like David. He can have or be anything he wants."

Her look carried a reprimand. "You know that isn't what I meant. Is Seth like you?"

Zach toyed with his food for a long moment, considering his words carefully. "Lisette . . ."

Her eyes fastened on his, acquiring an amber glow.

"What?" he asked, confused. Had he angered her?

"I don't think you've ever called me by my name before."

Because doing so felt intimate. "Forgive me. I should have asked—"

"No," she interrupted. "I like it. I'm sorry. You were saying?"

"Lisette," he began again, "if we . . . spend time together . . ."

"Yes?" she encouraged when he faltered.

How should he put this? "There will be things—about myself and about Seth—that I won't be able to share with you."

She looked down at her plate. "Because you don't trust me?"

"I wouldn't be here now if I didn't trust you." The trust he was willing to place in her astonished him. Were her safety not at risk, he suspected he would've answered every question she asked him.

"Then why?"

"For the same reason you don't tell your Second certain things. I can't risk your brother, or any other telepathic immortal, finding the information in your thoughts."

A full minute passed while she studied her plate.

"No protest?" he asked.

"No," she muttered. "Étienne has been in my head so much, I have a hard time keeping secrets from him. And I can't promise I'll never let my guard down. I get tired. I get wounded. I sleep. And my barriers fall." She speared some pasta, but didn't raise it to her lips. "Even with my barriers in place, Seth and David could read me if they wanted to."

Silence engulfed them. It wasn't a particularly comfortable one.

Zach scrambled for something to say. "Would you like me to leave?"

"No," she said without hesitation, but both her words and tone lacked pleasure. "If I were like Ethan, would you tell me? Would you answer my questions?"

"I fear I would, yes."

At last she met his gaze. "Why fear?"

He considered his answer. "I once heard Roland ask Seth—long ago, before you were born—what the source of *gifted ones'* advanced DNA was. Seth refused to answer. His explanation: that, if he did, bloodshed would follow."

A spark of interest lit her eyes. "Do *you* know the source of our advanced DNA?"

"Yes. But speaking of such things, as well as of Seth's origins and my own, always results in bloodshed."

"Why?"

"Because someone always shares the information with someone they shouldn't. Someone always *trusts* where he or she shouldn't. And the consequences are far greater than you could imagine."

"You say that as if you know from experience. Did you tell someone in the past?"

"No." After a short mental debate, he revealed, "Seth did. His wife."

Her eyes widened. "Seth was married?"

"Once."

"What happened?"

"She was slain. As were their children."

"Seth had children?"

"A son and a daughter. His son gave his heart and his trust to a woman who did not keep Seth's secret. She trusted where she should not have, told a friend, and . . ." Zach shook his head. "It unleashed a storm even Seth could not contain."

Lisette raised the pasta to her lips and slipped it within.

Zach almost forgot to eat as he watched the rhythmic motions of her jaw.

"Are you as powerful as Seth is?" she asked after a moment.

"No." Fury filled him. "But I *will* be."

"Why are you so angry with him?"

Hard for her not to pick up on, he supposed, since he tensed up and practically snarled every time she mentioned Seth's name. "Because he's the reason I was tortured."

"What?"

"He led the Others to me, knowing they would punish me."

"Why would he do that?"

"Because he blamed me for something I didn't do."

"I don't believe that. I can't."

Of course not. The Immortal Guardians all thought their leader infallible.

"Believe it." Glancing up, he saw confusion and disillusionment darken her eyes and sighed. "Sometimes the truth is too harsh to bear even for someone of Seth's age. It's easier, in such instances, to believe a lie."

Lisette said nothing. She seemed stunned by the possibility that her much-revered leader could have accused Zach of something he hadn't done.

"Is it not easier," he asked, "for a child to believe that Santa Claus exists than it is for him to believe his parents lied to him and betrayed him?"

"Seth isn't a child."

"Nor were you," he forced himself to say gently, "when your husband turned on you."

He might as well have slapped her.

She paled. "What?"

"You're telepathic," he continued, his voice as soft and coaxing as he could make it. "You must have known something was not right with him long before the night your husband attacked you and transformed you."

Resentment flared in her features.

"Was it not easier for you to tell yourself it was nothing?" he asked. "That his sudden, violent bursts of temper were the result of too much drink? Not enough sleep? Bad luck at cards? Anything that enabled you to ignore the madness that steadily claimed him?"

At first, he thought she might lash out and hit him.

Then her throat moved with a swallow. "Yes," she whispered painfully. "How did you know that?"

"I didn't. I knew only that your husband was vampire and turned you in a fit of madness. I guessed the rest."

She set her fork down and clasped her hands in her lap, clenching them until her knuckles turned white. "I should have said something." The pain in the eyes that met his surpassed the physical torment he had suffered these past few months. "If I had told Richart and Étienne what was happening . . ." She shook her head. Moisture welled in her eyes. "I was so ashamed. I *begged* Father to let me marry Philippe, to let me marry that . . . that monster. I couldn't bring myself to tell them. If I *had*—"

"They could have done nothing."

"They could have had him locked up in an asylum or . . ."

Zach reached over and covered her hands with one of his. "An asylum would not have held him, Lisette. You know that. He was vampire. The attendants would have been human. Their drugs would not have affected him. Their shackles would not have restrained him. They would have been helpless against his speed and strength." He squeezed her hands. "Had you told your brothers, they would have confronted him and been slain."

Her hands relaxed beneath his.

"Forgive me. I didn't mean to upset you," he said with genuine regret. "I merely wanted to help you understand why Seth did what he did, why he was so eager to leap to the conclusion that *I* had betrayed him." And Zach had damned near convinced himself to forgive the bastard in the process. What the hell was he thinking?

She unclasped her hands and sandwiched his between her own. "I'm sorry. It's a sore subject." A weary sigh escaped her. "I don't think I'll ever be free of the guilt of turning my brothers."

From what Zach had gleaned from his eavesdropping sessions, her brothers had offered her their blood after her transformation in an attempt to hide her condition, not knowing that repeated exposure to the virus in low doses would eventually cause *them* to transform as well. "Did it never occur to you that your brothers might also harbor guilt?"

"What do you mean?"

"They introduced you to your husband. They must have guessed, after the fact, how he had treated you as his insanity grew, that he had hurt you. They blame *themselves* for it all, not you."

Another long pause followed as she considered it. "You're just guessing. You can't—"

"I hear things," he interrupted. "I heard *them*."

"While you were up on the roof?"

"Pulling gargoyle duty," he said wryly. "You should harbor no guilt. Your brothers don't blame you. And both are revoltingly happy now."

She laughed. "Yes, they are." Still smiling, she smoothed her hand over the back of his, sending tingles of warmth dancing up his arm. "I thought you didn't like to be touched."

He found he had to clear his throat before he could speak. "I said I'm not *accustomed* to being touched." He drew a circle on her silky skin with his thumb. "Or to touching."

She cast him a flirtatious look through her long lashes. "Is it something you think you could get used to?"

He smiled. "With you? Absolutely."

Raising his hand to her lips, she pressed a tender kiss to his knuckles.

And Zach was lost.

"I have one more question, then I'll let you finish your meal."

He just hoped he would be able to answer it.

"Can you make me like Ethan?"

He quirked an eyebrow. "You wish to be cocky, arrogant, self-absorbed—"

She laughed. "I'll give you the cocky and arrogant part, but he isn't self-absorbed. And you know that isn't what I meant. Can you make it harder for other telepaths to read my thoughts and memories?"

He shook his head. "I don't know what makes him so

difficult to read. Anything you don't wish others to find, I would have to bury."

"So I would forget it, too?"

"Yes."

"Well, it was worth a shot."

Muffled rock music again filled the kitchen.

"Excuse me for a moment." Releasing his hand, she pulled her cell phone from her back pocket and answered the call. *"Oui?"*

"It's me again," he heard Tracy say. "I just wanted to let you know that Chris has called a meeting for tomorrow night, an hour after sunset."

"I'll be there. Do you want me to bring you anything?"

"No, I'm good. David has everything I need here. See you tomorrow."

Lisette tucked her phone away with a frown. "It must be about the vampires we fought tonight."

"The meeting?"

Nodding, she picked up her fork. "That's the second time I've come up against vampires like that. Not the skinny, slacker ones, but the large, ass-kicking ones. Some vampire must be following Dennis's example and raising an army."

Concern pricked Zach as he returned to his meal. "Did you notice anything different about the two tougher vamps?"

"Aside from their obvious fighting skills? No, not really."

"Did you read their minds?"

"Briefly. They were more lucid than the other two. They looked down on the older vampires and intended to kill them as soon as they lost their usefulness."

He drank several swallows of tea, buying time to decide how involved he could become without Seth's discovering his part. "Did you find any blank spots?"

"Blank spots?" she repeated, expression thoughtful. "Like the blank spots brain damage can cause?"

"Brain damage," he acknowledged, "or buried memories."

As soon as he planted the suggestion, he could have kicked himself. If she said one word at the meeting about the vampires having blank spots caused by buried memories, Seth would come gunning for Zach and the gloves would come off.

Lisette frowned. "I don't know that I would even recognize buried memories if I came across them." Her expression cleared. "Vampires can't do that, anyway. None of them are telepaths, so whatever vampire king is rising couldn't have buried the memories of his followers."

Zach resisted the urge to sigh. Even Lisette couldn't stomach the thought of an Immortal Guardian working against them. He would have to monitor the situation and see what developed.

Whatever happened, he would let no harm come to Lisette. From vampires, rogue immortals, *or* from Seth.

The sun rose as they finished their meal.

Lisette carried their dishes to the sink, then turned to lean back against the counter. "You *are* going to stay, aren't you?"

Once more his treacherous heart began to beat faster. "Do you want me to stay?" he forced himself to ask. He should go. He *really* should.

"Yes."

But even the Others couldn't drag him away now.

Zach rose.

"You can sleep in one of my brothers' rooms," she said, closing the distance between them, "or you can sleep downstairs with me."

"I'll sleep wherever you want me to sleep," he told her, voice hushed.

Taking his hand, she led him down to her bedroom. Once there, she hesitated. The uncertainty that entered her pretty features erased his own.

Zach squeezed her fingers. "I just want to sleep beside you, Lisette. Hold you in my arms, if I may."

Her smile returned. "You may."

The minutes that followed were enchantingly domestic. Lisette brushed her teeth and found a new toothbrush for Zach to use. Then she closed herself in the bathroom and emerged wearing a silky nightgown that fell to her knees and somehow managed to appear both modest and alluring at the same time.

Drawing the covers back, she climbed into bed and waited for him to join her.

Having declined her offer of a pair of sweats or shorts that belonged to her brothers, Zach settled himself beside her in his leather pants. Pain gripped him as he eased down on his side.

Lisette sat up and leaned over him to help him find a more comfortable position for his aching wings.

He sighed. Much better. "Thank you."

Smiling, she dipped her head and kissed his cheek. "Let me know if you need anything else."

Warmth filled him at the touch of her lips.

Turning off the lamp, she lay on her side, facing away from him, then eased back against him.

Zach spooned his large body around hers, her curves arousing him and making his blood sing despite the pain that battered him. Drawing her closer, he wrapped an arm around her and buried his face in her fragrant hair.

This, he thought, *is all I need.* And, after savoring the moment as long as he could, he let a healing sleep steal over him.

Chapter Six

Lisette's stomach fluttered with nervousness as she strode up the walk to David's front door. One of the last to arrive, she could hear the other immortals in the area gathered together inside, chatting with each other and their Seconds.

She had lingered in the forest a few miles distant, listening for the rest to ride or drive past, and timed her own arrival carefully. Not late enough to be late for the meeting. But late enough to, hopefully, prevent much conversation and keep Seth and David from having enough leisure time to pick her brain.

Étienne and Richart, along with their wives Krysta and Jenna, were already inside. Lisette bolstered her mental barriers as much as she could to keep Étienne from nosing around in there and finding Zach.

How she wished she could've remained snuggled up in bed with Zach instead of leaving him—still asleep—to attend this damned meeting.

Silently, she swore. *Don't even think his name*, she admonished herself. She couldn't risk the elders picking up on it and pouncing.

Several immortals and Seconds called greetings as she entered.

Smiling, she offered them a casual wave as she closed the door behind her.

"Hi, stranger." Sarah came forward and gave her a big hug. "It seems like I haven't seen you in ages."

Like every other immortal present, Lisette had a soft spot for Sarah.

Sarah had been the first *gifted one* in history to *ask* to be transformed so she could spend eternity with her husband. Though Roland was about as antisocial as they came, he had always been kind to Lisette, so she was thrilled that Sarah made him happy.

And it had been fan-freaking-tastic to finally have another female Immortal Guardian in the area. Too much testosterone was not always a good thing. Lisette had needed a break from it and had felt instantly comfortable with Sarah.

She forced a grin. "It's been so crowded around here lately, the only way I could quiet the voices and get some sleep was to spend more time at home." A solid explanation, she thought, for the many ears attuned to their conversation.

"Oh, right," Sarah said. "I keep forgetting it's hard for you to tune out all of our mental B.S. Since Roland and I have been doing the opposite and spending *more* time here lately, you probably got tired of my picturing him naked."

Across the room, Roland laughed.

Lisette did, too. "I *have* caught a stray image or two."

Several immortal males faked a shudder.

Grinning, Sarah linked her arm through Lisette's and drew her into the room. "Admit it," she ordered the males. "You're all just jealous because he's hotter than you."

Snorts and protests all around.

Tracy wound her way through the big, male bodies and

stopped before the two immortal women. "Excellent timing. I just heard Darnell give David a call."

"David isn't here?" Lisette asked, surprised. David loved Ami like a daughter—as did Seth—and had stuck very close to home since she had become pregnant.

"No."

Sarah shook her head and lowered her voice. "He and Seth are consulting a doctor in France. Melanie is with them."

Tracy looked at Sarah. "You know the immortals can all hear you, right?"

"Yes, but Ami can't."

Ami had just begun her eighth month. Since pregnancies on her planet lasted seven months and pregnancies here lasted nine, they had no way of knowing when the baby would or should come. Or what the state of its health would be. With extraterrestrial and *gifted one* DNA combined and the virus thrown in, no one knew what to expect.

And, like the other women on her planet, Ami was having an extremely difficult time carrying the baby to term. She would have lost it months ago without either Seth or David—both powerful healers—always on hand.

"Where *is* Ami?" Lisette asked. She couldn't see the petite Second for all of the tall males.

"Resting with Marcus in their room," Sarah supplied. "So far she's had a good day. No early labor pains or other complications."

"Good."

Roland wandered over, rarely far from his wife.

Richart and Jenna followed, holding hands like high school sweethearts.

"Hi," Jenna greeted Lisette with a smile.

"Hi. How's the training going?" Lisette asked.

"Great. I'm ready to start hunting."

"No, she isn't," Richart corrected with a scowl.

Jenna swung their hands between them. "Yes, I am. You're just being a worrywart."

"Seth put me in charge of your training," Richart insisted, "so *I* will decide when you're ready."

Jenna rolled her eyes. "*Seth* is the one who told me I'm ready."

Richart shot her a look. "He did?"

"Yes."

"Merde."

Everyone laughed.

Étienne and Krysta joined them. As usual, the pair stood close together with Étienne's hand resting on his wife's lower back. "You made it," he said with a quirk of his brow.

"Of course I did. Was there any doubt?"

He shrugged. "You haven't exactly been a frequent visitor of late."

Cameron, his Second, meandered over. "Yeah, what's up with that?"

Nearly everyone in the room followed.

Yuri and Stanislav. Their Seconds, Dmitry and Alexei. Krysta's brother, Sean, and his Second, Nichole. Edward and his Second, Desmond. Ethan, who gave her a quick once-over as if to assure himself that she was still in one piece, and his Second, Ed. Darnell, David's Second.

The only ones who didn't were Bastien and his Second, Tanner, who was Lisette's sports-viewing buddy.

Several voiced comments, wondering why she hadn't been around nearly as much and what—if anything—was wrong.

Lisette actually began to feel a bit panicky inside.

Especially when Seth and David appeared behind the group.

Together the two made an arresting sight and tended to draw stares wherever they went. Seth stood about six feet eight inches tall with broad shoulders, a leanly muscled form, beautiful patrician features, and long, wavy black hair (drawn back with a leather tie) that reached his waist. David stood about six feet seven inches with equally broad shoulders, a bit more muscle, the face of a pharaoh, flawless skin as dark as midnight, and pencil-thin dreadlocks that fell to his hips.

Both were totally drool-worthy. And both exuded power.

Melanie accompanied them, her five-foot form nearly eclipsed by theirs.

As Lisette tried to force down the fear that erupted within her, the two elders waited, expressions curious, for her to answer.

"What are you, her great-aunt Prudence?" Bastien drawled, quieting the throng as Melanie crossed to his side. "Don't you have anything better to do than bitch and moan because she doesn't visit as often as you'd like?"

In that moment, Lisette honestly loved that man.

Loud complaints erupted, accompanied by the usual slurs slung at the immortal black sheep.

Bastien shrugged them off as his gaze met hers.

Thank you, she told him telepathically.

His lips tilted up the tiniest bit.

Unfortunately, Seth and David both picked up on the thought and turned back to her with matching frowns, gazes sharpening.

Merde.

"Why *haven't* you been around lately?" Seth queried.

An expectant hush fell.

Really? Her absence had been *that* obvious? It had raised *that* many eyebrows?

She supposed she would feel flattered if she weren't so alarmed. "I've been around," she prevaricated.

"We haven't seen you in weeks," David said.

"And your Second has been spending more and more days here of late," Seth added.

Damn it. They *would* notice that. They noticed *everything.*

If Lisette didn't come up with something fast, they would probe her mind to find the answer themselves. And these two were aware of her concern for Ami. They knew more bodies and more thoughts filling the house wouldn't drive her away.

"I—"

"It's my fault," Tracy blurted.

All eyes went to Lisette's Second.

As did Lisette's. What the hell was Tracy going to say that Seth and David wouldn't know was a lie?

"I . . ." Tracy licked her lips and shifted her weight from one foot to the other. "I've been having a lot of . . . dreams lately and have been inadvertently pulling Lisette into them."

Everyone stared at her with *Yeah, so?* expressions.

"Erotic dreams," she continued.

Étienne suddenly swore, his eyes widening. "You've been having sex dreams about *Sheldon?*"

Tracy flushed a vivid red as gasps sounded and laughter erupted.

Seth eyed the immortals with disapproval. David shook his head at the others and offered Tracy a look full of sympathy.

Sheldon had made quite an impression as the proverbial kid brother here. Young. Full of enthusiasm. Not the brightest bulb in the box. And that first impression had lingered. No one here could imagine a woman seriously taking an interest in him.

"No wonder Lisette stayed away," Yuri chortled. "I wouldn't want to be pulled into those dreams either."

The comment sparked another round of laughter.

Every ounce of attention had been yanked away from Lisette, who wondered how the hell she was going to make this up to her friend. Tracy would *never* live this down.

Sheldon entered the living room with Jenna's son, John.

"What'd we miss?" Sheldon asked with a smile.

While Seth and David abandoned the group, all eyes went from Sheldon to Tracy to Sheldon to Tracy and back to Sheldon again.

It was like watching a tennis match.

And poor Tracy . . .

Lisette had never seen her look so stricken.

"Well?" Sheldon prodded, when no answer came.

Sean cleared his throat. "Tracy's been having sex dreams about you."

Krysta swatted her brother on the back of the head.

"Ow! What? Like no one was going to tell him?"

For a moment, Sheldon went utterly still. His eyes went to Tracy.

To her credit, Tracy didn't hide her face. She met his gaze straight on, face flaming.

Lisette stiffened, ready to kick Sheldon's ass if he made one of his usual smart-ass remarks and made Tracy even more miserable.

Tearing his eyes away, Sheldon directed a derisive snort at the others. "What, and you've never had one?"

Ethan grimaced. "Not about you."

More laughter.

Sheldon raked them all with a look of scorn. "Standing around, snickering like a group of ten-year-old boys looking at a dirty magazine for the first time. Grow the fuck up and leave her alone."

Several mouths fell open, including Tracy's.

Chris chose that moment to enter through the front door.

From the adjoining dining room, Seth said, "Shall we begin the meeting?"

No one moved. All were stunned that Sheldon hadn't pounced on the opportunity to . . . well . . . be himself.

Chris stopped short and raised his eyebrows. "What's going on?"

"Children," David prompted.

That got them moving. One did not ignore that tone.

Lisette wrapped an arm around Tracy's shoulders as they followed the others to the long dining table. *I can't believe you did that.*

Tracy sighed and leaned into her. *How red is my face?*

Remember that big baboon butt we saw on the news a few weeks ago?

Don't tell me . . .

It's redder than that.

Great.

Marcus and Ami entered as Lisette seated herself between Sarah and Tracy.

Ami looked the same as she used to—slender arms and legs encased in stretchy materials—except for her huge stomach. She looked, to Lisette, as though she had swallowed a beach ball. A tiny body with a big, protruding belly that offset her center of balance enough that she had to lean back a little and tended to waddle more than she walked.

Marcus walked with his arm around her shoulders and one of hers looped around his waist. Lisette didn't need to look into his thoughts to know he was stressed as hell, worrying about his wife, the baby, and what the hell would happen when Melanie and Dr. Kimiko gave the go-ahead and Seth and David finally let Ami go into labor.

Everyone greeted Ami with smiles and spoke kind words to her as Marcus seated her across from Lisette and sat beside Ami.

Once everyone settled, Seth turned to Reordon. "Chris?"

Chris nodded and addressed them all. "I called this meeting because a new problem has arisen. A couple of weeks ago, Lisette and Richart encountered a vampire with fighting skills that nearly matched their own."

Richart nodded. "He was skilled enough that I feared

for a moment he might be like Bastien, an immortal who mistakenly thought himself vampire."

Bastien frowned. "Was he?"

"No," Seth answered for them.

"But," Chris continued, "Lisette and Ethan encountered two more vampires with the same skills last night."

Lisette addressed the group. "All three vampires had been trained in martial arts and knew weapons as well as we do. The two last night were accompanied by a couple of your standard fare vamps—lanky and essentially useless—whom we swiftly defeated."

"The two with skills," Ethan added, "were a real challenge. They actually proved to be very difficult to defeat. It was like sparring with an immortal."

Roland leaned forward. "Sarah and I encountered a similar vampire a week ago."

Sarah nodded. "If I weren't as strong as Roland, I don't know that I would have defeated him."

Edward swore. "I came up against one, too. Just a couple of nights ago. I thought it was a fluke."

"One skilled vampire is a fluke," Chris said. "Five isn't. Five is a problem."

Roland looked to Lisette. "Were you able to read their minds?"

"Yes, but I could glean little more than that they thought the other vampires beneath them and intended to kill them once they proved to be of no more use to them."

"Sounds like Dennis," Ami commented. "The night he captured me, I saw Dennis lose it completely and hack several of his followers to pieces with a machete."

"Jeez!" Krysta exclaimed.

Chris sighed. "Clearly someone is amassing a new vampire army. And, based on the descriptions I was given of the fights, I suspect one of his or her goals is to capture an immortal."

Melanie frowned. "Why would that be a priority for vampires? Are they interested in immortals' advanced DNA?"

Bastien wrapped an arm around her shoulders. "I doubt vampires know about the DNA. Those I used to encounter when I thought myself one of them certainly never did. But I can have Cliff ask those he encounters outside of network headquarters some subtle questions to see if that's changed."

Roland cast him a disapproving scowl. "You're really taking him hunting with you?"

"Yes. And will allow him to roam freely a couple of times a week so he can connect with other vampires without them instantly going on the defensive when they see an Immortal Guardian at his side."

Marcus straightened. "You're going to let him roam freely? Are you crazy? He could tell them everything he knows. He could tell them about Ami! Any vampire wanting to get his hands on an immortal would be doubly eager to capture the only woman to ever successfully conceive a child by one."

Seth shook his head. "He hasn't told anyone, nor do I believe he will. David and I will take turns reading his thoughts each night after he hunts to make sure, but—as I said—I don't believe he will betray us."

Lisette watched Marcus absorb that with deep unease while the others compared verbal notes on the vampires they had come up against in recent weeks. She glanced at Ami to see how *she* was taking this.

Just then, Ami looked up at the ceiling for a long moment, then peeked at Seth with an *I hope he didn't catch that* expression.

Oh, crap. He wouldn't do it, would he?

Zach would *not* be so monumentally foolish as to follow Lisette to David's place and perch on the damned roof, knowing Seth was beneath it, itching to hand Zach his own ass again.

He wouldn't be that foolish, right?

Lisette kept her gaze on Ami.

Ami glanced at the ceiling again. A moment passed. She smiled, then lowered her head and rubbed her tummy.

Damn it! He had! What the hell?

Ami must have sensed his presence in that odd way she could. Had she spoken to him telepathically as well?

If so, how had she managed to do so without Seth and David picking up on it?

"Why would the vampires want to capture an immortal?" Marcus asked. "Why not just try to kill us as usual?"

Bastien leaned forward and braced his elbows on the table. "The vampires in the army I raised knew very little about immortals. I knew little of you myself." Would he *ever* consider himself one of them? "I knew Roland had to be as old as I was, but I had no idea immortals could live thousands of years."

Marcus frowned. "I'm not sure where you're going with this."

"Vampires may not know immortals have advanced DNA or how long-lived you are," Bastien said. "But they *do* know you're faster and stronger than they are. Some of the vampires who followed me firmly believed that drinking your blood would give them the same speed and strength, the same power. According to their reasoning, capturing an immortal and using him as a nightly donor would render the effects permanent. When I waged my war with you, I had a hell of a time convincing them to fight to *kill* instead of fighting to *capture*."

Chris studied him. "You've never mentioned this before."

Bastien shrugged. "I didn't think it pertinent. The vampires were all dead, save Vince, Cliff, and Joe. I didn't think their mistaken beliefs mattered."

Chris leaned back in his chair. "Well, that could be the answer. Some vampire out there with a lust for power may be telling his followers that they can become faster and stronger if they capture an Immortal Guardian and use him or her as a blood bank. And he's choosing the humans he transforms very carefully." He drew a picture out of the soft leather briefcase he often carried with him and held it up for all to see. "Lisette snapped a pic of the vampire she and Richart took out. I had some of my guys do a facial recognition search and came up with a former marine."

Lisette studied the picture of the soldier. "The two Ethan and I fought last night could have been ex-military as well. They certainly had been trained in hand-to-hand combat."

Chris nodded. "The vampire we're dealing with is still lucid and is no moron."

"We need to identify the source of this uprising," Seth said, "before it gets out of hand. If you come up against any of these more competent vampires, take them alive if at all possible. Start carrying auto-injectors that contain a vampire's dose of the sedative if you don't already do so."

"Younger immortals," David added, "should consider hunting in pairs again. For now, it's voluntary. If the situation escalates, however, it will become mandatory."

All nodded.

"Étienne and Lisette," Seth ordered, "read the minds of every vamp you encounter, lucid or manic. *Someone* knows who the leader is. We need to find that vampire."

Lisette nodded.

Her brother did the same.

"Anything else?" Seth queried.

Everyone waited expectantly, then shrugged and shook their heads.

"Fine. Meeting adjourned. Safe hunting tonight."

Lisette rose, intending to make a quick escape.

Seth caught her before she could and motioned Tracy over. As soon as Tracy reached them, Seth touched their shoulders and teleported them to . . .

Lisette looked around. "Where are we?"

"My castle in England."

"Really? It looks different." Almost modern.

He smiled. "You haven't been here in several decades. We've remodeled since then."

She pretended to take in the changes he'd made in the great hall while she wondered nervously why he had brought them there.

"I'd like to apologize for tonight," he said. "Had I not pressed you to explain your recent absence, Lisette, Tracy would not have had to reveal her secret and . . ."

Tracy sent him a wry smile. "Been thoroughly humiliated?"

He winced. "Yes. Again, I sincerely apologize." His gaze shifted to Lisette. "I know how concerned you've been about Ami. I know you've seen her dreams and have grown as protective of her as David, Marcus, and I are. So, when you abruptly ceased visiting, I feared something was amiss. Considering my age, it should come as no surprise to you that I'm a bit old-fashioned and tend to worry a little more about female Immortal Guardians than I do males."

Lisette and Tracy shared a look. *A little?*

He offered Lisette a sheepish smile. "Or a lot. There are so few of you."

Female Immortal Guardians were exceedingly rare. Most female *gifted ones* suffered torturous deaths at the hands of vampires before they could complete their transformation.

Seth shrugged. "Hell, for all I knew, you could have simply taken a lover and desired some privacy."

Tracy grinned at Lisette. "That would have been *awesome*. Do it! I'll give you all the space you need."

Seth laughed. "And I shall endeavor to mind my own business in the future."

Guilt poured through Lisette as she forced herself to

smile back. Since he seemed to expect a response, she uttered a simple, "Okay."

"Hey," Tracy said, "I don't suppose you'd be willing to bury everyone's memory of my dreams, would you? Or at least the subject of them?"

He offered her an apologetic smile. "Regrettably, no. I prefer not to alter someone's brain unless such is absolutely necessary. Burying memories can be tricky."

Tracy sighed. "It was worth a try."

He squeezed her shoulder. "You can't always judge a book by its cover, you know."

She frowned. "What do you mean?"

He winked. "If you look a little deeper, you may find that there is more to Sheldon than meets the eye."

Both women's mouths fell open.

"Are you playing matchmaker?" Tracy asked incredulously.

His smile vanished. "No. Definitely not. Not at all. And, if any immortal should ask you that, please tell them I'm not."

Okay. That was just bizarre. Had some immortal actually accused him of playing matchmaker?

Seth drew out a pocket watch, consulted it, and put it away again. "Tracy, you're welcome to continue spending the day at David's. Lisette, if you wish to continue sleeping at home without her, you need to check in with her frequently to assure her you're safe. I don't want to take any chances of your falling into the hands of the new vampire army with Tracy being none the wiser because you're spending less time together. She's your Second. Make sure you keep her informed of your every move so she'll know if you go missing."

Lisette nodded. "I will."

"Excellent." He touched their shoulders and returned them to David's place. "Safe hunting."

"You too," Lisette said.

He crossed to David's side. Lisette heard him mention something about Peru. Then he vanished.

"You want me to stay the day here again?" Tracy asked.

Hell no. Not after the embarrassment Tracy had just suffered. The jokes that would follow would be numerous and frequent.

But Lisette needed the house to herself. "If you really don't mind."

"Nah. Any bullshit they can dish out, I can take." Tracy *was* tough. "Is it okay if I go by the house and pick up a few things?"

"Sure."

"I'll head over there in a few then."

Lisette gave her a big hug. *I owe you one.*

Tracy smiled. *No, you don't.* She was a good friend.

Lisette called good night to the room in general and left through the front door.

Thankfully, no one followed.

When she reached her Busa, she studied the front of the house carefully to ensure no one peered out of any of the windows.

Nothing and no one. Good.

She cast a glance up at the roof and, *damn it,* there he was!

Perched in his usual spot on the roof, Zach tossed her a jaunty wave. Moonlight glinted on his beautiful wings (now healed) and silky hair.

Lisette clamped her lips shut and glared up at him as fury rushed through her. Pointing a stiff index finger at him, she then jerked a thumb over her shoulder, telling him without words to get the hell out of there and follow her.

A grin split his face.

Unbelievable.

Rising, he offered her a courtly bow and leapt into the sky.

It took considerable effort not to grumble under her breath as she retrieved her helmet, slammed it down over her head, and straddled the bike. As soon as the engine purred to life, she raced down the drive.

A full moon graced the night sky above her, unhindered by the sparse, wispy clouds that meandered across it.

Passing through the security gate at the end of the drive, she turned onto the main, two-lane road. Lisette burned up the pavement, a thousand thoughts and curses flooding her mind as the wind tugged at her coat.

A shadow passed over her, cast by the bright moon. Zach's shadow, wings spread, danced on the pavement, zigzagging across her path, almost playful in its antics.

Ten miles flashed past. Then ten more.

That should do it.

Having placed sufficient distance between them and David's place to ensure no immortal would overhear them and reduce the possibility of running into an immortal on his way out to hunt, Lisette turned onto a narrow dirt road, followed it several yards into the trees, and killed the engine.

Chapter Seven

Zach landed on the parched ground several feet away from Lisette and drew his wings in close to his back. He smiled as she removed her helmet and coat and stashed them on the bike.

Her movements, usually graceful, were now stiff with what he came to discern as anger as she turned to face him. "Are you out of your mind?" she came close to shouting.

"No," he answered. "Why do you ask?"

She growled—actually *growled*—with fury and stomped toward him. "What the hell were you thinking?"

Zach's heart began to beat faster.

Her alabaster skin seemed to glow in the moonlight. Luminous amber eclipsed her brown eyes. Color flushed her cheeks. The full breasts beneath her tight T-shirt rose and fell with swift, angry breaths.

Absolutely stunning.

"What's the subject here?" he murmured.

"Why did you follow me to David's?" she demanded, stopping only a couple of feet away. "You keep telling me Seth has it in for you, and then you show up at a meeting you know he will attend? What the hell?"

She smelled good, too, he thought as he surreptitiously

drew in her scent. "Technically, I didn't *show up* at the meeting. I eavesdropped upon it."

She waved a dismissive hand. "Don't bullshit me, Zach. Are you, or are you *not* on Seth's shit list?"

"I am."

"Then why were you at David's? If he had sensed your presence—"

"I was there for you," Zach interrupted, curling his hands into loose fists to keep from reaching out and touching her. There was something so . . . stimulating about seeing her like this: full of pique and energy and life. "I was there to protect you."

She blinked. "What?"

"Your mental barriers are no defense against Seth's or David's intrusion. If they were to read your thoughts and discover you've been meeting with me in secret, I wanted to be there to prevent them from rendering whatever punishment they thought your defection warranted."

Frogs and crickets competed in song while she stared up at him, lips parted in surprise. "You were there because you were worried about me?"

"Yes."

More frogs and crickets.

"Zach, if Seth and David had read my mind and decided to punish me, you couldn't have stopped them. As immensely powerful as you are, I don't see how you could defeat both Seth *and* David if they combined forces. And I know they would have. David and Seth are like this." She held up two fingers and crossed them.

Seth and David *were* close. But, after everything Zach had seen in the past year, he knew that Seth wouldn't *need* to combine forces with David to defeat him.

Something it galled Zach to admit. "It was a risk I was willing to take."

She threw up her arms. "Why?"

"I already told you. I was worried about you and wished to protect you."

"Well, you can't do that," she declared, confusion flirting with irritation in her features. "You can't just—"

He took a step closer to her.

She broke off.

He took another. "I want to try something."

She closed her mouth. Something flared in her incandescent eyes.

He had spoken the same words to her in her dream. Did she remember?

Her throat moved in a swallow. "What?" she asked, voice hesitant.

"I want to try something," he repeated, mere inches separating them.

"Okay."

Zach raised a hand to her face, slid his fingers over her soft, soft skin.

Her breath caught.

Dipping his head, he pressed his lips to hers.

Electric.

His heart leapt to life inside his chest, ramming against his rib cage.

Lisette's heart began to beat as fast as his.

Tilting his head, he increased the pressure, deepened the contact, and drew his tongue across her lips. She tasted *incredible*. Even better than she had in the dream.

Heat rushed through him when she parted her lips and touched her tongue to his. Looping an arm around her waist, he drew her closer. Every muscle tightened with need as she rose onto her toes and leaned into him. He thrust his tongue into her mouth, wanting more. And she met the intrusion eagerly, returning stroke for stroke.

Zach had never felt anything like it in his long existence. Fire ignited in his veins as she slid her arms around his neck and ground her hips into the erection that strained against the front of his leather pants.

And he didn't want it to end.

Breath coming fast, he raised his head.

She stared at him, face flushed with desire.

"You didn't pull away," he whispered.

Shaking her head slowly, she smiled. "Are you going to try something else now?"

Zach smiled and, after giving her cheek one last stroke, slid his hand down to palm her breast. Her eyes glowed a brilliant amber, brighter than he had ever seen them. He drew his thumb across a hardened peak.

Moaning, she rocked her hips against his.

Lust careened through him, making him crave more. More of her taste. More of her touch.

As if she had read his thoughts, she buried her fingers in his silky hair and urged him to lower his head again. Their lips merged, tongues stroking and tasting. Emboldened by her response, he tightened his arm around her. Curled his fingers around her braid. Pressed her closer. Kneaded her breast. Explored. Teased. And, with every touch, every lick, and every brush of her soft, full lips, he grew more desperate, wanting to rip the clothes from their bodies and feel her bare flesh against his.

Lisette lowered her arms and slid them around his waist, intending to explore his broad, muscled back, and encountered satiny feathers.

She broke the kiss, surprised, and lowered her heels to the ground. She had forgotten for a moment. . . .

"Lisette?"

She glanced up.

The need in his golden eyes turned her insides to liquid fire.

"Is it . . . is it okay to touch them?" she asked, unsure.

The beautiful wings disappeared.

"Touch *me*," he pleaded.

And any barrier that struggled to hold her back crumbled. Giving him a small smile, she nodded. Touch him? She could do that.

Lisette slid her arms around his waist and flattened her palms on his back.

She had been so distracted by his wings in the past that she hadn't noticed how ripped he was. Rising onto her toes, she brushed her lips against his. He responded hungrily as she explored his warm flesh with her fingers.

She had always appreciated strength. And Zach had it in spades. All muscle and sinew.

"You taste even better than I imagined," he murmured, sending a warm spiral of pleasure darting through her.

"So do you." And felt magnificent, too. Unable to resist, she drew her hands down and cupped his tight, leather-clad ass.

He groaned. Still kneading her breast, he thrust against her. *Mmmmmm.* So good. She wanted more. *Needed* more. Would he object to her jumping up and wrapping her legs around his waist? Because just the thought of opening herself to him, of settling the heart of her against his arousal, of gaining higher ground to give her easier access to his lips and tongue made her—

Zach stiffened and raised his head.

Lisette opened her mouth to protest.

Quiet, he cautioned.

It was the first time he had spoken to her telepathically, and the warm bass-baritone invading her mind, coupled with the body locked against hers, damned near made her orgasm.

Wrapping both arms around her, Zach eased them back into the dense trees.

Cool shadows engulfed them.

Lisette looked up at him, gradually becoming aware of a new tension gripping him.

His eyes focused on the canopy above them as he tilted his head and listened.

Lisette heard nothing but the usual nocturnal sounds that abounded in North Carolina.

Lips tightening, he looked over at her bike, illuminated by moonlight, thanks to a break in the trees.

He stretched a hand toward it.

Lisette's eyes widened when the Hayabusa silently rose into the air and floated over to join them in the shadows, the tires making only the faintest sound as he returned it to the ground.

That had been some display of power.

Meeting her gaze, Zach pressed a finger to his lips.

Desire receded, replaced by anxiety.

What did he hear? What was coming? Or who?

Was it the Others, whoever the hell they were? Had they found him?

She tightened her hold on him and waited.

The golden glow left Zach's eyes as he turned them up to the treetops once more.

Minutes passed.

Lisette heard the gentle flap of wings approach. Large wings, but not large enough to match Zach's.

A shadow flitted across the moonlit ground her Busa had formerly inhabited as something passed overhead.

Time ticked by, every minute feeling like an hour.

At last, Zach relaxed and patted her back. "It's okay now. We're clear."

Reluctantly, Lisette loosened her hold. "What was it? Or should I say *who* was it?"

"David, flying over in the shape of an owl."

Reality slapped her in the face.

Zach, too, by the looks of him. Releasing her, he backed away a couple of steps.

"Is he looking for you?" she asked. "Does he know you were at his home?"

"No. But if he had seen your motorcycle . . ."

"He would have come down and investigated," she finished for him.

"Yes. I thought it best to avoid a confrontation."

A wise course of action.

Lisette surveyed their surroundings, not really seeing any of it. A multitude of questions and fears and complaints bombarded her. *What if*'s and *why not*'s and *how*'s and *what will*'s.

"Lisette?" Zach spoke softly.

She shook her head, not looking at him. "How is this going to work, Zach?"

A long pause ensued.

"I don't know," he said at last, drawing her gaze. "I admit I'm still reeling from the discovery that you *wish* it to. Work, that is."

The honesty and vulnerability his words expressed pierced her heart.

"Well, think on it, will you?" she implored.

"I fear I shall think of little else."

Sighing, she found a smile. "Me too."

He shook his head. "You're such a puzzle to me."

"I don't know why. I'm just me." Nothing special. Just one of the guys as far as most of the other immortals were concerned.

"Why would you risk everything to be with me?"

Lisette thought Zach a far greater puzzle. He was one of

the most powerful beings on the planet, and yet he seemed heartbreakingly ignorant of his own worth. "I haven't felt like this in a very long time," she responded, "haven't been this drawn to a man since I was mortal. Perhaps not even then." Zach made her feel far more than her husband ever had.

She shook her head. "I can't just give that up without seeing where it can lead me. It's too rare. Too precious."

Nodding, Zach took one of her hands and lifted it to his lips for a gentle kiss.

She squeezed his hand and smiled. "Since David has killed the mood"—he might as well have dumped several gallons of ice water on them when he had flown over—"I suppose I should begin tonight's hunt."

He released her hand with obvious reluctance. "Shall I accompany you?" he asked as she donned her coat and helmet.

"If worry prompted that question, then my answer is I'm a big girl. I can take care of myself."

"Have you any of the auto-injectors that bear the sedative on you?"

She swore. "No. And I don't think we have any at the house."

"Then I shall accompany you."

She eyed him speculatively. "What would you be doing if you *didn't* accompany me?"

"Prowling around and seeing what the Others are up to."

Fear rose. "Zach—"

He held up a hand. "They won't let me go easily, Lisette. I know they're still searching for me. They *must* be. I need to know where and how. For my own safety and for yours. I need to know if they've discovered my connection to you. If they know you helped me. What exactly they intend to do if they find me."

"How can you do that without them capturing you again?" She had seen their brand of punishment and didn't want him to be subjected to it again because he worried they might come after her.

"When I'm at full strength, I can conceal my presence from them even when I'm in close proximity to them, the way I did with Seth and David earlier. They only know where I am if I *want* them to know."

"And you're at full strength now?"

"Yes."

"Not ninety percent or ninety-five percent," she clarified. "But one hundred percent?"

"Yes."

She could detect no uncertainty in his tone. "All right. Go then."

"I'd rather you not hunt alone when you don't have the sedative."

"It's just for one night. Watch." Tugging out her cell phone, she dialed Tracy.

"Yeah?" Disturbed's "Droppin' Plates" blared in the background.

"Where are you?" Lisette asked.

"On the road, headed home."

"Do we have any of the sedative at the house?"

Tracy swore. "No. I'll swing by the network on my way back to David's and pick some up."

"Thanks." Ending the call, Lisette arched a brow. "You see? All taken care of. It will be in my hands tomorrow night."

He crossed his arms over his chest. "I'd rather you not hunt alone tonight without it."

She groaned. It was like dealing with Seth or her brothers. "Are you going to be this stubborn about everything?"

"Everything that involves your safety," he said, unmovable.

"Fine. I'll go by the network myself and pick up the sedative, even though it will take over an hour away from tonight's hunt."

His face cleared as he lowered his arms. "Thank you."

"What about you?" she asked. Two could play the over-protective game. "What weapons will you carry with you when you go spy on the Others?"

"I have no weapons."

She stared at him. "None?"

"Not one. Though I know how to use them, I've never needed to carry them."

Well, screw that. Crossing to stand before him, Lisette gripped the lapels of her coat and opened it wide. A small arsenal hid inside, tucked into various and assorted loops and pockets and sheaths. "Take your pick."

His eyes lit with a faint golden glow. "I can have anything I want?" he asked in a silky voice that turned her insides to mush.

Her pulse leapt. "Yes."

"How you tempt me," he murmured. Stepping so close she could feel his warm breath on her forehead, he reached inside the coat on either side of her and drew two daggers from their sheaths. "Thank you. Be safe."

She kissed his chin. "You too."

As he backed away, his wings reappeared. "May I see you again tonight? After your hunt?"

She nodded. "Meet me at my place."

Offering her another courtly bow, he leapt up, drew his wings down, and sailed into the moonlight.

Lisette intended to swing by network headquarters and pick up the sedative. She really did. But, on her way there, she heard Étienne call out to her.

Lisette!

Yes?

Where are you?

On my way to the network.

Fuck the network. Come to UNCG. Krysta and I have come up against some of the vampires with skills, and I fear she'll be injured.

Do you have any of the sedative on you?

No, we were headed to the network to pick some up when we caught wind of the vamps.

I'm on my way.

Lucky for him, the new network headquarters was just outside of Greensboro. If she defied every speed limit and traffic law, she could be there in only a couple of minutes.

Richart, she called mentally. Even though he wasn't telepathic, she would hear his reply as long as the two were in the same state.

What? came his rather distracted reply.

Do you have any of the sedative on you?

Yes.

Can you get it to Étienne and Krysta at UNCG?

Jenna and I have come up against quite a large number of vampires at Duke.

Skilled vampires?

No, the usual fare. But I intended to use the sedative on some of them in hopes that they had heard something.

Save it for Étienne. He and Krysta are facing the new breed of vampires there and could use it.

All right. We'll be there as soon as we can.

Is Jenna fighting alongside you? Lisette asked as an afterthought.

Yes, he groused, *and I swear she's turning my hair gray.*

Lisette laughed as she reached UNCG's campus. Taking her Busa up onto the sidewalk, she followed the sounds of battle to her brother and his wife and plowed right through the vampires.

Bodies flew through the air. Blood splattered.

Krysta laughed. "Nice!"

Grinning, Lisette parked the bike, drew her shoto swords, and leapt into the fray.

A quick head count yielded over a dozen vampires. At least three bore thickly muscled physiques and brandished weapons with expertise. Étienne fought one and kept trying to engage another to keep him from joining the third, who battled Krysta.

Krysta, Lisette noticed, held her own better than Étienne did, thanks to her ability to see auras. While the auras of humans told her little beyond the man or woman's mood or health, the auras of vampires behaved differently. According to Krysta, they shifted and moved before the vampires did, alerting her to the vampires' intentions. So she could anticipate a vampire's every move and kick his ass. As she did now.

With a speed and strength that matched her husband's, Krysta dodged every strike of the muscled vamp she fought and inflicted wound after wound after wound with her own weapons.

Étienne didn't fare quite so well.

Lisette swung her swords in sweeping arcs as she raced forward, cutting the carotid and femoral arteries of a couple of the standard deranged vamps. Reaching Étienne's side, she then took on the second muscled vamp he struggled to keep away from Krysta.

Once more, battling the vampire proved to be a challenge. Had she, Étienne, and Krysta only fought the skilled vamps, Lisette thought the three of them would have triumphed more easily. But the damned psycho vamps proved to be dangerous distractions.

The large vampire Lisette fought was so adroit that she had to keep her attention focused on him at all times, which left her vulnerable to attacks from the other vamps. While she met the muscled vampire strike for strike, the less practiced vamps darted in and drew blood with wild slashes and stabs. If she took her gaze away from the adept vampire for even a second, he scored a hit.

Étienne swore.

They all did, encountering the same dilemma.

Their frustration mounted as wounds multiplied and stung. But they kept their cool as their training dictated.

Lisette spun away from the muscled vampire long enough to swipe the head from the body of a gangly vamp attacking her from behind and was rewarded by her primary foe with a cut across the neck. She hissed in pain and repaid him with two swift slashes to his right arm, hoping to hinder his swing.

Lisette? Étienne asked.

He nicked my carotid artery, she said, *but I'm okay*.

Okay and losing blood. Unlike a vampire, she wouldn't bleed out if a major artery was slashed. If she lost too much blood, she would simply slip into a sort of stasis or hibernation until a blood source came along. Fortunately, the cut the muscled vamp had inflicted was minor enough that the virus was able to seal it.

Her movements slowed, a result of blood loss.

From the sounds of it, Krysta was kicking her vampire's ass.

A lanky vamp shot forward and slashed at Lisette's legs. The sharp blade went right through her coat and sank into her thigh.

Stealing herself against the pain, she bent her knees, leapt up, somersaulted over the muscled vampire's head, and landed behind him. Her blade sank deep into his back before he could spin around. Leaving her shoto in place, she drew a dagger and tore into two of the slacker vamps as the muscled vampire struggled to reach behind him and remove the sword.

"Mine's down!" Krysta called and took on some of the vampires circling her husband.

As Lisette finished off the two vamps she fought, she scoured the muscled vampire's thoughts and found a chaos of rage and pain. She could see nothing of the one who had turned him or trained him.

She dipped low and cut the femoral artery of the last slacker vamp facing her. As she straightened, a blade sank into her side, narrowly missing her heart.

She cried out, the last comfortable breath she could take as blood began to fill her lung.

She turned to the muscled vampire.

His eyes glowed with triumph as he raised a long dagger above his head.

Dodging his downswing, Lisette drove her shoto sword up into his stomach, severing his abdominal aorta.

He froze, eyes widening, then stumbled backward, the movement removing his flesh from her blade.

Hunched over, Lisette watched his shirt turn crimson, watched him sink to the ground, and didn't turn away until he breathed his last breath and began to shrivel up.

A quick look around told her Krysta and Étienne would soon defeat the last of the vampires.

Gritting her teeth, Lisette reached under her arm, gripped the handle of the weapon still imbedded in her body, and drew it out. *"Ahhhhh!"*

"Lisette!" Étienne cried.

She stared in disbelief at the weapon in her trembling hand and turned to face her brother as he decapitated the last vampire standing and rushed to her side. "Bastard stabbed me . . . with my own . . . weapon," she wheezed, then spat a mouthful of blood on the grass.

Krysta darted over to her side and wrapped a supportive arm around her. "Are you okay? What can I do? Do you need blood? Étienne always brings some with us in a cooler now because he hates it when I'm injured."

As far as Lisette could tell, all of the blood that painted

Krysta was vampire. She barely had a scratch on her. "Blood would . . . be good . . . thanks."

Nodding, Krysta dashed away so fast she blurred.

"Damn it, Krysta!" Étienne shouted. "There could be . . . more," he finished with a sigh.

Lisette sure as hell hoped there *weren't* more vampires. Not unless they were of the typical easier-to-defeat variety.

Richart appeared, holding Jenna's hand as she leaned into his side. Blood speckled their faces and necks and saturated their clothing.

"Really?" Lisette hissed. Damn, it was hard to breathe. "You show up . . . *now?*"

"Where have I heard that before?" Richart muttered. His eyes widened as he took in her battered condition. "*Merde!*"

Étienne didn't look much better.

Jenna hurried to Lisette's side and carefully touched her back. "Are you okay? Can we do anything?"

Lisette shook her head, unable to speak and lacking the energy to *think* a response.

"I'm fine, by the way," Étienne drawled.

Richart snorted and said something derogatory.

Krysta reappeared with a couple of bags of blood in her hand. "I'm sorry. This is all we brought with us."

Lisette took one bag and motioned for Krysta to give the other to Étienne, who was stooped over a bit himself and held one side.

Étienne tried to refuse and insist that Lisette take it.

Lisette gave him the finger.

Immortal males tended to treat her as one of the guys until she was wounded and then—*holy crap*—the fuss they made over her! And her brothers were the worst. Étienne could be missing a limb and would *still* try to insist she take all of the blood herself.

Lisette sank her fangs into the lone bag she accepted. Sighing, she let them siphon the blood into her veins, replenishing some of that she had lost. It was enough to stop the bleeding of her wounds, but she would need more to heal them all. Her shallow, rapid breath evened out as her lung reinflated.

Étienne straightened as blood filled his veins. He lowered the bag and nodded at Lisette. "Did you read their thoughts?"

"Just the one I fought. I found nothing there."

"No plans? No image of the one who recruited or trained him? Nothing unusual?"

She shook her head. "Not a thing. Just anger and pain and a determination to kick my ass."

He frowned.

Richart approached her. "Let me take you home."

"No, thank you. I'm fine."

"You aren't fine. You look like shit."

"Well, I don't feel like it," she snapped. "And I don't want to leave my Busa behind."

"I'll come back for your damned motorcycle," he said.

"As rarely as you ride? I wouldn't trust you to get it to me in one piece."

"I can teleport it."

"And collapse afterward because it took so much energy? Forget it."

"I'll do it," Étienne spoke up. "Let Richart teleport you home so you can get more blood in you. I'll ride your bike to your place while you heal."

And have him run into Zach? Hell no. "You need to see to your own wounds."

Krysta looked at Jenna. "I don't know how to ride a motorcycle. Do you?"

"No."

"I could fetch Roland to heal you," Richart suggested.

"He still hurls daggers at you whenever you surprise him."

"Then Seth or David."

Hell no. "Stop fussing over me," Lisette griped and sheathed her shoto swords. "I'm a grown woman and can take care of myself."

Krysta raised her eyebrows. "I know that tone," she said with a wry smile. "It's the *my brothers are treating me like a baby and driving me crazy* tone. Sean used to wear my last nerve sometimes, worrying over me."

Jenna smiled. "Sons do the same thing. John *still* worries over me." She looked up at Richart. "You know, women *are* just as tough as men."

"I'm aware of that," her husband retorted.

"And yet I noticed you aren't urging Étienne to let you teleport *him* home or take *him* to a healer, and he looks as bad as Lisette."

Girl power! Lisette thought.

Richart and Étienne both held up their hands, unwilling to debate the physical equality of the sexes.

"Fine," Richart said. "Just call Tracy when you get home and let her know you arrived safely."

"I will," Lisette agreed, happy to be able to head home without them. "Will you catch Seth up on what happened?" Avoiding the elder felt wrong, but he had come very close to questioning her earlier. She didn't want to risk it again.

Or risk him smelling Zach on her after she had rubbed up against him earlier.

"Of course," Étienne said. "We're heading over there later anyway."

"Thank you." Lisette forced herself not to limp as she crossed to her bike. Clenching her teeth against the pain, she straddled the Busa and donned her helmet.

Krysta and Jenna returned to the subject of powerful women and stubborn men.

Starting the engine, Lisette tossed them all a wave and began the long ride home.

* * *

Wings tucked away, Zach listened to the night creatures sing their songs as he waited for Lisette to return. He had taken a chance and made himself at home. Mostly. Instead of perching on the roof, he sat on the front steps. His ass on the porch, he shifted his feet on one of the planks two or three steps below and rested his elbows on his knees.

It felt odd. Almost as if he were a guest. A *welcome* guest.

Frankly, he would feel much more comfortable pulling gargoyle duty, but thought Lisette might object if she caught him doing it again.

His lips quirked as he recalled the fury on her face when she had stepped outside David's sprawling home earlier, looked up, and seen him occupying his usual spot on the roof. It had been so hard not to laugh when she had pointed that accusatory finger at him and jerked her thumb over her shoulder, telling him to get the hell out of there.

She made him feel so much that was new to him.

All these millennia of existing, and he hadn't really begun to live until he had laid eyes on Lisette d'Alençon.

The faint rumble of a motorcycle reached his ears.

His smile widened. (He'd been smiling more, too, since he'd encountered her.)

Sitting straighter, he rubbed his palms against the soft leather covering his knees.

Would she let him kiss her again? Touch her?

His stomach fluttered with anticipation, then sank to the ground when she turned onto the long drive leading to him and he caught the scent of her blood. His smile vanished.

Her motorcycle's headlight flickered in and out of sight, brightening the brush and trees she passed. The engine slowed as she came around a bend and showered him with light.

Squinting, Zach threw up a hand to shield his eyes and

rose. Down the steps he strode, his concern growing with each pace.

She parked the bike and removed her helmet. Her clothes were saturated. He had seen them so before, but usually it was with *vampire* blood. Nearly all of that which painted her now was her own.

"Lisette?"

She offered him a tired smile, swung her right leg over the back of the bike, and dismounted, her movements stiff. "I needed that tonight."

"Needed what?" It looked as if someone had slashed her throat.

"To find you here waiting for me when I got home." Her smile broadened the slightest bit. "And *not* on the roof."

Bending, he whisked her up into his arms.

She sighed. "Thank you. I wasn't looking forward to climbing those steps."

His heart skipped a beat when she rested her head on his shoulder and wrapped her arms around his neck, snuggling close. "What happened?"

"We came up against some of the new irritatingly proficient vampires."

"We, meaning . . . ?" Hollow thuds echoed in the night as he climbed the steps and crossed to the front door.

"Étienne, Krysta, and I." Reaching down, she came up with some keys, unlocked the door, and turned the knob. "Well, Étienne and Krysta did. Then Étienne summoned me to help them."

Zach shouldered open the door and entered her home. "Why didn't you use the sedative?"

"They caught me on the way to the network. I didn't have time to pick any up before I went to their aid."

Two beeps emanated from the alarm touchpad set into the wall.

He kicked the door closed.

Two more beeps.

Lisette punched in her access code and stopped the beeps. "By the way, I always leave the indoor motion sensors off when I set the alarm. Tracy does, too. Otherwise Richart will set the alarm off when he teleports in."

"Why are you telling me this?"

"Because I want you to feel free to teleport inside any time you want to, instead of waiting on the front porch. Just listen first to ensure Tracy isn't home."

He stared down at her.

"What?"

He shook his head. She didn't know how rare her invitation was. Or the trust it indicated.

"Anyway," she continued, "Richart had some auto-injectors, but he and Jenna weren't able to join us until right after the last vampire fell."

"Do you need blood?" He could feel her trembling.

"Yes."

He headed into the living room and started to lower her onto the sofa.

"Not the sofa," she protested. "I don't want to get blood all over it. I'll be fine, sitting at the kitchen table."

How much blood had she lost?

Zach carried her into the kitchen, telekinetically drew a wooden chair back from the table, and gently lowered her onto it.

"Thank you," she said with another smile.

Uncertain how to reply, he turned to open the refrigerator door.

She laughed as he drew out the specially designed drawer she kept blood in and took out a trio of bags. "Sometimes you remind me so much of Roland."

Closing both the drawer and the door, he returned to her. "The immortal who tried to choke me with a piano wire?" Zach set the bags on the table and drew out the chair catty-corner to her.

"He was only looking out for Marcus." Sending him a contrite smile, she picked up a bag. "And, if you're going to blame someone for capturing and interrogating you, blame me. It was pretty much my idea."

It had happened months ago, after Lisette had caught Zach secretly conversing with Ami.

He seated himself and scooted a little closer. "You were worried about Ami. I can't fault you for that." And the *interrogation* had allowed him to speak to her directly for the first time.

She held the bag with one hand and sank her fangs into it. Her other arm rested on the table.

Zach didn't know how long it would take the virus to heal her wounds once her blood supply was replenished, but didn't wish to wait. Reaching out, he took her free hand in his own.

He heard her heart begin to beat faster at the contact, racing to match the increased thumping of his own. Raising her hand, still sticky in places with congealing blood, to his lips, he pressed a kiss to it, then covered it with his other hand.

Healing warmth grew within him and traveled from his body into hers.

Her breath caught.

He cursed mentally as his mind filled with an inventory of her injuries and images of the battle that had inflicted them.

His hands acquired a slight glow.

Face flushing, eyes wide, Lisette lowered the now-empty blood bag she held and stared at him. The tightness in her face eased as her wounds closed and healed. Yet her breath shortened.

The glow in his hands faded, as did the warmth. Once more, Zach raised her hand to his lips for a kiss.

"Did you . . . did you just heal me?" she asked, her lovely eyes now lit with amber.

"Yes." Every cut, puncture, bruise, and abrasion.

"Is that *all* you did?"

"Yes." When she continued to stare at him, he frowned. "Why?"

"Roland and Seth have healed me I don't know how many times over the centuries. David, too. But their touch . . . their healing warmth . . . *never* made me feel the way yours just did."

"How did mine make you feel?" he asked, unsure what those lovely eyes reflected.

"Like I want to tear your pants off, strip naked, and explore the Kama Sutra with you."

Zach stared at her, his body going rock hard as flames ignited within him. "My healing touch made you desire me?" He had never heard of such a thing.

"I desired you before you healed me," she said without missing a beat. "Now?" Her heated gaze roved him like a pair of hands. "Now I want to lick every inch of you."

His hands tightened around hers. All of the reasons he should keep her at a distance slunk back into the dark recesses of his mind as he imagined her doing just that and wondered how fucking fantastic it would feel.

A faint tremor shook her hand.

"You still need blood," he whispered, struggling to keep his head.

She blinked. Something like hurt flickered in her eyes before she lowered them and reached for a second bag.

When she tried to withdraw the hand he held, Zach clung to it. "Lisette, that wasn't a rejection."

She sank her fangs into the bag.

"I care about you," he went on, floundering and searching for a way to make her understand. "Your welfare will always come first with me. Your safety. Your comfort. It's why I accompanied you to David's. And why I didn't pounce upon your offer, which I didn't even know was an offer, just now. Your hand is cold. I felt you tremble and knew you needed blood. If my timing was off . . ."

She glanced at him from the corner of her eye. "It was a pretty blatant offer."

He shrugged. "I don't know what to say. I've never done this before and am clearly not well versed in it."

She lowered the empty bag. "Never done what?"

He took the bag from her and set it on the table beside the others. "I was going to say court a woman, but I don't think endangering a woman's life, then asking her to continue to risk it by consorting with me counts as a courtship."

She squeezed his hand. "You didn't ask me to risk my life. Aside from wanting me to pick up some of the sedative earlier tonight, I don't think you've asked a single thing of me."

"You know what I mean," he murmured. "Seth doesn't want you anywhere near me. You know the danger of betraying him."

"And I told you it's a risk I'm willing to take to know more of you."

"Why?" he asked helplessly.

"Because I've lived for over two hundred years and haven't felt this alive, this eager to greet each new night, since I was mortal. You make me feel things I never thought I would again, Zach."

The mere possibility astounded him. "And you make me feel things I never thought I *could*."

Her blood-streaked face filled with a tenderness he had never known as she stroked his fingers with her thumb.

Zach handed her another bag of blood.

Smiling, she took it. "Do you also take refuge in seeing to my safety and health when you aren't sure what to say or do next?"

"Yes." As much as she risked for him, she deserved honesty.

Chuckling, she sank her fangs into the bag and emptied it. Her fingers warmed. The tremors ceased. She set the bag on the table.

"Do you need more?" he asked, ready to fetch it if she did.

"No, thank you. I'm good."

Yes, she was. Too good for *him*.

Chapter Eight

Lisette watched Zach gather the empty blood bags and rise.

Her eyes widened as he turned away and walked in that long, languid stride of his over to the trash can to dispose of them.

He hadn't been lying. Or trying to make her feel better when his not "pouncing" on her offer had felt like a slap in the face. He really did want her. The evidence of it strained against the front of his leather pants.

Lisette didn't think she had ever desired a man more.

Grabbing the clean towel hanging over the sink, he held it under the faucet until the cool water ran warm. His broad muscled back, bereft of wings tonight, begged for her touch.

"Where are your wings?"

He shut off the water and approached the table. "I tucked them away once I arrived." Seating himself once more, he scooted his chair even closer until their knees brushed. "I admit I did so because I wanted you to see me as a man."

No problem there. "I've always seen you as a man."

"A *normal* man," he clarified. Clasping her chin in gentle fingers, he drew the soft damp cloth over her cheek, wiping away the blood that dirtied it.

The tender action touched her far more than flowers and chocolates would have. "I wouldn't know normal if it bit me in the ass. I'm not normal myself and never have been."

A smile lit his usually somber features as he shifted his attention to her other cheek. "I wish you could understand how surreal this is for me."

"How surreal what is?" she asked, *wanting* to understand.

"Sitting here with you in your cozy kitchen, the night's silence surrounding us. Talking with you. Touching you." He found a clean corner of the cloth to apply to her forehead. "Seeing the warmth in your eyes when you look at me, the . . . affection?" The last was spoken with uncertainty.

She nodded. "At the very least."

"I'm sure it all seems very unremarkable to you."

Like hell.

"But every aspect of it is new to me," he continued.

Every aspect of it?

"Zach," she began, then paused while he drew the cloth across her nose and upper lip. Her chin. Down her neck, a scowl creasing his brow as he cleaned the soft flesh the vampire had sliced open. "You said you've never courted a woman before . . ."

"Yes." Rising, he returned to the sink, rinsed the blood out of the towel, and draped it over the center divider.

"Does that mean you've never . . . ?" How should she put this?

Swiveling to face her, he leaned back against the counter and rested his hands on the edge of it on either side of his hips. "Lain with a woman?"

Lisette nodded and awaited his response with bated breath.

"Yes."

She stared at him. Zach had never made love with a woman. "You're thousands of years old." *A stupid comment,* she mentally berated herself. Zach knew how old he was.

"That's correct."

"How exactly does one go that long without . . . ?"

"Ask Seth," he countered.

"Seth was married once and had children. You told me yourself."

"But he has, to the best of my knowledge, remained celibate since the death of his wife."

It boggled the mind. It really did. Both men were incredibly handsome and radiated sex appeal. They could've easily gotten laid every night of the year. In *any* time period.

"I've shocked you."

"Yes," she admitted.

He shook his head with a self-deprecating smile. "So much for appearing normal."

"Normal is overrated," she told him. "If you had slept with one woman per year, which is definitely below the norm by today's standards, you would have slept with thousands of women by now. That is *not* an appealing thought," she concluded. "Guys may think it cool. But every woman I know would think it . . . gross."

He shook his head. "You are forever trying to put me at ease."

"I am forever prying and putting my foot in my mouth. I don't ever want you to feel uncomfortable around me, Zach. And . . . I won't lie. I'm also trying to distract myself from eagerly volunteering to be your first."

His hands tightened on the edge of the counter, knuckles whitening. "You want to be my lover?"

"Yes," she answered without hesitation.

"Because I'm a virgin?" He still couldn't seem to comprehend that *he* appealed to her, not what he was or wasn't or would never be.

"Your first or your five thousandth, I just want to be with you, Zach. Is that so hard for you to understand?"

His expression yielded the affirmative answer he wouldn't voice.

Rising, Lisette approached him slowly and held out a hand to him. "I appreciate your cleaning my face, but I need to take a shower and wash this grime off. Come with me. You can wait in my bedroom, keep me company in the bathroom, join me in the shower, whatever you wish. Whatever will make you happy."

A moment passed.

Straightening, Zach placed his large hand in hers and accompanied her from the kitchen.

Lisette led Zach down to her bedroom in the basement. The sheets on the bed were rumpled and still carried his scent.

"As I said," she told him. "The choice is yours. No pressure." Releasing his hand, she began to remove the small arsenal of weapons she carried.

Zach picked up one of her daggers and examined it.

"Are you skilled with weapons?" she asked. He had said as much, but she had never seen him use one and knew he could kill just as swiftly without them.

He nodded. "The Others thought it best to prepare."

She set her shoto swords on a wooden chair, stained many times over with the blood of vampires from similar disarmings. "Prepare for what? Seth?"

He shook his head. "Seth wasn't as powerful back then."

"Then, what?"

He set the dagger aside and helped her tug off her coat.

She pursed her lips. "Is this one of those things you can't tell me because all hell will break loose if someone reads my mind and spreads the word?"

"Yes."

She sighed. "That sucks."

"I don't like it any more than you do." His brow furrowed as he neatly folded her coat and draped it over the back of the chair. "Keeping secrets never bothered me until I met you."

She gave him a teasing smile. "So it's all my fault, is it?"

His face lightened. "I can go with that."

Laughing, she unfastened her belt, drew it through the loops, and dropped it on the chair with her weapons. "You haven't said what you learned tonight when you spied on the Others. Are they still searching for you?"

He nodded, face sobering.

"And?" she pressed.

"They are determined to capture me."

Not what she had been hoping for.

"Fortunately, concealing my presence from them truly *has* become second nature," he continued. "They received not so much as a hint of my whereabouts while I was unconscious and have no idea where to look for me."

At least there was that.

"They don't know I've sought refuge with you. They don't know who you are or that you've helped me." Something new entered his gaze. "Nor do they know what you mean to me."

That got her pulse jumping again.

She started to ask what the Others would do to him if they caught him, but—considering the night she had had—decided to save that unpleasant reality for another time. Instead, she turned her attention to her shirt and began unfastening the buttons along its front. Her heart fluttered with a sudden hint of nerves as his gaze shifted to the pale flesh exposed as the fabric parted down the middle.

Ethan was the only man who had seen her naked in the past century. Lisette wanted to be bold like the women of this time, but . . . as sheltered as her upbringing had been over two centuries ago, she was surprised she had even had the temerity to flirt with Zach upstairs and lure him down here.

She shrugged the shirt off, wishing vampire blood didn't coat so much of her skin or stain her lacy white bra red.

Zach's dark brown eyes turned a dazzling gold as she lowered her fingers to the button on her pants. She heard his heartbeat quicken, saw his hands curl into fists as if he fought the need to reach out and touch her.

Down her zipper went. Then she pushed the soft material down to her ankles and stepped out of it, facing him in only her bra and panties.

"You're beautiful," he whispered.

"So are you." Stepping closer, she rose onto her toes and kissed his cheek. "Remember, no pressure."

Turning, she strode into the adjoining bathroom.

Zach stood as still as a statue, frozen by the sight of Lisette, barely clothed, strolling away from him. His hands burned with the need to touch her. His skin tingled where her lips had brushed him.

He didn't breathe again until she entered the bright tiled room and left his view.

A door opened. A faucet turned. Water struck tile in a hot waterfall. Tendrils of steam slithered past the doorway, then ducked into the bedroom, seeming to beckon him with a curling finger.

Zach slowly approached the doorway and entered.

Lisette's delicate bra and panties lay discarded on the floor.

Through frosted glass, he saw her slender form. Head back, elbows aimed at the ceiling, she combed the cleansing water through hair that now tumbled down to her hips in a curtain of black silk.

Zach's pants, boots, and socks swiftly landed beside her

bra and panties. Grasping the handle of the shower door, he pulled.

Lisette's chin dipped. Her arms lowered. Moisture-spiked eyelashes framed eyes that flared bright amber as they met his.

Stepping into the cocoon of steam, he closed the door behind him.

Blood no longer stained her. Water had already rinsed it away, leaving flawless alabaster skin dotted with clear, shining droplets that raced each other down her curves.

Neither spoke.

Zach closed the distance between them until he could feel her warmth. He settled his hands on her waist, heard her heart begin to pound. As he slid his hands up her sides, over the faint ridges of her rib cage, he still found it hard to believe that he was here with her, touching her, skin to skin, nothing between them.

Her perfect breasts beckoned. Zach cupped one in the palm of his hand, heard her breath catch as he smoothed a thumb across its taut peak.

Touching his chest, she slid a small hand up to curl around the nape of his neck and drew his head down.

He eased even closer, his erection brushing her stomach and sending a shock of pure pleasure through him the same instant her lips met his.

Everything he had endured up to this point . . .

The millennia spent locked in a stark and lonely existence.

The confusion that had gripped him when he had lost faith in the path he had chosen.

The torture to which he had been subjected when he'd turned his back on the Others.

It had *all* been worth it for this moment.

Thousands of years of control began to slip away as Zach curled an arm around Lisette and drew her against him. So warm and soft and enticing.

She rose onto her toes, wrapped her other arm around his neck, met his lips with increasing hunger. It felt so good. Everywhere her long, lithe body pressed against his, he burned with delicious heat. And the more she touched him, the more he wanted to explore.

He hated to abandon her breast, but needed to get closer to her. And closer. He couldn't *get* too close and crushed her against him, his thoughts full of nothing but *needs* and *wants* and *must haves*. He slid a hand down over the beautiful ass she hid too often beneath her long coat and squeezed.

Moaning, she arched her hips against him.

While Lisette wasn't a short woman, Zach still towered over her at six foot ten and couldn't reach and touch and taste everything he wanted to.

Turning them, he lifted her up and pressed her back against the wall.

The cold tile against her skin didn't cool Lisette's ardor even the slightest. It seemed as though she had wanted this for months.

Wrapping her legs around Zach's waist, she ground her core against his erection.

He groaned and dragged his lips from hers, scorching a path down her neck to her breasts. First one, then the other, he tongued and nipped and drew on hard. There was nothing tentative in his explorations. No uncertainty or any of the timidity that had plagued *her* the first time she had made love. Zach was bold, his touch firm, his hands aggressive as they roamed her bare body.

And she had never wanted anyone more, never felt such intense heat and need.

"Zach, please," she gasped. "I need you."

He raised his head . . . and Lisette was mesmerized by the intensity in his golden gaze. He had no difficulty supporting her with one hand as he positioned his hard cock at her entrance.

Wet and desperate for him, she held her breath, waiting.

When he plunged inside, a cry of pure pleasure escaped her. Zach was a big man, filling her with such delicious friction that she nearly came from the first penetration. All the way to the hilt he pressed, then ground against her as if he wanted to go even deeper, get even closer, rubbing against her clitoris.

Lightning crackled through her, heating her blood even more.

Then he withdrew almost entirely and plunged inside again. And again. Driving into her with hard, powerful strokes. His hands once more roving and exploring. His lips and tongue tasting . . . everything.

All Lisette could do was hang on and try to breathe as the pleasure and pressure continued to mount. Her fangs descended as they sometimes did when she experienced strong emotion. Her legs tightened around his hips, urging him on. Her fingers clutched his hair.

His tongue rasped across her nipple. At the same time, he slid a hand between them and stroked her clit. Ecstasy claimed her. Her body clenched and unclenched around his.

Zach stiffened as an orgasm gripped him.

Her climax seemed to go on for minutes, wringing the last of her strength until Lisette collapsed against him, hanging limply in his arms, breath coming in gasps.

Zach seemed a bit weak in the knees himself, resting his forehead on her shoulder as his breath slowly calmed.

Water continued to pound the tiles in the shower as she drew her fingers over his slick skin in languid movements.

He raised his head.

She met his golden gaze, saw the fierce emotion that lit his eyes, and . . . everything changed. *Everything*.

Framing his stubbled jaw in both hands, Lisette couldn't find the words to express what she felt for him in that moment.

He dipped his head. Their lips touched.

Her stomach growled.

Both laughed.

"I can't help it," she said. "I'm always hungry after a hunt. Fighting with preternatural strength and speed burns a lot of energy. And this fight burned more than usual."

Shaking his head, Zach withdrew from her and gently lowered her until her feet touched the floor. "Then let's see if we can't do something to replenish that energy." As he reached for the soap and washcloth, he sent her a smile she thought half shy and half sly. "You'll need it later."

She grinned. "How about dinner in bed? We could make a couple of sandwiches, grab some chips, and have a picnic down here."

His smile broadened. "I like the sound of that."

"Even though we'll get crumbs in the bed?" she teased.

He lathered up the cloth. "You could crush an entire bag of potato chips, sprinkle them on the sheets, and—as long as I held you in my arms—I wouldn't notice."

Damn. He must be the only man on the planet who could make crumbs in bed sound romantic. "Maybe while we eat, you can explain to me how you can be so good at something you've never done before."

He winked, the handsome rogue, and motioned for her to turn around. "I might not have done it, but I spent a *lot* of time thinking about it."

Lisette laughed as he began to wash her back.

Seth leaned over David's desk, perusing the page full of barely understandable gibberish before him. At his elbow, David sat in his usual comfy chair and held the large medical text open to the passage he wished to discuss.

Weariness dragged at Seth, weighing his body down and forcing him to read the same damned paragraph several times before he could understand it. He couldn't remember the last time he had slept. Usually, he spent hours teleporting from this country to that, handling whatever crises arose and seeing to the various and assorted needs and concerns of Immortal Guardians worldwide, then sought sleep whenever his phone stopped ringing.

Now, instead of seeking rest, he returned to David's home to be near Ami, to monitor her condition, to prevent her from going into premature labor, and to pour over every medical textbook that might provide even the tiniest smidgeon of helpful information.

In the living room, someone cracked another joke about Tracy's racy dreams of Sheldon.

"Poor Tracy," he murmured.

David grunted.

Seth knew the immortals and their Seconds meant no harm. They were just blowing off steam and easing tension the way so many family members did: by razzing and teasing each other mercilessly. But sometimes jests could cut deep.

And Tracy's figurative wounds were leaving her pretty battered.

"Do you want me to step in?" David asked softly.

That would put an abrupt end to it.

"Perhaps. Let us see how it plays out." Frankly, Tracy's continued presence at David's home surprised Seth. Every chance encounter with Sheldon had to aggravate the situation, though Seth gave the boy credit for the kindness he had exhibited toward her. Sheldon had been nothing but respectful and had even leapt to her defense several times, ordering the others to cut the crap.

Seth wondered why Lisette hadn't insisted that *Tracy* be the one to stay home alone while *she* spent the day at David's. As long as the two didn't sleep in the same house, the dreams wouldn't affect Lisette. Lisette could easily avoid the erotic dreams *and* spare Tracy the humiliating jokes by staying here in her stead until some other titillating bit of gossip distracted the household.

Unless Tracy's dreams weren't the real reason for Lisette's absence.

Seth frowned at the thought.

A knock sounded on the closed study door.

"Enter," David called.

Étienne strode in, his face liberally flecked with blood. Numerous cuts and tears marred his clothing, which glistened with wet patches. The younger immortal closed the door behind him and, a bag of blood held to his mouth, approached the desk.

"Everything okay?" David asked.

Étienne tossed the empty bag in the trash can. *Can we talk in one of the quiet rooms?*

Seth motioned Étienne forward, then touched his and David's shoulders and teleported them to a secluded, moonlit beach.

Étienne looked around. "Where are we?"

"Rio de Janeiro." Seth studied him. "What's troubling you?"

"Well, two things, actually. One, I fucked up. Sort of. Krysta and I didn't have any of the sedative on us. Or at the house."

Seth scowled his displeasure.

"So we were headed to the network to pick some up," Étienne hastened to add. "But, on the way there, we caught wind of some vampires at UNCG and detoured to take care of them before they could get their hands on any humans."

David considered him thoughtfully. "Were they the new breed of vampires?"

"Three of them were."

"How many total?" Seth asked.

"A dozen. Maybe a couple more. Anyway, I summoned Lisette to help us out."

At least he had done that. Two young immortals against so many vampires at once could yield either victory *or* defeat.

"Did Lisette sedate them?" David asked.

"N-n-n-no," Étienne responded with reluctance. "She didn't have any either." He relayed the battle and subsequent victory for them.

"Did you and Lisette read their minds?" Seth asked, his concern growing. There had been vampire armies in the past, but none with such skilled fighters. Even Bastien's army had not been so well-trained.

"Yes. And that's the other thing that troubles me." He shifted restively, a puzzled frown forming on his brow. "I found no information on the vampire who recruited them or trained them. Nothing on their plans beyond a desire to capture an immortal, which we already knew. But I *did* find blank spots. Not the kind that result from the brain damage the virus yields. The kind that indicate buried memories."

Seth and David shared a sharp look. "You're sure?"

"Yes."

"Lisette saw it, too?" Seth asked.

"Actually, Lisette said she only had time to read the mind of the vampire she fought and didn't find anything odd. Just the usual rage and pain."

"Yet you did."

"Yes."

"Let me see what you saw," Seth said.

Étienne nodded. "Just close your telepathic eyes if you come across any images of Krysta naked up there."

Forcing a smile, Seth perused Étienne's memories. The battle replayed itself before him, as did the conversation that had followed it. He sensed David's presence in the young immortal's mind and knew he saw the same.

"What does it mean?" Étienne asked.

Seth said nothing.

"Are these vampires men we've encountered in previous battles?" he pressed. "I know we let some humans live the first time we came up against Donald and Nelson, and you two buried their memories."

"I don't recognize them," Seth said.

"Nor do I," David pronounced.

"Only a telepath can bury memories," Étienne said, "so a vampire couldn't have done it." Once more, he shifted his weight from one foot to the other, every movement expressing unease. "Could there be another Bastien out there, Seth? Another *gifted one* whose transformation you missed?"

There were three phenomena Seth always felt internally, no matter how far away they took place. The birth of a *gifted one* produced a sort of breathless tingling sensation in his chest. The death of either a *gifted one* or an immortal provoked a feeling of emptiness. And the transformation of a *gifted one* into an immortal prompted a sick feeling of dread. If Seth focused on that dread, the individual's fear and pain would serve as a beacon he could follow to track him or her down. While Seth had no control over the first two, he had *always* felt and followed the third, guiding each newly initiated immortal through the difficult transition and helping him understand his new existence.

With one exception: Bastien. So many immortals had been transformed that year, so many voices had called out to him, that Seth had somehow missed Bastien's.

Or *had* it just been the one exception?

"I don't know," Seth responded at last.

A heavy silence descended upon them.

"I didn't want to say anything in front of the others," Étienne murmured.

David nodded. "We appreciate your discretion and will look into it."

Étienne just seemed glad to end the conversation.

"Thank you," Seth added. He teleported Étienne back to David's study, then returned. "Could I have missed another one?" he asked David, dismayed by the thought. If he had missed two *gifted ones'* transformations, how many others might there be? How many other immortals had lived their lives believing themselves vampires destined to descend into madness?

"No," David answered, utter conviction in his voice. "Could Zach have returned?"

Seth shook his head. "Even the merest *hint* that Zach might defect as I did and meddle in mortal affairs would have made the Others shit their shorts. After his little deviation a few months ago, they will have taken him well in hand and won't let him loose again. You can consider him under house arrest for the rest of eternity."

"He couldn't escape?"

"With so many eyes constantly monitoring him? I don't see how."

"Perhaps all eyes aren't monitoring him."

"What do you mean?"

"All of the Others are telepathic. Tampering with vampires' memories would be child's play for them. Perhaps one of *them* is guilty of raising this army."

"To what end? You know how fanatical they are. The Others believe any interaction at *all* with humans is dangerous. It's why they live in total isolation. They observe. They don't act. They *never* act. They fear even the slightest contact with humans would interfere with the natural course of mankind and bring about not only their *own* destruction, but that of the world."

"The irony, of course, is that if *you* had not strayed and dabbled in mortal affairs, vampires would have roamed unchecked and would have long since slain every human on the planet."

"And brought about the end of the world. Or at least, would have ended humanity's role in it. But the Others don't see it that way and never will. They believe humans must make their own destiny. And have good reason to think thusly."

"I admit they do."

Seth shook his head. "When I abandoned the path we all chose, they spent years trying to capture me and force me back into the fold. And, when that didn't happen, they spent years trying to kill me. And I was *helping* humans. The rest of them stayed true to their beliefs. Thousands of years have come and gone, and I was the only one who deviated."

"Until Zach."

"Until Zach." Seth looked out over the darkened ocean. "If there is such a thing as lockdown mode where the Others reside, they will have instituted it for the long haul. I do not doubt that, even as we speak, Zach is being tortured for his defection. And all he did was unbury the memories of two men. He played no role in the rest of their game."

"Well, whoever we are facing now isn't just tampering with vampires' memories. He's raising and training the army himself. *Choosing* them himself. *Infecting* them himself."

"The Others would never allow so great a defection to take place again. I am their cautionary tale. They still believe I will bring about Armageddon with my meddling. Do you really think they would allow another to leave the path?"

"No. You're right. It can't be one of the Others. I just . . . don't like the alternatives."

Seth paced toward the soft waves that stroked the sand a few yards distant. "I must have missed another *gifted one's* transformation."

"You didn't."

"What other explanation can there be?" he asked. "As Étienne said, the vampires' memories had to have been buried by a telepath." And if Seth, David, Zach, and Étienne hadn't done it, that only left . . .

David met his stare, face somber.

"No," Seth said, "I refuse to believe it."

David nodded. "The thought sickens me as well."

"Lisette wasn't the one who betrayed us by restoring Donald's and Nelson's memories. She has no reason to betray us now."

"I agree." A moment passed. "So why has she been avoiding us?"

"You didn't buy the Tracy explanation either?"

"No. If Tracy's dreams were bothering her, Lisette would have simply continued to spend the day at my place while Tracy slept at home. Not the reverse. Which would also have allowed Lisette to continue to keep an eye on Ami, as we both know she has been doing almost obsessively until recently."

Lisette's odd behavior disturbed Seth as well. "Why didn't she want Richart to take her home after the battle?"

"I don't know, but it had nothing to do with her motor-cycle."

"Perhaps she's taken a lover?"

David frowned. "Wouldn't Ethan be behaving oddly if she had taken a lover?"

"I would think so." Ethan was crazy about her. "Why didn't she want them to summon you or I or Roland to heal her?"

"I understand the Roland bit—"

"I'm *really* going to have to have another talk with him about that."

"—but I don't know why she would forgo *our* aid."

"Perhaps it was as Krysta said? She simply didn't like them offering her special treatment because she's a woman." Seth thought it a weak premise. She had never refused their aid in the past.

"Why do you think she didn't mention the blank spots?"

"She must have missed them." Seth sighed. "And *I* must have missed another *gifted one's* transformation."

"You didn't."

"I wouldn't have believed I had missed even *one* before Bastien raised his army and waged war with us. Who's to say I didn't miss more?"

"I say it," David insisted.

"You would be happier believing Lisette guilty of such treachery?"

"No." More silence. "You might have missed Bastien's transformation, but you didn't miss his birth."

Seth turned to him. "So?"

"We've kept meticulous records of every *gifted one's* birth. I'll pass the names and dates on to Chris and have him look into it. If there are any other anomalies like Bastien, he'll find them. Then we'll know who the culprit is and can use Chris's connections to help us track down the unknown immortal."

"What if he doesn't find any anomalies?"

Only the lapping waves answered.

Chapter Nine

Lisette sat atop Davis Library, a faint smile pulling at her lips as she recalled Zach's manner in bed earlier that day. There had been no need to "show him the ropes" sexually. He had taken the ropes firmly in hand and had enjoyed testing them since that first explosive foray in the shower several nights ago. Sometimes he was slow and tender. Sometimes he was demanding and aggressive, driving her to unbelievable heights as he took her in ways that both shocked and thrilled her. And sometimes, like today, he was playful and affectionate.

Lisette thought she liked the last the most, simply because he seemed happier in such moments. And she thought happiness foreign to him.

Around her, UNC Chapel Hill's campus slumbered peacefully. No parties raged at the frat and sorority houses. No students blearily stumbled along the sidewalk after cramming long hours for exams or working the late shift. Even the animals all seemed to have sought their beds, no strays or pets out seeking mischief.

She had slain two vampires shortly after midnight. Both had been the usual vampire fare. Raving lunatics. So drunk with power they didn't realize they couldn't match *hers*.

It had been an easy victory. No new vampires in the mix.

Zach was off checking on the Others, who still seemed intent on hunting him down and capturing him, and he would likely be gone until daybreak, so she lingered at UNC to see if any more vampires might show their faces.

"Lisette," a voice spoke behind her.

Gasping, she leapt up, spun around, and drew her weapons all in one motion.

Seth stood behind her, his face impassive.

"Seth! You startled me." Why hadn't he called ahead the way he often did?

She frowned. How had he even known where to find her?

Reaching out, he touched her shoulder.

The pretty college campus vanished, replaced by a moon-lit meadow.

No structures or landmarks gave her any hint of their new location.

Releasing her, Seth turned and walked away several steps. Tension radiated from him.

Lisette tightened her hands on the grips of her shoto swords, then asked herself what the hell she was doing.

"You may put away your weapons," he said, his back to her.

Anxiety rose within her.

Her hands began to shake as she slipped the swords into the sheaths on her back. "What's going on?" she asked, unable to sound as casual as she would've liked.

He stopped and stared at the ground. "I might ask you the same thing," he said finally and swiveled to face her.

Ice filled her veins.

He knew. He *must.*

His eyes acquired a faint golden glow as he stared at her, unblinking.

Lisette didn't think she had ever been so afraid in her life.

"You fear me now," he said evenly.

Hell yes, she feared him.

"Why?"

She watched him helplessly. "Seth . . ."

This man had been nothing but kind to her. He had given her a life when she had thought hers had ended. He had given her a purpose and a confidence in herself that she had lacked as a mortal. He had given her warmth and affection and a huge extended family.

Clouds gathered overhead, blocking out the moon.

He had given her everything except that which she had found with Zach.

And she had repaid Seth with betrayal.

She shook her head, not knowing what to say.

Thunder rumbled, vibrating through her chest. The trees began to bend and sway as wind found its way through them, building in strength.

Seth's eyes glowed brighter.

Lisette took a step toward him. "Seth—"

He held up a hand. "Stay back," he warned. A muscle in his jaw jumped as he clenched his teeth and visibly struggled for control.

Heart pounding in her chest, she inched backward. One step. Two. Fighting the urge to turn and flee. Her breath quickened.

"Tell me you didn't do it," he gritted.

She couldn't find her voice.

He squeezed his eyes shut for a moment, something like agony rippling across his features.

Her vision blurred with tears. It killed her to know she had disappointed him. That she had hurt him this way. He had asked so little of her during her lifetime. And had given her so much.

He opened his eyes and speared her with his gaze. "Then tell me you did and break my heart."

Her breath hiccupped in a sob.

Lightning streaked across the sky and struck a tree atop a distant hill. A drop of cold rainwater fell to her shoulder. Another followed. Then more. Large drops dappled the ground around her, making swishing sounds as they multiplied and struck the trees and grasses.

Seth blurred, reappearing inches away from her. He raised a large hand and gripped her chin, his touch firm, but not painful.

Lisette almost broke down entirely when she saw tears shimmering in his luminescent eyes.

"Then I'll find the answer myself," he declared hoarsely as the rain wet their hair and saturated their clothing.

He did nothing to conceal his entrance into her mind, but his presence there caused her no discomfort. Even as furious as he was, he didn't harm her.

Yet.

She waited miserably while he combed through her memories, not knowing how many or which ones he accessed.

Would he let her see Zach one last time? Before he killed Zach for whatever bad blood was between them? Before he killed *her* for betraying him?

Both had known it could come to this. Both had known it likely *would* come to this.

But it had been worth the risk. It had been *so* worth the risk.

Shock flitted across Seth's features. His eyes widened. His lips parted.

Lisette swallowed hard as he released her and staggered back a pace. When she blinked, tears spilled over her lashes and mingled with the cold water on her face. "I'm so sorry," she finally managed to force past the lump in her throat. "I know I betrayed you. But I never wanted to hurt you."

He said nothing, just stared at her with a look of stunned disbelief.

She shook her head and swiped impatiently at her cheeks.

"I love you, Seth. You know I do," she said over the raging storm. "I owe you everything. But . . . for so many decades it seemed as though I were sleepwalking, just going through the motions. Then Zach came along and . . . woke me up. He made me *feel* again. And I haven't felt anything but guilt and weariness for so long."

Seth shook his head. "I thought . . ." Turning, he walked away.

"I don't know what bad blood is between you," she went on, desperate to make Seth understand. "He tried to warn me. Zach tried to push me away. He said you didn't want him anywhere near me. And I know you told me to stay away from him. But . . . I couldn't do it. I couldn't walk away. I *wanted* to feel again. I wanted to have what Richart and Étienne have found. I wanted to experience love again. To find just a few moments of happiness after two hundred years of . . ." She shook her head. "I couldn't let that fall through my fingertips. Even knowing how angry you would be, how disappointed. Even knowing I'd be punished. And, even if Zach is right and the punishment is death, it will have been worth it." Thinking of the long day they had shared— making love, laughing and teasing each other—she nodded and again swiped at her cheeks. "It was worth it."

When Seth said nothing and stood with his back to her, she broke down and began to sob.

"I'm so sorry I hurt you, Seth. I never wanted—"

He returned so fast she didn't even see him move. One moment he stood several yards away. The next, he wrapped his arms around her and gathered her against him in a tight hug. "Shhhh." The thunder ceased. The wind abated. The rain slackened, turning to a slow drizzle.

As Lisette buried her face in his chest, Seth cupped the back of her head in one large hand.

Would he kill her now? Snap her neck?

His hold tightened. "I'm not going to kill you, Lisette."

She relaxed against him, fisting her hands in his wet coat.

"This is *my* fault, not yours," he said. "I should have killed Zach when I had the chance."

She stiffened. "What?" Lisette pushed him away. "No."

Seth shook his head. "Zach isn't what you think he is."

"Yes, he is," she insisted. "He's like you."

"He *isn't* like me. *Never* say that he is. If he were like me, I wouldn't have told him to stay the fuck away from you."

Lisette wiped the tears and rainwater from her eyelashes so she could see Seth better. "Why are you so angry with him?"

"Because he betrayed us," he announced with a bitterness she had never heard him express before. "He betrayed us all."

"How?" she asked, needing to know the source of their animosity.

"Chris's tech team didn't miss anything when they cleaned up after we defeated Donald and Nelson and their mercenary army the first time."

Confusion eradicated the last of her fear. "I thought they missed a backup server."

"They didn't. I lied. I didn't want to have to explain . . ." He shook his head. "I read Donald's and Nelson's minds before David and I dispatched them. Zach restored the memories we had wiped. Zach helped them remember us and resume their war with us."

Her heart stopped. "No," she denied. "He didn't. You're wrong. He wouldn't do that."

"He did."

"You actually *saw* him do it in the mercenaries' memories?"

"No," Seth admitted, "but he didn't deny it when I confronted him about it."

Why would Zach let Seth think he had betrayed them in such a way? Lisette didn't for a minute believe Zach guilty of the deed. "If for no other reason, Zach wouldn't have done it because it put Ami in danger."

"He put *all* of you in danger," Seth corrected.

"Seth, I'm telling you, he didn't do it."

"There were only five telepaths in North Carolina at the time: you, Étienne, David, Zach, and me. Who—of those five—do you think is responsible?"

Okay. That was pretty damning. "Could there be a telepath in the area you aren't aware of?" she asked, grasping at straws.

"No. I checked."

"Perhaps a telepathic *gifted one*?" She knew it was a stretch even as she suggested it.

"No mortal *gifted one* would possess a telepathic gift strong enough to alter memories. At best, he or she would be able to read thoughts."

She shook her head. "I don't know what the explanation is, but it couldn't have been Zach."

"It was," Seth insisted, utterly implacable. "And he has betrayed us again."

"What do you mean?"

"Étienne told me he found blank spots in the memories of the vampires the two of you fought last week."

"*All* vampires have blank spots. The brain damage the virus causes—"

"Étienne said those vamps hadn't been infected long enough to produce that kind of damage. He said the blank spots indicated that some of their memories had been buried."

She frowned. "How would Étienne even know what buried memories look like? Neither of us has ever seen them."

He studied her. "You've never read the mind of a mortal after David or I buried his memories?"

"No. Neither has Étienne."

"Yes, he has. He was there when I buried the memories of the military veteran Chris recruited from Donald's army." He looked thoughtful. "That explains why Étienne said you claimed you had seen nothing out of the ordinary when you scanned the vamps' minds."

"I didn't claim it. I—" She stiffened. "Wait. When you brought me here tonight and told me to tell you I didn't do it, you weren't actually . . ." Hurt stabbed her in the chest. "Did you think *I* had done it? That *I* had altered the vampires' memories? That I was in league with them?"

Arms at his sides, Seth spread his fingers in a *What else could I think?* gesture. "Coupled with your long absences and odd behavior of late—the discomfort that bordered on fear you exhibited whenever you were in my presence or David's—I didn't know what to think," he said.

"So, this wasn't about Zach at all," she pressed, needing to clarify it in her own mind before she went ballistic. "You thought I had taken up the sword Bastien dropped and was secretly raising a vampire army?" Her voice rose with each word.

Seth's face tightened. "I didn't know what else to think."

"You didn't think at all!" she yelled, then gasped at her temerity.

"I know!" he shouted and gave her his back. "I know I didn't! I don't know what the fuck is happening!" Dragging a hand through his long wet hair, he paced away from her. "I can't think straight anymore!" he growled with such frustration, such anguish.

Lisette stared.

He stopped and rubbed his eyes with the heels of his hands, seeming infinitely weary all of a sudden. "I can't think straight anymore," he repeated softly.

And all of the anger building inside her—or most of it anyway—fled.

Lisette approached him with care. "Seth . . . how long has it been since you slept?"

"I don't know." He lowered his hands. "Weeks, I think."

"Because you're worried about Ami?"

The drizzle stopped, but heavy clouds lingered.

"Because I'm worried about Ami. Because keeping her

from losing this babe has been a constant struggle. Because her babe is dreaming of torture."

"What?" Horror filled Lisette. "Is the babe dreaming of her mother's torture?" Lisette had been pulled into Ami's dreams often enough to know that the torture Ami had endured sometimes returned to haunt her in nightmares.

Seth shook his head. "That's the puzzle. Ami isn't the one being tortured in the dreams."

"The baby is dreaming of her *own* torture?" That was even worse! Was Ami's daughter precognitive? Was she seeing her future? A future in which she would be tortured like her mother?

"No. The one being tortured is a man. And, before you ask if it's Marcus, I don't know. I can't see his face because the dreams seem to be from his perspective."

"No wonder you aren't sleeping."

A sad laugh escaped him. "Those are just the highlights. I've also seen the future." He studied the puddles forming around his big boots. "More specifically, I saw Ami and Marcus in the future. Two years hence."

"Then you know Ami will survive childbirth." That was a good thing, right?

"Yes. Ami will," he whispered. He said nothing of the babe.

Dread soured Lisette's stomach. "Was the baby with them? In your vision of the future?"

His Adam's apple bobbed up and down. "No."

She could think of no response.

"I know it doesn't necessarily mean . . ."

"Of course not." Lisette tried to sound confident, but failed miserably.

"Now this new vampire army is rising. And . . ." He turned to face her. "I thought Zach was out of the picture, and it tore me up inside to think you had betrayed me."

"I would never betray you," she responded automatically, then bit her lip.

He raised one eyebrow.

"Okay, *other* than boinking your enemy, I would never betray you," she qualified.

He huffed a laugh. "Boinking?"

"I believe that's one of Sheldon's terms."

He nodded, amusement gradually receding and leaving his handsome face pensive as he searched the horizon. "I can't seem to keep you all safe anymore," he murmured. "It weighs heavily on me."

"You keep us safe."

"Lisette, I've left *you* more vulnerable than anyone. Zach is toying with you. I don't know why, and I don't know what his endgame is or even how he escaped the Others, but . . . surely you realize now that, having betrayed us once before, he must be the one who has raised this new army. He's burying their memories so we can't identify him."

"It *can't* be Zach, Seth," she said, determined to convince him. "This army didn't spring up overnight. Someone has been raising and training it for months. If you read my memories, then you know that Zach was imprisoned and tortured by the Others and didn't escape until the night before Ethan and I encountered the two new vamps."

"I also know," he responded, "that Zach communicated with you through dreams while he was imprisoned. He could have done the same with the vampires."

"Communicated? Possibly. Turned them and trained them? I don't think so."

"Zach is more powerful than you know."

"Is he *that* powerful?"

His brow furrowed. "If not Zach, then who?"

There must be some other explanation. "Could you have . . ." She trailed off. "Could you have missed another *gifted one*'s transformation? Like you did with Bastien?"

He didn't flinch. Nor did hurt cross his features as she had feared it might. "No."

"Are you sure?"

"Yes. I didn't want to believe you had betrayed me. And I thought Zach well in hand. So I assumed it must be another Bastien. David gave Chris the names of every *gifted one* ever born, and Chris put his research team on it. Every *gifted one* has been accounted for. Bastien was the only one I missed."

"If you missed the *transformation* of a *gifted one,* could you not have also missed the birth of one? Could there be one not on your list? One who has transformed?"

"No. Of that, I'm certain."

Then there seemed to be no explanation.

"Exactly," he said.

"It wasn't Zach."

"You would have me believe Immortal Guardians are rising up against their own kind?"

"Immortal Guardians plural?"

"A teleporter would have to carry the betrayer in and out of the area for the telepath's movements to remain undetected."

"Honestly, the idea that at least two of our own may have betrayed us is as unpalatable to me as your belief that Zach has," she said.

"Pluralitas non est ponenda sine necessitate," he uttered.

"Occam's razor?"

He nodded. "The simplest explanation is usually the better one. Zach can teleport, bury memories, and has been closely surveilling Immortal Guardians for some time now."

"The same could be said of the Others."

He stared at her for a moment. "What has Zach told you about the Others?"

"That they're hunting him, intent on recapturing him and punishing him."

"Because he interfered in mortal affairs?"

"Is that why he was being punished?" she asked. Zach had never told her.

Seth swore, as if he had said too much and regretted it. "You didn't know?"

She shook her head.

He sighed and seemed to weigh his speech carefully. "The Others don't interact with humans, Lisette. They *observe* humans. They sure as hell wouldn't *transform* humans and raise an army of insane vampires."

"Well, I don't know who is responsible, Seth, but Zach didn't do it." Reaching out, she touched his arm. "Couldn't you just talk to him? And by talk I mean *talk,* not"—she motioned to the waterlogged landscape and overcast sky—"confront."

He glanced around with a grimace. "This was not well done of me. I apologize for frightening you."

Now that she no longer feared he would punish her, Lisette noticed the lines of fatigue that creased his face. Seth looked exhausted. She hadn't even known an immortal *could* look exhausted and wondered just how much sleep one would have to miss for such to occur.

She squeezed his arm. "You're forgiven. Just, please, don't ask me to stop seeing Zach."

"Lisette—"

"He makes me happy, Seth."

Lifting a hand, Seth gently stroked her face with the backs of his fingers. "That's all I've ever wanted for you." He lowered his hand with a sigh. "Why couldn't it have been Ethan?"

She stopped breathing. "Why would you say that?"

He arched a brow.

"You knew about Ethan?"

"Of course I knew about Ethan."

"You never said anything."

He shrugged. "Neither did David."

"*David* knew?"

"Of course."

"Does anyone else know?"

"Do you really want me to answer that?"

"No."

"Well, there you have it."

"Back to the subject at hand," she said, eager to abandon that of her affair with Ethan. "Would you please talk to Zach? Maybe he can help you figure out who is working against us."

His look told her he knew who was working against them: Zach.

"Have you no faith in my judgment?" she pressed.

"Love can make us blind to the obvious. Love can make us trust where we should not."

"Did you not see, in my memories, how he treats me? How loving he is? Zach wouldn't endanger me by waging war with you. He wouldn't endanger Ami either. He considers Ami his friend. And . . . I don't think Zach has had many friends during his long existence."

Seth mumbled something that sounded like *with good reason*.

"If Zach truly were your enemy, Seth, would he not have exposed all your secrets? Would he not have told me what you are? What you *both* are?"

His gaze sharpened. "I'm immortal."

"I think we both know you're more than that, that you're different from the rest of us. I know Zach is like you. Yet, when I asked him what he is, if you have wings like his, what the source of *gifted ones*' and immortals' advanced DNA is, he wouldn't tell me. He didn't want to expose your secrets to me and to anyone who could read my mind. And, when he told me you were responsible for his capture and torture, he even offered an excuse. He said sometimes the truth is too harsh to bear even for someone *your* age. That it's easier, sometimes, to believe a lie."

Minutes passed. Did Seth search her memories again?

"I'll consider it," he said at last. Disturbed's "Down With The Sickness" rose on the night. Seth took out his cell phone and gave it a glance. "Duty calls. I must go."

"You aren't going to insist I stop seeing Zach?"

"Would it do any good?"

"No."

"I assumed it wouldn't."

Lisette hugged him again. "Get some sleep, Seth."

He pressed a kiss to the top of her head. "Be careful."

"I will."

When he released her, they were atop Davis Library once more.

Seth vanished without another word.

Fury thrummed through Zach.

Beside him, Lisette sighed as they strolled through Duke's quiet campus. "It's been days, Zach. I wish you would just let it go."

If Lisette hadn't all but begged him not to, Zach would have confronted Seth and done his damnedest to beat the shit out of him after she had mentioned the little *conversation* the two of them had shared. "He accused you of betraying your brethren."

"Well, you have to admit I *have* been behaving suspiciously of late."

"He frightened you." That fueled his temper more than anything—that she had experienced even one millisecond of fear because of that bastard.

"I hate to break it to you, but you aren't exactly making me feel all warm and fuzzy yourself right now."

He looked down at her in surprise. "You fear me?"

"No. Not really. But your eyes are glowing and you look like you really want to kill something."

"Not some*thing*. Some*one*."

"Well, let's put those violent urges to good use. About a dozen vampires are headed our way."

Shocked, Zach realized he had been so distracted he hadn't even smelled them coming.

A smile slid across Lisette's pretty face. "Oh, you're going to love this. They're all the new breed."

He followed her gaze to the figures making their way through the shadows. Indeed they were. Strange. "I don't suppose I could talk you into letting me handle this on my own," he said, palming two daggers.

She drew her shoto swords. "Don't start treating me with kid gloves, Zach. My brothers do it, and it drives me crazy."

As soon as the vampires spotted them and the weapons they held, the vamps attacked. There was no talking. No boasting. No bullshit. Just what appeared to be a single-minded determination to capture Lisette. Zach, too, once they realized that—despite his lack of hunting garb—he bore the speed and strength of an immortal.

Planting his back to Lisette's, Zach started carving the vamps up with the weapons she had insisted he carry. Oh yeah. This was just what he'd needed.

Cries of pain sounded behind him. All male.

Zach smiled. He loved that Lisette could fight and found her strength a fascinating complement to her vulnerability.

Crimson liquid slapped him in the face as he opened arteries. These vamps bordered on expert warriors. They fought as a team with order and a cold calculation that the vampires he had seen Seth and his immortals fight in the past had lacked. Even those led by Bastien had not achieved this expertise.

Nevertheless, three vampires soon lay on the ground at their feet, shriveling up as the others stumbled over them.

Lisette's back left his.

Lisette? he asked.

I'm fine, she assured him. *I just needed a little more swinging room so I could—*

Her presence in his thoughts abruptly vanished.

Spinning around, Zach saw her shoto swords fall from limp fingers.

Eyes closed, knees buckling, she crumpled where she stood.

"Lisette!"

Hurling his daggers into the throats of the vampires in front of her, he lunged forward and caught her before she could hit the ground. "Lisette?" He gave her a little shake.

No response.

Lisette? he thought desperately and delved into her mind.

Dead silence.

Fear struck with frightening force as he sank to his knees and waited for her to dissolve in his arms, certain she was dead.

But she didn't. Beneath Zach's ragged, panicked breaths, he detected the faintest beat of a heart.

Not dead. Not yet.

Like sharks scenting blood, the vampires moved in for the kill. Or the capture.

Rage so raw it seemed to scald his skin rose within Zach. Clutching Lisette to him with one arm, he thrust the other toward the vampires in front of him. All five fell to the ground and began to rapidly shrivel up.

He turned to the last two, who regarded him with wide, terror-filled eyes.

When they started to flee, he froze them in place.

The tendons in their necks stood out as they stiffened and strained to break his telekinetic hold.

"I don't know what you've done to her," Zach spoke as he rose, Lisette cradled in his arms, "but you're going to pay for it in blood."

* * *

In a rare moment of tranquility, Immortal Guardians and their Seconds kicked back and relaxed in David's large, cozy home. There used to be far more of these moments. The insurgencies and enemies who had risen up against the Immortal Guardians in recent years, however, had stolen them away.

Most of the usual frequent visitors were present, lounging on the sofas and in the chairs that filled the huge room. Roland and Sarah occupied a love seat near Marcus and Ami, who shared a sofa with Seth. David relaxed in a wingback chair across from them, feet propped on the coffee table, the latest Stephen King novel in his lap. Bastien and Melanie chatted with Richart and Jenna near the fireplace. Seconds Sheldon, Tanner, and Nichole laughed on another sofa as they viewed something on Sheldon's laptop. Tracy surreptitiously peered over their shoulders and smiled. Darnell joined the trio and laughed.

Ethan was almost curious enough to get up and go see for himself, but really didn't want to leave the comfy leather chair in which he slouched.

Étienne called something to his brother, who flipped him the bird. Beside Étienne, Krysta and her brother Sean laughed. Jenna did, too, as she leaned into Richart's side. Edward smiled as he studied the chessboard on the table between him and his Second, Desmond, over in the corner.

Yuri and Stanislav carried on a conversation in Russian while they raided the refrigerator, out of sight. Their Seconds, Dmitry and Alexei, headed in there to comment and filch some food.

It had been a good night, Ethan thought. An uneventful night.

He used to think uneventful nights boring. Now he *preferred* them. No one suffered any injuries on uneventful nights. Tense faces relaxed with smiles on uneventful nights. Laughter flowed freely on uneventful nights.

As it did now.

The immortals had all gotten their hunting over with early, each encountering only a slacker vamp here or there. Tracy and Tanner had prepared a delicious meal for the group. Everyone had enjoyed it so much that not a crumb had remained.

For once . . . for this moment . . . all was right in the world. All were safe. All were happy.

Except for Ethan, who didn't like that Lisette was yet again absent. He hadn't seen her in days and couldn't help worrying, even though Tracy frequently touched base with her and claimed all was well.

Yuri and Stanislav returned with two platters piled high with fruits and breads and cheeses.

Immortals and mortals alike pounced.

Hell, even Ethan couldn't resist that temptation and snatched some snacks before sinking into his favorite chair again.

Mmmm. Good food. Good company. Good conversation.

He smiled at a joke Darnell cracked, then grinned when Ami's baby began to hiccup in the womb. It was odd, being able to hear the babe's movements. Even odder to imagine an unborn baby getting the hiccups. Yet Jenna, Melanie, and Dr. Kimiko insisted it was normal.

Marcus rubbed a hand over Ami's big belly and gave her a tender smile.

Seth and David both watched with affectionate indulgence, then abruptly turned their heads toward the front of the house, all levity in their faces draining away. Seth's eyes flashed a bright gold milliseconds before he closed them. When he lifted his lashes, his eyes were brown once more.

Had Ethan not been staring right at him, he would've missed it.

What the hell?

Seth shared a look with David, then turned a smile on Ami. "Marcus, Ami has spent too many days and nights cooped up inside. Why don't the two of you go for a ride? Roll down the windows. Get some fresh air. Enjoy the night."

Ami's face lit up.

Marcus eyed Seth (long enough that Ethan suspected Seth had just told him to get Ami the hell out of there) and forced a smile. "Sounds good to me. Are you up to it, sweetling?"

"Absolutely!"

David tossed Marcus his keys. "Take my car. More room for you both to stretch your legs."

Everyone called cheerful good-byes as the couple left through the back door.

It didn't take long for the others to catch on that something was wrong.

Silence fell. Tension gripped the room as all eyes went to Seth and David.

Outside, David's car started and tore off down the drive, accompanied by Ami's fading laughter.

The two elders rose as one. Their faces turned to stone.

"Everyone out," Seth ordered.

"What's going on?" Roland asked, rising.

Ethan rose, too.

Everyone rose.

But none left. All sensed what Ethan did, that something was coming. And they would be damned if they were going to leave and let Seth and David face it—whatever the hell it was—alone.

The air began to crackle with static electricity.

The hair on Ethan's arms and the back of his neck rose.

Thunder rumbled on the night.

Seth shook his head, his eyes beginning to glow. "No time. Just go."

"Use the escape tunnels in the basement," David instructed from beside him, his eyes glowing a vibrant amber. Ethan had not seen that very often. "Don't return until we summon you."

"Fuck that!" Bastien said, echoing Ethan's thoughts. "I don't know what the hell is coming, but we aren't going to leave you to face it alone!"

"Just go!" Seth snapped. "Get the Seconds out while you can. They—"

The large bay window facing the front of the house exploded inward. Shards of glass rocketed through the living room, finding purchase in mortal and immortal flesh, as a body catapulted inside as though it had been shot from a cannon.

Sheldon tackled Tracy as Immortal Guardians flung themselves out of the way, the married men all placing their bodies between their wives and the threat.

A coffee table splintered as the bloody body struck it. The unconscious male hit the floor and rolled twice before coming to a halt, lips parted to reveal fangs. A second body flew bonelessly through the bay window, knocking more shards free as it went and widening the hole in the window. It hit the floor just beyond the first. Another vampire. Unconscious. His face and form shredded and bloody.

"There!" a voice bellowed outside as wind whipped the curtains.

As though the one word shook them all from their shocked paralysis, everyone present lunged for the weapons they had removed and braced themselves for a fight.

Everyone except Seth and David, who glared daggers into the night through the broken window.

Lightning flashed across the sky, momentarily illuminating the figure who strode toward the house, still yards away, a black construction paper cutout with wings spread, carrying something or someone in his arms.

"There's your fucking proof!" he shouted.

Ethan's eyes widened. *Holy shit!*

The male, standing six foot ten, leapt through the gaping hole and faced them with furious defiance. Little bits of feather, sliced away by the fragments of glass that remained in the window frame, floated on the breeze and settled quietly on the floor.

Zach. Eyes glowing golden like Seth's. Face full of pure, animalistic rage. Lisette's limp form cradled in his arms.

"What the hell?" Étienne shouted and leapt forward, swords flashing.

Zach looked at the French immortal.

Étienne seemed to hit an invisible wall, then flew backward.

Richart vanished and reappeared behind Zach, daggers raised.

Without even turning around, Zach sent him flying, too. "She tried to warn you it wasn't me!" he snarled at Seth. "She tried to tell you I couldn't have raised the new vampire army because I was too busy being fucking tortured!"

Roland, Yuri, and Stanislav leapt forward.

A wave of power rippled through the room like the blast wave of an A-bomb, Zach at its epicenter.

Ethan swore as he and every mortal and immortal present, save Seth and David, were swept off their feet.

"I didn't . . . fucking . . . do it!" Zach roared. "And, because you wouldn't believe us, because you couldn't believe one of your *precious* Immortal Guardians would betray you, the new vampire army *I didn't fucking raise* grew unchecked! Well, there's your proof!" He nodded at the vampires. "Read their minds! Unbury their memories! You won't find me in any of them!"

All waited with bated breath.

Seth held out a hand, palm facing out in a *just stay calm* motion, and slowly backed toward the vampires. Kneeling, he placed a hand on the first vamp's blood-soaked head.

Minutes ticked past. Seth touched the other, every second he took to scan them seeming an hour, then rose.

"You see?" Zach demanded, the two words filled with wrath.

Seth shared another look with David. "What have you done to Lisette, Zach?"

"Watched over her. Tried to protect her when you wouldn't."

That arrow hits its mark.

David's eyes lost their glow.

Seth's dimmed. "What happened tonight?"

"Lisette and I went hunting together."

Seth opened his mouth.

"That's right! Together!" Zach bellowed before Seth could speak. "Did you think I was going to leave her unprotected while you pissed away your time and let the vampire army grow in strength and numbers? Let them get their shit together? Let them nearly capture her?"

All Ethan could do was watch with wide eyes and think, *Shit!*

"The two of you were hunting," David said, his voice so full of calm it made Ethan feel better just to hear it. "What happened next?"

"We took on a dozen of the new breed of vampires. I thought with me at her back she would be safe. But . . ."

"You can defeat a dozen vampires without lifting a weapon," Seth pointed out.

"Killing one or two with a thought wouldn't draw any notice. But the kind of power it would take to kill a dozen would have alerted the Others to my location. If they found out about her, learned what she means to me—"

"You just exerted more power than that here."

"They'll assume it was you."

"Fuck this," Ethan blurted when he could stand it no longer, and clambered to his feet. "We don't have time for if-I-woulda-coulda-shouldas. What's wrong with Lisette?"

Zach swallowed, nostrils flaring, moisture rising in his eyes. "I can't wake her." He clutched Lisette closer, rubbed his chin across her hair. "Her presence in my mind vanished, and when I turned around . . . she was falling."

Seth took a step forward. "Give her to me."

"Fuck you! I'm not letting you anywhere near her! Not after that little conversation you had with her." His gaze circled the room. "Do your Immortal Guardians all know you accused *her* of collaborating with the vampires?"

Richart's and Étienne's heads snapped toward Seth. "What?" they both demanded.

Ethan stared at Seth.

Seth's face remained impassive. "If you don't want me near her, why did you bring her to me?"

"I didn't." Zach looked at Melanie. "I came here for you." His gaze shifted to Bastien. "And for you."

Melanie glanced at Seth and David, waiting for their approval before she moved.

Bastien didn't wait. He just sheathed his weapons and strode forward, broken glass crunching beneath his boots.

Ethan thought him either the ballsiest or stupidest immortal on the planet.

Melanie approached Zach with caution and felt Lisette's pulse. Peeling Lisette's eyelid back, Melanie then looked for whatever the hell it was doctors looked for in eyes. Pupillary response? Lack of response? Dilation? He didn't know. "Any major arteries severed?" She began checking them herself even as she asked.

"No."

"So not a lot of blood loss?"

"No. Most of the blood that coats her is vampire."

Seth took a step forward. "You didn't give her your blood, did you?"

Zach glared daggers at him. "Of course not. I'm not an idiot."

What the hell did *that* mean?

More calmly, Zach told Melanie, "We were holding our own against them very nicely before she collapsed. She suffered no major injuries as far as I could see, hear, or smell."

Melanie glanced around at the debris-covered room, then motioned down the hallway. "Could I get you to place her on a bed in the infirmary so I can examine her more thoroughly?"

Zach's arms tightened around Lisette as his eyes flashed brighter.

Melanie raised a hand. "Okay. It's okay. I'll just . . . see what I can learn here for now so you can have another minute to . . ." She floundered. "So you can have another minute."

Ethan wouldn't know what to say either. Zach looked pretty feral. How the hell was Melanie going to get Lisette away from him?

Bastien seemed to be dividing his attention between helping his wife check for injuries and keeping an eye on Zach to make sure he didn't threaten Melanie in any way.

Ethan glanced around.

The downed immortals had all risen to their feet. Mortals rose more slowly and with the aid of their immortals. Or, in Tracy's case, with the aid of Sheldon, another Second.

Richart and Étienne looked as if their heads were about to explode.

Ethan had to admit he was pretty pissed, too. How could Seth have thought Lisette capable of such treachery? Had he discovered she had slept with Zach? Because clearly the two were lovers now. And that chafed a hell of a lot. But big fucking deal. Bad judgment in lovers wasn't tantamount to betraying everyone you know and love.

Seth kept his gaze trained on Zach, Lisette, and the two immortals now examining her.

David glowered at everyone else, effectively shutting down any tirade they might wish to launch. David didn't blow his stack often, but when he did—*Whew!*—it was best not to be around.

Melanie tried to examine Lisette as best she could under the circumstances. She ran her fingers over Lisette's arms and legs, across her abdomen, applying pressure here and there along the way. When her fingers slipped between Lisette and Zach's chest, she gasped and jerked her hand back.

Bastien stiffened. "What?"

A bead of blood formed on the tip of one finger. Frowning, Melanie slowly felt along the same path, then drew her hand back.

Dread curled in Ethan's stomach when she held up a tranquilizer dart.

It couldn't be.

Melanie listed to one side, eyelids drooping.

Bastien hastily wrapped his arms around her, his face darkening with concern. "Melanie? Sweetheart?"

She squeezed her eyes closed and shook her head. "I'm okay," she said, but slurred her words as though drunk. Unsteady on her feet, she clung to the arms Bastien wrapped around her. "I just . . . I just pripped . . . pricked my finger."

A pinprick had done *that? Shit!* How much sedative had been in that thing?

"They must've . . . must've upped the dosage again," she continued.

Utter silence took the room. Men and women turned to mannequins, shocked into stillness. *They,* meaning the mercenaries who were all supposed to be dead, had upped the dosage *again?* The last time they had done that, it had taken double the usual dose of the antidote to enable immortals to rouse and function again. And they hadn't functioned normally. They had functioned, at least briefly, as if they were high on coke or something. Juiced up. Heart racing. Not thinking clearly before they acted.

Seth strode forward. "That isn't possible."

"Stay back!" Zach barked.

"Fuck off!" Seth took the tranquilizer dart from Melanie's limp fingers and brought it to his nose. He drew in a deep breath. His eyes flashed gold again, and thunder rumbled outside. "How the fuck can this be?" he growled with a fury and disbelief Ethan suspected they all felt. "We didn't even bother to bury memories this time. We killed fucking *everyone!*"

"It doesn't matter how it happened." Bastien spoke, the only calm voice and clear head present, it would seem, aside from David's. "Not right now. We need to get Melanie a small dose of the antidote and see what, if anything, we can do to revive Lisette."

If anything. The words hung like a pall over the room.

Keeping one arm around his wife, Bastien shifted to stand at Zach's side. He reached around and touched Zach's back beneath his wings, giving him a sympathetic pat. "Come on. The infirmary is just down this hallway. Let's make Lisette comfortable and see if we can't help her."

Ethan had only ever heard Bastien speak so compassionately to Melanie and Ami.

The immortal black sheep had to give Zach a gentle push to get him moving.

Stiffly at first, as though his feet had grown roots and didn't want to leave the floor in front of the bay window, Zach allowed Bastien to lead him from the room.

Seth followed.

A raindrop hit the grass outside with a swish. Another

followed. Then more, racing each other to their doom until the sky opened up and pummeled the land with liquid fists.

David eyed them sternly. "Not one word."

Étienne glowered at him. "David—"

"Not. One. Word," the elder repeated. "Your grievances will be heard at a more appropriate time. For now . . ." He motioned to the vampires. "Richart, take these two to the network and place them in separate holding rooms. Bring Chris back with you when you return. He needs to know what's going on. And ask him to send someone out here to replace my window. The rest of you, see to your wounds, then clean up this mess."

He turned without another word and headed down the hall, disappearing through the infirmary's doorway.

Darnell and Tracy followed, closing the door behind them.

Ethan looked at the others.

Everyone seemed as shell-shocked as he felt, and he knew a hell of a lot more about what was going on than they did. They didn't even know who Zach was.

"You heard him," Roland said. Turning to his wife, he began to brush the glass from her clothing, cutting up his hands—Ethan was sure—in the process. "Now isn't the time for questions." He speared the d'Alençon brothers with a warning glare. "*Or* for recriminations. Now is the time to circle our wagons. We don't know who or what might come through that window next."

Stanislav nodded. "We should post guards in case another of his ilk should follow."

Not a bad idea, Ethan thought, since Zach had mentioned that *the Others* were searching for him, whoever the hell they were.

Roland nodded. "As the strongest present, Sarah and I will patrol the grounds. Stanislav, you and Yuri go below and keep your ears open. Ensure no one enters through the escape tunnels."

The two nodded and zipped down to the basement.

"Étienne and Richart, I know you're concerned about Lisette, but do not go into that infirmary unless you can keep your shit to yourself. Am I understood?"

Jaws clenching, the brothers nodded.

"Richart, take care of the vampires as David instructed first."

Richart crossed to the vampires, hoisted them over his shoulder, and vanished.

"Jenna and Krysta, stay here and stay sharp. Keep your eyes and ears peeled for anything that might indicate an intruder got past us. Your husbands are distracted and may not notice a sound or a shadow that doesn't belong."

They nodded.

"Edward, you stay with them."

Edward nodded.

"What about me?" Sean asked. He was the newest inductee into the Immortal Guardians' ranks, having been turned at his request shortly after his sister Krysta had transformed.

"Arm yourself heavily, then track down Marcus and Ami. Make sure they're safe and guide them to network head-quarters. If anything has happened to them, *anything,* call me immediately." He rattled off his cell phone number.

"What should I tell them?" Sean asked.

No one knew what would happen if Ami were upset. For all they knew, it could cause her to go into labor again, and Seth and David needed to be able to focus their attentions on Lisette.

And Zach.

Roland looked to the others. "Any ideas?"

Ethan thought furiously. "Some of us were sparring," he suggested. "Bets started flying. Things got a little out of hand. And Seth and David want her to hang at the network until the mess is cleaned up."

Sarah looked at them. "You guys *do* bet a lot."

Roland nodded. "Good enough for now. I'll call Marcus and fill him in later."

Ethan looked to Roland. "What do you want me to do?"

No one questioned Roland's command. The British immortal was hundreds of years older than the rest of them and had led men into battle even as a mortal.

"Clean up the broken glass, then—"

"We'll do it," Sheldon said, stepping forward. "The Seconds will take care of the cleanup. As soon as we're finished, we'll arm ourselves out the ass and help Jenna, Krysta, and Edward keep watch."

Roland nodded. "Then, Ethan, you take the back door. No one," he said, catching every eye, "and I mean *no one* gets in this house unless he or she is a regular visitor."

Nods all around.

"Okay. Let's do this."

Chapter Ten

The infirmary was larger than Zach had anticipated. A wall—tiled from the floor to about waist high, then double-paned glass above with blinds in between that could be closed—divided the room in two. The room on the right sparkled, antiseptically clean, beneath lights so bright they hurt his eyes. Several surgical or exam tables occupied much of the floor space, bordered by a conglomeration of machines whose purposes eluded him.

The room on the left bore a row of neatly made beds, bracketed by comfortable-looking chairs and bedside tables. Large-screen televisions hung at intervals upon the opposite wall. Shelves beneath them bore all kinds of electronic gaming devices, along with a couple of rather tattered decks of cards and a large selection of books.

"Zach," Seth prodded.

Ire rose at just the sound of Seth's voice.

Zach followed Melanie, Bastien, David, and Seth into the room on the right. The mortals who had trailed after them in the hallway filed into the room on the left and stood just on the other side of the window.

Bastien led Melanie over to a counter and leaned her

against it. Opening a drawer, he drew out a syringe and a small bottle of clear liquid.

Zach remained motionless, Lisette still cradled in his arms, as Bastien filled the syringe with the antidote and turned to his wife.

Taking one of her arms, Bastien pushed up her sleeve and positioned the needle at the bend of her elbow. "Say when," he said softly, his eyes locked on hers.

She nodded.

Pushing the needle into her flesh, he began to slowly inject the liquid.

"When," she said.

Withdrawing the needle, Bastien tossed it into a nearby step-on medical waste bin and cupped her face in his hands. "Okay?"

She straightened with a smile. "I'm okay."

He pressed a gentle kiss to her lips, then released her and stepped aside so she could see to her patient.

Zach stiffened as she walked toward him and motioned to one of the surgical/exam tables.

"Would you please place Lisette on the table?" she asked, her voice and demeanor so gentle she almost made Zach forget he wished to kill the eldest member of their party.

Everything inside him balked at the idea of relinquishing his hold on Lisette.

"It's okay," Bastien said, stepping up behind his wife and meeting Zach's gaze. "Melanie will take good care of her. And you can still touch her and hold her hand if you need to."

Zach decided that, aside from Lisette, Bastien was his favorite of all the Immortal Guardians. With monumental reluctance, he lowered Lisette onto the exam table.

Bastien zipped across the room, grabbed a metal stool on wheels, and rolled it across to Zach. "Here. You can sit on this."

"Thank you." Zach parked his butt on the stool and leaned his elbows on the table. Fearing his wings would get in the way in the enclosed space, he retracted them. Then, taking one of Lisette's hands in his own, he brought it to his lips for a kiss and clung tightly to it as Melanie renewed her inspection.

"Are you telepathic, Zach?" Melanie asked. "I'm sorry. May I call you Zach?"

"Yes to both questions."

"See if you can reach her telepathically."

"I've tried," he told her, despondent. "I've *been* trying. Over and over again. There's nothing there. No response. No thought. No dreams. Just silence."

She looked to Seth. "Seth, can you reach her?"

Seth stared at Lisette for a full minute. "No. It's as he said."

"I've never seen one of you slip into stasis before," she murmured. "Does it look like this? Could that be what this is?"

Zach had forgotten about that, the eerie state of hibernation immortals would slip into if they lost too much blood. They wouldn't die like vampires. Rather both their breath and their pulse would slow to the point that even an immortal couldn't discern them. Zach had never seen an immortal in such a state, but thought hours could pass between heartbeats.

"Her pulse would not be detectable as it is now if it were stasis," Seth responded. "And blood alone would bring her out of it."

"You're sure she was hit with the same drug the mercenaries used?" Melanie asked.

"Yes."

"Bastien, honey, would you please get me a double dose of the antidote?"

Bastien retrieved two auto-injectors from another drawer and handed them to his wife.

Melanie injected Lisette with the first.

No response. No increase in pulse. No increase in breath. No sudden burst of thought in her subconscious.

She injected Lisette with the second.

All held their breath.

When Krysta had received a double dose of the antidote, she had reacted instantly. Leaping up, she had happily jumped back into battle, heart racing, breath short, judgment a tad hampered.

Lisette's pulse picked up and began to race. Her chest rose and fell with short, choppy breaths. But her eyes remained closed. Her limbs didn't move. Her delicate fingers didn't squeeze Zach's. And he heard nothing in her mind.

Melanie looked at each of them. "I can't risk giving her another dose."

Zach's heart sank. A lump rose in his throat.

"I can give her blood—"

"Give her mine," David said and looked to Seth.

Seth nodded. "Do it."

Melanie nodded. "I'll set up an IV for her. Bastien, would you draw some of David's blood for me?"

"Of course."

"I could infuse her with my fangs," David suggested.

Melanie shook her head. "I don't want you exposed to the drug. Why don't all of you head into the next room and do it there. Send Tracy in when you do, and we'll clean Lisette up and make her more comfortable."

Bastien grabbed everything he needed and headed into the next room, David right behind him. Tracy entered and stood back, face uncertain.

"Seth," Melanie spoke kindly, "I'm pretty sure Lisette wouldn't want you to see her naked."

"You're right, of course," Seth said. "Zach?"

"I've already seen her naked," Zach muttered, his eyes clinging to Lisette.

Seth sighed. "I meant—"

"I'm not leaving her."

Something unspoken might have passed between Seth and Melanie. Zach wasn't sure and really didn't care. Then Seth retreated into the next room.

"Tracy, would you please close the blinds?"

Lisette's Second closed the blinds.

"Draw the curtain, too," Melanie instructed, "in case Richart and Étienne come in."

Tracy pulled a curtain Zach hadn't even noticed across the doorway. As the mortal woman approached the exam table, her eyes filled with moisture. "I can't believe this is happening."

Nor could Zach as he rose. Moving to the end of the table, he unlaced one of Lisette's boots, pulled it off, and let it fall to the floor with a thump. Her sock was wet at the ankle from the blood that had dripped down and soaked it. Her skin beneath was cold.

Zach removed the sock and cupped her small foot between his hands, trying to warm it. When he looked up, he found Tracy watching him.

A tear spilled over her lashes and raced down one cheek. "Are you the reason she needed the house to herself?"

He nodded.

"You care about her?"

"Deeply," he responded, voice hoarse.

She offered him her hand. "I'm Tracy, her Second."

Zach removed one hand from Lisette's foot long enough to shake Tracy's. "Zach." He shifted his attention to Lisette's other boot and began to unlace it.

Tracy turned her tragic gaze on Melanie. "Will David's blood help her?"

"I don't know," the doctor confessed.

Another tear slipped down Tracy's cheek as her throat

moved in a hard swallow. Nodding, she stepped up to the table, took the angled scissors Melanie handed her, and applied them to the sleeve of Lisette's coat.

Seth teleported to the lobby of the network.

John Wendleck, head of security, greeted him with a smile, having been forewarned with a call. "Good to see you again, sir."

"Good to see you, John. Do you, by any chance, know where I might find Marcus and Ami?"

John touched the walkie on his shoulder. "Todd?"

"Yes, sir?"

"What's the immortal's latest pos?"

"He and his wife are in Cliff's apartment."

"Thanks. Seth is on his way down."

"Yes, sir."

Whenever Seth and the other immortals visited the East Coast hub of the human network that aided them, they refrained from teleporting unless an emergency warranted it. They also moved around at mortal speeds. Such not only reduced the unease some of the employees felt in the presence of the powerful beings, it also aided the soldiers and guards manning the hallways in telling friend from foe and cut back on surprises that could cause itchy trigger fingers.

Seth took the elevator down to the fifth sublevel.

Every human guard on the premises wielded an automatic weapon and a tranquilizer gun, more necessary than ever now that seven vampires resided there.

Seth greeted Todd and the other guards and strode down the hallway to Cliff's apartment. He offered the young vampire a courtesy knock.

"Yeah?" Cliff called.

"It's Seth."

"Come in."

Seth waved a hand over the security pad. A clunk sounded, and the heavy door swung open.

Marcus, Ami, and Cliff sat shoulder to shoulder on the sofa, wielding PlayStation controllers as bright images flashed on the large-screen television across from them.

"Hi, Seth," Ami called cheerfully.

"Hello, sweetheart."

"Did you get everything cleaned up?" she asked, eyes still on the screen.

Marcus looked at Seth over his shoulder, needing no words to convey his doubt of the sparring tale.

"Almost," Seth said. "You mind if I borrow Marcus for a moment?"

"As long as you tell me whatever you're going to tell him when you get back. I'm not as fragile as you think, you know, and am getting a little tired of everyone treating me like I am."

"I don't think you're fragile, Ami," Cliff threw in. "I bet, even pregnant, you could kick my ass."

She laughed and motioned to the television. "I can at *this* anyway."

He groaned.

Marcus joined Seth out in the hallway and closed the door. They crossed to Melanie's empty office and sealed themselves inside.

"What happened?" Marcus asked. "I figured it must be bad if you wanted me to get Ami out of there so quickly."

"I wanted you to bring Ami here to keep her safe." All had agreed Ami should not be teleported while pregnant. "*And* so I could tell you something in private in case you blew a gasket."

Seth relayed the events of the night.

"Lisette didn't awaken after Melanie infused her with David's blood?"

"No."

"Shit." Marcus paced away. "How could *vampires* have gotten their hands on the only drug that can sedate us?"

"That's what we're trying to piece together."

"And who the hell is Zach?"

Seth didn't really know how to answer that one. "You might say he's my cousin."

"You have a cousin?"

"For all intents and purposes, yes."

"Okay. Why have I never heard of him? Immortal Guardians that age—"

"Because he isn't an Immortal Guardian."

Marcus studied him. "He isn't one of us?"

"No."

"You don't like him."

"I don't trust him."

"And he's at David's house. Right now."

"Yes."

"Then I'm sure as hell not taking Ami back there."

"Zach won't harm Ami."

"How can you be so sure?"

"Because they know each other."

Marcus's eyes narrowed. "Know each other how?"

"Ami has met with him secretly on half a dozen occasions up on David's roof."

"What?"

"The anger flooding your face right now is why I'm telling you this privately."

"You're damned right I'm angry! What the hell?"

"Marcus, calm down. Ami would never cheat on you—"

"I'm not worried about Ami cheating on me. Ami loves me, and I trust her. I'm worried about why this asshole you don't trust has been luring her up onto the roof. And while she's *pregnant?* Who the hell *is* this guy? What does he want?"

"He's one of her strays," Seth attempted to explain.

"One of her strays?"

"Like Bastien," he clarified. "You know how tender-hearted Ami is. The months of torture she endured at the hands of Emrys left her full of sympathy for anyone or anything that suffers at the hands of others. It's why she took to Bastien so swiftly when I pretty much imprisoned him in my home in England in an attempt to win him over to our side. She knew he was in pain, both mentally and physically. And it's why she loves your manic cat."

"Slim isn't manic. Not all the time, anyway."

At least Marcus seemed to be listening. "The same sympathy drew her to Zach. Zach didn't lure her up onto the roof. She sensed his pain and went looking for him."

"What pain?"

"He was riddled with wounds the first night she met him."

"If he isn't an Immortal Guardian and doesn't hunt vampires, how was he injured?"

"That's a story for another time."

Marcus considered that for a minute. "Fine. Why didn't Ami say anything to me?"

"Gee, I don't know, could it have anything to do with your inclination to be overprotective?"

Since Marcus couldn't protest the accusation, he remained silent.

"You don't even like it when she spends time with Bastien, Marcus. And there really isn't that much to tell. Lisette has been worried about Ami and, while watching over her, saw the two together on the roof. I read it in Lisette's thoughts a few months ago."

"You could have said something," Marcus grumbled.

"It wasn't my place. And, as I said, there isn't much to tell. The meetings never lasted long. There was very little, if any, conversation. Ami just offered Zach a lollipop and kept him company for a few minutes, then went back inside. Plus,

Zach told her I wouldn't be pleased to learn he had been visiting, and she knew I would read it in your thoughts if she told you about him."

Marcus's brow furrowed with uncertainty. "You aren't angry that she kept it from us?"

"I'm more angry at myself for making her feel she had to."

"I hate it when you're right."

"Now, when I tell her what happened tonight, her concern will be twofold. She'll fear for Zach and Lisette *and* she'll fear your jealousy and anger."

"There won't be any jealousy or anger."

"Good. And don't stir up trouble with Zach when you meet him. I'll handle Zach myself." Although he sure as hell hadn't handled him well thus far.

When Marcus nodded, Seth clapped him on the back.

Lisette? Please, answer me, love, and tell me you're all right.

Zach squeezed her hand when, yet again, no response came.

David's blood seemed to have done nothing to help her. It didn't even warm her cold feet. When Zach had repeatedly expressed his concern over her chilly toes, Melanie had found a heating pad and applied it, along with several blankets.

Not knowing how else they might help her, they had moved Lisette to a bed in the next room, where she would be more comfortable while they watched and waited.

Bastien and Melanie had followed Darnell to David's office. Low murmurs of conversation fluttered to Zach's ears while the three consulted this immortal doctor or that network doctor over the phone.

David had been called away to solve some crisis in South Carolina, but not before he had ordered Richart and Étienne to cut the crap when they had continually objected to Zach's presence . . . *and* his holding Lisette's hand.

Zach would be damned if either one of them would usurp his place at her bedside.

And, if his holding her hand pissed them off, what the hell would they do when they found out about all of the marvelously wicked explorations he had made of her body?

Tracy occupied a chair on the opposite side of the bed, keeping Zach and Lisette quiet company. Lisette's two brothers glared holes in the back of Zach's head from their seats over by the televisions.

Knowing worry and weariness would eventually drive him to exacerbate Seth's ire by hitting both males with enough preternatural force to make their eyes swell shut if he kept catching glimpses of their scowls, Zach leaned over and rested his head on the bed next to Lisette, pressing his face to the hand he refused to relinquish.

Lisette, sweetheart, please answer me.

"Zach?"

His heart leapt at the feminine voice, then plummeted when he realized it wasn't Lisette's. Raising his head, he looked toward the doorway.

Ami stood there, her big belly preceding her. Behind her loomed Marcus and Seth.

"Seth told us what happened," she said, her gaze taking in Lisette's still form, as well as Zach's desperate hold on her hand. "Are you okay?"

"Yes," he said for the benefit of their audience. *No,* he told her telepathically. *I'm not. She won't wake up.*

Ami hurried forward, arms extended.

Zach looked to her husband as Ami wrapped her arms around him and hugged him.

Marcus crossed his arms over his chest and watched the two impassively.

Hmm. Zach leaned into her embrace and wrapped his free

arm around her. Burying his face in her neck, he let her comfort him.

"I didn't realize you two were seeing each other," she said softly, rubbing his back.

It's only been a few weeks. He didn't say it aloud. The others could kiss his ass. It was none of their business. *But she means everything to me.*

"There's been no response?"

"None."

Lisette? he heard her call mentally. *It's Ami. Can you hear me?*

Ami's belly jumped against his own as the baby kicked, but Lisette remained still and silent.

Ami hugged Zach tighter. "She'll come back to us. I know she will."

Somehow the confident words conveyed only worry.

Ethan entered the infirmary on silent steps.

Lisette lay as still and pale as death in her bed, a mound of blankets piled atop the cold feet over which Zach had been obsessing. Her brothers slept in two of the other beds the room boasted, their wives curled into their sides. Zach . . .

Ethan stared at him.

Zach sat on the same stool he had occupied for the past three nights and days, his head on the covers beside Lisette's hip, her limp hand clutched in his. His longish hair concealed his eyes, but Ethan thought they were closed. Something about him seemed . . . off.

Ethan looked to Seth, who slouched in a chair on the opposite side of the bed, his hand pressed to Lisette's shoulder. That hand, Ethan couldn't help but notice, bore a golden glow.

Ethan nodded at Zach. "Is he asleep?"

Seth shook his head. "Unconscious. He keeps pouring

every ounce of energy he has into healing her, then passes out. When his strength returns, he tries again to heal her and, when his energy flags, he passes out. He tries again when he awakens. Then again."

Any doubts Ethan had borne that Zach truly cared for Lisette flew out the window. The idea of her loving another man still cut like a knife, but at least Lisette had found someone who would give everything he had to help and protect her.

Ethan studied Seth. Frankly, he didn't look so good. Ethan hadn't realized Immortal Guardians could appear weary. Sure, they could *feel* weary. But the virus usually kept the telltale signs of exhaustion from manifesting in their countenances.

Not so with Seth. If Ethan hadn't known any better, he would have taken one look at Seth and assumed him on the brink of collapse. Dark circles created hollows beneath his eyes. Lines creased a formerly pristine face. His long hair fell in loose, untidy waves to his hips as if he had lacked the energy or will to bind it and had settled for merely dragging a comb through it. Once.

"What about you?" Ethan dared to ask.

"What *about* me?"

"Can you really afford to expend the energy you are by trying to heal her again?"

Seth stared at him, his face set in stone. "What else would you have me do?"

Sighing, Ethan sank into the chair Tracy had abandoned when Darnell and Sheldon had forced her to get some rest. "I don't know."

Three days. Three days, and Lisette hadn't opened her eyes. Melanie had even tried administering another double dose of the antidote today.

There had been no change other than Lisette's heart pounding rapidly in her chest as her breath shortened. She hadn't so much as twitched otherwise. Hadn't murmured in her sleep. Hadn't spoken telepathically. Hadn't dreamed.

Ethan had heard one of the doctors Melanie had consulted over the phone ask if she thought Lisette might be brain dead.

"It isn't possible, is it?" he asked, stomach heavy with dread.

"What isn't?"

"An immortal's being brain dead?"

Seth returned his attention to Lisette. "Such would be a first."

That didn't reassure Ethan as much as it would have five years ago.

There had been a *lot* of firsts lately.

Too many, perhaps.

Silently he prayed this wouldn't be another.

Lisette? Can you hear me, love?

Zach's deep voice carried to her through the darkness, bringing Lisette some much-needed warmth.

Yes, she responded.

Why was she so cold?

Pain shot through her fingers and up her arm.

Why are you crushing my hand? she asked.

The pressure eased.

Forgive me. Soft, warm lips bathed her sore fingers with kisses. *Can you open your eyes for me, sweetheart?*

Inwardly, she frowned. *Of course.* Only, when she tried, her lids didn't seem to want to lift. Alarm pulsed through her. *What's wrong with me? I can't open my eyes.*

It's okay. Don't panic.

Don't panic when she couldn't move or open her eyes and Zach clutched her hand to his chest like a lifeline? Easier said than done.

"She's speaking to me telepathically," she heard Zach tell someone. "But she can't move or open her eyes."

The panic multiplied.

Lisette? Seth's bass-baritone voice filled her head.

Merde.

The chuckle that inspired carried relief, not humor. *Not the response I was hoping for, but I'll take it.*

Zach? she called, fear rising.

I'm here, love.

What the hell are the two of you doing in the same room? You are *in the same room, aren't you?*

Yes.

Has Seth hurt you?

A sigh. *You toss two bodies through David's bay window, and she asks if I* hurt *you,* Seth griped.

You did what? she demanded.

She wasn't conscious when I . . . delivered the vampires, Zach said. Then, to Lisette, he added, *You were tranqed, love.*

Shouts of denial pummeled her head. *That's not possible.*

It is and you were, Zach insisted gently.

Is that why I can't move?

Yes.

Why haven't you given me the antidote?

A long pause ensued.

We did, Seth informed her. *Melanie gave you double the dose. Twice. You didn't respond.*

Four doses? Fear crept in. *I thought four doses would kill an immortal.*

Melanie seems certain that it would, Seth acknowledged, *so she administered double the dose the night you were tranqed, then waited forty-eight hours before administering it again.*

Forty-eight hours?

"Her fingers just tightened around mine," Zach spoke, voice full of excitement.

How long have I been out? she asked.

Five days, Zach answered, his telepathic voice full of anguish. *Five long, terrifying days.*

A thousand questions flooded her mind as energy gradually flowed into her limbs. The anvils holding her eyelids closed lifted, allowing her to pry them open. Pain pierced her head, driving her to close them once more.

"Too bright," she muttered.

The room instantly dimmed to near darkness.

Lisette valiantly forced her eyes to open again and focused them on the man sitting at her side.

Zach's hair was a bit of a tousled mess, as if he had finger-combed it one too many times. Shadows formed dark pools beneath eyes bracketed by lines of fatigue. And, in those eyes, she saw love. Love and fear and such stark relief that tears rose in her own.

"It's okay," she whispered, mustering what strength she could to tug him closer.

As he rested his head on her chest and wrapped his arms around her, she combed her fingers through his hair. "It's okay," she repeated, voice raspy. "I'm okay now."

The doorway went black as Immortal Guardians garbed in hunting gear poured through it, Richart and Étienne at the front of the pack.

Her brothers looked from her face, to her arms wrapped around Zach, and back to her face.

She tightened her hold on Zach.

Don't look so worried, Étienne told her as they approached the bed. *That's all we needed to see.*

What is?

You, weak as a kitten, looking as fierce as a lioness preparing to protect her cub.

She frowned. *You aren't going to . . . ?*

Lecture you endlessly? Complain ad nauseam about your keeping him a secret from us? Rant over your falling for

*the one immortal Ethan claims is on Seth's shit list? Oh, yes.
We will definitely do all of that. But try to come between the
two of you?* He shook his head and gave her shin an affectionate pat. *No. He may be even more antisocial than Roland
and annoying as hell, but—after watching him with you,
seeing him give everything he had over and over again in an
attempt to heal you—we don't doubt his feelings for you.*

She smiled. *Thank you.*

Richart cleared his throat. "Do you mind?" he asked
Zach with unconcealed impatience. "We'd like to embrace
our sister now."

If anything, Zach tightened his hold on her. "I'm not
letting go until I'm good and ready."

Lisette's smile broadened. She had no problem with that.

Even when it took Zach hours to become *good and ready*
and finally step back.

Chapter Eleven

Lisette glanced around David's long dining table. Only Seth and David were absent. The rest of the Immortal Guardians and Seconds in the area had long since taken their seats. Even Cliff had joined them, she was both surprised and pleased to see. It was the first time a vampire had ever been invited to one of their meetings.

Beside her, Zach shifted in his chair. This was all new to him, too. He would probably feel much more comfortable pulling gargoyle duty up on the roof. Particularly since the other immortals didn't seem to know quite what to do with him. Zach's tense relationship with Seth left them floundering for no other reason than this was the first time they had to wonder if befriending the new guy would alienate Seth.

Lisette didn't think it would. Seth had said nothing of the sort in the two days since she had awakened and had even conversed with Zach on occasion. She just didn't think Seth trusted him fully yet. The fact that Zach had been included in the roll call of this meeting was more a testament of Seth's faith in Lisette than of his belief that Ami and Lisette had won Zach over to *their side*.

Étienne, seated between Krysta and Richart, shifted in his chair.

There seemed to be a lot of that tonight. No talk. Lots of restless movement.

Lisette didn't have to guess what was on Étienne's mind. His thoughts came through, loud and clear, without her even having to attempt to read them. As did Richart's. Both d'Alençon brothers wore scowls and broadcasted every furious complaint they wished to lodge, though they probably didn't realize it.

She frowned. Tonight they didn't focus on Zach. Tonight it was all about Seth. They couldn't forgive him for accusing her of treachery.

Hell, *she* had forgiven Seth. Why couldn't they?

In fact . . . "If *I* can forgive Seth," she spoke into the leaden quiet, "why can't you?" She looked around the table. "Why can't *all* of you?"

Bastien crossed his arms over his chest. "I don't see that there's anything to forgive."

Richart leaned forward. "He accused her of fraternizing with vampires."

"I lived with vampires for two hundred years," Bastien drawled.

Melanie nodded. "I fraternize with vampires every day."

"You know what I mean," Richart snapped.

Bastien's eyes lit with amber fire. "Watch your tone when you speak to her," he warned.

Melanie patted his arm. "I can take care of myself, sweetie."

Étienne leaned forward. "He didn't just accuse her of fraternizing with them. He accused her of leading them. Of pitting them against us."

Bastien raised a finger and opened his mouth.

"Oh, shut up!" Étienne growled. "You were actually guilty of it."

On Lisette's other side, Ethan spoke. "So Seth made a

mistake. Get over it." She was happy to see Ethan had gotten over *his own* anger at Seth.

Cliff dared to enter the fray. "Yeah, are *you* so perfect?"

Ed nodded. "I agree. The possible sources of this new uprising were A, B, C, or D. When the possibilities of A, B, and C had all been explored and eliminated, that left only D. No matter how unpalatable he found it, Seth would've been remiss if he hadn't looked into it."

"He would have been better served," Richart gritted, "looking into E."

"There *was* no E," Zach said, his deep voice startling her.

Lisette hadn't expected him to join the conversation. *Or* defend Seth . . . which he seemed to be doing. She stared.

"You don't know that," Richart countered.

"Yes, I do. You think Seth, David, and Chris wouldn't have come up with an E if there had been one?" He looked to Chris.

Chris scrutinized Zach a moment, then nodded. "There wasn't an E. We covered all the bases."

"Donald and Nelson's mercenary army was obliterated," Zach said, ticking the possibilities off on his fingers. "None were left alive to launch their war again. *I* was shackled and being tortured round the clock, so I could not have been responsible. Bastien is the only *gifted one* whose transformation Seth has ever missed, so it couldn't have been some other immortal outside the fold who believed himself a vampire."

Chris nodded. "We checked to be sure."

"Every other telepath in the area was accounted for at all times," Zach continued.

"*Lisette* was accounted for, too," Richart said. "She was right here . . . with us."

"Actually, she wasn't. Not here at David's, anyway. Lisette's behavior of late has been outside the norm for

her. It's my fault. She didn't want Seth—or the rest of you—
to know we were seeing each other. But, as much as I hate
to admit it and as much as it chaps my ass to defend Seth, it
did breed grounds for suspicion."

Lisette thought Seth's mouth would have fallen open had
he been there.

Zach stared at the brothers. "You just don't like anyone
maligning your sister in any way, even if accidentally. Seth
apologized. Lisette moved past it. I did, too . . . somewhat."
At her repeated urging. "Now you should as well."

Étienne started to rise. "Who the hell are you to tell us—?"

Krysta locked a hand around his arm and held him in his
seat. "Étienne, I love you. But I think you're being a little hard-
headed about this."

That didn't go over well. "How can you say that?"

"Honey, I tried to decapitate you when we first met. In
fact, technically I tried to do it twice. You forgave me for
that, but you can't forgive this?"

His brows drew down in a deep V. "You thought I was a
vampire. Of course, I forgave you."

She smiled and patted his arm. "That's right. I was operating on the only information I had at the time. As was Seth
when he confronted Lisette."

Jenna looked to Richart. "And *you* forgave John for
telling me he thought we should wait for the sun to rise, then
shove your ass out the door."

Richart's eyes widened. "John said that?" he demanded.

Jenna bit her lip. "I, uh, I never told you about that?"

"No."

"Then, yes. He did."

"When?"

"The night you accidentally teleported to our living room,
covered in blood, with your fangs out and eyes glowing,
then collapsed."

"Oh. Well, that's understandable. He thought I was a vampire."

She raised her eyebrows. "And was operating on the only information available to him?"

The two brothers sighed and sank back in their chairs. "Fine," the twins said in unison. "We'll apologize."

"Good," Zach said, then addressed the table at large. "The rest of you . . . I can read your every thought." He narrowed his eyes at Ethan. "Except for you."

Ethan gave him a sarcastic salute.

Zach shook his head. "You all find the notion that Seth could believe one of you guilty offensive. Well, guess what. One of you *is* guilty. Maybe not one of you at this table. But one of the Immortal Guardians. Likely two. Only a telepath could have buried the vampires' memories. And he or she had to have had help slipping in and out of North Carolina undetected."

Grim faces all around.

"So get a grip. Cut Seth some slack. And think what it must feel like for him to believe that men or women he has offered safe harbor for hundreds or thousands of years have now turned on him *and* you and are waging this new war that holds more potential than ever of destroying one of you. He's doing everything he can to keep you safe and doesn't need to deal with your bullshit on top of that."

Under the table, Lisette took his hand and rested their twined fingers on her thigh.

The front door opened. David strolled in, closing and locking it behind him with a thought. "I couldn't have put it better myself," he said as he joined them. He speared Zach with a look as he took his seat at the head of the table. "Nor could I be more surprised that Seth's staunchest defender tonight is you."

"What can I say?" Zach said, deadpan. "I'm an enigma."

"Indeed."

And he tried to keep the peace, Lisette knew, for *her* sake, not out of any love for Seth.

Beside David, Darnell drew out his cell phone.

David halted him before Darnell could dial and addressed those present. "No accusations or recriminations will be spoken this night. Am I clear? No one here is without fault. Seth does a million things right every day and has done so for thousands of years, far longer than any of you can imagine. Not one of you would exist today, were it not for the things he has done right. Denouncing him for making a single mistake is nonsensical. So get your shit together before he arrives. And marshal your thoughts."

Lisette watched her brothers for their reaction.

David raised a brow. "Richart? Étienne?"

"We'll apologize for giving him a hard time," Richart vowed.

Étienne nodded. "We'll apologize."

David nodded to Darnell.

As Darnell dialed, David turned to Zach and spoke softly. "I'm surprised you joined us tonight."

Zach's lips turned up in a wry smile. "As I said, I'm an enigma."

Lisette grinned . . . until she caught Marcus scowling at Zach. "What?" she asked.

Marcus directed his response to Zach. "Do you have something against shirts?" His eyes dropped to Zach's bare chest.

"Yes," Zach retorted.

Tracy laughed. "I can live with that."

"Me too," Sean's Second, Nichole, said with a smile.

And the mood, at last, lightened. Stress flowed from the room. Shoulders relaxed.

Good. Lisette loved Seth and knew what a hard time he was having with everything. He had always been quick to try to alleviate their suffering. What had they done to alleviate his? If ever there were a time for them to give more to Seth than they took from him, it was now.

Thank you, David spoke in her head.

She smiled.

Plump snowflakes fluttered to the ground. Some didn't quite make it, landing instead upon Seth's broad shoulders or alighting upon his thick eyelashes.

Swaying where he stood, he rubbed gritty, no doubt bloodshot eyes.

Fatigue clawed at him, doing its damnedest to drag him down. Little sparkly things kept flickering at the edges of his vision. A first, for him. He couldn't remember that ever having happened before. Yet he couldn't rest until he discovered who waged this new war.

Lisette could have perished. The heavier tranquilizer dose had nearly destroyed her. Had she been younger, Ethan's age or Krysta's, perhaps it *would* have destroyed her. They had no way of knowing. Just as they had no way of countering it on the battlefield.

Seth contemplated the snowy landscape around him. So tranquil and quiet. ·

Even this could not bring him peace. Not while such danger loomed.

He spent both his days and nights checking in with every telepath in the world. Sometimes they greeted him with a smile when he appeared, chatting and laughing with him while he secretly combed their thoughts for anything that would indicate they had been the ones who had erased those vampires' memories. Sometimes they had no idea he had even visited, either sleeping through it or carrying on with their hunt or whatever they were doing while he watched and waited and sought the tiniest fragment of guilt from the shadows.

Younger telepaths, like Lisette and Étienne, were fairly easy to read, willing or nay. Older telepaths often had much stronger barriers that he couldn't always breech without them knowing. Seth wasn't sure if he wanted to go there yet, if he wanted to confront them, force down their barriers, and sift through their thoughts. Once he did, once he took that step, word would spread like wildfire that he suspected an Immortal Guardian of treachery. The many who weren't guilty would likely react as those in North Carolina had. They'd be shocked, disturbed, pissed, and wonder if he suspected *them*. The immortal or immortals who *were* guilty, if they got the news before he could identify them, would hunker down or, worse, do something rash that might result in deaths.

How had it come to this? To one of his own rising up against him?

Sighing, he dragged his hands down his face, fingers rasping on the heavy stubble that coated his cheeks and chin. He hadn't shaved in days. Too damned tired.

Disturb's "Down With The Sickness" violated nature's hush.

Too late. No time to shave now. That would be Darnell, calling to let him know they were ready to start the meeting.

"Yes?" he answered.

"We're ready," Darnell said.

"I shall be there shortly." Seth tucked away his phone.

How he dreaded this. Seeing the accusation and condemnation on all of their faces.

Bracing himself as best he could, he teleported to David's dining room.

Conversation ceased.

Seth nodded to all present, avoiding their eyes and the

recriminations they must certainly bear, and crossed to his chair.

Étienne rose as Seth passed him. "Seth, I was an ass about the whole Lisette thing. I hope you'll forgive me."

Seth's steps faltered as he turned his disbelieving gaze on Étienne. No accusation. Just genuine remorse.

Richart nodded as he rose. "Me too. Everyone makes mistakes. We shouldn't have condemned you for yours. And, after all of the trouble our sister has gotten us into over the centuries, I would've suspected her myself, had I been thinking clearly."

"Hey!" Lisette protested with a laugh and stood. Circling around to them, she linked her arm through Seth's and escorted him to his chair. "Believe it or not, it's actually kind of a relief for us to discover that you aren't infallible. Perfection can be annoying sometimes."

"*All* of the time," Marcus corrected with a smile. "It's good to know we aren't the only ones who screw up on occasion."

"I never screw up," Stanislav boasted with false disdain.

Everyone hurled insults at him.

Seth just stared at them as he let Lisette gently push him down into his chair.

As she returned to her own seat, the dark figure beside her shook his head.

"Zach," Seth greeted him cautiously. "I'm surprised you joined us."

"Apparently, he's an enigma," Marcus drawled, the words dripping with sarcasm.

Seth actually felt the urge to smile.

"And you're the luckiest bastard on the planet," Zach declared. "They love you, faults and all."

Seth met every glance, examined every face, and found none of the anger he had expected. No condemnation. Only acceptance. And, as Zach had claimed, love. He really *was* the luckiest man on the planet.

Feeling lighter than he had in weeks, Seth smiled and shook his head. "Shall we get down to business?"

Lisette hoped she had made it clear to everyone present that she harbored no anger toward their leader.

Seth looked like hell, at least as much as he *could* look like hell. Lines of fatigue creased his face. Dark shadows created hollows beneath his bloodshot eyes. His chiseled jaw hadn't seen a razor in days.

The last thing he needed was to deal with hostility from his immortal family.

"So," Seth began, "we seem to have a problem."

The men and women present nodded and murmured their agreement.

"A vampire army, more powerful than any we've fought before, is amassing, and even their thoughts don't reveal who leads them," Seth told them. "Étienne found blank spots in the minds of members of this vampire army. Blank spots that he thought indicated buried memories. However, the specimens Zach so thoughtfully provided us with a few nights ago revealed that at least some of the memories had not been buried. They had been permanently removed."

Lisette wished she could have been conscious when Zach had tossed the vampires through the bay window. She glanced at him from the corner of her eye. *Magnifique*.

Roland scowled. "Doesn't that cause brain damage?"

"Yes," Seth said, "which is why David and I prefer to *bury* memories rather than erase them. The vampires whose memories have been removed will descend into madness at a much swifter rate, because they are suffering brain damage spawned by two different sources: the virus *and* our new enemy."

"Clearly our new enemy isn't concerned about the health or longevity of his army," Roland drawled.

Seth's gaze circled the table. "Any ideas regarding the identity of this mysterious foe?"

"An Immortal Guardian with a grudge?" Zach suggested.

"Anyone know of such an individual?" Seth asked. "Or two? Or three?"

Lisette sure as hell didn't. The only immortal she had ever met—aside from Zach—who didn't credit Seth with every ounce of happiness he had found since transforming was Bastien. And he seemed right as rain with Seth.

Stanislav cleared his throat. "We all owe you a great debt, Seth, for aiding us in finding contentment in our new existence. I don't know *anyone* who would wish you ill."

Darnell folded his hands on the table, his handsome face troubled. "I haven't seen anything on the Web site that would indicate animosity. No subtle digs or stray comments that might indicate discontent."

"I haven't either," Chris mentioned. "There's also the problem of how this new army came to possess the sedative."

"Not only that," Marcus tossed in, "but how they knew that they needed to increase the dosage."

Roland leaned back in his chair and looped an arm around Sarah's shoulders. "Once more, I say it's someone at the network. If an immortal can dirty his hands in this venture, it isn't out of the realm that he would seek the aid of a human."

As expected, Chris's face mottled with anger. "It isn't someone at the network. We checked and double-checked and triple-fucking-checked that the last time this came up and have since instituted even stricter protocols for handling both the sedative and the antidote."

David caught Roland's eye. "I read the mind of every mortal employee myself. None were guilty of betraying us."

"It might be worth reading them again," Roland suggested,

"to ensure none have changed their minds. Or to ensure no one has changed their minds for them."

Hell. Lisette hadn't thought of that. Could an elder telepathic immortal have manipulated the thoughts of a network employee to get what he wanted, making him or her his unwilling minion?

David looked to Seth.

Seth nodded. "No stone should go unturned."

David looked to Chris. "We'll discuss how to go about it after the meeting."

Chris nodded, more worried now, it seemed, than pissed.

Yuri cleared his throat. "So essentially we're looking for a telepath."

"Yes," Seth agreed.

"Can you not read their minds and discover who the culprit is?" he followed.

"I've been doing little else since the vampires nearly killed Lisette," Seth stated. "I've yet to discover the betrayer."

Lisette frowned. "They must be guarding their thoughts exceedingly well."

Seth nodded. "I'm inclined to believe it is an older immortal. But those with the strongest mental barriers will know when I've invaded their thoughts and forced their barriers down."

"And word will spread." Ethan's glance flickered to Richart and back to Seth. "Have you read the minds of the teleporters?" He sounded apologetic, as though he hated to suggest it in front of Richart. "The telepath would need a teleporter to get him in and out of the area undetected, wouldn't he?"

"If he can't teleport himself, yes. Although I still have a number of telepaths to scan, I've read the minds of all but a handful of the teleporters," Seth replied. "None appear guilty, and none have blank spots that would indicate *their* memories have been erased."

"Is that possible?" Lisette asked, unsettled. "Can a telepath erase portions of an immortal's memory?"

"I have never attempted such," Seth said, "so I'm not sure."

"I would think the virus would prevent it," Lisette said.

Melanie shook her head. "Not necessarily. If erasing a memory damages the brain, then the virus could conceivably heal it in an immortal. But the virus can't restore what isn't there to recover. Once the memory is gone, it's likely gone forever."

Roland swore. "So an immortal may not even realize his brain has been tampered with?"

"Yes," David concluded, face grave. "And Seth and I would find only an undamaged brain when we scanned him. We would have no way of knowing he's missing a memory or two or that anyone had tampered with his thoughts."

"Shit," Ethan breathed.

"Precisely," Seth said. "Seconds, I want you to keep your ears to the ground. If an immortal is behaving oddly, his or her Second may mention it online."

"Unless the immortal blanked his Second's memory, too," Roland countered.

Tracy shook her head. "Immortals rarely pay attention to what their Seconds do online. We should chat up the Seconds of telepaths and see if anything leaks."

Seth looked to Chris. "Can you get them a list of all the Seconds who serve telepaths?"

"The Seconds who serve teleporters, too. I can have it in their hands tonight."

"Excellent."

Zach shifted. "You should expand your scrutiny to include shape-shifters and their Seconds."

"Why?" Lisette asked.

Rising, Zach took a step back from the table and released his wings. "With these and preternatural speed and strength, I can race a commercial jet."

Sheldon stared up at him in awe. "Really? You're that fast?"

"Were the Concorde still flying, I could give it a run for its money."

"Damn," someone whispered.

Zach's wings vanished (Lisette hoped he would tell her one day how he did that) as he retook his seat at the table.

David eyed Seth. "He makes a valid point. While no shape-shifter other than you or Zach would be able to carry another across an ocean in a mere three and a half hours, if the distance weren't that far and they had all night . . ."

Lisette looked up at Zach. *Are you really as fast as the Concorde was?*

He reclaimed her hand with a faint smile. *Shall I show you later?*

Hell yes!

"Include the Seconds of shape-shifters," Seth agreed. "I'll commence reading shape-shifters' minds tonight."

After you get some sleep, Lisette implored mentally.

Seth sent her a tired smile. *I'll sleep when I've identified this latest threat.*

"Are you sure," Roland asked, "that the man we're looking for isn't sitting at this table?" His gaze, full of suspicion, slid to Zach. "If Zach is as old as you are, he is certainly capable of teleporting and erasing a few memories."

Lisette held her breath, not knowing how Zach would respond.

Zach's lips curled into a smile, but his expression held no mirth.

Even Lisette found it a little scary.

"This vampire army nearly took Lisette from me," Zach responded. "Had I raised and trained it myself, I would have done to these vampires what Bastien tried to do to you. I would have staked every one of them to the ground in an open field and let the sun roast them."

All but Roland seemed satisfied.

"It wasn't Zach," Ami said, entering the conversation for the first time.

Roland gave her a gentle smile. "You've a kind heart, Ami, and sometimes have difficulty seeing the bad in people." He glanced at Bastien as he said it. "Zach might not have shown you his true face when you met him."

Judging by Marcus's expression, he feared the same.

Roland looked to Seth.

"It wasn't Zach," Seth said.

Lisette couldn't help but wonder if Seth really believed that.

Chris took a small notebook out of his pocket, along with a stubby number-two pencil, and began making notes. "I'll add shape-shifters and their Seconds to the list. Be subtle when you contact them. Darnell, would you coordinate their efforts? I don't want some teleporter's Second to wonder why a dozen Seconds from North Carolina are suddenly chatting him up and mention it to his immortal."

"Of course." Darnell addressed the other Seconds. "Once you've received your list, examine it closely and let me know which names are familiar, which Seconds you've communicated with in the past. A top-five list will do for now. Then I'll get back to you and let you know with whom you should touch base."

Nods.

"Cliff," Seth said.

The young vampire's eyebrows flew up. "Yes, sir?"

"Have you had any luck recruiting the vampires with whom you've been rubbing elbows?"

"None so far. The ones I've encountered are either so far gone they would be too dangerous to recruit or recently turned and so high on using their new strength and speed to kill that they think themselves invincible. Any suggestion otherwise, any insinuation that they would be better off joining you guys, usually results in mockery, hostility, and my coming dangerously close to getting my ass kicked. I can't seem to find any middle ground, any vampires who are beyond that first burst of power, but not yet to the he-could-snap-at-any-minute stage."

"Have you encountered any of this new breed of vampire?" David asked.

"No, sir. Not yet. Should I . . ." Cliff looked back and forth at the elders. "If I do encounter one, should I try to infiltrate the group? Try to join them and gather whatever—"

"No," Bastien interrupted. "It's too dangerous."

Cliff contemplated the immortals seated around the table. "No offense, but you don't seem to have a lot of avenues open to you right now. No stone should go unturned, remember? If I come across one of these bad-ass vamps and feign interest in his cause—whatever the hell it is—then I could find out faster than anyone else who exactly you're dealing with."

"It's too dangerous," Bastien repeated.

Cliff shrugged. "I don't have that much to lose."

Melanie reached past Bastien and touched Cliff's arm. "Please don't say that, Cliff."

"Look," he continued, resolute, "the Immortal Guardians have been good to me. You all helped me hold my shit together a lot longer than I would have if I had been left to fend for myself. If I'm gonna go out—and we all know it's gonna happen some day in the not too distant future—then being taken out while helping you conquer the bad guy wouldn't be such a bad way to go."

"Actually," Zach countered, "it could be a *very* bad way to go."

Seth nodded. "Whoever our new nemesis is reads and alters the minds of every recruit. He would know the instant he met you that you were there to collect information for us. I doubt he would reward you with anything less than torture."

A brief flicker of fear entered Cliff's brown eyes. "Been there. Done that. Would rather not do it again."

"And," David added, "he could use what he finds in your mind against us."

"Okay." His disappointment palpable, Cliff consulted the elders. "So what should I do if I encounter one? I don't think they would expect immortals to have a vampire as an ally. It just seems like you ought to be able to use that to your advantage in some way."

Chris's face brightened. "Do you think you could plant a tracking device on one?"

"You mean like slip it in his pocket?"

He shook his head. "The tracking devices are magnetic. If you can get close enough to attach it to one of their weapons, it might go unnoticed long enough for us to find whatever lair their leader keeps erasing from their memories."

"Yeah. I should be able to do that."

"I don't like it," Bastien spoke dourly, ever protective of his vampires. "If the vampire realizes what's happening, he could destroy Cliff. That or turn him over to his leader."

"Bastien's right," Seth agreed. "Let the Seconds do their digging. I'll continue to scan memories and see what I can learn myself."

"And the rest of us?" Lisette asked.

"Hunt in pairs. *All* of you. Even the elders. I don't want *any* of you to hunt alone until further notice. Am I understood?"

Nods all around.

"If you encounter one of these new vampires, don't even try to engage him. Just tranq him and call me. If he attacks before you can tranq him or if he tranqs one of you first, the hunting partner should tranq him or kill him as swiftly as possible, then get the fallen immortal to the network. Don't buy time and try to read his thoughts or emotions. Don't try to capture him or question him. Just kill him or tranq him.

Period. Any immortal who doesn't leave the house with auto-injectors containing the vampire's dose of the sedative in every pocket will answer to me, *if* you live long enough to do so."

Lisette looked to Étienne and Krysta. That last part had probably been directed at them. Three immortals with not one auto-injector between them?

Yeah. They had screwed up.

Krysta cleared her throat. "It might be a good idea, too, for immortals to do as the mercenaries we fought last time did and check in with our Seconds at the top of every hour. That way if both immortals are tranqed . . ."

Seth nodded. "Do it."

The danger had never been so great.

Melanie raised a finger. "One more thing. I don't think Lisette should hunt tonight. I think she should rest for a couple more days before she jumps back into things."

Seth looked at Lisette. "You heard her."

Lisette thought it best not to complain.

Seth visually consulted the rest of those present. "Anything else?"

Grim silence.

"Then our meeting is adjourned. Safe hunting to you all."

"Are you sure you're all right?" Zach asked. Wrapping an arm around her, he guided Lisette up the steps to her home.

She smiled. "For the hundredth time, I'm fine, Zach."

"I think you should have spent another day under Dr. Lipton's supervision."

"Melanie said I'm fine."

"If you were fine, she would have cleared you to hunt tonight."

"So she'll clear me tomorrow or the next night. And we'll both sleep better here."

Lisette now knew what it must feel like to live as a lab rat. All of those eyes studying them and scrutinizing them twenty-four hours a day. Immortal and mortal alike. Every mind bursting with questions they wished to launch.

Fortunately, Zach tended to be rather intimidating.

It had taken her a day and a half to regain most of her strength. The knowledge that their current enemy possessed a drug that could do that to an immortal—could completely incapacitate him or her for days—terrified her. Lisette couldn't even remember the battle that had resulted in her being tranqed. The drug had stolen the memory of it from her. Zach had replayed the battle for her mentally, letting her see what had happened from his perspective.

Étienne had *shown* her what had happened afterward.

She still couldn't believe Zach had tossed two bodies through David's window.

And Seth, perhaps the greatest surprise, had shown her the rest: Zach's refusing to leave her side and rendering himself unconscious over and over again in his attempts to heal her.

Once inside, she ditched her keys and let Zach remove her coat.

"Do you want me to fix you something to eat?" he asked as he hung it up and turned back to her.

She shook her head and smiled up at him. "I want you to take me to bed."

His dark brown eyes lit with golden desire. "Don't tempt me."

"I'll more than tempt you," Lisette promised. Leaning into him, she wrapped her arms around his waist. "Since I don't have to hunt tonight, I intend to ride you hard and put you away wet." She frowned. "Wait. Is that how that saying goes? It didn't sound right."

Zach wrapped his arms around her. "It doesn't matter. I didn't hear anything after *ride you*."

Laughing, she leaned up and nipped his chin. "So what are we waiting for?"

His brow furrowed as he brushed her hair, left loose, back from her face. "Are you sure you're up to it?"

She *did* feel a little weak. Or maybe a lot. "Okay, I'll ride you another time."

He hid his disappointment fairly well as he loosened his hold.

Lisette linked her fingers behind his back instead of releasing him. "You'll have to ride me instead."

The golden flames flared brighter. He was already hard for her. "I nearly lost you, Lisette. I don't want to push things if you need more time to recover your strength."

"The truth is," she said, abandoning all levity, "I don't care how we do it, Zach, I just want to feel you inside me."

His arms tightened.

"What happened—finding out I was trapped in that sea of nothingness for five days and came so close to not waking from it—scared the hell out of me." She rested her head on his chest and closed her eyes. "I'm still cold from it and need to feel your warmth all around me."

Hugging her close, Zach kissed the top of her head.

Her bedroom replaced the foyer as he teleported them and flicked on the lights with a thought.

"We'll take it slow then," he said, his fingers reaching for the buttons on her shirt.

"I'm going to have to start wearing T-shirts again," she murmured, "so you can just yank them over my head."

He shook his head. "I like the buttons." He slipped the first through its corresponding buttonhole, parted the material, then moved on to the next. "I like the slow reveal." He freed the next, his warm fingers brushing her cool skin. "Like seeing your beautiful body exposed an inch at a time."

She was beginning to like it, too.

With the last button unfastened, he drew the soft cotton

material down her arms and let it fall to the floor. Her breath shortened at the look in his iridescent eyes as he reached around behind her and unfastened her bra. The lacy material fell away, exposing her breasts.

"Touch me," she whispered.

"Soon." He tucked his fingers in the waist of her pants, unfastened the button in front, and drew the short zipper down.

Kneeling, he drew one of her feet onto his thigh and went to work on the laces of her boots.

Lisette braced a hand on his shoulder and combed the other through his soft hair.

One boot and one sock hit the floor. The others soon followed. Then he drew her pants and underwear down to her ankles and watched her step out of them.

"Your turn," she said, eager to feel his naked body against hers.

Rising, he doffed his boots, socks, and leather pants.

She loved that he went commando under the last. "Now take me in your arms and make me forget the cold."

Chapter Twelve

Zach's chest tightened at the vulnerability reflected in Lisette's amber eyes. Wrapping his arms around her, he drew her up against him.

Concern rose. "You *are* cold," he said, the chill in her flesh nearly making him shiver. She must be weaker than she had let on if she couldn't even regulate her body temperature.

Lisette said nothing, just rested her head upon his chest and snuggled against him.

Rubbing his hands up and down her back, Zach infused her with heat until the chill left her skin.

She sighed. "Thank you."

Were he a stronger man, he would've refused to make love to her until she returned to full strength.

But she seemed to need him as much as he needed her.

And Zach *really* needed her.

Lifting her into his arms, he drew back the covers on the bed with a thought and settled her on the sheets. As soon as he lay down beside her, he drew the soft material up again to keep her warm.

She curled into him, drew a slender leg up his, and hooked it over his hip, opening herself to him and ratcheting up his need.

"Slow and easy," he insisted, though his body craved more. She nodded.

It felt almost as though they were making love for the first time. Zach took his time, sliding his hands over her soft skin and relearning every curve, dip, and hollow. Even when his pulse increased, his breath shortened, and his body screamed for release, he moderated his touch, delivering unhurried strokes that made her tremble with desire. He caressed her breasts and gave one hard, tempting peak a pinch.

Lisette arched into him with a moan.

Another pinch and her leg over his hip flexed, urging him closer.

Zach caressed his way down her stomach to the heart of her, slid his fingers along her slick entrance. She was already wet for him, her heat and scent driving him mad. He found her clit with his thumb, circled it, stroked it.

She bucked against him, tunneling her fingers through his hair. "Zach."

He slipped a long finger inside her. So warm and tight. He added a second, pumping them in and out as he continued to torment her with his thumb.

"So good," she moaned, the tips of her fangs peeking out from between her lips.

He buried his face in her hair, muscles tightening with the need to bury himself inside her. *Slow and easy,* he reminded himself when instead he wanted to flip her over onto her hands and knees and take her from behind.

Her breaths became pants as he continued to work her with his fingers.

Zach kissed his way up her slender neck, his resolve weakening.

* * *

When Lisette could take no more of the sweet torture, she rolled onto her back, bringing Zach with her. Yes! She tried to pull him down to her, but he had other ideas.

Easing lower, he took the tip of one breast between his lips while his fingers resumed their torment.

Pleasure whipped through her, stealing her breath.

He nuzzled her rib cage just beneath her breast, eased farther down, disappearing beneath the covers as he kissed his way to her stomach. Her blood heated, as did the rest of her. His tongue teased her navel, then descended lower. Lisette flung back the covers and watched as he slid his arms beneath her bent knees, sent her a look that scorched her, then—his fingers still buried deep inside her—lowered his lips to her clit.

Moaning, she arched up against him. The things he did with his tongue . . . licks and flicks and undulations. And his fingers . . .

How the hell could he be new to this?

She cried out as ecstasy swept through her, so intense that—for a moment—she thought her pounding heart had stopped. Then, panting, she collapsed against the pillows.

His muscles tense, his erection straining toward her, Zach withdrew his fingers and rose above her. "Are you up for more?" he asked, settling his hips between her parted thighs, careful to keep the bulk of his weight off of her.

"Hell yes," she assured him, sliding her hands down over his muscled ass.

Needing no further encouragement, he drove his hard cock inside her.

Lisette gasped. Wrapping her legs around his hips, she drew him down until his muscled chest brushed her breasts with every powerful thrust and dispelled the cold.

Not so slow and easy now.

Need swiftly rose again as she strained against him and urged him on. Faster. Deeper. Harder. Rising to meet him.

Thrust for thrust. Until she climaxed again, swept away on a tide of pleasure that drew Zach under as well.

He called her name as he came. Then, rolling them to their sides, he drew her head to his chest.

The frantic heartbeat beneath her ear gradually returned to normal. Her own pulse slowed.

Lisette closed her eyes and savored just being held in Zach's arms. How she loved him. If she hadn't been certain before, she was now. Not just because he had given so much of himself to help her while she had been rendered unconscious by the drug. And not because he had risked everything simply by taking her to David's house to seek help. But because he brought her peace. Contentment. And a happiness she had not even known as a mortal.

The night sounds outside quieted.

Her thoughts fell silent.

Zach's heartbeat, slow and steady, began to fade away to nothingness . . .

Jerking, Lisette forced her eyes wide open, fear plowing through her and speeding her pulse.

Zach cuddled her closer. "It's okay," he whispered, pressing his lips to her hair. "It's okay. It's just sleep."

Fighting tears, she nodded. The first time she had fallen asleep after rousing from her coma (if that's what it had been), they had had difficulty waking her again. And, for a moment, just now, she had feared . . .

"It's just sleep," he assured her again. "Dr. Lipton said the drug has finally left your system. It's just sleep, Lisette. You won't have any trouble waking this time."

The confidence in his voice lulled her into relaxing against him.

"Don't worry. I'll watch over you," he vowed, his low voice filled with fierce affection.

At last, she let her heavy lids close.

* * *

Zach awoke in an instant, his senses on high alert. Curled on his side, his body spooned around Lisette's bare, tempting form, he lay motionless.

The sounds that met his sensitive ears were of the usual sort one heard at dawn. Bird song, accompanied by the occasional flapping of wings. The murmuring of insects. A squirrel bitching at some creature that had strayed too close to its nest. The shuffling and scuttling of animals foraging for morning snacks.

Nothing alarming. Then . . .

A single heartbeat.

Zach's eyes went to the ceiling.

Not Tracy. She had remained at David's to give them some privacy. And this heartbeat was slower than a human's.

Not vampire. The sun had risen. No vampire could withstand even the slightest exposure.

And not one of the Others. Had they discovered Zach's whereabouts, they would have come *en masse* and would not have been subtle.

Slowly, he uncurled his long legs and rolled toward the edge of the bed.

Lisette reached back and grabbed his arm. "Where are you going?" she mumbled, still half asleep.

Leaning forward, he smoothed the hair away from her face and kissed her cheek. "I'll only be gone a moment."

Giving his arm an affectionate stroke, she settled back into sleep once more.

Damn, he loved her. And was not thrilled over having to leave her, even briefly.

Tugging on the leather pants he had discarded earlier, Zach took his time and scaled the stairs at mortal speeds.

Bright light framed the curtains that covered every window.

His bare feet carried him silently across the cool bamboo floor to the back door. Zach punched in the security code

Lisette had given him and stepped out onto the back deck. Morning dew glistened on every blade of grass below him. A cool fog slowly crept across the ground.

Releasing his wings, Zach let them carry him up to the roof.

Another winged figure already occupied it. This time *Seth* performed gargoyle duty, his butt parked in the same spot Zach had so often occupied.

Zach settled himself beside the Immortal Guardians' leader and squinted into the rising sun. "Shouldn't you be sleeping?"

Seth grimaced. "Don't *you* start on me. David has been riding my ass for days, trying to get me to rest."

"Perhaps you should listen to him."

Seth responded with a cranky growl.

Minutes ticked past. Minutes Zach would have vastly preferred to have spent in Lisette's arms. "You're hanging by a thread, Seth," he commented at last.

Seth loosed a heavy sigh.

"David's right. You need to get some sleep. Clear your head. And David isn't the only one who sees it. Lisette sees it. Darnell sees it. Chris sees it. I think even Ethan sees it. It's only a matter of time before the rest do, too. If they weren't so distracted by everything that's been happening, they would have already noticed."

"Can you read Ethan's thoughts?" Seth asked, his weary voice carrying curiosity.

"No. I gave him a nosebleed trying until Lisette stopped me."

Seth nodded. "You know Ethan and Lisette used to be lovers, right?"

Zach's hands tightened into fists as jealousy tore through him. "No," he snarled. "I would have given him more than a nosebleed had I known."

"There's no reason to be jealous. She never loved him. And he'll soon realize he doesn't love her, at least not as more than a friend. They were just lonely and needed someone they could cleave to whenever they craved comfort."

Zach fought the urge to take to the air and hunt Ethan down. He didn't know what he would do to the American immortal when he found him, but . . .

"Don't even think about it," Seth warned. "If you kill him, Lisette will never forgive you. And, as I said, there's no reason to be jealous. It's clear to me that her heart belongs to you."

Zach forced his fingers to uncurl, his muscles to relax. "They were friends with benefits?"

Seth glanced at him, eyebrows rising. "I'm surprised you even know that term."

"Roland explained it to me."

Seth's look turned speculative. "I've been dying to ask you for some time now. . . . Why did you let them capture you that night? Why let Roland, Sarah, and Lisette interrogate you?"

"Why do you think?"

"Lisette?"

Zach nodded. "I had never been close to her before she crept up behind me that night and tried to tranq me." It seemed so long ago. Years rather than months. "Letting them take me gave me a chance to spend time with her, to speak to her."

"You love her." The simple statement conveyed both surprise and conviction.

"Yes, I do."

Seth faced the sun once more.

A bird alighted upon the edge of the roof. Two men with wings must have been a confusing sight for the little creature. Twittering a good-bye, it fluttered down to one of the bird feeders Lisette hung on the front porch and treated itself to a crunchy breakfast.

Zach wondered idly if any of the immortals, aside from David, had ever seen Seth's wings.

Seth sighed. "It *wasn't* you, was it?"

Again with the vampire army?

Oddly, it didn't upset Zach this time. Perhaps the weariness in Seth's voice took some of the sting out, because Zach actually found himself feeling a bit sorry for him. "No," he denied one last time. "It wasn't me. I didn't raise the new vampire army. And I didn't restore Donald's and Nelson's memories."

Seth rubbed his eyes. "I realize that now. I'm sorry I drove a dagger into your chest and led the Others to you."

Ahhh, there it was: the anger and resentment over the months of suffering he had endured because of this man. Without turning his head, Zach drove his fist straight out to the side and slammed it into Seth's jaw.

Head snapping sideways, Seth grunted as bone cracked.

Zach let a grim smile tilt his lips.

Seth laughed and spat blood. "Feel better?"

"A little."

"Good."

Zach studied him.

Seth's broken jaw didn't heal as swiftly as it should have, yet another indication that he desperately needed rest.

Zach heard Lisette roll over in bed, feel the sheets for him, then settle back into sleep.

Again he looked at Seth and mentally muttered every swear word he knew. Such continued for quite a while. Then he loosed a sigh of defeat. "What do you want me to do?" he asked with no enthusiasm whatsoever.

Seth spat blood again, then drew a bright white handkerchief from one pocket and dabbed at his lips and chin. "What do you mean?"

"You need sleep. You're off your game. And, with this

new threat, you need all of your wits about you to figure out who the hell you're battling. David can hold down the fort here in North Carolina and in surrounding states. What do you need me to do elsewhere to free up some time for you to take your ass to bed and get your shit together?"

Seth stared at him as if Zach had suddenly sprouted a second head. "Seriously?"

"Yes. I can hunt with Lisette at night, then do whatever it is you need me to do during the day."

"Well . . ." Seth's brow furrowed as if he were trying to decide if this were a joke. "You could read the minds of the shape-shifters and their Seconds for me. Without them knowing you're doing it and *without* harming them, that is."

"No nosebleeds?"

"No nosebleeds."

"Fine. What else?"

The utter disbelief in Seth's gaze began to grate a little. "You could go back and read the minds of the telepaths and teleporters to ensure I didn't miss anything. Their Seconds, too."

"Done. Just get me a list of who and where. What else?"

"Help David?" Seth suggested, features uncertain. "He can't stray too far from Ami so, if an emergency arises elsewhere—and one always does—"

"Give me your phone," Zach interrupted and held out a hand.

Seth stared at him. "Let me read your thoughts."

Zach arched a brow. "Let me read yours."

Stalemate.

After a moment's indecision, Seth handed over his phone.

He must *really* be exhausted. As in dangerously near collapse, something his Immortal Guardians would never dream could happen.

Zach pocketed the phone. "I'll be you for the next two days."

Seth frowned. "You don't mean you'll *appear* as me, do you?"

Zach snorted. "Like I want to look like you. Hell no." He sent Seth a dark smile. "I'll simply tell them I'm your long-lost cousin recently welcomed back into the fold."

Seth smiled, the lines of fatigue beneath his eyes becoming deep creases. "Just be patient with them."

"Would I be anything else?"

That prompted a laugh. "I think we both know you would."

"Fine. No spankings if they misbehave."

Seth shook his head. "Why would you do this for me after I let the Others torture you?"

"I'm not doing this for you. I'm doing it for Lisette," Zach told him. "I nearly lost her, Seth. Those bastards nearly killed her. I'll befriend whomever I fucking have to, to discover who set those dogs on her. I'll do whatever I have to do to ensure they never come near her again. And"—he grimaced—"if spending the rest of eternity with her means I have to play nice with you and your precious immortals, then I'll damned well play nice."

"If the sun weren't up"—Lisette spoke in her bedroom in the basement—"I would race up there and cover you with sloppy kisses."

Both men grinned.

Zach hadn't realized she had awoken. "Go to sleep, love."

"Okay, but hurry back," she urged sweetly.

Soon her breathing deepened.

Seth shook his head. "You really *do* love her."

"Yes," Zach confirmed again.

"Is it all you thought it would be?"

Zach faced the sun once more and shook his head.

"I didn't even know what love was until I met Lisette. And I *never* could have imagined anything like this. It is so much more than I ever guessed." He locked eyes with Seth. "I would have died inside if that damned drug had destroyed her."

Seth nodded. "It was the same with my wife."

Another bird joined the one at the feeder, the two chirping hellos to each other.

"Do you still miss her?" Zach asked.

Seth looked away into the sun. "Every damn day."

Zach frowned at the golden ball as a vulture with a truly impressive wingspan swept through its rays.

Seth glanced at him from the corner of his eye. "*Now* what's wrong. You're scowling again."

"I don't know," Zach said, puzzled. "For a moment I just felt this peculiar . . . I don't know . . . *non*-murderous connection to you or something."

"It's called kinship, asshole."

"Ah."

In the basement, Lisette laughed.

"I thought you were asleep," Zach said, his whole being lightening at the sound.

"Who can sleep with you two chatterboxes up there yakking away?" she retorted. "Come inside, and I'll fix us all something to eat."

Zach looked at Seth. "The woman is always hungry."

"I heard that," she said.

Laughing, Zach and Seth rose.

Lisette donned a nightgown and robe and met them in the kitchen. Her heart swelled as the two men entered, Seth tugging on a T-shirt.

What a sight. Seth, standing six feet eight inches tall. Zach, standing six feet ten inches. Both with shoulders as broad as the doorway. Bodies slender, but ripped with muscle. Chiseled faces more handsome than any she had ever seen. Jaws unshaven and bearing a deliciously rough, dark stubble that, in Zach's case, would have left marks on her skin from their torrid lovemaking had she been human. Eyes so dark and full of history and pain and power, framed by amusingly feminine, long lashes.

They made a swoon-worthy pair.

Seth seated himself at her table. Zach did, too, after catching her hips in his hands and pulling her to him for a brief kiss.

"Do you want something hot or cold?" she asked as she crossed to the refrigerator.

"Cold," both said.

Though autumn had replaced summer, temperatures had been a trifle warm of late.

Lisette opted for cold sandwiches and went to work.

A trebly version of "Down With The Sickness" filled the room.

Zach retrieved Seth's phone and, brushing Seth's out-stretched hand aside, answered. "Seth's phone."

An uncertain pause followed. "Seth?" a male voice Lisette didn't recognize asked.

She hadn't realized until then how alike the two elders sounded.

"Seth isn't available," Zach said. "I'm filling in for him. What do you need?"

"Who the hell is this?"

Zach opened his mouth.

Lisette waited for a blistering response.

He looked at Seth, then sighed and droned, "His long-lost cousin recently welcomed back into the fold."

She laughed.

Seth rolled his eyes. "This isn't going to work."

"Was that Seth?" the male asked.

"Yes," Seth responded without raising his voice or taking the phone. "I have some business I must attend to, so Zach will be handling my calls for a couple of days, Lucius."

"Oh. Is he a healer?"

Zach scowled. "He can answer for himself. Yes, I am."

"Then I could use your help."

Zach vanished.

Lisette stared. "Where did he go?"

"To heal Lucius, I imagine."

"He can follow the cell signal or whatever it is you follow? He's that powerful?" Richart could only do that with her and Étienne, she assumed because they were siblings.

"Apparently."

"You don't look too happy about that."

"Because I still find his new position as an ally . . ."

"Too good to be true?"

"Yes."

"After my history with men," she said, assembling sandwiches, "I fear he's too good to be true myself at times. I just refuse to let that interfere with the happiness he brings me. Do you want jalapeños on yours? I know you usually like your meals spicy."

"Yes, please."

Zach reappeared, his right hand wet with blood. "Done." Striding over to the sink, he washed away the red and dried his hands on the towel Lisette offered.

She motioned for him to reclaim his seat at the table and finished building the sandwiches.

Seth grinned when she set his on a plate before him. The thing was massive, so crammed with vegetables and organic meats that it would be a struggle for him to fit it in his mouth.

Zach received one of the same proportions.

Lisette carried a pitcher of tea and three glasses to the table, then joined them with her own gargantuan sandwich.

"What?" she asked when the two males shared a look full of amusement.

Seth shook his head. "I just love a woman with a healthy appetite."

Zach nodded. "As do I."

Lisette shrugged. "Fighting vampires burns a lot of calories." She cast Zach a sly glance. "As do certain other activities."

He winked.

Each of them took a big bite and chewed in happy silence.

This is nice, Lisette thought to them.

Both nodded, mouths full, though there remained some reticence between them.

"Down With The Sickness" filled the kitchen once more.

Frowning, Zach retrieved the phone and answered. "What?"

Lisette stared. This time, he had altered his voice so that it had sounded exactly like Seth's.

"My Second is down," a distraught immortal male said. "He'll bleed out before I can get him to the network."

Zach dropped his sandwich and vanished.

"I admit," Seth mentioned, "that I thought at one point you and Tanner might get together."

Tanner had been Bastien's Second since his vampire leader days and had warmed up to Lisette faster than he had to the others when he and Bastien had joined their ranks.

She shook her head. "Tanner and I are just friends. We both love sports and . . ." She shrugged. "We flirt and tease, but Tanner's a wounded soul. I don't think he's ready to allow himself to be happy again."

Seth nodded. "He thinks, because he was unable to save his son from the horrible end he met, that he doesn't deserve to be happy."

"And, after my own past, I just couldn't let myself fall in love with a human."

"I understand."

They ate in silence for a few minutes.

"Would you like to sleep here, Seth?" Lisette asked, feeling closer to him than she ever had. Ironic, considering she had feared he might kill her not so long ago.

"I wouldn't want to intrude."

"You wouldn't be. Tracy is still staying at David's. Zach and I will be gone most of the time. And we can be extra quiet while we're here."

"I suspect, once I close my eyes, I'll be dead to the world and won't hear a thing anyway," he replied with a wry smile.

"Then do it. I know you'll worry if you aren't nearby. And you won't get any rest at David's."

After a moment, he nodded. "Thank you. I think I will."

"Good."

He took another bite of his sandwich.

He looked so damned weary it broke Lisette's heart. "Do you need blood?"

"No, thank you. I'll be fine with a little rest."

She took a bite of her sandwich and studied him while she chewed. It just wasn't normal for an immortal to evince so many symptoms of fatigue.

Krysta had mentioned once that Seth's aura didn't look like theirs. Instead of being a swirling mixture of white and purple, she said his was just blindingly white.

"Do you *ever* need blood?" Lisette asked before she could stop herself.

His chewing slowed. "I'm an immortal. What do you think?"

"I think I've never seen you infuse yourself before. I've never seen you infuse anyone else either. And I've never known an elder immortal to . . ."

"To what?"

"To look so tired," she finished apologetically. "Blood and the virus usually keep us from showing signs of weariness."

"I look that bad, do I?"

"Not *bad*," she answered honestly. "Just in need of sleep."

Zach reappeared, both hands bloody. Crossing to the sink, he washed his arms up to the elbows, then returned to the table and sank into his chair. He eyed the two of them as he took a big bite. Chewed. Swallowed. "Why so serious? What did I miss?"

Lisette produced a smile. "Me asking questions that Seth can't answer."

Zach looked at Seth. "I hate keeping things from her."

"But you understand the necessity of it."

Zach nodded.

"I do, too," Lisette said with a sigh. Half a sandwich later, she asked Seth, "Is there anything you *can* tell me about Zach?"

Mischief entered her leader's eyes. "I can tell you that Zach isn't short for Zachary. It's short for Zachariah."

Zach grimaced. "I didn't like the name when it was popular, and I don't like it now."

"It's not that bad," Lisette teased with a grin. Leaning toward him, she said in low, sultry tones, "Kiss me, Zachariah. I need you, Zachariah. I *want* you, Zachariah." Wrinkling her nose, she straightened. "I see your point. Doesn't really work, does it?"

"I don't know," Zach responded, his eyes glowing faintly. "I kinda like it now."

Seth laughed.

"Down With The Sickness" sounded once more.

"Seriously?" Zach demanded, retrieving the phone and taking the call. "What?"

"Zach," Darnell said on the other end, "what the hell are you doing with Seth's phone? Why are you taking his calls?"

Seth smiled. "I have business I must attend to, Darnell," he said, raising his voice so the mortal could hear him. "Zach has offered to field my calls for a couple of days."

"Oh." Lisette suspected Darnell knew exactly what Seth's business entailed. "Is there anything I can do? Do you want me to screen your calls? Chris and I can handle the nuisance calls, and I can forward the emergencies to Zach."

"Aren't they all nuisance calls?" Zach drawled.

Lisette kicked him under the table.

"I would appreciate that, Darnell," Seth said. "Thank you."

"Great. I'll get right on it."

Zach set the phone on the table.

Lisette arched a brow. "Nuisance calls?"

Seth smiled sheepishly. "A term Darnell has coined, not I."

"And those entail . . . ?"

Zach arched a brow. "Brothers bitching about their sister being accused of something she didn't do?"

Seth laughed. "More like Seconds complaining that their immortals keep trying to protect *them* instead of vice versa. Or an immortal wanting to be assigned a new Second because his Second snores and keeps him awake all day. Or a newbie immortal bitching about having to change his diet and go organic because his favorite foods don't taste the same now that his senses are heightened."

Lisette laughed. "I've heard Melanie complain about that. Makes me glad I was transformed when organic foods were all that was available. I didn't have to change a thing diet-wise."

"Down With The Sickness" filled the kitchen.

Zach scowled. "I'm already beginning to hate that song. What?"

Portuguese, a language she recognized, but had never learned to speak, flowed over the line.

Rising, Zach grabbed half of his sandwich. "I'm taking this with me," he grumbled and vanished.

Lisette glanced at Seth. "Is it always like this?"

"Yes." He downed half of his glass of tea.

"I had no idea you were so inundated with calls."

He shrugged. "I turn my phone off at meetings and let David, Darnell, or Chris answer them when I spend time with Ami."

They ate in silence.

Zach reappeared, sandwich gone, hands bloody. He washed them in the sink and returned to the table. Before he could sit down, "Down With The Sickness" sounded once more.

The air turned blue with curses. *"What?"* he growled into the phone.

Urgent Swahili flowed across the line.

Sighing, Zach vanished.

Lisette looked at Seth. "It's going to be a long two days."

Chapter Thirteen

Cloaked in darkness, Zach watched the immortal seek his bed. Outside, the sun crested the horizon and bathed the earth with golden light.

Though shadows had been Zach's friend for thousands of years, he found no comfort in them now. He had not slept in two days, thanks to Seth's precious Immortal Guardians. Nor had he made love to Lisette.

The last irritated him far more than the first, of course. Zach craved her touch like a cat craved catnip. His existence had always been so bereft of affection and passion and tenderness that—now that Lisette had given him a taste of it—he constantly wanted to drink more in, to bathe in it and relish every kiss and touch and gasp of ecstasy.

The immortal sprawled on the bed and fell still. Soon his breathing deepened as sleep claimed him.

He was older than most of the Immortal Guardians in North Carolina. A Mayan who could unravel the mysteries surrounding the prophecy about which so many doomsday enthusiasts speculated. A powerful telepath with mental walls Zach couldn't breech without the Mayan's being aware of his presence. Not while the Mayan was conscious.

Zach silently stepped forward and waved a hand over the immortal's face.

While the Mayan was unconscious however . . .

Zach took a mental sledgehammer to the walls the telepath had erected. The power and time it took to topple them impressed the hell out of Zach, as did the mental push it took to keep the Mayan unconscious. Once the walls fell, Zach dove in and began his search.

Many minutes later, he appeared on the roof of a building at Duke University, where it was still night.

Lisette stepped from the shadows. "What took you so long?" Wrapping her arms around his waist, she leaned into him and rested her chin on his chest.

"You're splattered with blood," he said in lieu of an answer. "You weren't supposed to hunt without me. What the hell were you thinking?" Locking his arms around her, he held her tight.

"Relax. Three of the usual psycho vampires caught a couple of eggheads who were stumbling back to their apartments after studying late. I couldn't just let the vamps kill them."

"Lisette—"

"None of the new vampires were with them. I made sure of it before I attacked. And I didn't stick around after saving the humans. I called Chris's cleanup crew in to tidy things up and take the guys home."

Zach grunted.

Leaning back, she looked up at him. "What about you? You didn't say what took so long. Is everything okay?"

"Yes."

She lost her smile. "Uh-oh. What happened?"

"What do you mean?"

"You look guilty as hell. What did you do?"

"Why would you assume I did something?"

She arched a brow.

"All right," he conceded. "I *might* have *accidentally* made a telepathic immortal's nose bleed. A lot. While forcibly intruding into his mind."

"Zach!"

"I said accidentally."

"Was it an accident?" she asked.

"No."

She pushed out of his arms. "Damn it, Zach! Seth told you to be subtle and not to alert the immortals to your intrusion when you read them."

"Don't worry. The immortal won't remember having his thoughts read." He'd made sure of it.

"What did you do to him?"

"I didn't kill him, if that's what you're thinking. I merely commanded him to sleep through it. And I stopped his nosebleed and cleaned him up afterward, so there will be no indication that anything happened."

She stared up at him.

"I can't read your expression," he said after a moment. "What are you thinking?"

"You said you'd play nice."

"I did play nice. I let him sleep through it."

"Zach—"

"What would you have me do, Lisette?" He paced away, tension beating him. "I've read every immortal on the list who can easily be read and keep coming up empty. There is nothing more incriminating in their minds than lusting after this person or that or cheating at fucking cards. Only the elders remain. Those whose minds, like Ethan's, are extremely difficult to read. And no stone can go unturned."

"Okay," she said softly. "It's okay. Come here, *mon coeur*."

Sighing, he returned to her and welcomed another embrace.

"I know this is all new to you and that you're frustrated,"

she said, her small hands roaming his back. "I shouldn't have criticized."

"And I shouldn't have snapped." He rested his chin on her hair and closed his eyes.

"So you didn't find anything in the telepath's mind?"

"Nothing." He heaved a heavy sigh. "I don't understand this. Something is wrong. Something is off. But I can't put my finger on what it is. Why can't we find out who the enemy is? Why is there no trace of him in any immortal's thoughts? *Someone* has to know who he is. *Someone* has to be complicit."

"Have you read the thoughts of everyone on the list?"

"Almost. Only three remain, all older than the one I examined tonight. And those I must read before Seth awakens."

Seth had slept soundly for going on two days now, waking only twice to ask if all was well.

"Why do you have to do it before he awakens?"

"Because I'm not confident he will do what's necessary to seek the information we need."

Her hands stilled. She leaned back. "Zach . . ."

"He told me not to force it, not to give anyone nosebleeds. Do you think it will be easier for him to do it himself?"

She sighed. "No. As long as you can do it without them knowing it or causing permanent damage, you may actually be doing Seth a favor by taking care of it yourself." She smiled. "And I know how much you *love* to do Seth favors."

He groaned. "I hope you know what torture this is for me."

Instead of laughing, she bit her lip. Her face turned pensive. "Is it really?" she asked. "I know being with me requires you to do things you'd rather not do . . . like play nice with Seth and the others."

"You're worth it." Cupping her face in his hands, he pressed a tender kiss to her lips. "I would do anything for you, Lisette." He kissed her again. "If you told me tomorrow that Tracy had inadvertently thrown away your favorite throwing star, I would fly to the nearest landfill and comb through the mountains of reeking, dripping garbage until I found it." He thought about it for a moment. "Actually that would probably be a lot less irritating than dealing with your immortal brethren has been for the past forty-eight hours."

She laughed. "Poor baby. You're just not a people person, are you?"

"Not by any stretch of the imagination."

Tightening her hold on him, she rested her head on his chest. "That just makes me appreciate everything you're doing for us, and for Seth, all the more."

He grimaced.

"You're going to have to stop doing that, you know," she said.

"Doing what?"

"Grimacing every time I mention your helping Seth."

"How did you know I grimaced? You weren't even looking at me."

"Because I know you."

He smiled. She did. She knew him better than anyone else in the world. He supposed that should unnerve him, but it didn't.

She leaned back. "For example, even if I couldn't feel how tense and bunched up your muscles are, I would know you're feeling stressed."

Stressed didn't quite cover it.

Peeking up at him between her lashes, she drew a circle on his chest with one finger. "Maybe I can do a little something to help you relax."

Every muscle in Zach's body tightened as she drew that finger down his abdomen and tucked it into the waistband of his pants.

"You know, I'm still not used to seeing you in so many clothes," she purred, and flicked open the button.

Zach swallowed, already hard and aching for her. While

performing Seth's duties for the past two days, Zach had dressed as the Immortal Guardians did: black pants, black shirt, long black coat, wings tucked away.

"It's almost like I have two different lovers," she continued, taking his zipper in her hand and lowering it an inch, knuckles brushing the erection straining against the black material. "A mysterious Other who comes to me bare-chested and embraces me with wings as soft as silk." She lowered the zipper another inch. "And a hunter, who comes to me dressed all in black and loaded down with weapons."

Hell, he'd come to her dressed as a party clown, if she would just finish lowering the damned zipper.

She laughed. "I heard that."

"You did?" He was slipping more and more around her, letting his guard down without even realizing it.

"Never let it be said that I won't give you what you want." She drew the zipper all the way down, freeing him at last, and took him in her hands.

Zach moaned as she tightened her hold and squeezed her way to the sensitive head of his cock.

She sank to her knees in front of him.

His pulse raced. His heart pounded erratically in his chest.

She touched her tongue to the sensitive crown, licked it, teased it, closed her lips around it, and sucked him deep.

Sssshit!

Coherent thought fled as she used fingers, lips, and tongue . . . her warm, wet, talented mouth . . . to drive him to the brink. Zach had never experienced anything like it.

"You taste so good," she murmured, then resumed her exquisite torment.

Her phone rang.

Zach groaned.

She ignored it.

"I love you so much," he vowed.

Her eyes lit with amusement as she winked up at him.

"Down With The Sickness," a song Zach had really come to hate, filled the air.

Damn it. Darnell only forwarded the emergency calls, so Zach couldn't ignore it.

Fumbling in his pocket, he retrieved the phone. "What?" He bit back another moan of ecstasy.

"Why isn't Lisette answering her phone?" Richart demanded.

Zach glanced down at her. She did something just then with her tongue that damned near made him come. "I don't think you want to know the answer to that," he gritted.

The call ended.

Zach stuffed the phone back in his pocket and buried his fingers in Lisette's hair, unraveling her neat braid with a thought so he could bunch the thick waves up in his hands and urge her on.

Richart and Jenna appeared a couple of yards away. Their jaws dropped.

"Ahhh!" Richart spun around and gave them his back, then reached over, took his wide-eyed wife by the shoulders, and turned her back to them, too.

Scrambling to her feet, Lisette wheeled around. "What the hell are you doing here?" she demanded, her face darkening with absolute fury, her French accent more pronounced than usual.

"I did *not* need to see that," Richart said. "I mean I *really* did not need to see that. Jenna, honey, grab one of my daggers and poke out both my eyes."

"Richart!" Lisette barked.

Zach mentally mumbled every curse word he knew, tucked himself away, and carefully raised his zipper, throbbing and trembling on the precipice. Just one more minute. If they'd just had one more minute . . .

"You're my sister!" Richart shouted in dismay.

"I know that, jackass. Why are you here?"

"You didn't answer your phone!" he complained.

"And it never occurred to you that I might simply want a little privacy?"

"I wish to hell it had. You think I wanted to see you . . . like that . . . with him?"

"Oh, please. Like what you just saw was any worse than what Étienne and I overheard the first time we spent the night at your place after you and Jenna married."

Richart turned to face them and frantically drew a hand back and forth across his neck.

Jenna gasped. "What?" When she turned to Lisette and Zach, her face flamed with color. "You could hear us?" she asked, voice high with mortification.

Zach looked down at Lisette in time to see her bite her lip. As much as she must have wanted to shove it down her brother's throat, she clearly did not want to embarrass Jenna. Not any more than she already had, anyway.

Jenna looked up at Richart. "You said you soundproofed our bedroom because I was having trouble sleeping with my new heightened hearing."

"I did."

She narrowed her eyes.

"And . . . because Étienne said they could hear us when we made love," he finished miserably.

Jenna covered her face with her hands. "Richart! Why didn't you *tell* me they could hear us?"

"I wasn't thinking about *them* when we made love. How could I? I was so caught up in you and your delectable body that it didn't even occur to me that they might hear us."

"I am *never* going to be able to look your siblings in the eyes again without blushing."

He took Jenna's wrists and tried to pull her hands away from her face. "Oh, come on, sweetheart. It's not that bad," he cajoled. "We just caught Lisette down on her knees with Zach's cock in her mouth, and *she* isn't blushing."

Zach bit back a bark of laughter.

Through gritted teeth, Lisette said, "I'll blush as soon as the desire to decapitate you has passed."

Zach held up his hands in a placating gesture. "All right. All right. So everyone is embarrassed . . . except for me. I'm just very, very frustrated."

Lisette elbowed him.

Jenna lowered her hands and offered him a tentative smile.

"Since I'm playing problem solver again tonight," Zach went on, "why don't I simply bury everyone's memory of this, send Richart and Jenna back to wherever they came from, and Lisette and I can go back to what we were doing?"

"Zach," Lisette warned.

"Fine. I won't bury anyone's memories. Can I still send Richart and Jenna back to wherever they came from so we can go back to what we were doing?"

Jenna laughed.

Richart relaxed.

Lisette just shook her head. "I think that ship has sailed."

Zach groaned.

"That's just wrong," Richart said.

Lisette gaped at him. "After you just . . . And all that bitching and moaning . . . You can't . . ." She clenched her teeth. "Tell me again why you're here?"

In much calmer tones, Richart repeated, "You didn't answer your phone."

"So? I let it go to voice mail all the time."

"So, a week ago you were incapacitated by a tranquilizer dart and we nearly lost you."

"Oh." All hostility fled. "Right."

"When you didn't answer your phone," Richart continued, "I feared you had been sedated again. So I called Zach and mistook the strain in his voice for anger."

Zach frowned. "You thought I'd harmed her?"

Richart shrugged. "I don't know you, Zach. I have no idea what you are or aren't capable of or how you treat Lisette when the rest of us aren't around."

And Lisette had once had a husband-turned-vampire who had beaten her on a regular basis. All without her brothers' knowledge.

They hadn't learned the truth until the night her husband had turned her.

Well, that killed Zach's erection.

Wrapping an arm around Lisette, he drew her into his side. "In the future, when you call to inquire about her, I will endeavor to be more specific."

"But not *too* specific," Richart requested with a smile.

Zach laughed.

Lisette sighed. "Unless I'm fighting vampires, I'll start answering my phone whenever it rings. At least until we've conquered this new enemy."

"Thank you."

"Anyone else smell that?" Jenna asked suddenly, her nose wrinkling.

Lisette looked down at her shirt. "What? The blood on my clothing?"

Zach shook his head. "The vampires headed our way."

Though Jenna was younger than anyone else present, she had been transformed by Roland at Richart's request. So, like Sarah, she had the power of a nearly millennium-old immortal and was far stronger and faster than the French siblings, with more acute senses.

"Ugh." Lisette grimaced. "I smell them now."

The four of them eased back into the shadows.

Eight vampires loped into view. Scraggly, unkempt hair partially concealed eyes glowing from a recent kill. Multiple blood types stained clothing that reeked of stale sweat and unwashed bodies.

With her sharp eyes, Lisette could see dirt and she didn't want to know what else caked beneath their fingernails. Some hands still bore the blood of their latest victims, sticky and glistening like strawberry jam.

All were of the usual variety of vampires, infected for a few years by the looks of them and well on their way to becoming totally psychotic. All but one.

One vampire ate up the ground in long, confident strides rather than slump-shouldered lopes or shuffling steps. Both his body and his clothing were clean, his hair cropped short and recently shampooed. He walked at the back of the pack, curling his lip at the others while he studied his surroundings with a razor-edged gaze.

One of the new breed of vampires is with them, Lisette thought to the others.

Richart took Jenna's hand.

Lisette, Zach spoke in her mind, *does Seth intend to awaken tonight?*

She glanced up at him. *Tonight or tomorrow.*

Zach's eyes narrowed as he watched the vamps.

Why?

Because I want to try something.

Apprehension pricked her. *Zach—*

Remain here, he said. This time she could tell he directed the command at all three of them.

Richart held up a hand. *Seth said not to engage any of the new vampires.*

Seth told you *not to engage the new vampires,* Zach corrected. *Not me. Have you a tranquilizer gun with you?*

Lisette, Richart, and Jenna each drew one and held it up.

Lisette's had just been delivered by the network that morning. Usually she only carried EpiPen-like auto-injectors full of the sedative.

Only use them if you have to, Zach ordered.

Zach! Lisette protested, afraid he intended to do something reckless.

Dipping his head, he brushed a light kiss across her lips. *I'll be fine. Stay here.*

He vanished, then reappeared only a few feet in front of the pack.

Lisette raised the tranquilizer gun and aimed it at the big vamp.

The vampires shuffled to a halt.

"Who the fuck are you?" one demanded, either too insane or too stupid to be afraid.

Zach smiled. "It doesn't really matter. You won't live long enough to tell anyone." Drawing katanas, he shot forward.

Lisette gasped as he tore through the vampires like a tornado.

Holy shit, he's fast! Richart thought and took a step forward, his fascinated gaze glued to the tempest below.

It didn't take long.

Zach stilled in the center of the pack, knees bent, blades dripping, face marbled with blood. Seven vampires sank lifelessly to the ground, their bodies spread around him like the petals of a flower, as the virus went to work and they began to shrivel up like mummies.

The newbie vampire, eyes wide, swiftly raised a tranquilizer gun nearly identical to the one Lisette carried and aimed it at Zach's chest.

Zach straightened and lowered his arms to his sides, hands loosely clasping the hilts of his swords. Face impassive, he arched a brow. "Well?"

What the hell is he doing? Richart demanded.

Lisette's heart began to pound. *I don't know.*

The vamp pulled the trigger.

Lisette expected Zach to leap aside and dodge the dart,

or drop a sword and catch the dart between two fingers. He certainly possessed the speed required to do so.

Instead, he just stood there.

The dart lodged itself in Zach's chest.

She bit back a cry.

Zach stared at the vampire and shifted his shoulders a bit. Tilting his head, he pursed his lips. "Sort of tickles."

The vamp's eyes widened. He pulled the trigger again.

Zach's face darkened in a blink, twisting into a snarl of rage that caught even Lisette off guard. He dropped a sword, caught the dart, and let it fall harmlessly to the pavement. Before the vamp could get off another shot, Zach zipped forward. Wrapping the fingers of his free hand around the vampire's neck, he shoved him up against the nearest building.

The vampire struggled at first, swinging a meaty fist that connected with Zach's jaw, then went still.

Dangling in Zach's hold as though paralyzed, he stared at Zach with eyes full of terror. His mouth opened in a silent cry as his face contorted with pain. Blood began to trickle from one nostril. The trickle became a streaming rivulet.

Lisette lowered her gun. Striding forward, she stepped off the roof.

Richart and Jenna appeared beside her.

"I told you to stay on the roof," Zach snapped.

None of them moved.

Blood emerged from one of the vamp's ears and slipped down to soak his collar. His other ear began to bleed, too. Then his eyes.

Zach's hand at the vampire's throat began to glow.

Lisette could only stare.

Veins soon stood out on the vamp's temples and forehead as his face mottled. The cords of his neck stood out as he snapped his teeth together and ground them with a moan. Blood oozed from his mouth.

Zach, as far as Lisette could tell, didn't breathe. Not until he opened his fingers and let the vamp fall to the ground.

The vampire's body instantly began to shrivel up as the virus went to work. Soon he would be as the other vampires: no more than a pile of clothing.

Air rushed from Zach's lungs in a whoosh. His chest rose and fell as though he had been running.

Lisette took a cautious step toward him. "Zach?"

Face set in harsh lines, he turned to them. "The next time I tell you to stay on the roof, you'd better *stay on the fucking roof!*"

Jenna nodded swiftly, Richart more slowly.

"The battle was over," Lisette said. And she had wanted to get a closer look at what Zach was doing, wanted to see for herself that he was okay after being tranqed.

"There could have been more of them lingering downwind," Zach said.

True. She had been so distracted she hadn't thought of that.

Face taut with anger, he surveyed their surroundings. "We have to get out of here."

He blurred, moving past her like a breeze, sweeping up the vampires' clothing as he went. Lisette heard a Dumpster lid clang off to their right. Then Zach returned and tucked the vampire's tranquilizer gun in the back of his pants.

He looked to Richart. "Go home. Now."

Richart touched Jenna's back and teleported the two away.

Zach took Lisette's arm, his hold less than gentle.

"Are you okay?" she asked.

"The Others will have felt the power I just wielded and will be here momentarily." Bending, he picked up the dart he had dropped.

The campus around them dissolved into darkness, and

Lisette found herself in David's home. More specifically in David's study.

Talking on the phone, David took one look at them and told whomever he spoke with that he would call them back. "What happened?"

Zach released Lisette and handed the dart to David. "Courtesy of one of the new breed of vampires. A full dose for Dr. Lipton to study."

David took the dart. "Do I even want to know how you got this?"

"I caught it before it could hit me." Reaching back, Zach retrieved the tranquilizer gun and placed it on the desk. "There should be more in here."

David ignored the gun and lowered his gaze to the dart still poking out of Zach's chest. "And that one?"

"Didn't affect me. So it won't affect Seth." Yanking it out, Zach tossed it in the wastebasket. "It *is,* however, strong enough that it will likely affect *you.*"

"Good to know." David set the dart down on his desk between the gun and yet another thick medical tome. "Will it knock me out or just leave me groggy?"

"Groggy."

"Groggy's not a problem. I don't suppose you were able to tag him with a tracking device."

"By the time I finished with him, there was nothing left to tag."

"You destroyed him?"

"Yes."

"Could you maybe *not* destroy the next one?"

Zach responded with a terse nod.

David studied him. "So, how are you otherwise? You're looking a little . . . tense."

One hell of an understatement. Lisette thought that, if

Seth's phone were to ring in that instant, Zach's head would explode.

"I told them to stay on the roof," he gritted.

"Them meaning . . . ?"

"Lisette, Richart, and Jenna. I told them to stay on the roof, and they didn't fucking stay on the roof."

David nodded. "Welcome to our world." He looked at Lisette. "Next time stay on the roof."

"I will."

"See that you do. And impress upon your brother how displeased I will be if he and Jenna don't do the same."

She nodded. One did not gainsay David anymore than one did Seth.

David met Zach's gaze. "Are we good?"

At last, Zach's shoulders relaxed a little. "Yes, we're good."

David smiled. "Go get cleaned up and relax for a bit. You can use one of the quiet rooms below. I'll have Darnell redirect Seth's calls to me for the next couple of hours."

"Thank you," Zach said, much to Lisette's surprise. "Let me know if you need me to teleport you."

"I will."

Capturing one of Lisette's hands in his own, Zach led her from the room and headed down to the basement.

Lisette didn't say a word. She almost wished she could peek into his thoughts so she could better read him, but wasn't sure she would like what she found up there at the moment.

Sheldon passed them in the hallway, Tracy's scent all over him.

Interesting. Lisette made a mental note to remind Tracy of Immortal Guardians' heightened sense of smell.

Zach took them unerringly to an empty quiet room.

Lisette didn't know if Zach had just made a lucky guess—most of the quiet rooms had been occupied of late—or if he was so powerful that he could hear what the others couldn't and had known no one slept within.

Into the large bedroom he guided her, then closed the door behind them.

Butterflies fluttered in Lisette's belly. This was the first time Zach had truly been angry with her. She wasn't sure how to deal with it.

"Zach—"

She only managed to get the one word out before he backed her into the door, slipped a hand around to cup the nape of her neck, and brought his lips down on hers in a ferocious kiss.

Fire flashed through her, igniting her blood and shortening her breath. She parted her lips, her insides melting at the first stroke of his tongue. Rising onto her toes, she wrapped her arms around his neck and leaned into him.

"Zach," she whispered.

He bent his knees and locked an arm around her. When he straightened, he took her with him, her feet rising to dangle a good foot or more above the floor.

Abandoning her nape, he lowered his hand to her ass and urged her to wrap her legs around him.

Lisette did so eagerly, already wet and aching for him as she rubbed against the hard bulge of his arousal.

Zach's lips left hers. His eyes shone a vibrant gold as he stared down at her, the emotion they contained a mystery. "Don't ever . . . ever . . . *ever* defy me again," he ordered, voice hoarse.

She frowned. "Zach—"

"I'm not saying it to be a hard-ass. I'm saying it because . . ." He buried his face in her neck and squeezed her tighter against him. "You don't know what it did to me to see you fall that night. To not be able to awaken you. To reach into your thoughts and find nothing but silence. Darkness." His grip tightened to the point of pain as he swallowed hard.

"To hear that same silence, day after day after day and not know if there would ever be anything else. To not know if you would ever again open your eyes. Say my name. Wrap your arms around me and dispel the cold."

Moisture blurred her vision as his agonized voice rumbled in her ear.

"You can't let yourself be tranqed again, Lisette. You can't."

"I won't," she vowed.

He shook her slightly. "Don't make promises you won't keep. If I tell you to stay on the roof, then stay on the fucking roof. If I tell you to run, then run," he commanded, his torment carrying to her loud and clear. "We have no way of knowing if they'll up the dosage again. If they increase it even a *little bit* and you're hit with a dart, we may not be able to bring you back."

Chilled by the thought, she nodded. "I will. I'll do as you say." She would rather duck and run for the first time in her immortal life and let Zach fight her battles for her than end up lost forever in a dark mental void. Or destroyed. Particularly since the drug didn't affect him.

"I don't want to be left with nothing but a pile of your clothing, Lisette," he murmured. "I don't think I could handle it." He fisted a hand in the back of her shirt. "I think I would lay waste to the world if I lost you."

Tears burned her eyes. "I'm sorry," she wheezed, chest constricted by his words as much as his tight hold.

Giving a little start, he relaxed his grip and raised his head to peer down at her with furrowed brow. "I'm sorry. Was I hurting you?"

She smiled. "It's okay."

"No, it's *not* okay. I don't *ever* want to hurt you."

"Zach, you were just cutting off my air a little. Don't worry about it." When he opened his mouth to protest, Lisette stole a quick kiss. "I'm sorry I didn't take greater care earlier.

I should have listened to you and not let my curiosity get the better of me."

"Curiosity?"

"I wanted to see what you were doing to the vampire."

"I was turning his brain to mush, searching for answers."

She wrinkled her nose. Then a disquieting thought arose. "Wait. You didn't do that to the telepath you gave a nosebleed, did you? You didn't turn his brain to mush?"

"Of course not."

Whew! "Just checking."

He smiled. Easily supporting her weight with one hand, he raised the other and drew gentle fingers down her cheek. "I really do love you, you know."

Her heart swelled in her chest. "I know. I love you, too."

"I would've thought that, after waiting thousands of years, it would take longer."

"What would?"

"Falling in love." He brushed a tender kiss across her lips. "Surrendering my heart." Another kiss. "My body."

She nipped his chin. "Having your first blow job interrupted by your lover's brother?"

He laughed. "That's going to be a tough one to forget."

Yes, it was, damn it. But she'd worry about that later.

Lisette sent him a flirtatious smile and arched against him.

He groaned as desire leapt to life once more in his luminous eyes.

"We could pick up where we left off earlier," she suggested. She was eager to taste him again. To see the ecstasy ripple across his handsome face as she tongued him and teased him and—

"I need to feel you under me first."

Sounded good to her. All of that delicious weight pressing down on her, muscles bunching as he drove into her again and again, urging her toward a climax. His wings, when he released them, hovering above them and filling the room with the scent of rain and snow and sunshine all at once.

"Then what are you waiting for?" she demanded, not bothering to hide her need.

He hesitated.

"What?" she asked, wishing they were already naked.

"Don't take this the wrong way," he began.

Uh-oh. "Okay."

"When I'm inside you, driving into you and tasting every inch of your soft, soft skin . . ."

Her gaze dropped to his lips. She could almost feel them on her now. "Uh-huh?"

"I want to smell *you,* not the vampires we killed tonight."

Lisette laughed. "Yeah. We do sort of reek, don't we?" And her skin, beneath her clothing, was probably streaked with vampire blood. As was his. "Okay. Why don't we . . . play with each other in the shower until we're both clean and mindless with lust? Then, once we make it to the bed and you have me under you, you can do anything you want to me."

His eyes flashed brighter. "Anything?"

She drew her tongue across his lips. "Anything."

Their clothes fell away as he turned and crossed to the bathroom.

"How did you do that?" Lisette asked. His hands hadn't moved.

"Telekinesis."

Lisette decided she loved that ability. With their clothing strewn across the floor behind them, his long, hard erection now teased the heart of her, sending sparks of pleasure dancing through her with every step. "Hurry," she pleaded.

He responded with a wicked chuckle that made her shiver. "I don't think so. David gave us two hours." Entering the bathroom, he turned on the shower with a thought. "And I intend to spend every last minute of them worshipping your lovely body."

Chapter Fourteen

When Lisette and Zach teleported to her home two hours later, sated and relaxed, they found Seth in the kitchen, sipping tea from a huge Looney Tunes mug.

Lisette stared.

He wore only a pair of black pants that rode low on slender hips. No shoes. No socks. (It felt oddly intimate to see his big feet uncovered.) Just bare muscled chest, rippling washboard abs . . . and wings nearly identical to Zach's.

Folded in against his back, Seth's were a little bit darker. But then his skin was too, always appearing sun-kissed and naturally tanned. Like Zach's, the feathers of Seth's wings were the same color as his skin at their base and darkened to black at their tips. Seth's long hair, pulled into a ponytail at the nape of his neck with a leather tie, was still damp from a shower and nearly disappeared amidst the dark, silky wings.

Zach touched the tip of an index finger to the bottom of Lisette's chin and applied gentle pressure, closing the mouth she hadn't even realized had fallen open.

A quick look up, and she saw disapproval into those deep brown eyes.

"What?" she asked in her defense. "I'm just not used to seeing him this way."

Seth turned to face them.

"And wish you were?" came Zach's caustic reply.

She gave his shoulder a shove. "Oh, please. Wipe that jealous look off your pretty face. You know you're the only man I want to lick from head to toe."

Golden flames dispelled the darkness in his eyes. During their two-hour interlude, she had done just that until he had shouted her name in climax.

Seth set his mug on the counter and reached for a black T-shirt that lay over the back of a chair. "Forgive me. I didn't expect you home so soon."

Lisette held out a hand. "No. Leave it off, Seth. There's no need to don it on my account. I'm guessing you don't let many people see you like this, and I want you to be comfortable." She knew, from her mortal past, how hard it could be to maintain a facade among friends and family. "In fact, I want you to consider this a second home. A place where you can be yourself."

He hesitated. "You would offer me that after I accused you of betraying me?"

She waved a hand. "Pfft. Water under the bridge. You were tired. I was behaving oddly. And, technically, I *did* betray you because I ignored your warning to stay away from Zach."

Still, Seth hesitated.

Zach released a heavy sigh. "You may as well. She's already seen your wings."

"Do *you* want this to be a second home for me?" Seth taunted with a faint smile.

"Hell no. But I love her and will tolerate your ass as often as I have to if it will make her happy."

"It will," Lisette said.

Zach dipped his chin in an abrupt nod. "Then park said ass at the table and finish your tea."

Seth grinned. "Actually, I was just about to cook some pasta. I can make enough for all of us, if you'd like."

"I could eat," Lisette said. Her stomach rumbled in anticipation.

Smiling, Zach rolled his eyes. "Didn't I tell you? The woman is always hungry."

"Hey," she admonished playfully, "unless you object to how I *worked up* my appetite, don't complain about it."

Zach held both hands up in surrender.

Shaking his head, Seth took a couple of boxes of multicolored fusilli down from an upper cabinet.

Lisette let Zach tug her coat off her shoulders and draw it down her arms.

As he left to hang it up on the coat hooks near the front door and remove his own, she studied Seth.

No stubble adorned his cheeks. Nor did circles hover beneath his eyes or lines of strain bracket his mouth. His shoulders and stance seemed relaxed. His lips still curled in a faint smile.

"You look better," she ventured gently.

He glanced at her as he stirred the pasta, his expression somewhat chagrined. "I *feel* better." When Zach rejoined them, Seth held out his hand. "My phone, please."

Zach handed it over with unmistakable relief.

Seth tucked it in a back pocket. "I have to admit, I expected you to crush it mere hours after I gave it to you."

"I was sorely tempted," Zach retorted without remorse.

Seth motioned for them to sit at the table.

Each took a turn at the sink first, washing and drying their hands.

"Ami and the babe are all right?" Seth queried.

"Yes," Lisette assured him. "Dr. Kimiko and Melanie

both seem pleased with how well Ami is doing *and* by how the baby's lungs are coming along."

"Excellent." He looked to Zach. "Marcus hasn't tried to kick your ass?"

Zach smirked. "He isn't that stupid."

"Marcus has been keeping his distance," Lisette said, warning Zach with a glance not to stir up trouble.

He winked, the rascal.

Zach held the chair at the head of the table for Lisette, then seated himself on one of the new bench seats she'd had Tracy purchase.

Seth served them each a plate piled high with the colorful fusilli and topped with homemade sauce Lisette had prepared earlier, then took his own plate and settled himself on the second bench across from Zach.

"So," Seth said as they tucked into their meal.

Lisette didn't know if it was the vampire hunting or the lovemaking or a combination of the two, but hunger gnawed at her and drove her to wolf down the delicious meal faster than she normally would have.

"So?" Zach repeated before he slipped a forkful of pasta into his oh-so-talented mouth. Perhaps it *was* the lovemaking. He seemed as hungry as she.

Seth caught Lisette's eye. "How did he do?"

Her mind still on lovemaking, she paused. Then she realized Seth was asking how Zach had done filling in for him. "Very well. I'm proud of him."

Zach sent Seth a *See, I told you I could do it* look.

"He didn't kill anyone?" Seth asked, voice full of doubt.

"Only vampires. No immortals, *gifted ones,* or humans."

Seth nodded, satisfied, and addressed Zach directly. "How did the search go? Have you read the minds of all the immortals on the list?"

"Yes."

"Without giving anyone nosebleeds? I'm impressed."

Lisette and Zach looked at each other.

And, of course, Seth saw it. Seth saw everything. "Without giving anyone nosebleeds?" he repeated, his deep voice acquiring a hard edge.

"Actually . . ." Zach said slowly.

"Damn it, Zach! I told you not to hurt any of them!"

"I—"

"I told you not to tip any of them off either!"

"I didn't," Zach protested. "They all slept through it. And I healed the damage done once I was finished."

Lisette rested a hand on Seth's strong forearm. "He did it for *you,* Seth. They're elders. Their minds are very difficult to penetrate. Zach knew it would tear you up to hurt them like that yourself. So he . . . hurt them for you." This wasn't sounding as good as it had in her head. "I mean, he knew you needed the information and the only way to get it was to force it. . . ." She looked at Zach. "I'm not helping, am I?"

"You don't need to defend me, love. Seth knows it had to be done and is secretly relieved he won't have to do it himself."

Lisette eyed Seth doubtfully.

Seth stared at Zach, his fingers clenched around the fork he held. "What did you find?"

"Not a damned thing," Zach told him.

Seth's brow furrowed. "I'm torn between feeling relieved that I didn't miss anything and utterly confounded. How is that possible?"

"That would be the billion-dollar question."

Seth poked at the pasta on his plate. "You found no evidence of guilt in *any* of their minds?"

"Nothing."

"You read the shifters, too?"

"Yes."

"And found nothing?"

"Nothing. Although . . ."

Seth looked up.

"There *was* one telepath," Zach murmured, face troubled, "whose barriers were stronger than any of the others'." Setting his fork down, he leaned forward and drew a folded sheet of paper out of his back pocket. He spread it on the table in front of Lisette.

A quick glimpse revealed it to be the list of immortals he had been given, both names and where to find them.

"This one," he said, pointing to a name on the list. "The Celt."

"Aidan," Seth murmured.

Curious, Lisette leaned forward to view the name. "Aidan?" The only Aidan she knew spelled it with an *e*. "Aiden O'Kearney?"

Seth shook his head as he studied the paper. "Different Aidan. This one's been stationed in Denmark for some time. Keeps to himself."

"He's an elder?"

Seth nodded. "Born around seven or eight hundred B.C." His eyes met Zach's. "And he can read minds *and* teleport."

Zach picked up his fork and resumed eating. "Among other things."

"You say his barriers were stronger than the others'?"

Zach nodded.

"How much stronger?"

"*Too* much. Enough to tell me he's been working on strengthening them. I couldn't penetrate the strongest of them without giving him more than a nosebleed. With your *permission,*" he drawled, voice dripping with sarcasm, "I'll return and find out what the hell he's hiding."

Seth immediately vetoed that one. "No, I'll do it."

"Bad call," Zach said with a shake of his head.

"Not wanting you to kill him is a bad call?"

"I wouldn't kill him. I'd just hurt him. And an Immortal Guardian as old as he is will recover quickly."

"No."

"Stop being such a hard-ass," Zach said. "When you fucked up before, you could blame it on not having slept for two months."

Lisette looked at Seth. "You told me weeks, not months!"

Seth glared at Zach.

Zach continued. "Fuck up now that you're rested, and it'll just be poor judgment."

"I'm not going to let you—"

"There's a reason surgeons aren't supposed to operate on their own relatives," Zach interrupted, voice mild. "Their emotions are too invested and may lead them to make mistakes, to *not* do something they should for fear they'll cause their spouse or father or daughter pain." He pointed his fork at Seth. "Try to do this yourself, and you'll pull back the instant Aidan manifests discomfort."

Lisette nibbled her lower lip and watched Seth. "He has a point."

Something flickered in Seth's eyes, there and gone in an instant. "You question my ability to carry out my duties?"

"Absolutely not," she assured him, squeezing his arm before she withdrew her touch. "Unlike Zach, I think you'll do whatever it takes to find out what Aidan is hiding because the lives of the rest of us depend upon it. But I also know that you aren't as cold and ruthless as Zach can be."

Zach frowned. "Ummm . . ."

Seth's lips twitched.

"Being the instrument of pain that will extract the information you need from Aidan will torment you endlessly. Zach won't give it a second thought."

"Now, wait a minute," Zach protested.

Lisette rolled her eyes. "Don't even try to deny it. If I hadn't stopped you, you would have erased Bastien's and Ethan's memories of you and given them brain damage."

Seth scowled. "What?"

"To protect you," Zach ground out. "I was going to do it to protect you."

"And you're willing to hurt Aidan why?"

A moment passed. Zach sighed in defeat. "To protect you. Fine. I'm ruthless."

She smiled. "It's one of the many things I love about you."

His face lightened. "Good." He looked to Seth. "So, am I doing this, or what?"

Lisette could almost hear Seth's stomach churning at the prospect.

"Fine," Seth said at last. "You can do it. But we go together."

"If you go, you'll just—"

Seth held up a hand. "We go together," he repeated, words clipped. "And not just so I can be assured you won't kill Aidan. Have you forgotten the Others are hunting you?"

"Hell no. They're like fucking bloodhounds. Every time I expend more energy than usual, they come running and I have to disappear."

Lisette stared at him. "*Every* time? You didn't tell me that. I thought it was just tonight."

He shook his head. "I didn't want to worry you."

"Zach . . ." How long would they hunt him?

And how long could he continue to elude them? Lisette feared she would never see Zach again if the Others succeeded in recapturing him.

"As long as I'm gone when they get there and have left nothing behind that carries my scent," he said, "they have no way of knowing for sure whether it was me or Seth. And, since I can still conceal my presence from them, even if they figure out it was me, they can't follow me once I teleport."

Seth grunted. "Expending the amount of energy you'll need in order to topple Aidan's mental barriers is sure to draw their notice. If I sense the Others coming before you're finished, I'll take over, and you can disappear so they'll think it was me the whole time. In fact, even if you finish before they arrive, I'll linger after you leave, just to throw them off a little."

Zach nodded. "Sounds good."

Lisette continued to fret.

"We'll go as soon as we finish our meal. It's daytime in Denmark, and Aidan will be sleeping."

They returned to their pasta, silent, somber.

"Someone want to tell me why my phone isn't ringing?" Seth asked out of the blue.

Lisette forced a smile. "David volunteered to take your calls for a bit. I think he saw how on edge Zach was and decided he could use a break."

"Ah."

Zach grunted. "That reminds me. I learned a couple of things from one of the new breed of vampires tonight."

Seth frowned. "I thought I told you not to engage them."

"You told your *Immortal Guardians* not to engage them. And they didn't. We came across one of the new vampires traveling with seven of the usual vamps. I ordered Lisette, Richart, and Jenna to remain on the roof nearby while I dispatched the psychotic vamps and confronted the new one myself."

Seth raised his eyebrows and met Lisette's guilty gaze. "Did you remain on the roof?"

"No," she confessed, "but the danger had passed. Zach had already taken out the insane vampires and incapacitated the newbie when we joined him."

Seth shook his head. "There could have been—"

"More lurking downwind. I know. Zach and David already read me the riot act, so stop looking at me like that. I won't make the same mistake twice."

"David read you the riot act?" Seth asked, lips quirking.

"In his quiet, gentle, don't-make-me-lose-it-like-the-Hulk way," she said.

Seth smiled and returned his attention to Zach. "What did you learn?"

"First, that even with the dosage upped, the drug won't affect you or me, although it *is* strong enough to make David groggy."

"Will it knock him out?"

"One dose won't, no."

"Good to know. What else?"

"The immortal you're looking for is definitely an elder and very powerful. Yet another reason to delve more deeply into Aidan's mind. Because your immortal enemy doesn't just erase the memories of the vampires in his army. He plants commands in their subconscious to get them to do what he wants."

Lisette had never heard of such a thing. "You mean like hypnosis?"

"More like hypnosis times a hundred," Zach confirmed. "These are impulses so deeply implanted that the puppet couldn't ignore them no matter how strong his will to do otherwise."

Seth took a bite. Chewed. Considered Zach's words. "That explains how the vampires can carry out duties without revealing anything about the one commanding them. But such behavioral modification would take great power."

Zach nodded. "If I didn't know how loyal he was to you, I would suspect David."

"David would never betray me."

"I know. The big question is who would?"

Seth sighed. "A question for which I still have no answer."

"But we've narrowed it down."

"To one of the elder telepathic immortals. Aidan is the most powerful."

"And is harboring secrets. If he's strong enough to bend someone's will, he may be strong enough to keep you or me from finding what we seek in his mind. That barrier I encountered may be too strong even for *us* to topple. At least not without destroying him."

Lisette looked from one to the other. "Even while he's sleeping?"

Both males nodded.

"Then how can you find out who it is?"

"Did you plant a tracking device on the vampire?" Seth asked Zach.

"No. His brain was Swiss cheese by the time I finished with him. Have you pissed off Aidan or any of the other elder telepaths recently?" Zach asked.

"Actually, yes," Seth said. "But I didn't think their anger had lingered."

"You have?" Lisette asked, surprised.

He shrugged. "Rumors of the recent marriages that have taken place here have circulated the globe. Like other immortals, the elder telepaths have become suspicious regarding the unusually high number of *gifted ones* that seem to populate North Carolina."

Lisette looked from Zach to Seth. "I admit I've been a bit curious about that myself."

Seth sighed. "David and I always steer *gifted ones* toward areas that bear network headquarters. It makes it easier for us to keep them safe in the event their advanced DNA is discovered."

"Ahhhhhh. No wonder."

"Aidan requested a transfer a few months ago."

Because he had hoped to find love and happily ever after himself?

Zach grunted. "A transfer you denied."

"Yes."

"So we have motive."

Lisette knew well how lonely this existence could be, but . . . "Do you really think your denying Aidan a chance to meet and fall in love with a *gifted one*—something that would still be a long shot, even if he were here—would drive him to retaliate by trying to destroy us all?"

Seth shook his head. "You've only been immortal for two centuries, Lisette. You don't know how wretched it can be to live thousands of years without love."

Zach nodded. "It is."

"Yes, but . . ." She looked at Seth. "You make it sound like you're a marriage broker or something and have intentionally denied Aidan and the other elders spouses."

"I decide which immortals are stationed here. And I'm responsible for guiding *gifted ones* to the area. Even David suspects there are immortals out there who think I'm playing favorites. I'll have Darnell look into comments made online, see if he can differentiate between the disgruntled and the furious. Aidan's wasn't the only transfer I denied recently."

A sobering thought. Lisette had heard of men killing for love. She supposed killing for being *denied* love wasn't so far out of the realm of possibility.

"Down With The Sickness" interrupted them.

Zach growled. "I *hate* that *fucking* song!"

Laughing, Seth retrieved his phone. "I guess this means David is off the clock." He took the call. "Yes?"

"Is this Zach or Seth?" Bastien asked on the other end, voice taut.

"Seth. What's up?"

"Cliff tagged one of the new vampires."

Seth vanished.

Zach touched Lisette's shoulder and teleported, following Seth to the field that used to support Bastien's lair.

Lisette staggered to one side as her feet connected with the ground.

Zach steadied her and bit back a grin when she glared up at him.

"Next time at least let me stand up and set my fork down first," she demanded. Her angry words lost much of their impact, however, when she raised the forkful of pasta she held to her mouth and stuffed it in.

Smothering a laugh, Zach turned to Seth and the others.

Bastien stood facing them, his feet braced apart in a warrior's stance and his face set in stone. At his side, Cliff shifted constantly, as if he couldn't bear to stand still, his features pinched with anxiety.

Seth addressed the young vampire. "Are you injured?"

"No," Cliff answered.

Seth looked to Bastien. "I thought we had decided it would be too dangerous for Cliff to try to tag one of the new breed."

A muscle jumped in Bastien's jaw. "I changed my mind. We needed information. I thought it worth the risk."

"Bullshit!" Cliff exclaimed, mirroring Zach's thoughts.

If Zach had learned nothing else about Bastien, he had learned that the immortal black sheep was fiercely loyal to those he loved. And he loved Cliff like a brother. No way would he have let the young vampire, who clung to sanity by his fingertips, try to tag one of the new breed of vampires and risk being captured again.

Bastien shot Cliff a warning glare.

"I did it myself," Cliff said. "On my own. Bastien didn't know about it."

Leaden silence.

"If you did it on your own," Seth said, "how did you get your hands on a tracking device?"

"I gave it to him," Bastien answered.

"No, he didn't," Cliff denied. "I stole it."

"He's lying to protect me," Bastien continued. "He knows I went against your orders—that we had agreed not to do it—and doesn't want to see me punished."

Seth looked to Cliff. "Is that true?"

"No, sir, it isn't. You can read my thoughts if you don't believe me."

Bastien turned on Cliff. "Would you shut the hell up?"

"No! I'm not going to let you take the fall for this, Bastien, not after everything you've done for me!"

Bastien swore.

Cliff turned back to Seth. "And after all the Immortal Guardians have done for me, I wanted to help. I wanted . . . no, I *needed* . . . to do one fucking good thing in my life before I lose my mind and have to be put down like a rabid dog."

"I've been in your thoughts," Seth said, more calm than Zach would've expected when faced with such insubordination. "You've done *many* good things, Cliff, both as a mortal and as a vampire. You have already helped the Immortal Guardians in countless ways for which we can never fully repay you. Humans, too."

Lisette nodded. "The night the mercenaries attacked network headquarters you saved dozens of human lives and put yourself in harm's way to do it. You're a hero, Cliff. Even mortals at the network, who are leery of vampires, think so."

He shook his head. "Don't say that."

"It's true. We immortals couldn't have fought the mercenaries *and* saved the network's employees. Most wouldn't have made it out alive if you hadn't rescued them and helped them evacuate."

Zach's heart went out to the young man, who so badly wanted to be known and remembered for something good rather than the bad they all knew lurked just over the horizon.

"Anyone would have done that," Cliff murmured.

"Joe didn't," Bastien said. "Joe ran."

Silence.

"Where did you get the tracking device you planted?" Seth repeated.

"At the network," Cliff admitted with a miserable glance

at Bastien. "They don't keep them guarded and locked away the way they do the sedative and antidote. It was actually pretty easy to sneak one out."

Seth sighed. "Chris is going to freak."

"Then don't tell him," Bastien came close to pleading.

Seth shook his head. "The rules are there for a reason, Bastien. After all Chris does for us, I won't undermine his authority by lying about a security breach."

Again Bastien swore.

"Don't panic. I'll suggest leniency this time." He gave Cliff a stern look. "But you're on notice, Cliff. No more bull-shit. No more following Bastien's example and breaking the rules. No more putting yourself at risk because you think you have nothing to lose. You'll follow protocol and abide by our decisions, or I will revoke your hunting privileges."

Cliff nodded. "Yes, sir."

"Now tell us what happened."

"I found a group of vampires over by the Morrisville Walmart."

There weren't that many places open twenty-four hours a day in North Carolina. Those that were, like a select few Walmarts, tended to be vampires' second-favorite hunting grounds. College campuses being their first.

"There were half a dozen nutcases who were really far gone and three huge guys I could tell had only recently been turned. All three of the big vamps carried tranquilizer guns and looked like friggin' marines, so I knew they were the new breed. While the crazy ones were running their mouths the way they do, I sidled up to the other three and asked if they were all together."

Bastien grumbled something indecipherable.

Cliff ignored him. "They said they had just met the crazy ones and figured they should band together for safety's sake. Hunt in larger numbers, you know? A couple of the crazy vamps started fighting. I pretended to try to break it up and let them push me out of the way. I stumbled into one of the stoic vamps, planted the device on his tranquilizer gun, told them they might want to think twice about hooking up with the psychos, then got my ass out of there."

"Did any of the vampires follow you?" Zach asked.

"No. The older ones were too busy scrapping. The younger ones must have thought they would have a better chance of running into an Immortal Guardian if they hung out with vampires guaranteed to go on a killing spree."

Bastien nodded. "I heard no signs of pursuit when he caught up with me."

"Could they have tagged you with a tracking device?" Seth asked Cliff.

"Vampires have tracking devices?"

"They haven't used any thus far. But, since they have the drug, we can't rule it out."

"If they did, I didn't feel it."

"I shall return momentarily." Seth vanished.

The swish of tree leaves rustling in the breeze was the only sound for many long minutes. That and the frogs, insects, and other creatures that embraced the night.

Zach studied the vampire.

Cliff seemed to be calming a bit. Perhaps he had feared Seth would execute him for disobeying.

"You did a good thing," Zach told him.

A faint smile curled Cliff's lips as relief that *someone* thought so crept into his features.

"Don't encourage him," Bastien snapped.

"I believe *you* are the one who encouraged him."

"I didn't tell him to do this!"

"Are you not his mentor?" Zach studied the irate British immortal. "How many times have you broken, trampled upon, then set fire to the rules by which the other Immortal Guardians live, as well as the rules Chris Reordon has painstakingly created to keep those at the network safe?"

"*You* would lecture *me* on following the rules?" Bastien demanded incredulously.

Lisette nodded her agreement. "It *is* sort of the pot calling the kettle black."

Zach shrugged. "I don't pretend to be a leader. I'm just saying, if you want to protect your vampire followers, then lead by example."

"They're my friends, not my followers. I no longer command an army of vampires."

"Yet those at the network look to you for leadership."

"I'm beginning to wish I hadn't bound your wounds when you were injured," Bastien groused.

Zach grinned.

Lisette smiled up at him. "You two are so alike."

Cliff laughed, finally at ease.

Seth reappeared with Chris Reordon.

Before anyone said a word, Chris stepped forward and waved a metal detector over Cliff. "Clear." He stepped back. "So, Seth says you tagged one of the new vampires?"

"Yes."

"You can tell me about it in a minute. Right now, we need to get you back to network headquarters so I can start tracking the bastard."

"Down With The Sickness" overlapped his words.

At the same time, Bastien's phone bleated.

He and Seth shared a look of concern as they answered their phones.

"Ami's water broke," Marcus and Melanie said in unison, Marcus to Seth and Melanie to Bastien.

"I'm on my way," Seth told Marcus.

"We'll be there soon," Bastien promised his wife.

Seth put away his phone and looked at Chris. "Ami's water broke."

Zach spoke up. "Go. I'll get Chris and Cliff back to the network."

"Thank you. Come to David's afterward. Dr. Kimiko said once Ami's water broke, there would be no turning back, that we couldn't risk putting the delivery off any longer for fear of Ami or the baby developing an infection. So she'll have to deliver tonight, and I want every healer in the area on hand."

Zach nodded. "We'll be right behind you."

Seth crossed to Bastien, grabbed his shoulder, and teleported them away.

Zach, Lisette, Chris, and Cliff stared at each other in somber silence.

"I hope she'll be okay," Cliff said softly. "The baby, too."

Suddenly his insubordination seemed meaningless.

Zach commanded the others to close in, then teleported them all to network headquarters.

After the kindness Ami had shown him, he wanted to be there for her in case she should need him.

Chapter Fifteen

Over a dozen immortals and their Seconds occupied David's living room in what felt to Lisette alarmingly like a deathbed vigil.

Every available chair, love seat, sofa, coffee table, and footstool was occupied.

Lisette sat in a flat-wing chair with Tracy wedged in beside her. Like children awaiting punishment by a stern parent, they held hands and tried to will strength and hope into the small mortal woman laboring in the next room.

Utter silence reigned, broken only by Ami's labored breaths.

Zach, Seth, David, Marcus, Melanie, and Dr. Kimiko were all with her in the delivery room. Roland and Sean had been asked to linger in the recovery room, ready to rush forward in the event the babe should require healing once delivered. The other three healers might be either too sapped from pouring their healing energy into Ami or too busy trying to keep Ami from slipping away from them to heal the babe themselves.

Marcus whispered words of love and praise and encouragement to his wife and, by all accounts, had not released her hand since discovering her water had broken.

Melanie and Dr. Kimiko monitored Ami every second, guiding her through breathing exercises as contraction upon contraction gripped her, murmuring medical nonsense to each other, and assuring Ami she was doing well. But an underlying thread of tension resided in their voices that led Lisette and the other immortals listening to believe that all was *not* well.

What's a cervix? Zach asked her suddenly.

Lisette blinked. *What?*

What's a cervix? Apparently Ami's has stopped dilating despite the hard contractions, which I gather is not a good thing.

Ummm . . . It's a . . . female thing . . .

I already knew that. What is it and where is it located?

I don't know, Lisette admitted.

How can you not know? You're a woman.

Yes, a woman born in a time when women didn't sit around discussing their lady parts.

He swore.

Hang on. She turned to her Second. *Tracy?*

Slumped beside her, face pensive, Tracy looked over at her. *Yeah?*

What's a cervix?

Her eyebrows flew up. *It's . . . ummmm . . .* Her eyes roved the room as she thought about it. *Actually, I'm not sure.*

Lisette didn't feel so bad now. "Does anyone know what a cervix is?" she asked the room at large, frustration mounting. Since Ami was mortal, Lisette didn't fear her overhearing them. And, if Zach needed to know, Lisette would do whatever she had to, to find out for him, even if she had to use Darnell's laptop to look it up on the damned Internet.

Everyone present stared at her with *what the hell* looks.

"A cervix?" she repeated. "Anyone know what it is?"

Sheldon slowly raised his hand.

Tracy rolled her eyes. "Sheldon, put your hand down. Watching porn does *not* teach you what a cervix is."

He grinned. "I didn't learn it from porn. I read up on pregnancy and childbirth after Seth told us Ami was pregnant."

Tracy's face lit with surprise. "Oh."

"The cervix is the lower portion of the uterus that opens into the vagina. During pregnancy it closes to hold the baby inside the uterus. During labor, it dilates or widens to allow the baby to pass from the uterus into the vagina."

Everyone stared.

Yuri looked around. "Anyone else think that was too much information?"

Every male save Sheldon raised a hand.

Did you hear that? Lisette asked Zach.

Yes. Thank you.

His presence in her mind receded.

Once more, Lisette waited with the others.

Stanislav cleared his throat. "How bizarre is it that Sheldon knows more about a woman's body than the women present do?"

Sheldon smiled.

More waiting.

More unbearable tension.

Several knees bobbed up and down.

Anxious teeth abused fingernails.

Stanislav's Second, Alexei, paced back and forth and back and forth until several voices shouted at him to sit the hell down.

Suddenly, Zach swore.

What? Lisette asked, unable to remain silent.

Dr. Kimiko is recommending a cesarean.

Seth studied Dr. Kimiko. "Is there no other way?"

She shook her head. "I fully understand the ramifications

and wouldn't recommend this if it weren't absolutely necessary."

He looked to Melanie.

Melanie nodded.

Marcus's eyes, when they rose to meet Seth's, carried fear and dread and a desperate need for Seth to assure him that everything would be okay.

How Seth wished he could make that promise.

Seth leaned down and stroked Ami's hair. "Sweetheart, the babe is being stubborn. Dr. Kimiko and Melanie think a cesarean is necessary to bring her into the world."

Ami nodded, her sweet face pinched with pain as she breathed through another contraction. "Do it."

"You know they can't sedate you or numb you. Because the babe carries both alien and *gifted one* DNA, we have no way of knowing how the medication would affect her."

"I know. It doesn't matter."

"David and I may have to—"

"Just do it," she commanded. "I endured six months of torture. I can endure this." She looked at the doctors. "Do it. Whatever it takes. Just keep her safe."

That was all they needed to hear. The two women went to work. Sterile drapes replaced the lightweight hospital gown that covered Ami's belly and the monitors strapped to it.

Melanie placed a short screen above Ami's abdomen that blocked her view. "To keep the field sterile," she told Ami with a smile, then looked to Seth. *And so she won't have to watch us cut her.*

Seth and David had been monitoring Melanie's thoughts ever since they had arrived so she could think concerns to them that she didn't want to voice in front of Ami and Marcus.

Melanie wheeled a tray of surgical instruments closer to the table while Dr. Kimiko scrubbed for surgery. Seth hadn't even thought about germs, assuming he could heal any infection that resulted if Ami's own incredible regenerative capabilities failed her. But he supposed Dr. Kimiko had some concerns for the baby. None knew what kind of immune system the child would possess. Or if she would even possess one. None knew if the babe was infected with the virus. Ami had had such difficulty carrying the baby to term that testing the babe in utero had been deemed too risky.

Seth retook his position beside David at Ami's head and placed a hand on her shoulder. He met David's gaze and saw the same dread reflected in his dark eyes that Seth felt himself.

He nodded to Dr. Kimiko.

Dr. Kimiko made a horizontal incision on Ami's lower abdomen.

Ami stiffened and clutched Marcus's hand so tightly her knuckles turned white. Pain contorted her features. Her breathing turned harsh. But she made no other sound, didn't scream or moan, her ability to remain silent a holdover from the torture she had endured.

Marcus leaned so close to her their noses practically touched, maintaining eye contact. Seth overheard Marcus speaking to her mentally and knew Ami listened to every word, drawing what comfort she could from it.

Before Dr. Kimiko could make another incision, the first began to heal and seal itself. She met Seth's gaze.

Steeling himself against the pain he knew he was about to inflict, he refocused his energy and used it to *prevent* Ami from healing. The temperature in the room rose a degree as David, then Zach, threw their energy into the mix.

Seth's eyes burned as he felt Ami's pain magnify tenfold.

Lisette, and everyone else present, cringed at the first whimper that escaped Ami. Another followed. And another. Then a moan.

She heard sniffles and could almost see the tears trailing down Ami's pale temples.

Which was more painful, Lisette wondered: Being cut? Or Seth and David's preventing Ami's body from doing what it did naturally and healing itself?

Another whimper.

She feared it was the latter.

Ami cried out in agony.

Darnell leaned forward and buried his face in his hands, his bald, brown head gleaming in the overhead light. Closer to Ami than anyone else in the room, he was clearly terrified for her.

Tracy tightened her hold on Lisette's hand. "Anything?" she whispered.

Lisette shook her head. Zach hadn't said a word since the cesarean had begun, and Lisette didn't dare distract him. She didn't know how large a role he played.

Icy fear abruptly breezed through her like a winter wind.

Lisette stopped breathing.

Not *her* fear. Zach's.

The babe isn't breathing, he told her.

Lisette's eyes burned as tears welled.

"What's happening?" she heard Ami ask, voice trembling.

"What's wrong?" Marcus asked in clipped tones. "Is the babe okay? Why isn't she crying? Shouldn't she be crying?"

"Roland. Sean," Seth bit out.

Jenna turned her face into Richart's chest. Richart wrapped his arms around her and held her tight.

Tears slipped down cheeks as Marcus repeatedly asked about the babe, each question growing more frantic than the last.

Ami began to sob softly, her questions growing weaker.

"Roland," Seth pressed.

"I'm trying," Roland snapped.

"What's happening?" Darnell asked, face still hidden in

his hands. Like the other mortals present, he couldn't hear the terse comments issued in the infirmary. He knew only that Ami's cries had ended.

Lisette could barely swallow past the lump in her throat. "The babe isn't breathing," she whispered, almost afraid that saying it aloud would make the horror more real. "Roland is trying to help her. Sean, too, I think."

Krysta buried her face in Étienne's shirt. Étienne buried his in her hair and clutched her close.

Moments passed, so long and filled with tension that Lisette wanted to scream.

Then the high-pitched wail of an infant broke the silence.

Lisette's breath escaped in a whoosh. Tears blurred her vision and spilled over her lashes.

Several others breathed sighs of relief. Heads dropped back against chairs.

Darnell raised his head, his eyes red and full of moisture.

"She's okay," Roland said in the infirmary, his voice full of relief and exuberance. "She's okay. She's breathing on her own now. She's okay."

"The baby's breathing," Lisette told Darnell and the others.

Some of the tension left the room.

Some, not all. They had yet to learn if the babe were infected with the virus.

"You hear that, Ami?" Marcus murmured, elation brightening his words. "She's okay." He laughed. "And listen to her work those lungs!"

Lisette smiled through her tears. The poor babe sounded pissed.

"Ami?" Marcus said, the jubilance draining from his voice. "Ami, sweetling?"

Everyone tensed.

"Ami?" Marcus called, his panic palpable. "Why isn't she responding? What's wrong with her?"

"Dr. Kimiko," Seth said.

"Ami, can you hear me?" the doctor asked. In a lower voice, she said, "The incisions aren't healing. Are you still blocking her regenerative capabilities?"

"No," Seth answered.

"Is she bleeding internally?"

"No."

"Her pulse is thready. Are you trying to heal her?"

"Yes. I'm pouring as much strength and energy into her as I can," Seth said.

"As am I," David added.

"And I." Zach said.

Minutes ticked past. Minutes during which the babe's cries quieted to snuffles. Since the doctors were occupied with Ami, Lisette assumed Roland and Sean were cleaning up the baby. Wrapping her in a warm blanket. Doing . . . whatever it was that doctors and nurses did to newborns.

"Ami?" Marcus repeated, his voice choked and barely climbing above a whisper. "Come on, sweetling. Don't do this to me. Don't leave me. Please."

"The incisions are starting to heal," Dr. Kimiko announced. "Her pulse is getting stronger."

"Her blood pressure is improving, too," Melanie murmured.

Lisette conveyed the latest to the Seconds present.

More minutes.

More knees bobbing up and down.

More nail chewing.

"She's stable," Dr. Kimiko announced.

"Seth?" Marcus asked.

"I think Ami has slipped into her healing sleep," Seth told him.

"You think or you know?"

A pause. "I think. If she has, it's different this time, perhaps because we depleted her energy and kept her from healing long enough for the babe to be born."

"Is she going to be okay?"

"Yes."

"Seth," Zach said, a faint reprimand.

"She'll be okay," Seth insisted, "if I have to feed her energy twenty-four hours a day until she wakes up. She'll be okay."

Seated at his desk in network headquarters, Chris Reordon rubbed eyes that burned from fatigue. He'd pulled too many all-nighters lately, trying to help Seth track down whoever the hell was betraying the Immortal Guardians. Now one of the vampires had admitted to leaving the area he was allowed to roam at headquarters and had stolen high-tech equipment, so Chris had to watch last night's surveillance video to see what else the young vamp might have gotten into.

Dragging his hands down his face, he eyed with longing the cushy seven-foot sofa that had been his sleeping place more often of late than his bed at home. He looked at the clock.

No. He needed to get this shit done, so he could fill Seth in as soon as Seth finished helping Ami. Another concern.

Sheldon, of all people, had been thoughtful enough to text Chris and send him updates. According to the last, the babe was breathing (it had been a long damn wait for that text after Sheldon had texted him that the babe *wasn't* breathing), but Ami had slipped into what Seth and the others *hoped* was a healing sleep and remained unresponsive.

Seth continued to try to revive her.

Chris forced himself to refocus on the computer screen. Nearly the size of one of the large-screen televisions every sports fan dreamed of owning, it bathed his office in faint blue light. A sleek desk lamp provided a small circle of sunny illumination in which his trusty notebook and pencil rested.

Multiple windows divided the monitor's screen, each offering video surveillance footage from the cameras on sublevels four and five. Chris touched the space bar on the keyboard and set all of the videos into motion.

He had feigned anger earlier when the young vampire had admitted his deed, but it had just been for show. Since Cliff, one of the first three vampires ever to reside at network headquarters, had made this his home, he had won Chris's respect. Descending into madness was a harsh price to pay for a stupid mistake made in one's teen years. And Cliff had succeeded longer than any of the others in staving off the insanity. The young man had a will as strong as iron. Courage, too. And honor. Chris couldn't help but like him.

Did Chris like that Cliff had flagrantly disobeyed the rules and stolen from the network?

No. But Chris sure as hell admired the kid's reasons for doing it. And the tracking device Cliff had planted would provide them with invaluable information. Chris's tech team already worked on tracing the newbie vampire's return to what they hoped would be the vampires' lair.

Chris was curious to see what the lair of such well-trained vampires would comprise.

He grunted when the footage he sought finally rolled around. "There he goes," he murmured, scribbling the camera number and video time code in his notebook.

Biting into an apple, Cliff strode down the hallway toward the open door of Melanie's office and headed inside. Anyone not specifically looking for it would have missed the barely noticeable blur that shot from the room a few minutes later.

Chris turned his attention to the camera focused on the elevator doors and rewound the video several frames. Dr. Whetsman stepped off the elevator and greeted Todd and the other guards. At the last possible moment before the elevator doors slid closed, Cliff swept inside. A couple of guards looked around with a frown, but most hadn't noticed the breeze the vamp created as Dr. Whetsman distracted them with his latest bitch fest.

Millisecond by millisecond, Chris was able to piece together and track the shrewd vampire's progress as he sped through the fourth sublevel to the room the techies used to store the expensive toys they designed for immortals, Seconds, and network guards.

The kid was smart.

By all appearances, Cliff had only taken two tracking devices (one of which he had returned to Chris earlier), then had gone right back to Melanie's office on the fifth sublevel. But Chris couldn't afford to take chances. He needed to be certain. So he grasped the hot, steaming mug of coffee he hadn't noticed his assistant place at his elbow, downed a few scalding gulps, reached for the sandwich she had also thoughtfully provided, then continued to watch the video.

Hours ticked by as he scoured footage from all five sublevels, then moved on to the ground floor.

The texts from Sheldon stopped around sunrise. Still no change in Ami.

Chris couldn't bring himself to ask about the baby. Was the little one infected with the virus? Was she vampire?

Something caught his eye in the footage provided by the camera aimed at the large granite desk. The guards seated behind it cleared every employee who entered and exited the building, ensuring no one who didn't belong got past the foyer.

The big bite of sandwich Chris had taken nearly flew out of his mouth.

"What the hell?" He rewound the video. Played it forward in painfully slow increments. Gaped at what it revealed.

Shoving the sandwich plate aside so forcefully it skidded

across his desk and tumbled to the floor, Chris wrote furiously in his ever-present notebook.

Two hours later, he sat back and stared at the computer screen.

He needed to talk to Seth, but—last he had heard—Seth was still pouring energy into Ami, trying to heal her or revive her or whatever it took to get her to open her eyes. David probably was, too.

Picking up the phone, he dialed Darnell's number.

"Yeah?"

"Hey. How's Ami?" Chris asked.

"Still unresponsive," Darnell said, voice grave. "Seth said she didn't even rouse when Melanie put the baby to Ami's breast to see if she would nurse."

"The baby's . . . okay?" Chris forced himself to ask.

Darnell lowered his voice to a whisper. "No fangs or glowing eyes, if that's what you're asking. And Roland said he couldn't smell the virus on her."

"What about Seth or David?"

"They can't either, but"—his voice quieted even more—"they're both exhausted. I don't know how they're even still conscious. They haven't stopped pouring energy into Ami since her labor began."

Shit.

"What's wrong?" Darnell asked when Chris went silent.

"I need to talk to them."

"Can you do it here?"

"Can I use your laptop?"

"Of course."

"Then, yes. Hey, did the baby nurse?"

"Tried to. Ami's milk hasn't come in. But Melanie said that's normal, that—for human women—it can take three or four days."

Which didn't necessarily mean Ami's milk would follow the same timetable or come in at all. It sounded as though they weren't even sure Ami would live. "Okay. I'll be there shortly."

Zach.

Zach's eyes flew open.

Curled up beside him in bed in the quiet room they had claimed for the day, Lisette slept deeply.

They hadn't made love before retiring. Both had felt too drained: Zach drained of energy and Lisette drained emotionally from the hours of worry and anxiety that had gripped her as Ami had labored. Instead they had clung to each other, absorbing the peace and comfort it brought them.

Zach, Seth repeated in his head.

What?

Meet me in David's study.

Zach glanced at the clock beside the bed. Only an hour had passed since he and Lisette had drifted off to sleep. Sighing, he gently lifted the arm Lisette had thrown across his chest and rested it on her side, then tried to ease out from under the thigh she had draped over him. He swore as he grew hard from the sweet contact.

Lisette slid her arm back across his chest and scooted closer. "What are you doing? Don't go."

"I have to. Seth needs me."

She lifted her head.

Zach smiled.

Her long raven hair, loose and tangled, obscured most of her face. Her adorable features contorted in a frown as she batted it out of the way and peered up at him with heavy-lidded eyes. "Is it Ami?"

"I don't think so. He told me to meet him in the study."

"Oh. Okay."

With great reluctance, Zach slid out from under her and

stood beside the bed. "Go back to sleep." He leaned down and pressed a quick kiss to her lips.

"Hurry back," she murmured, and dropped her head onto his pillow, hugging it to her chest.

Zach brushed a hand over her hair, then donned a pair of pants and slipped from the room.

Across the hall, Roland Warbrook eased from the bedroom he and Sarah shared, his feet bare like Zach's, his hair tousled from sleep.

The two men shared a look.

Roland had never apologized for choking Zach with a piano wire when he, Sarah, and Lisette had captured Zach and interrogated him. But Zach didn't hold it against him.

"Infirmary?" Roland asked. Apparently he had been summoned for a different purpose.

Zach shook his head. "David's study."

They headed upstairs.

Roland continued on to the infirmary. Zach turned into David's study.

Darnell waited within. "Hey."

Zach nodded.

When Darnell motioned to one of the chairs in front of David's desk, Zach sank down in the comfortable leather and unashamedly eavesdropped on the infirmary.

"What's up?" Roland asked.

"David and I need to meet with Chris. Would you sit with Ami and feed her healing energy until one of us returns?"

"Of course. Has there been any change?"

"No. Get some blood in you first to strengthen you."

"Do you want me to bring some for you and David?"

"I'll take some," David said.

"None for me, thanks," Seth refused.

Several minutes later, Seth and David strode into the study.

David looked as he always did, but walked with slower steps and bore an air of fatigue.

Seth . . . looked like shit. His shoulders slumped with exhaustion. Dark circles had once more found a home beneath his eyes. Lines of strain bracketed his mouth. His skin bore a sickly pallor. His cheeks seemed hollower.

"Zach," Seth greeted him. He even sounded tired.

"How long do you intend to keep this up?" Zach asked. Unlike David's, Seth's strength and energy couldn't be restored with a simple blood infusion.

"As long as I can." Seth sank into the chair beside him.

Sighing, Zach held out his hand. "Give me your phone."

"I'm fine."

"Bullshit. You're expending energy like there's no tomorrow. Teleporting all over creation to rescue your precious Immortal Guardians on top of that will totally deplete you."

David paused beside Seth's chair and rested a hand on Seth's chest.

Seth gasped and gripped the arms of his chair. The lines in his face smoothed out. The dark circles vanished. Color returned, not quite healthy, but certainly *healthier*.

Relaxing once more, Seth stared up at David. "I didn't know you could do that."

David shrugged and patted Seth's shoulder. "Neither did I. I really didn't expect it to work." He started around the desk and staggered.

Seth jumped up and gripped David's arm to steady him. "Darnell."

"I'm on it." Darnell hurried from the room.

Zach watched Seth guide David to the comfortably worn chair behind the desk.

David boasted more power than Zach had realized if he could replenish so much of Seth's energy that soon after losing his own and needing blood.

Darnell rushed back into the room, bearing bags of blood he piled on David's desk.

Chris entered on his heels, a battered-all-to-hell leather

briefcase in one hand and a cooler in the other. He frowned when he saw David sink his fangs into a bag of blood. "Everything okay?"

Seth nodded. "What's in the cooler?"

Chris set the cooler on the desk and opened the top. Zach and the others leaned forward to peer inside.

Lined up in neat rows were over a dozen plastic bags, each roughly the size of a soda can, full of white liquid.

"What's that?" Darnell asked.

"Breast milk," Chris replied.

Seth's eyebrows rose. "Whose breast milk?"

"Jasmine Harris donated it. She works in medical at the network."

All stared at him.

"And she just happened to have some breast milk on hand?" Zach asked.

"Of course not. A couple of months ago I consulted her about newborn babies' needs. She's a doctor and a mother, so I figured she would know best. Turns out she's still breast-feeding her toddler. I like to prepare for every possibility. So I asked her if she would be willing to donate some milk. She said yes without even asking for whom. So"—he waved a hand over the cooler—"*voilà*. And there's more where that came from, should you need it."

Zach looked at Seth. "He really *does* think of everything."

Seth nodded.

Chris turned to the door. "Linda?"

Linda, a friend of Melanie's and another doctor from the network, poked her head in. "Yes?"

"Would you please put this in the fridge?"

Smiling, she entered.

The men all smiled and nodded to her as she took the cooler from Chris.

After she left, Chris leaned forward and lowered his voice. "I knew Melanie and Dr. Kimiko were probably resting and assumed you guys wouldn't feel comfortable helping Marcus get the baby to latch on every two or three hours when it's time to feed her."

Didn't babies just latch on naturally? Zach thought, then blinked. Wait. Newborns fed every two or three hours? "If you're going to bottle feed her, why do you need Linda?"

"Dr. Harris suggested we let the baby nurse for a bit first, *then* bottle feed her the milk. Something about avoiding nipple confusion, whatever the hell that is, and reducing the chances of the baby refusing to breastfeed later when Ami's milk comes in?" Chris said, phrasing it as a question, as if he were as clueless as the rest of them.

Only Seth seemed to know what it all meant.

"Any luck tracking the vampire?" David asked.

"Some. He's holed up with nine others in a house outside of Pittsboro. One that's too small to be the main lair."

"Are you sure there aren't extensive tunnels beneath it like Bastien's?" Seth asked.

"Yeah. I had one of my contacts do a satellite thermal-imaging scan. There were only ten men, all with the cooler body temperatures of a vampire, so we're waiting to see if they'll lead us to the lair once the sun sets."

Zach frowned. "Won't they find the tracking device in the meantime?"

"It's a risk we'll have to take," Seth murmured. "Their minds will yield no information. And moving in now and killing them will net us nothing."

Nevertheless, it didn't sit well with Zach.

"Was that why you wanted to see us?" Seth asked Chris.

"No. I need to show you something. Darnell, can I use your laptop?"

Darnell opened a laptop on the corner of David's desk and, moving some medical texts aside, slid it toward the center.

Chris circled the desk and stood beside David. Pulling a

small metal device from his briefcase, he connected it to the computer and began dragging his finger across the smooth touchpad on the keyboard.

Seth waved Zach forward.

Zach joined them behind the desk.

David sat up straighter as the blood went to work restoring his strength.

The image on the computer screen changed from a tranquil Zen garden to what appeared to be a hallway in network headquarters. Zach had visited the network several times during his stint as "Temporary Seth" and recognized it as the fifth sublevel.

Chris straightened. "I've been pouring over surveillance video, wanting to see if Cliff ventured anywhere else he shouldn't have while he was off swiping the tracking devices."

"Did he?" Seth asked.

"No. Here's the video, in slow motion, taken from every camera he passed on his foray." He pressed a button on the keyboard.

Zach watched the blurry, indistinct form (which moved too quickly for the camera to catch clearly) zip from the fifth sublevel up to the room the tracking devices were stored in on the fourth floor. Once the vampire pocketed the devices, he raced back to the fifth sublevel, making no other stops.

Chris pressed a key and paused the video just as a shot of the lobby appeared. "I wanted to make sure he didn't make any other excursions later on, so I kept looking and found this." He pressed the key again, restarting the video.

The lobby was decorated in shades of gray, the only color provided by potted peace lilies. The central focus of the camera was a large granite-topped security desk. Half a dozen guards sat behind it, their eyes fastened to monitors hidden from view. A few yards beyond them, over a dozen more guarded elevator doors.

A tall figure, garbed in a long black coat, suddenly appeared in front of the security desk.

The men behind it jumped and reached for their weapons. Before they could draw them, the figure waved a hand.

The guards' expressions went blank. They retook their seats, their posture relaxed.

One of the guards nodded and spoke to the figure.

"The cameras don't record audio," Chris mentioned apologetically.

The dark figure strolled over to one of the elevators. The guards there didn't appear to see him.

The doors slid open. The figure stepped inside.

The scene cut to surveillance footage of the elevator.

The figure kept his head turned away from the camera. Bearing the dark hair, height, and build common among immortal males, this man could have been any of them.

The video cut from scene to scene, following the mysterious figure to a room full of file cabinets.

"He stayed in the records room for the longest," Chris said, "always keeping his face turned away from the camera." The video sped up, showing the immortal pulling out this drawer or that and removing file folders.

Seth leaned forward and planted his hands on David's desk. "He isn't even *trying* to hide his presence. If he were, he would be doing all of this at preternatural speeds to avoid being videotaped or having it show up on the security monitors."

"He didn't have to," Chris said. "None of the guards have any recollection of encountering him. None saw anything unusual on the surveillance cameras. So none of us would have ever looked at this footage twice if Cliff hadn't stolen the tracking devices."

Zach caught Seth's eye. "Mind control? Memory wipes?"

"Had to be either one or the other."

The figure returned to the first floor and traveled down a hallway Zach hadn't seen before, all of Zach's visits having taken him below. The figure waved a hand, bypassing security locks each time he encountered them, and ultimately entered a swanky, modern office.

"Where is he now?" Zach asked.

"My office," Chris said, his jaw clenching. "He must have known where all of the other cameras were located by reading the guards' minds because he missed a couple here. There are hidden cameras in my office that only *I* know about."

The immortal crossed to a row of tall file cabinets that lined one wall and began to draw out files. Upon finding whatever he sought, he turned and leaned a shoulder against the cabinets while he perused the papers.

Whatever camera Chris had hidden caught a perfect image of the immortal's face.

"Aidan," Seth said.

David swore.

Chris eyed them with sympathy. "Looks like we've found your traitor."

"I don't understand," Seth muttered. "All this because I wouldn't transfer him to North Carolina? I know I told Lisette it was possible, but . . ."

Brooding silence.

"You already knew he was hiding something from you," Zach mentioned.

"Lisette was hiding something from me, too, and look how badly I misjudged *her.*" Seth straightened. "I don't want to make the same mistake twice." He looked at Zach. "Or thrice. I misjudged you, as well."

Zach snorted. "I don't count. Even *I* would have suspected me."

"*I* sure as hell did," David added.

Seth shook his head. "Aidan is damned near as even-tempered as David. It just seems out of character for him to . . . to do something so heinous."

Chris motioned to the laptop. "The proof is indisputable. If memory wipes damage brains, he just damaged the brains of several of my men to keep them from remembering his little visit." And Chris was pissed.

"If Aidan feels I've wronged him," Seth demanded, "why not come after *me?* Why endanger *all* Immortal Guardians by raising this vampire army?"

"Because he knows your weakness," David murmured. "We *all* know your weakness."

Seth turned to him.

David's expression gentled. "Everyone knows the surest way to hurt you is to harm one of your Immortal Guardians."

"*One* of my Immortal Guardians. This threatens you all. This threatens humans, as well. If vampires were to gain the upper hand . . ."

He didn't have to finish.

"Has any immortal ever gone crazy from too much solitude?" Chris asked.

Seth shook his head. "Never. One of the reasons I started assigning Seconds to immortals in the first place, aside from knowing they needed someone to guard them and take care of business for them during daylight hours, was to keep immortals from leading too solitary an existence. I wanted them to have friends and companions to help keep the loneliness at bay."

Roland spoke in the infirmary. "I went hundreds of years without having a Second, and *I* didn't go crazy." He must have been listening. "But there's a big difference between insanity and bitterness. Bitterness can spawn a madness all its own . . . as you well know, Seth, having walked me back from that edge a few times over the centuries."

Seth closed his eyes and pinched the bridge of his nose. "Zach."

"What?"

"Can you capture Aidan and incarcerate him at network headquarters?"

"Yes."

"On your own?"

"Yes."

"Without killing him?"

"If I must."

"Then do it. If I did it myself and he were to fight me . . ." He sighed. "I don't have as much control over my powers when I'm this weary and don't want to inadvertently kill him before I can interrogate him."

Zach wasn't nearly as tired as Seth and suspected he would have a hard time reining himself in, too. He wanted the bastard dead in the worst way now that he knew Aidan was guilty. He turned to Chris. "Can you do anything to prevent Aidan from freeing himself by using mind control on the guards and getting them to unlock his prison door once he's in custody at the network?"

"Yes," Chris responded. "Teleport me there now and give me a couple of hours. I'll have my guys weld the door of one of the holding rooms closed so the guards won't be able to free him even if they want to."

"What's to keep him from teleporting out?" Zach asked.

Chris swore. "Can you sedate him when you capture him?"

"Yes."

Seth spoke up. "Use the same dosage the new vampires used on Lisette. Even as old as he is, it should knock him out for a day or two. Have Melanie prepare an auto-injector for you before you leave."

"I'll do it now," Zach said.

"No, let her rest a little longer. Chris needs the extra time to weld the door shut anyway. And chain Aidan with the strongest chains available. If he should awaken earlier than we expect and is chained, he won't be able to teleport without taking the whole damned building with him."

"Oh, I'll chain him." Dark anticipation rose within Zach. "Trust me. He won't escape. As soon as Chris calls me and lets me know they're ready for him, I'll bring his ass in."

"Don't kill him," Seth reiterated.

"I won't," Zach promised.

He never said he wouldn't hurt him.

Chapter Sixteen

Aidan sat in darkness. Alone. Waiting.

He had sent his Second on a series of errands that would keep him away until sunrise, so the modest home they shared was quiet.

Aidan knew what was coming.

Or *who* was coming.

The soft leather of his favorite wingback chair, worn smooth by the many hours he had spent in it over the decades, creaked as he slid his booted foot off his knee and planted both feet on the floor.

His arms rested upon those of the chair, his hands dangling over the ends.

Aside from the beating of his own heart and the nearly undetectable rustle of his clothing as his chest rose and fell with each breath, no sound infringed upon the night.

Quiet, once a balm, now pricked him like needles.

He had to force himself to remain still, to suppress the desire to pace. To rage. To commit violence.

Someone had been inside his home.

He had known the instant he had awoken. Someone had been inside his home *and* inside his head.

Aidan had found a single drop of blood on his pillow. Had felt something . . . off in his mind. In his thoughts. And he'd known.

Only one immortal could've entered his home without alerting Aidan's Second. Only one immortal could've then forced Aidan into a virtual coma while he dynamited the walls Aidan had erected in his mind, prowled around, and stole memories that didn't belong to him.

Seth. Leader of the Immortal Guardians.

Once a friend.

A friend no longer.

Aidan's fingers curled over the ends of the chair arms and gripped the leather.

He had heard that some hitherto unknown immortal had been fielding Seth's calls for the past couple of days. Rumors had been flying over why. *And* over the mysterious immortal's identity. Apparently he was ancient. Yet no immortal had ever heard of him.

Aidan didn't know the who, but—unlike the others—he didn't have to speculate on the why. Seth knew. He knew an immortal had betrayed him and, like a bloodhound, had been sniffing out the culprit.

Aidan didn't know why Seth hadn't confronted him after scouring his damned brain. Something must have called him away. Perhaps the mortal woman, Ami, whom Seth had come to love like a daughter. Rumors abounded over her, too. But Aidan didn't concern himself with such.

Seth knew.

And, when he returned, there would be a reckoning.

Aidan tensed as he abruptly heard the heartbeat of another.

His eyes pierced the darkness, his vision sharper than a cat's, yet failed to find the elder.

He rose. "I know you're there. You may as well show yourself."

The silence stretched, broken only by that slow, steady heartbeat.

"Seth . . ."

The air stirred. A fist plowed into Aidan's face, striking him so hard that Aidan flew backward and went through the wall behind him. A shadow, moving so quickly that even Aidan couldn't see him clearly, poured through the gaping hole he had created and delivered another blow. And another.

Aidan fought with nearly three thousand years of training at his back and barely managed to land a punch. It was like trying to fight a tornado.

Fingers wrapped around his throat, lifted him, and slammed him down so hard the wooden floor buckled and Aidan damned near fell through to the first floor.

As Aidan lay there, choking on the blood pouring down his throat from loose teeth and his broken nose, his assailant's face swam into view.

Shock seized him.

"Who the fuck are you?" he wheezed.

Zach stared down at the traitor, wanting so badly to kill him, *needing* so badly to kill him.

This bastard was responsible for Lisette's nearly dying.

Rage burned his stomach like acid as Zach leaned in close and gripped Aidan by the throat. "I'm the dog Seth sicced on you."

The room around him fell away as Aidan teleported them to a darkened mountain range.

Zach's hold didn't loosen. "Anywhere you teleport, you take me with you, dumb ass."

Aidan fought harder, using telekinesis to hurl large stones

and other objects at Zach, as he pried at the fingers closing off his air.

Zach merely tightened his grip.

Aidan teleported them again, this time to a sunny vale.

Warmth washed over Zach's back . . . which remained unblemished. Minutes passed while Zach continued to choke Aidan, fending off his blows and repaying them with many of his own. Eventually Aidan began to sunburn.

Zach didn't and saw the surprise in the younger immortal's eyes. "That's right, asshole. Like Seth, I'm impervious to daylight."

Aidan returned them to his home.

A dagger leapt from a stand on the wall and slid into Aidan's grip. Aidan slashed at Zach and managed to draw blood before Zach closed his hand around Aidan's on the dagger and made Aidan stab himself in the arm.

Furniture shattered as the struggle continued, Aidan taking nearly all of the damage.

Zach had a *lot* of anger to burn.

"Where's Seth?" Aidan gritted.

"Seth was furious enough that he feared he might kill you, so he sent me in his stead." Tired of playing, Zach pinned Aidan in place with a powerful telekinetic push.

Aidan's eyes widened.

Zach sneered down at him. "How I wish I could kill you myself." He drew an auto-injector from his back pocket. "Or maim you in ways the virus can't heal. Let you suffer as others have suffered because of your perfidy. Alas, it isn't my fucking place to do so."

Zach jabbed the auto-injector into Aidan's neck with more force than necessary.

Just as Lisette had, the immortal instantly went limp.

* * *

Wrapping a towel around herself sarong-style, Lisette looked up from tucking the end between her breasts as the bedroom door swung open.

Zach strode in, clad in his usual leather pants and boots.

She smiled. "Damn, you look good."

He grinned. "I *feel* good now that I'm with you." Halting, he swore and closed the door behind him.

"What?"

"I missed it."

"Missed what?"

"You. Naked in the shower. Water cascading down over your soft-as-silk skin and skimming off the tips of your bewitching breasts." His eyes began to glow as a noticeable bulge rose behind his zipper.

Lisette started toward him, then noticed his bruised and bloodied hands, the red smears on his arms and chest. "Zach! What have you done now?" she asked, propping her hands on her hips.

"Moi?" he asked, his expression as innocent as a choirboy's. Until he followed her gaze to the blood. "Oh." He winced. "Right. That."

She rolled her eyes. (Was this how Melanie felt, constantly having to deal with Bastien's crazy antics?) "Explain."

"We found him."

"Found whom?"

"The immortal who has betrayed us."

Lisette didn't let him see how thrilled she was to hear him include himself in the Immortal Guardian family. "Was it Aidan?"

"Yes."

"You read his mind?"

"We didn't have to. Reordon has surveillance tape of Aidan breeching network headquarters, using mind control on the guards, wiping memories—"

"*Merde!*"

"—and helping himself to confidential files in both the records room and Reordon's private office."

They had known an immortal had betrayed them, had even suspected Aidan, but . . . it still confounded.

"What happened? What did you do?"

"Seth asked me to capture him and incarcerate him at the network."

She looked pointedly at his hands, which finished healing even as she spoke. "And you—what?—scraped your knuckles on the doorframe on your way in?"

"I might have kicked his ass a little first."

"Zach—"

His face darkened. One second he stood by the door; the next he loomed over her, his eyes glowing with rage. "He hurt you."

"He wasn't even there the night—"

"He has probably been culling information from the network for weeks. Perhaps months. And he used that information to up the dosage of the sedative so it would bring you to the brink of death."

An experience she never wished to repeat. "So you kicked his ass."

"And wanted to kill him so badly I could taste it," he growled. "I wanted him to pay, Lisette. I wanted him to pay in blood. I wanted to do to him what the Others did to me."

Biting her lip, she leaned forward and raised her arms to embrace him.

Zach backed away before she could. "Hold that thought. I need to wash his filth off me." He vanished. Water began to flow.

Lisette turned to face the bathroom. Through the open door, she saw steam rising inside the shower as soap-suds flew.

The cascade of water ceased. Zach stepped out and grabbed a towel.

Not even a full minute had passed.

He met her gaze. Blurred. Then slowed and tossed the damp towel on the counter beside the sink. Naked, aroused, his gaze a brilliant gold, he strode toward her. "Drop the towel."

The towel hit her feet. Lisette was so entranced by the heat pouring off of him and the sight of his leanly muscled body as he drew closer that she wasn't sure if *she* had released the towel or if Zach had used telekinesis to rid her of it.

Stopping inches away, he drew his knuckles down her cheek. "I believe you once promised to ride me hard?" He quirked a brow.

Lisette grinned. "I believe you're right."

Lifting her up so she could straddle his waist, he fell backward onto the bed.

The sound that bubbled up from Lisette as she tumbled down on top of him could only be described as a giggle. To hear such a happy, youthful sound emerge from her after two centuries of guilt and weariness and violence and know that *he* had coaxed it forth meant the world to Zach.

Her long raven tresses, which she must have blown dry just before he had arrived, spilled down around them in a midnight curtain as she straddled him and settled her core directly over his erection. Hunger rose, as did the desire to feel her warm, slick walls enfolding him and squeezing him tight.

He settled his hands on her thighs, every muscle tightening with need.

She braced her hands on his chest, her lovely eyes shining amber as she gazed down at him. Humor faded. Her smile turned wicked. She toyed with his nipples, gave them a pinch, then curled her hands into claws and drew her nails lightly down his chest and abdomen and—*shit!*—it felt good.

Pulse pounding in his ears, he slid his hands around to cup her ass and lifted his hips to grind against her.

Lisette moaned, her eyes closing as her head fell back. She rocked against him, already wet, gliding along his length and driving him mad.

He slid his hands up and cupped her breasts. Squeezed. Kneaded. Teased her nipples with his thumbs before he delivered little pinches.

She gasped and covered his hands with her own.

"Take me inside you," he rasped. "I need you."

She stared down at him, eyes blazing with desire. "I need you, too." Rising above him, she reached between them and curled her fingers around his aching cock. Now *she* squeezed and stroked and played and tormented.

"Lisette," he gritted when he could take no more.

Guiding him to her entrance, she lowered herself down on him, inch by slow, torturous inch. So hot and wet and tight. Until they were fused together, breath held.

Her hands found their way to his chest again as she began to move, holding his gaze as she rode him. First slow and easy. Then faster. Harder. Stealing his breath as his hands roamed her. Explored her. Fondling her breasts, her ass, her thighs. Then sliding in between. He teased her clit with his thumbs, stroking her in time with her movements and luring little cries from her that fired his blood even more.

She stiffened above him. Calling his name. Nails digging into his chest as her slick walls clamped down and spasmed around him, milking him until he came with a roar.

Her light weight collapsed atop him. Her warm breath bathed his chest as her pulse—racing as fast as his own—fought its frantic pace and began to slow.

Quiet embraced them. The calm after the storm.

"Why couldn't I have found you two hundred years ago when you were first made immortal," he murmured, and felt her smile against his chest.

Sliding his hands down over her ass, Zach raised his head and buried his lips in the hair above her ear. "I want to try something," he whispered.

Her heartbeat picked up again. "Okay."

For days, he had been contemplating introducing telekinesis to their lovemaking. But he hadn't been certain how she might react. Now, with her body pliant against his, her warmth still embracing his hardness, he thrust his hips up against hers and telekinetically stroked all of her erogenous zones at once with the speed and force of a vibrator.

She climaxed instantly, once more clenching and unclenching around him for so long he came again himself.

"What the hell was that?" she panted.

"That," he said, "is one of the perks of making love with an elder."

Raising her head, she smiled down at him, her face still flushed with pleasure. "Why *couldn't* you have found me two hundred years ago?"

Zach laughed and hugged her closer, never wanting to let her go.

Seth teleported to Melanie's lab at network headquarters, his stomach full of dread. She and Bastien were there with Cliff, Stuart, and the five newer vampire recruits. All seemed on edge, and Seth soon ascertained why.

Out of sight, in one of the holding rooms, Aidan hurled constant curses at the top of his lungs and banged the hell out of . . . something.

"Good evening, Melanie," Seth said.

When the room's occupants turned to face him, every expression screamed, *Finally!*

"Hi, Seth," Melanie greeted him with unconcealed relief. "Umm . . . your prisoner's awake."

"So I hear." That had been fast.

Aidan's voice quieted, but the loud clanging noises increased.

"He's been a little loud," Melanie said, the words carrying an apology. "It's starting to irritate the vampires."

"We passed irritated half an hour ago," Cliff said. "Now we're just pissed and want to kick his ass."

"Yeah," Stuart added. "Would you please shut that guy up? He's giving me a headache. And I didn't even know vampires could *get* headaches!"

Melanie muttered something indecipherable. "Do you want me to sedate him?"

"I'd be happy to knock the bastard out for you," Bastien offered courteously. "No drug necessary."

"Honey, you've said that like ten times since he woke up. You're not helping."

"I'll take care of him," Seth assured them.

Melanie smiled. "Thank you."

Nodding to them, Seth stepped out into the hallway and followed the racket to a holding room several doors down.

No guards stood before it. Instead, they all congregated at the opposite end of the hallway in front of the elevator and the door to the stairwell.

Smart fellows. Mind control tended to require close proximity.

All nodded a greeting to Seth as he approached the holding room door. As promised, Chris had welded it shut.

Seth teleported inside.

He wasn't sure what he had expected to find, but it wasn't Aidan doing his damnedest to free himself.

The immortal appeared to be somewhat groggy. Though

the effects of the drug had worn off enough for him to awaken, his telekinesis and other gifts seemed to be hampered.

That didn't, however, dampen his determination to escape.

Zach had shackled each limb twice and bound Aidan to the wall with titanium chains the width of a muscular man's biceps. Even if Aidan were strong enough to teleport, he couldn't do so as long as he was connected to the wall without taking the entire building with him.

So Aidan had opted to remove the shackles.

Lacking the strength needed to break them and robbed of his telekinetic ability, he had instead broken what appeared to be every bone in his hands to force them through the two tight wrist cuffs on each side. Both arms were free, his hands a mangled mess only barely, sluggishly beginning to heal.

Now Aidan sat on a cement floor splattered with his own blood, trying to toe off his boots.

"You should have removed them before you broke your hands," Seth said.

Aidan's head snapped around. Leaping to his feet, he backed away and eyed Seth warily. Chain links rattled with his every movement. "You had me chained to the wall like a lowly vampire," he accused.

"Dude," Stuart said in the lab, "we can hear you."

Aidan's brow furrowed as he cast a fleeting glance at the door.

Seth studied him and wondered what truths would unfold in the coming minutes. Had loneliness stolen Aidan's sanity despite the companionship of Seconds? Had bitterness driven him mad as Roland had suggested? Or was Aidan simply pissed? Seth didn't recall ever having seen the Celt lose his temper.

"Well?" Seth said when the silence stretched. "Have you nothing to say to me?"

Aidan stiffened. "What are you waiting for? That bastard who captured me said you wished to kill me."

"I thought I would let you have your say first. So talk while I'm still of a mind to let you."

A moment passed. "Why didn't you tell me an immortal was plotting against you?" Aidan asked.

Seth arched a brow and crossed his arms over his chest.

Aidan's eyes flickered with something Seth thought might have been hurt. "How could you think it was me? After all the years we've known each other, how could you think I would betray you like that?"

"Are you saying that wasn't you I saw on the network's surveillance footage, wiping the memories of network guards and exerting mind control over them?"

Aidan's lips tightened. "It isn't what you think."

"You didn't breach network headquarters and violate every protocol put in place to protect the humans who help us?"

"I know it looks bad, but—"

"You didn't fuck with the guards' minds," Seth continued, anger rising, "possibly giving them brain damage, and roam the compound freely?"

"I—"

"You didn't comb through the records room, then make yourself at home in Chris Reordon's office, searching confidential files for information you could feed the vampire army you've raised as well as the scientists you've commissioned to increase the dosage of the tranquilizer?"

"I didn't—"

"Don't lie to me!" Seth bellowed.

Everything went quiet.

Aidan.

The vampires in the lab.

Melanie.

Bastien.

Even the guards in the hallway fell into silence, so Seth's voice must have carried through the thick walls.

"It isn't what you think," Aidan insisted.

"You made the network your playground, endangered all of the humans who work here by compromising the guards and security, and helped yourself to an ass-load of confidential information and research. At the same time, a surprisingly adept army of vampires rose against us and miraculously gained access to the *only* sedative that works against immortals. A sedative that can only be obtained on these premises, along with a detailed compilation of dosages and their effectiveness, culled from the research performed here. Quite a coincidence."

"Seth—"

"That tranquilizer was used against Lisette," Seth snapped.

"The French immortal?"

"She nearly died, Aidan! She lay comatose for days! She's a telepath, yet even her mind was quiet."

Aidan stared at him. "When did this happen?"

"You know damned well when it happened!"

"It isn't what you think," Aidan repeated.

"Then why don't you tell me what it is?"

The minutes stretched. Every once in a while, Seth heard bone scrape against bone as the virus struggled to heal Aidan's hands, but not a flicker of pain touched the Celt's impassive face.

"Well?" Seth prodded.

"Do you know why poor people play the lotto, Seth?" he asked at length.

"What?"

"Wealthy people on the news are always condemning poor people for playing lotto, saying they should take that one dollar a week and invest it in whatever the hell rich people think will miraculously eradicate poverty. A savings account that will accrue a Lilliputian amount of interest by the end of the year. Four dollars more a month put toward paying down debt. They say lotto players are irrational. They say they're stupid. They think all lotto players mistakenly believe that they have an excellent chance of winning big. They call lotto players sheep and accuse them of playing for no other reason than that everyone else seems to be playing and they want to be part of the "in" crowd. I've even heard them accuse poor people who play lotto of being greedy and self-destructive. And do you know why?"

Before Seth could ask him what the hell he was talking about, Aidan continued.

"Because they don't get it. Because they've never had to struggle. They don't know what it's like to work two jobs you hate just to pay the rent and put food on the family's table. They don't know what it's like to have a car so old and in such poor condition that you say a prayer every time you turn the key, hoping it'll start. They don't know what it's like to not get to attend college because there aren't enough government grants to go around and their parents can't afford tuition. They don't get what it's like to work the same low-paying, dead-end job day after day, having to take shit from a boss who fucks with his employees' lives for no other reason than he's an asshole who likes to fuck with peoples' lives and is in a position to do so, and to know that this is what their lives will always be like because they can't do a damned thing to change it. They don't know what it's like to live without hope."

That caught Seth's attention.

"They can't comprehend," Aidan said, his tone almost begging Seth to understand, "the fucking stress and depression a life without hope dumps on a person. They can't understand that for just a few minutes, when that man or woman buys a lotto ticket, the stress that constantly tightens their shoulders eases just a bit. That just *imagining* winning the power-whatever, imagining all of their financial woes disappearing, imagining being able to quit their shit jobs and tell their asshole boss to go fuck himself gives them a desperately needed moment of happiness, of peace, and helps them get through the day. That every time their jackwad boss treats them like shit, they can think of that ticket and of the drawing at the end of the week and how awesome it would be to win, slim though the chances may be, and—again—get a brief mini-vacation from the stress. That *that* one-dollar ticket gives them something nothing else in life has. It gives them hope."

Seth stared at Aidan in silence.

Aidan raised his arms a few inches, then let them fall back to his sides. "I need my lotto ticket, Seth," he said with near desperation. "I need hope. I've lived too long without it."

"And you thought raising a vampire army—"

"I didn't raise a fucking army!" Aidan shouted, features mottling with fury. "I breached network headquarters and violated Reordon's protocols because I was looking for a list of *gifted ones!*"

Seth could detect no deception in his tone and saw none in his posture or expression.

"You wouldn't transfer me," Aidan said, both his voice and face full of anguish.

"Five *gifted ones* have been transformed in recent years, so we have five new immortals in the area. We don't need—"

"I don't give a flying fuck how many immortals are in the area! If you have more than you need, then send the Brits and their wives elsewhere and transfer *me* here. I *know* the chances of finding a *gifted one* who can love me and who will transform for me are as slim as the chances of winning the lotto, but I need the hope, Seth." He shook his head, swallowed hard. "I've lived without it for nearly three thousand years. I broke into the damned network and risked your wrath because I can't live without it any longer. If you wouldn't transfer me here, then I wanted to acquire a list of *gifted ones* I could look up myself. I wouldn't hurt them. I wouldn't scare them. I would just . . . bump into them at the grocery store. Help them change a flat tire. Whatever the hell I had to do to just have that chance meeting and see if, by some miracle, a spark might flare between us. If I had to teleport here every night before hunting to manage it, I would do it."

Shit.

"I didn't raise a vampire army. I just . . . wanted to purchase a lotto ticket." Aidan held out his bloody hands. "Whatever the cost."

Seth stared at Aidan, one of the most powerful warriors he knew, and felt his chest tighten when moisture glinted in the other man's eyes. "Lower your barriers," Seth commanded.

"What?"

"Your mental barriers. Lower them."

Aidan nodded slowly. "It's done."

Seth delved into the immortal's mind. Every barrier toppled, letting Seth see the loneliness and desperation that had driven Aidan to rebel. Not by raising a vampire army. But by combing the network's records in search of the names and addresses of female *gifted ones*. Had Aidan tried to hide anything, Seth would've seen it.

There was nothing. Aidan hadn't even known a vampire army had risen against the immortals until he had awoken chained in this holding cell and heard Bastien and Melanie discussing it . . . and naming *him* the betrayer.

Yet again, Seth had misjudged one of his immortals.

Closing his eyes, he bowed his head and pinched the bridge of his nose. "Fuck." Would this never end? Would he never discover who was waging war with them?

Aidan released a long sigh. "I'm sorry I defied you."

Seth shook his head. Opening his eyes, he crossed to

Aidan and placed a hand on the younger man's chest. Though Seth was low on energy from healing Ami, he poured what he could into Aidan and healed both of his hands.

While Aidan flexed his fingers, Seth drew back his hand and waved it toward Aidan's feet.

The shackles opened and fell away.

"Thank you."

"Why didn't you tell me?" Seth asked. "When you requested the transfer, why didn't you tell me how bad things were?"

Aidan sank down on the narrow bed behind him. "Too proud, I suppose. Too ashamed. I don't know. Too angry, maybe, that you didn't see it. Hell, Seth, after all these years, you know me better than anyone."

Sighing, Seth sat beside him and leaned back against the wall. "You're right. I didn't see it."

"Now that I know what you're dealing with here, I understand why."

And Aidan didn't even know about Ami. "It's no excuse. I should have realized."

"Seth, you can't be everywhere at once," Aidan said, the words oddly familiar. "Because you *seem* to know everything, some of us sometimes forget that you don't and . . . I don't know . . . expect perfection. Miracles. Though we are far from perfect ourselves."

"If it helps, even after seeing the surveillance video, I had a hard time believing you guilty."

"You're sure it's an immortal?"

"Yes. Whoever it is can erase memories."

"Shit."

"Everyone in the area has been cleared, so a teleporter must be involved."

"And I can erase memories and teleport." Again Aidan swore. "Who else can?"

"Chaahk and Imhotep. Their thoughts bore nothing perfidious. You were the only one who hid something behind unusually strong barriers."

"Thanks for the nosebleed, by the way," Aidan commented with a wry smile.

Seth laughed. "Actually that was Zach."

"The bastard who captured me?"

"Yes."

"Who *is* he? He clearly is an elder. And older than I, judging by the ease with which he kicked my ass."

"You might say he's my cousin."

Aidan whistled. "He's as old as *you* are?"

"Yes. And thank you for that." As if Seth didn't feel ancient enough.

"Is he as powerful as you are, too?"

"No. But, in time, he'll come close."

"I sense you don't want to talk about him."

"I don't. Maybe later. I have too much on my mind right now."

"Do you trust him?"

"I can't believe I'm saying this, but yes."

And once more, Seth and the others were back to square one. If the tracking device Cliff planted on that vamp didn't lead them to the vampires' lair . . .

"Let me help you," Aidan said.

Seth shook his head. "You don't have to earn a transfer, Aidan. It's yours. Just don't tell anyone how you went about securing it. And Bastien, I expect you, Melanie, and the vampires to keep our secret as well," he said, knowing they eavesdropped.

They agreed.

Aidan held out a healed hand. "Thank you, Seth."

Seth clasped Aidan's arm and pulled him into a hug,

clapping him on the back. "The North Carolina bunch is a lively one," he warned.

"Sounds like just what I need."

"And we have other secrets we will ask you to keep as well."

"Whatever you need me to do, I'll do it. I'm sincere in my desire to help you, Seth. And I won't betray you again. I vow it."

Seth nodded.

They sat quietly for several moments, Seth puzzling over . . . everything. Frowning, he looked at Aidan. "What do *you* know about being poor? You haven't been poor since you were transformed and I took you under my wing. And you weren't even poor before that."

"You caught that, did you?" he said with a smile, then shrugged. "My best Seconds have always been those you rescued from poverty."

"I didn't rescue them. I just offered them a well-paying job I knew would suit them."

"And they appreciated it and never took the perks for granted the way some do."

"Am I the jackwad boss who likes to fuck with people's lives in your analogy?"

Aidan laughed. "No. As far as bosses go, you kick ass."

"When I'm not kicking *your* ass? Or sending my henchman to do it for me?"

"Don't dwell on it, Seth. *I* don't intend to. I'm too old and weary to hold a grudge. And you've lived thousands of years. You were bound to make a mistake *some*time."

"Three mistakes. You're the third immortal I've wrongly accused."

His eyebrows flew up. "Really? Damn. I've been missing all the fun. We have a true mystery on our hands if the evidence has pointed you in that many directions."

"You make it sound exciting."

"It is. Hell, just the idea of encountering vampires who aren't the same old same old sounds exciting to me."

"Even when they endanger younger immortals' lives?"

"No. That just sounds infuriating." Aidan smiled. "Aren't you glad you'll have me around now to help you take care of them?"

Smiling, Seth shook his head. "I believe I am."

Chapter Seventeen

Lisette smiled when Zach took her hand and twined his fingers through hers.

He had just rocked her world, as Americans were fond of saying, more than once, yet this simple act—holding hands—made her heart leap with joy.

He closed the door to the quiet room David had invited them to use and headed for the stairs that led up to the ground floor.

Keeping pace with him, Lisette admired the broad shoulders and muscular chest left bare by his usual wardrobe of black leather pants and boots. Now that he no longer subbed for Seth or wore hunting garb, Zach refused to carry katanas or anything else that would require looping scabbards over his shoulders or back. He didn't want anything to interfere with his wings when he released them. So, instead, he wore a beltlike bandolier around his hips with daggers and throwing stars tucked into sheaths and loops.

As he traveled the corridor in long, ground-eating strides, Zach looked like what he was: a bold, powerful warrior of old. Strong and regal and utterly edible.

He glanced down and caught her staring. "What?"

She shook her head. "I just love you. That's all."

He stopped short. Turning to face her, he locked an arm around her waist and dragged her up against him. His lips crashed down on hers, stealing her breath and kick-starting her pounding heart.

Lisette's body reacted as though they hadn't just made love. Twice. Heating up and straining against him.

"Dude. Seriously. Get a room."

Zach raised his head. Lisette saw Sheldon, standing just outside the training room.

Sheldon must not have liked what he saw in Zach's eyes, because he swallowed and ducked back into the room.

Zach's eyes glowed with golden fire when they met hers. "You don't know what hearing you say that does to me," he said, voice guttural.

"I have a pretty good idea." She arched into the hard length of him, hissing in pleasure.

He groaned and closed his eyes. "I don't think I'll ever get enough of you."

"Good. Because I *know* I'll never get enough of *you*."

Yuri's voice, thick with a Russian accent, floated out of the training room. "Well, I've had enough of the both of you. Either return to your bedroom and go at each other like rabbits, or continue on and spare us all the love and lust you're oozing."

Stanislav laughed. "Go easy on them, Yuri. They've only just found each other."

Yuri grumbled something in Russian.

Zach smiled and shook his head. Still clasping Lisette's hand, he stepped back.

She sighed as cool air swept between them, dampening her ardor. A little.

By the time they climbed the stairs and reached the ground floor, Zach had gotten his body under control.

Lisette wished *she* had been as successful.

They entered the infirmary and, again, stopped short.

"You've got to be fucking kidding me," Zach snarled.

Seth and David sat beside Ami, pouring energy into her as usual. Marcus sat on the other side of her, the babe snoozing in his arms. At Ami's feet, stood a male immortal Lisette had never seen before.

"Aidan didn't betray us," Seth announced.

This was Aidan? The Celt? The one Zach had captured?

Zach's hand tightened almost painfully around Lisette's. "We saw the surveillance video of him breeching network headquarters, using mind control—"

"He breeched network headquarters for another reason," Seth said. "He is in no way connected to the new vampire army that has risen against us. I read his thoughts. *All* of them. Even those you couldn't access without killing him."

"Then who is?" Lisette asked, at a loss. "Who is our enemy?"

"I don't know." Seth sighed. "I feel like I'm being fucked with."

She nodded. First the evidence had pointed to Zach. Then to her. Then to Aidan.

"Perhaps that's the point," Zach suggested, still scowling.

Aidan nodded. "Someone may be trying to sow seeds of dissent, to pit you against the ranks."

"How could they have known I would accuse the wrong Immortal Guardian? Three times," Seth added with self-disgust.

"Technically," Zach said, "I'm not an Immortal Guardian."

"You'd damned well better be. You answered my calls for two days."

"Oh." Zach looked surprised. "Okay."

Lisette nudged him with her shoulder. "Welcome to the ranks."

"Anyway," Aidan addressed Seth, "it's just fortunate that you accused *us*."

Zach grunted. "How the hell is that fortunate? I got my ass kicked because he thought I was guilty."

"As did I," Aidan reminded him darkly.

Lisette grinned. "I didn't. I got a hug."

The men laughed.

"Down With The Sickness" filled the air.

"I'm not kidding, Seth," Zach warned. "I'm going to crush that phone if you don't change the ringtone."

Smiling, Seth answered the call.

"Can you come and get me?" Chris asked. "I want to show you something, and I'm too tired to drive."

"I'm on my way." Seth released Ami and disappeared. Seconds later, he reappeared with Chris by his side.

Chris handed a cooler to Marcus. "I brought more milk."

"Thank you." Rising with the baby cradled in one arm, Marcus took the cooler to the kitchen.

Chris nodded a greeting to Lisette, Zach, and David, glared at Aidan, then held something up for Seth to inspect. "The tracking device Cliff planted."

Seth frowned. "How did *you* get hold of it?"

"I expected movement once the sun set. When nothing happened, I ordered an infrared satellite scan of its location. The scan found no signs of life, so I sent men to the scene to check it out."

"You should have let me do it," Seth admonished.

"It wasn't necessary. I knew no one was there, so the risk was minimal."

"Your new contacts provided you with the satellite imagery?"

Launching a satellite into space tended to attract attention, so the network didn't itself own one they could use when needed. That was where Chris's contacts came into play: men and women recruited from agencies, bureaus, and other groups shrouded in secrecy who were willing to risk all to help the Immortal Guardians whenever they needed special intel.

"Yes."

"How did that go?" Seth asked.

"Smoothly for them. Hard as hell for me."

Chris's last group of contacts, as well as their spouses and children, had either been tortured to death or shot execution style by Donald and Nelson's mercenaries. A quick peek into his thoughts told Lisette that Chris feared history would repeat itself.

"Speaking of which . . ." He drew a cell phone from his back pocket and held it out to Seth. "I instructed the men who got me the satellite photos to call this number if they have even the tiniest suspicion that they're being followed or have been compromised."

Taking the phone, Seth nodded. "I'll teleport them and their families to safety if such should occur. Then you can work with the other network heads to create new identities for them and relocate them, preferably out of the country."

"Thank you."

"What did your men find?" Lisette asked.

"It was a small frame house. The little bit of furniture we found inside was broken and turned over. From the looks of things, the vampires scuffled. You know how volatile their tempers can be, even when newly turned."

All nodded.

"We found the tracking device under a chair and assume it came off during the fight."

Lisette shook her head. "That was our only lead."

"I know," Chris said. "And Cliff risked a hell of a lot to get it for us. I didn't tell you at the network, because I didn't want him to overhear."

"Give me the tracking device," Zach ordered.

When Lisette looked up, she damned near took a step back at the fury she saw reflected in his face.

Chris frowned. "What?"

"It still works, doesn't it?" Zach asked.

"Yes."

"Is it waterproof?"

"Yes. My tech guys made it damned near indestructible."

"Then give it to me, and I'll make sure it doesn't fall off the next vampire."

"How exactly do you plan to do that?"

Tired of waiting, Zach took the tiny device from Chris. "I plan to shove it down his fucking throat." He tucked the tracker in a front pants pocket. "If the vampire swallows it, it won't fall off. It can't be knocked off in a fight. He can't lose it. And I'll make damned sure he doesn't remember swallowing it. This shit needs to end." Zach looked to Seth. "Does that work for you?"

Seth nodded. "Sounds good. And, since he'll swallow it, the virus won't view it as shrapnel and eject it."

Lisette tightened her grip on Zach's hand. "I'm going with you."

"The hell you are," he denied.

"Then let me put it this way," she said sweetly. "I'm going hunting tonight, with or without you. If I should happen to come across one of these new supervamps, I'll try to tag him myself. I can't make him swallow a tracker because I can't wipe his memory or do the mind control thing, but I guarantee you I'll get close enough to plant it on him *somewhere*."

Zach swore.

She grinned. "You can't love that I kick ass, then try to keep me from kicking it."

"Why the hell not?" he grumbled.

She laughed.

"Fine. *I'll* shove it down his throat. *You* can cheer me on." Lisette winked. "Let's just see how it goes, shall we?"

* * *

Zach and Lisette found no newbie vampires that night. Or the next. On the third, they fought two skirmishes with the usual vampire fare. Few in number. Easy kills. Zach spent more time admiring Lisette during the fights than he did combating the vampires.

She was such a fascinating combination of fragility and strength, of vulnerability and ferocity. The way she wielded her shoto swords, the agility with which she evaded the weapons of her opponents . . .

It just made him want to pounce.

The last vampire in the second battle fell.

Zach collected the vampires' weapons and tried to get his mind off all of the things he would be doing to Lisette if they were in the privacy of her bedroom.

The bowie knives, folding knives, and machetes were all of poor quality. Some of the blades had broken upon contact with Lisette's superior shoto swords. "What do you think?" he asked, holding them up. "Toss them?"

She nodded.

Zach zipped away to toss them in a Dumpster, then returned to her.

Lisette finished tucking her weapons away and handed him his.

"Thank you."

She smiled and grabbed the vampires' sticky clothing.

"What?" Zach asked as he helped.

"Nothing. It's just . . ." She straightened. "I like that you let me be me," she said with a shrug. "I like that you think I'm strong."

"You *are* strong."

"But you also appreciate my femininity."

"I *more* than appreciate it," he said with a leer.

She grinned. "Yet you aren't overprotective like my brothers and Seth, all of whom can drive me up the wall sometimes."

"Oh, but I am. I cringe every time a battle arises. And my inner Neanderthal awakens whenever I think you're in danger."

"Your inner Neanderthal?"

He nodded. "I believe you met him when I ordered you to never defy me again."

She winked. "Your inner Neanderthal gave me multiple orgasms."

And wanted to give her more.

"And if you really *were* Neanderthal-ish, you would have found some way to keep me at David's and gone hunting without me these last few nights."

"I knew you would never forgive me if I did," he admitted. "And I didn't want to—I don't know—stifle you."

She crossed to him and rose onto her toes to kiss his cheek. "You see? You let me be me."

"Because I love you as you are. Even when you scare the crap out of me by putting yourself in danger."

"Sweet-talker."

He brushed a kiss across her lips, then a second and a third. "You are so tempting."

"Do you want to call it a night?"

"Yes."

"But?"

"We need to find a newbie vampire to tag. It's taking too long. And I was serious when I said I want this shit to end."

She nodded, face full of regret. "Me too. Let's get going then and tag one of these bastards before another immortal gets tranqed."

"Where do you want to search next? UNCG?"

"I think Krysta and Étienne are hunting there tonight."

"Duke?"

"Sounds good."

Looping an arm around Lisette's waist, Zach drew her up

against him. "Too tempting by far," he said with a smile and teleported them.

As soon as the darkness faded and Duke's campus materialized around them, a foul breeze struck, carrying with it the scents of blood and death.

Zach stiffened and looked around.

Whimpers sounded in the distance, accompanied by growls and laughter.

He jerked his chin to the north. *That way.*

Lisette nodded, face grim.

Zach took off, streaking through the campus at speeds he knew Lisette could match, always conscious of her at his back.

In the loading dock behind a building Zach wasn't familiar with, half a dozen vampires crouched in the shadows. Zach drew daggers and peered around the corner, motioning for Lisette to stay behind him.

Like jackals, the vampires feasted on two females, lips locked on every major artery. The girls appeared to be college students. As did the two males, who had been disemboweled and tossed aside like discarded toys. One was dead. The other died seconds after Zach's arrival. The heartbeats of the females, if they lived, were too faint for Zach to hear above the snarling and bragging and bullshit spouted by the vampires, one of which bore the appearance of a newbie.

How many? Lisette asked in his head as she drew her shoto swords.

Half a dozen. Only one looks to be of the new breed of vampires.

Let's do this then.

Zach and Lisette stepped from behind the building.

The newbie vampire saw them and rose.

The other vamps followed his gaze and dragged to their feet.

"Who the fuck are you?" one demanded, his mouth and chin slick with blood.

"Is he an Immortal Guardian?" another asked uneasily, and bent to pick up a discarded bowie knife.

"Immortal Guardians don't walk around shirtless, dumb ass," the first sneered.

The newbie vampire ignored them and reached behind him.

Zach shot forward, his daggers finding flesh before the vamps even had a chance to react to his first step. As maddened vampires sank to the ground amid a river of blood, the newbie vampire drew a tranquilizer gun from behind his back.

Zach dropped a dagger and grabbed the vamp's wrist, forcing the barrel of the gun up.

Behind him, Lisette huffed, "Damn it! You didn't leave any for me!"

Zach said nothing, just stared into the eyes of the newbie, who reached for a tactical knife on his belt.

As the vampire drew his knife, his body relaxed. His fingers uncurled and dropped the weapon. When Zach released the vamp's other arm, it fell to his side, still clutching the tranquilizer gun.

"You encountered no Immortal Guardians tonight," Zach told him.

After a pause, the vampire said, "I couldn't find any Immortal Guardians."

"The vampires with whom you chose to band together proved to be too volatile," Zach continued.

The vamp nodded. "Those vamps were freakin' crazy."

"So crazy they turned on you, leaving you no choice but to kill them."

"I had to," the vamp agreed. "It was kill or be killed."

"Once they were dead, you found no others with whom you could band together, so you ended your hunt for the night."

"I'll start fresh tomorrow."

"Good. Now open wide."

The vampire dutifully tilted his head back and parted his lips.

Zach drew the tracking device from his pants pocket and dropped it in the vamp's mouth. "Swallow."

Closing his mouth, the vampire swallowed.

"A piece of candy one of the women dropped when the other vampires attacked her," Zach said. "Strawberry flavored. Delicious. You wish she had been carrying more."

Again the vampire nodded and worked his mouth as though he could still taste it.

Zach stepped back. "Run along. You saw neither me nor my companion tonight."

Tucking the tranquilizer gun in the back of his pants, the vampire loped off up a darkened sidewalk.

Zach turned and found Lisette watching him.

"How do you do that?" she asked.

"It takes a great deal of power."

"Enough to attract the Others?" The threat they posed loomed always in the periphery of her thoughts.

"Not when I only do it once and for such a brief time."

She tucked her shoto swords away. "You could have let *me* take care of the weasels while you did your mind-control thing."

"I wasn't willing to take the chance. Thus far, none of the standard-fare vampires have carried a tranquilizer gun, but that could change if the new vampires keep failing to capture us and decide to recruit the slacker vamps instead of just using them as bait."

She drew out her phone, a faint smile toying with the corners of her lips.

"What?" he asked.

"You said *us*." She dialed a number. "You're one of *us* now. You're an Immortal Guardian. You're one of the family."

He was? Seth had said as much earlier, but . . .

Zach thought about it for a moment and nearly staggered in shock as he realized he *did* think of himself as one of them.

"Chris?" she said. "Lisette. We need a cleanup crew at Duke."

Zach heard a security guard strolling their way and sent him in a different direction as Lisette let Chris know where on the campus they could be found. *Can you inform him we tagged a vampire without Cliff overhearing?* he asked, knowing the vampires who resided at network headquarters could hear both sides of the conversation if they were listening.

She nodded and started pushing buttons on her phone. A few seconds later, she returned it to her pocket. "I texted him. He'll understand why. And a team will be here in five."

Zach nodded.

"You look thoughtful," she commented, bending to check the pulses of the females.

Both were dead like the males, he knew. Once the vampires had fallen, he had heard no heartbeat other than his own and Lisette's. But Lisette was kindhearted and always hoped their ears deceived them when they were too late to save a mortal.

"What's on your mind?" she asked as she rose, absently wiping her bloody fingers on her new coat. The old one had suffered too many slashes and stains in recent weeks to be salvaged.

"Nothing really. Just wondering what it's like."

"What *what* is like?"

"Being part of a family."

She smiled and walked into his embrace. "You'll know soon enough. Seth and my brothers are already beginning to think of you as such. The rest will, too, in time."

Zach kept a sharp gaze on the campus around them, ears attuned to anything that might indicate another newbie vampire lurked nearby. "I'm not so sure."

Two college students strolled in their direction. Zach mentally guided them away.

"Is that what you want?" Lisette asked.

The hesitance in her voice made him pause his vigil and look down at her. "What?"

"Is that what you want—for the rest of the Immortal Guardians to accept you into the fold?" Her gaze dropped to his chest. "We've never really spoken of the future. Not long-term, anyway."

"My future is with you," he said simply. He could no longer conceive of one without her.

Her eyes rose, snaring his. "I want you to be happy, Zach."

Smiling, he drew the fingers of one hand down her soft cheek. "I didn't know what happy was until I met you."

Taking his hand, she pressed her lips to his palm. "Nor I until I met you. But . . ." She shook her head. "Zach, if you aren't happy here, in North Carolina, mingling with the other Immortal Guardians, we can go somewhere else."

"You would do that for me?" he asked, touched that she would leave her brothers.

She nodded. "You've said little of your past, but what you *have* said has led me to believe you've spent much of your existence . . . isolated. If you aren't comfortable dealing with over a dozen immortals and their Seconds on a nightly basis, I can request a transfer. We can go someplace more remote—"

"It doesn't matter where we live, Lisette," he interrupted softly. "Or how many of your brethren surround us. It won't even matter if they can't come to accept me as one of them. All I need to be happy is you. All the *family* I need is you."

Rising onto her toes, she brushed his lips with a kiss. "Weren't the Others like your family?" she asked.

"Not really. We got along and were friends for the most part. But it was friendship that was forced upon us by our circumstances rather than a friendship we chose. We didn't share the affection Immortal Guardians hold for each other."

"You never talk about them, aside from letting me know they're still hunting you," she said softly. "Do you miss them?"

"The Others? No." He sure as hell didn't miss their judgment or their punishments or their fanatical determination to refrain from any and all interaction with . . . well . . . everyone else on the planet.

"Why can't they just let you go?"

He shook his head. "They fear what will happen if I decide to follow Seth's example and start dabbling in the lives of humans. They already believe Seth's actions will one day bring about their downfall. Allowing a second to stray and threaten their existence is unacceptable, so they are determined to capture me and show me the error of my ways. So determined, in fact, that I felt one do a flyby over David's earlier tonight when we were making love." Zach still couldn't believe they had resorted to such. The Others must be getting desperate, with no clue as to where they might find him.

She stiffened. "Did he sense you were there?"

"No. As long as I'm at full strength, they can't sense me."

"But you've been pouring so much energy into Ami."

"Forgive me. I should have said as long as I retain my powers, they can't find me. Even while sleeping or drained of energy I should be safe. Only large bursts of power expenditure will tip them off now." And while he had been guilty of a few of those while helping Seth search for the betrayer, he had thus far managed to teleport away before the Others could pinpoint his location and catch him.

He smiled down at her. "Besides, the one who flew over earlier was searching for a cold, distant Other, not a man making passionate love to the woman he adores. I would have seemed a stranger to him had he felt my presence."

"Will he come back?"

"I doubt it. I'm surprised he even dared to venture so close this time. Seth's and David's homes have pretty much been designated no-fly zones. Violating that is tantamount to issuing a threat that could incite Seth's wrath."

"Do they fear him that much?"

"They don't fear Seth. They fear the destruction he would unleash if they pushed him too far. They fear the attention it would draw and the consequences that would follow. I'm not sure why Seth is so much more powerful than the rest of us, if it's simply because he has worked hard to increase his strength and extend his gifts, or if it's more that we've suppressed our own for so long. But when his temper fully erupts . . ."

She grimaced. "I know. I've seen it."

"No, you haven't. You've only had a tiny taste of it. When Seth's wife and children were slain so long ago . . ." Zach shuddered, remembering the carnage. "It took all of us—all of the Others—*and* David combined to reel him in. And we took a lot of damage doing it."

"David was alive way back then?"

"Yes. I don't think we would have been able to reach Seth without him."

"What did you do? Did you . . . torture him the way *you* were tortured?"

Zach snorted. "No. We were too broken and bloody ourselves. We combined our own powers and used them to drain Seth of his. It was a temporary fix. Or punishment. Call it what you will. But it protected the world from his wrath long enough for him to get his shit together."

He heard the rumble of an approaching vehicle.

"Can they do that to you?" she asked and tightened her hold on him. "If they find you, can they drain your power and take you away from me?"

Yes, they could. And would, if he wasn't careful.

Zach rested his chin on the top of her head and rubbed her back. "That isn't going to happen, Lisette. I won't let it."

He had too much to lose.

Kidneythieves singing "Before I'm Dead" drew Lisette from slumber. She had been having the most marvelous dream about Zach. He had been laughing—his handsome face carefree, his manner playful—as he walked backward and tugged her after him through a forest. She had been laughing, too, but couldn't remember why. Just that she had been happy to have his fingers curled around hers and awed by the brilliant rays of sunshine that streamed through the branches and dappled them with light.

Light that didn't harm her.

Opening her eyes, she found herself stretched on her back on her bed at home. Naked. The covers bunched around her hips. Zach sprawled facedown beside her, pressed up against her side, his head on her chest, a heavy arm draped across her stomach.

"I'm going to kill whoever is on the other end of that line," he muttered groggily.

"You'll hear no complaint from me." She fumbled for the phone she had placed on the bedside table.

"I was having the best dream," he continued, voice gravelly from sleep.

She looked to see who was calling. Tracy.

"We were in a forest." He snuggled closer.

Lisette smiled. "Were you holding my hand and pulling me after you?"

He lifted his head. "Yes."

She winked at him. "I was there."

He smiled, so damned irresistible with his hair tousled.

"What's up?" she asked her Second.

"Chris has called another meeting. Everyone needs to be at David's an hour after sunset."

"Thanks. We'll be there." She returned her phone to the bedside table.

"Perhaps the vampire we tagged produced some fruitful intel."

"I hope so." She brushed his hair out of his eyes. "You've been pulling me into your dreams, haven't you? Intentionally?"

He nodded. "I knew you missed the sun and wanted to share it with you."

Her eyes burned as tears rose. "Thank you," she whispered.

He brushed a kiss across her lips. "Anything for you."

Chapter Eighteen

Immortal Guardians and their Seconds once more gathered around David's long dining table. Ami's chair remained empty as the coma, as Dr. Kimiko and Melanie now called it, continued to hold her in its grasp.

Was this, Lisette wondered, what it had been like for the others when *she* had been trapped in that awful darkness? The waiting. The wondering. The worrying.

They had at least had some hope that the drug would eventually wear off in Lisette's case. With Ami, none knew what to expect, because none were certain what was causing her coma. Every day that she lay unresponsive, hope suffered another blow. When she had been gravely wounded early in her relationship with Marcus, she had completely recovered within twenty-four hours without any help from Seth or David, her alien DNA having given her incredible regenerative capabilities.

Now, even their aid seemed incapable of returning her to them.

Roland and Sarah had coaxed a weary Marcus into leaving his wife's side long enough to attend the meeting. Linda now sat with Ami in his stead.

Seated at the table, Marcus cradled his infant daughter to his chest.

Lisette didn't think she had seen him set the babe down once other than to change her nappy, something for which Jenna had praised him endlessly.

I loved John's father, Jenna had said, *but that boy wouldn't have changed a dirty diaper if someone had offered him a million dollars to do it.*

Marcus had exhibited no such reluctance, though he had been pretty intimidated by the babe's tiny size the first few times.

His daughter stirred and opened her eyes, a beautiful green like her mother's.

Beside Marcus, Roland smiled and reached over to cup the soft, downy head in his large hand and give it a gentle stroke. He alone, of all the men present, had had children in his mortal life.

Lisette thought she detected a certain wistfulness in his dark eyes and wondered if he were wishing he and Sarah could have a child together.

Zach squeezed Lisette's hand under the table. *I'm sorry we can't have a baby.*

She smiled up at him. *Me too.* Immortal Guardian couples had never been able to conceive children.

Conversation floated around the table.

Only David and Seth were absent. David remained in the infirmary, channeling healing energy into Ami until the meeting began. Seth was . . .

Actually, she didn't know where Seth was. But, based on the two days Zach had spent walking in the shoes of the Immortal Guardians' leader, she assumed he was taking care of some emergency.

The front door opened.

Chris Reordon strode in, his usual battered briefcase in

one hand and what looked almost like a rifle carrying case gripped in the other.

Darnell rose and crossed to take the rifle case.

"Thanks." Chris nodded a greeting to everyone and joined all of them in the dining room. "Is David with Ami?"

"Yes." Darnell set the case on the table across from Lisette and Zach, who occupied two chairs near the end beside Seth's empty seat.

Chris dropped his heavy briefcase on the floor with a thump and reached for the rifle case.

Wondering what it contained, Lisette watched him flip the latches and open it.

Long rolls of paper the size of posters were stacked on top of each other inside, along with wooden sticks she watched him assemble into some sort of display easel.

While Chris positioned the easel on Lisette's side of the table near Seth's chair, Darnell left the room. He returned a moment later, carrying a large corkboard he leaned against the nearest wall.

When Chris nodded, Darnell phoned Seth and let him know they were ready.

Seth appeared at Zach's elbow seconds later.

David entered from the hallway, his expression telling them there was still no change in Ami's condition. Face somber, he seated himself at the head of the table.

Seth took the seat at Zach and Lisette's end and adjusted his chair a bit so he could see whatever Chris intended to show them on the easel.

Immortals and Seconds shifted their seats.

Chris removed a poster from the rifle case and began sliding off the rubber bands that kept it tightly rolled. "All of you probably know by now that Cliff tagged a vampire with a tracking device."

Lisette was pleased to see the young vampire included in their meeting again.

"Well, last night we hit pay dirt. The vamp finally led us home."

Those who knew that Zach had had to tag another vampire remained silent, wanting Cliff to have his moment.

Chris placed the large corkboard on the easel, then unrolled the paper and fastened the corners to the corkboard with thumbtacks. "This is where he led us."

When he stepped back, Lisette felt her heart drop into her stomach.

"Tell me that isn't what I think it is," Roland gritted.

"It's a mercenary compound," Chris announced, inciting a new round of swearing. "Or rather it's *part* of a mercenary compound." He grabbed another poster roll, stripped off the rubber bands, and attached it atop the first.

Lisette stared.

"Shhhhhit!" Ethan exclaimed.

The satellite image provided them with a faintly blurry bird's-eye view of an enormous compound, encompassing she-didn't-know-how-many acres, with multiple buildings.

Warehouses. Hangars. Training fields.

"Is that a runway?" Sheldon asked, wide-eyed.

"Yes. And a helipad." Chris bent and removed a file from his briefcase, along with a handful of thumbtacks he dropped with a clatter onto the table. One by one, he tacked up eight-and-a-half by eleven-inch satellite images. "I called in aid from damned near every contact to get these. There's a runway. Airplanes. Military helicopters. Civilian helicopters. Tanks. Humvees. Armored personnel carriers. Various and assorted other kick-ass vehicles. Warehouses. We believe these two buildings here house the soldiers. We estimate each is at least forty-thousand square feet."

"Shit!" someone else—Stan's Second, Alexei?—exclaimed.

"There are dozens of firing ranges that rival those down at network headquarters in size and sophistication. A breeching range."

"What's a breeching range?" Lisette interrupted.

"Doors—indoor and outdoor—and iron fences soldiers use to practice breeching buildings. There's also a tactical driving track. Small town and maritime mock-ups. This is the main building here. Aside from jumping the razor wire-topped fence or entering by plane or helicopter, there is only one way in or out. This road here. And, naturally, it's heavily guarded. It's also probably outfitted with bear claws to keep unauthorized vehicles out."

"How big is the compound?" Darnell asked.

"Roughly four thousand acres."

Stunned silence took the room.

"Exactly," Chris said. "These guys are who Donald and Nelson aspired to be. These guys are doing their damnedest to give the big guns a run for their money."

Seth studied the pictures. "Are they affiliated in any way with the government?"

"We haven't gotten that far, but it wouldn't surprise me at all if they've landed government contracts."

It was damned close to the worst-case scenario.

"Who are they?" Sheldon asked.

"Shadow River."

The name meant nothing to Lisette.

Judging by the expressions of the other immortals, it meant little to them as well.

The mortals in their midst, however, looked worried.

"I've heard of them," Tracy said. "They don't call themselves mercenaries. They call themselves a global security company. And their reach really does extend overseas."

Chris nodded. "From what we've been able to ascertain thus far, they're often hired to protect foreign dignitaries and important figures both here and overseas, to train foreign soldiers or police forces in war-torn areas, to protect American contractors. That sort of thing. But you haven't seen the worst of it yet." He removed another poster and tacked it up.

"I had one of my contacts do a thermal-imaging scan of the compound this afternoon." He stepped back. "The red figures on the training fields and scattered about the compound are human. The yellowish-green ones here in this housing building are vampire."

Lisette traced her gaze over dozens of green figures who clearly slumbered in beds. Rows and rows and rows of them.

Those vampires weren't prisoners.

Chris turned to Seth. "Do you still have that phone I gave you?"

Seth nodded.

"If any of my contacts call you, we'll know just how far this company's reach extends. If Shadow River is in bed with the military or has close ties with the government, my contacts' actions won't go unnoticed."

A heavy silence ensued, as though all waited with bated breath to see if Seth's phone would ring.

"The vampires on the compound . . ." Cliff said. "Do you think the mercenaries recruited them or turned them?"

Lisette answered. "Based on the skill with which these new vampires fight, I'd say they're turning their own men. Any vampires they *didn't* turn themselves were likely captured for study and so the mercenaries could acquire the virus."

Chris nodded and took the seat across from Zach. "Shadow River has done what Donald and Nelson didn't have the chance to do. They've implemented the virus and begun to build an army of supersoldiers. Whether they intend to hire them out to the highest bidder globally and rack up billions or land a big-ass government contract is anyone's guess."

Aidan shook his head. "You're sure an immortal is helping them?"

David nodded. "They couldn't have acquired the sedative—the *only* drug that affects us aside from the antidote Melanie developed—without an immortal's assistance. Nor could they have known that the previous dose of the sedative wasn't strong enough to incapacitate an immortal to such an extent that the antidote couldn't counter it."

"It's inconceivable," Étienne muttered.

Ethan cleared his throat and cast Zach a nervous glance. "Could it be one of the Others?"

Lisette held her breath.

Did anyone else present even *know* about the Others?

"No," Seth and Zach answered in unison.

Bastien frowned. "Who the hell are the Others? Other *what*?"

Seth shared a look with Zach and sighed. "Zach is not the only elder immortal out there who is not one of us. Or who *wasn't*."

"Wait," Marcus said, voice low so he wouldn't disturb the babe. "There are other immortals as ancient as you two?"

"Yes," Seth said.

"Why is this the first time we're hearing of them?"

"Because, as I said, they aren't Immortal Guardians. They don't spend their nights hunting and slaying vampires. They chose a different path thousands of years before your birth and live in total isolation."

Zach nodded. "They have no contact with mankind. Fight no battles. Choose no sides. And they believe Seth has been treading the wrong path all these years."

"So . . ." Ethan frowned. "You're saying they just sit on their asses and do nothing?"

"Yes," Zach confirmed. "They merely observe."

David leaned forward, drawing everyone's gaze. "Have you ever seen one of the many time-travel movies in which those who travel back in time are warned to alter nothing? They're told that even so tiny an action as killing a butterfly or stepping on a bug in the past could have a ripple effect that could change the present in disastrous ways."

Nods all around.

"That is how the Others view immortal interaction with humans. They think it dangerous on any level and, in those early decades, tried numerous times to kill Seth for daring to stray from the path. Fortunately for us, he prevailed and grew so powerful they couldn't touch him. Zach, on the other hand, is risking his life to join us and be with Lisette."

"Seriously?" Sheldon asked.

Zach nodded. "The first time I met Ami, she found me up on the roof, riddled with wounds and afflicted with so much pain that I nearly shook with it. Do you know what transgression warranted such punishment?"

"What?" Marcus asked, his gaze piercing.

"The night the mercenaries attacked network headquarters I found Seth in South Korea and told him his phone was broken."

Lisette had heard none of this and was as stunned as everyone else at the table.

"That's it?" Marcus questioned.

"I also mentioned that his people here in North Carolina were trying to reach him."

"And for that you were punished?"

"Yes."

Seth leaned back in his chair. "Because he interfered."

"By telling you your phone was broken?" Étienne asked incredulously. "You would've figured that out on your own fairly quickly."

Richart nodded. "It's not like Zach joined the battle or anything."

"But he killed the butterfly. Or stepped on the bug. However you wish to view it. He took an action, minute though it may seem to you. And the Others are fanatical about not doing *anything* that might interfere with the natural course of mankind."

Roland donned his usual scowl. "What the hell do they think will happen?"

"If they interact with humans?" Seth said. "Armageddon."

Leaden silence.

"No, seriously," Sheldon said. "What do they think will happen?"

"They think any contact with humans could kick-start the Apocalypse," Seth repeated.

Étienne turned to Zach. "You believed that, too?"

"Until recently, yes."

"Why?"

"Believe it or not, there was compelling reason to believe it. But I won't elaborate."

Étienne fell silent for a moment, during which Lisette suspected he unsuccessfully tried to read Zach's thoughts. "What changed your mind?"

"Your sister."

Étienne shifted his gaze to Lisette.

Smiling, she shrugged. "I am woman. Hear me roar?"

The women present all laughed.

"When the Others learned Zach had met with me again," Seth continued, "they tortured him for months and would likely *still* be torturing him had he not escaped."

Guilt suffused Lisette. "Did they know you saved my life? Is that why they captured you?"

Zach shook his head. "They knew nothing about that. All they knew was that I had spoken with Seth."

"And for that you were tortured," Bastien stated. "Again."

"Yes."

Lisette leaned into his side. "Because he has strayed from the path again to be with me, the Others are hunting him."

Marcus shot Seth a look. "Will their search bring them here? Is it safe?"

"They won't touch David's home or harm any of you. It's Zach they want."

"Okay," Ethan said. "So . . . I think it's safe to say they aren't involved in this. Which means it *has* to be one of our own." He looked to Seth. "What do you want us to do?"

"Nothing yet. I'll leave momentarily to check out the compound and—"

"Alone?" Lisette asked. David had always accompanied Seth before.

"Yes. David needs to remain here with Ami."

"I'll go with you," Zach offered.

Chris spoke up. "Checking it out tonight is good. But I think, when it comes to eradicating the place, we should go in during the day. Since the mercenaries are new to the whole vampire thing, chances are good they haven't developed protective suits yet for their supersoldiers. The vampires will be vulnerable and will have to remain in their residence, while the suits you'll wear will give you free run of the compound and shield you to some extent from the darts. I've had my guys make a few modifications."

If that was the case, Lisette wouldn't complain about having to wear a protective suit. She did *not* want to get tranqed again. Zach had scared the hell out of her when he'd pointed out that the enemy could up the dosage even more.

"I'd also like a few days to do some recon," Chris told Seth. "Learn their routine so we'll know where their men are during the day. The damned place is so huge, if we don't know their training schedule and how spread out they are on a regular basis, it could bite us in the ass."

"How may days do you need?" Seth asked. "Every day we delay, we risk their gaining enough confidence in this venture to reveal their seemingly indestructible army to potential buyers."

"Three," Chris said. "A week would be better, but three days will tell us more than we know now. Plus you guys are going to need a hell of a lot of support from the network to ensure that every inch of the fence that surrounds *all four thousand acres* isn't jumped by fleeing mercenaries. I'll need a little time to coordinate that *and* to call in every Special Ops man we have to scour the grounds while you hit the main buildings."

"So be it." Seth started to say something else, but stopped. His brow furrowed with what looked to be puzzlement.

"Marcus?"

Lisette gasped at the tentative inquiry and looked toward the hallway that led to the back of the house.

Ami stood there, pale and fragile, her coppery curls forming a disheveled halo around her face. A demure white nightgown fell to her knees. Her limbs were thinner than Lisette remembered, her cheeks gaunt. Her body seemed to bear none of the extra weight or roundness a woman who had just given birth *should* have. Her tiny feet were bare against the cold bamboo floor. Her hands curled into fists.

Lisette looked to Marcus, who had gone so pale she feared he might pass out.

Roland must have feared the same, because he hastily took the baby from Marcus and cradled her against his chest.

Marcus rose slowly and staggered a few steps toward his wife as though afraid she were an illusion. "Ami?"

She nodded.

Rushing forward, Marcus took her in his arms and crushed her against him.

"Careful," Seth cautioned as he and David rose.

Loosening his hold, Marcus sank to his knees in front of Ami, buried his face in her chest, and wept.

Ami's green eyes glimmered with moisture as she wrapped her arms around him and rested her chin atop his head. Her gaze sought Seth. "Is it . . . ? Did the baby . . . ?"

Seth circled the table, pausing long enough to take the babe from Roland. Then he and David approached the couple.

As soon as Ami saw the small, swaddled bundle in Seth's arms, her face lit with hope.

"Your daughter," Seth told her with a smile.

Tears spilled over her lashes and trailed down her cheeks. "She's okay? She's healthy?"

He nodded. "There's no trace of the virus in her blood."

Marcus gained his feet and took his daughter from Seth to present her to his wife.

"She's beautiful," Ami professed.

"Just like her mother," Marcus rasped, drawing her into a family hug.

Zach squeezed Lisette's hand under the table.

Blinking back tears, Lisette rose and joined the others who migrated over to the couple and welcomed Ami back.

Ami was so thrilled about the babe and so concerned about Marcus that her usual shyness, which bordered on fear (a lovely parting gift from her captivity), fell away. She even smiled through the multiple embraces the immortals and their Seconds foisted upon her.

Everyone spoke at once. No one minded.

Even the baby, awakened by the cacophony of voices surrounding her, took it in stride, peering around with curious eyes.

Lisette nearly wept when Ami held her baby for the first time and received a toothless smile.

"Zach," a voice spoke behind Lisette.

Turning, she saw David issue Zach a hard look.

"Come with me."

Unfazed, Zach smiled at her and gave her back a quick caress. "I'll be back in a minute."

Lisette watched with trepidation as the two slipped out the front door.

* * *

Zach followed David several miles away to a meadow that was little more than a small break in the dense trees that covered David's land.

"I've been with Seth for thousands of years," David said without preamble.

"Yes," Zach acknowledged when David seemed to expect a response.

"I know pretty much everything there is to know about him. Which means I know everything there is to know about you."

Zach shook his head. "You may *think* you do, but you don't know me, David."

"I know you can be slain."

Surprise flitted through him. "Are you threatening me?"

"I may not be as powerful as you," David said, taking a step forward and daring to crowd him. "But trust me when I say that, if you betray Seth, you will never see me coming."

"Trust *me* when I say I will."

"I wouldn't be so sure. Even Seth can't always tell when I come and go. And, should I not succeed, I shall summon those who will."

Zach stiffened.

"That's right. I will broadcast your every movement to the Others until they come for you."

That was a threat he couldn't ignore. "You wouldn't know how to reach them."

"Oh, I know how to reach them. I've done it before; remember? When Seth lost it after his wife and children were slaughtered. And I can and *will* do it again, should you drive me to it."

A sobering thought. "You would endanger Lisette?"

"No. I would endanger *you*."

"Once they know what she means to me—"

"They won't touch Lisette. She's one of Seth's. And their fanatical determination to remain apart from the rest of the world and to stay off the proverbial radar will keep them from creating the chaos of violence that harming her would spawn." A chilling smile tilted his lips. "They'll leave Lisette alone, turn all of their wrath upon you, and will ensure you never see her—or anyone else—again. There will be no escaping them a second time."

Zach could see why the other immortals were reluctant to raise this one's ire. David could be a formidable opponent.

"Sheath your claws," Zach told him. "I won't betray Seth or stab him in the back or whatever it is you fear I'll do. I'm one of *you* now and intend to remain so for the rest of my days. Or for as long as Lisette can tolerate me."

David stared deeply into Zach's eyes.

What did he see there?

The dark Egyptian's smile went from chilling to friendly in a heartbeat as he took a step back. "Then we're good." Clapping Zach on the shoulder, he turned and raced through the trees toward his home.

Zach stared after him.

"That was scary."

Jumping at the sound of a voice behind him, Zach spun around and watched Lisette step from the trees.

"Yes, it was," a deeper voice agreed.

Issuing a squeak of surprise, Lisette did a one-eighty. Her mouth fell open as Seth stepped from the trees behind her. "How long have you been there?"

"About as long as you have." His features darkened with feigned disapproval. "Really, Lisette? Eavesdropping? *Tch. Tch. Tch.*"

Smiling, Zach shook his head. "Aren't you guilty of the same?"

"Yes," Seth said as he and Lisette strode forward. "But now that everyone knows I'm not infallible, I can get away with it."

Lisette laughed.

"Are you ready to do this?" Seth asked.

Zach nodded and gave Lisette a quick kiss.

"Be careful," she ordered.

"I will," he promised.

Her brow furrowing with worry, she stepped back.

"Let's shift now," Seth said.

"What form?"

"A hawk. Average-sized. Nothing that will draw notice."

Zach grimaced. Shape-shifting was a lot easier when you shifted into something roughly your own weight. Significantly smaller animal shapes were more difficult to maintain.

The worry on Lisette's face vanished in an instant when he and Seth shifted. Her eyes widened. Her beautiful lips stretched in a grin. "I so wish I could do that!"

Laughing inside, Zach leapt into the air and began their flight to the compound. *We could have teleported, then shifted when we were closer,* he commented mentally as he and Seth rode the breeze.

There's so much we can't share with Lisette, Seth replied. *I wanted to show her something we could.*

Thoughtful bastard.

Seth's laugh floated through Zach's mind.

It didn't take long. Zach marveled over how accurately the satellite images had represented the impressive compound. *Was Donald and Nelson's compound like this?*

Hell no. It was a cheesy motel compared to this place.

Movement on the training fields over which the two soared drew Zach's attention. *Is that what I think it is?*

Vampires training like military soldiers? Yes.

The vamps were newly turned and exploring the extents and limits of their abilities. They were also high on the power they now wielded.

The humans in their midst responded with both awe and irritation as the vamps' taunts and showboating increased.

Scuffles nearly broke out at least half a dozen times while Zach and Seth passed overhead.

They're already having difficulty controlling them, Seth said.

Zach agreed. *It must be why they're so determined to get their hands on an Immortal Guardian. They hope to discover what keeps immortals from going insane so they can prevent it in their own army. Power mixed with volatility is a disaster waiting to happen.*

Near the heavily guarded entrance to the compound, a vampire argued with a human soldier. The more the vampire tried to convince the human he was obsolete, the more heated their words grew.

"I can see in the dark, dumb ass," the vampire bit out. "You need night-vision goggles that cost thousands of dollars."

"Bull*shit* you can see in the dark. You just see *better* in the dark," the human retorted.

With preternatural speed, the vamp yanked the soldier's weapon away from him, aimed it up at the sky, and fired.

The bullet slammed into Zach's shoulder, damaging his wing. Unable to shift without blowing their cover, he tumbled to the hard ground.

Are you okay? Seth asked, flapping his wings in feigned panic before veering away.

Zach groaned. *Yes.* He peered through the tall grasses at the vampire who had shot him.

"You see that, asshole?" the vamp crowed. "Can *you* do that? I don't think so. Like I said . . . you're obsolete."

"Oh yeah?" the human retorted furiously. "Well, let's see you do that during the day!"

The furious vampire yanked the soldier forward and sank his fangs into the man's neck.

Vampire and human soldiers alike raced forward, some to break it up, some to incite more violence.

I think we've seen all we need to see, Seth said. *Can you teleport to David's place?*

Not without changing forms first.

Seth fluttered down and landed beside him. Brushing a wing across Zach's back, he teleported them to David's front lawn.

Relief rushed through Zach as he retook his usual form, instantly teleporting on the leather pants he had left in the forest several miles away when he and Seth had initially shifted. The burning pain in his shoulder began to fade. The bleeding, at last, slowed as the wound began to close. As long as he had to focus the bulk of his energy on maintaining another form, there wasn't enough left over to heal injuries, which was best not done until he was in his natural form anyway.

He sighed. Much better.

Also clothed, Seth motioned to the front door. "Shall we?"

Nodding, Zach followed him inside.

Tension thrummed through Lisette while she waited in David's living room for Seth and Zach to return.

Richart crossed to her and looped his arm around her shoulders.

She looked up at him.

"So," he said.

She arched a brow. "So?"

The room darkened and fell away as a familiar weightlessness engulfed her and she found herself teleported to the quiet room Étienne and Krysta had claimed as their own. Étienne lounged in a chair, waiting for them.

Lisette glared up at Richart. "You know I hate it when you do that." If she wanted him to teleport her somewhere, she'd tell him.

"We wanted to speak with you privately," he responded with a shrug.

"About what?"

The twins shared a look.

"How *are* you?" Richart asked at length.

"I'm fine," she said, puzzled. "Why?"

Étienne rose. "You're hiding something from us. You've been shielding your thoughts for weeks."

Lisette took a moment to ensure her mental barriers were well in place. "If you want to know what I'm hiding from you," she said, "ask Richart. He and Jenna both got an eyeful."

Étienne laughed. "I heard about that. Made me glad I can't teleport."

Richart grumbled something.

"So, what are you hiding?" Étienne repeated.

"That's it," she said. "That's what I'm hiding." And technically it wasn't a lie. Yes, she hid all of the things she'd learned about Seth recently. But she also hid her intimate relationship with Zach, because it was none of their business.

And because she had been raised in a time when such things were not discussed. Ever. They were kept private, a sentiment that had remained with her.

"If I opened my thoughts to you," she told Étienne, "you would be flooded with details of my relationship with Zach that I wish to keep private. You don't need to know all about our lovemaking."

Étienne grimaced and looked at his twin. "I can see why you asked Jenna to poke out your eyes. I don't even want to *think* about it, let alone see it."

Lisette rolled her eyes. "Then stop trying to read my thoughts. Your relationship with Krysta is almost as new as mine is with Zach. How often do you think about making love with her?"

"Constantly."

"Then there is your answer."

Again the twins shared a look.

Lisette sighed. "Just say it."

"Does he treat you well, Lisette?" Richart asked, his face grave.

She smiled, affection replacing exasperation. "Very well," she assured him. They just wanted to make sure history wouldn't repeat itself. "I love him. He makes me happy. And he would do anything to keep me safe. Zach would never hurt me the way Philippe did."

The two smiled, mirror images of each other, though she had never had difficulty telling them apart.

"That's all we wanted to hear," Étienne said.

"Then can we go back upstairs now?"

"Of course."

Zach followed Seth inside and closed the door behind them with a thought. David's house was still crammed full of Immortal Guardians and their Seconds.

Lisette and her brothers emerged from the darkened hallway on the opposite side of the living room. As soon as she saw him, Lisette raced forward. "What happened? Are you okay?"

Grimacing, Zach clutched his bloody shoulder.

Concern flooded her pretty face. Taking his uninjured arm, Lisette draped it across her shoulders and wrapped an arm around his waist. Had he been younger, he likely would have *needed* to lean on her. He had, after all, lost quite a bit of blood. As it was, however, he just reveled in her form pressed against his own.

He issued a faint moan.

"Come on," Lisette said. "Let's get you to bed."

Hell yes!

Seth cast him a reproving look.

Zach grinned at him over her head.

Rolling his eyes, Seth turned toward the dining room. But not before Zach saw him smile.

Zach let Lisette guide him a few steps toward the hallway, then noticed her brothers standing there, arms crossed over their chests, brows drawn down into V's. Sighing, he stopped. "It's all right, sweetheart. The wound is healing now that I've resumed my natural form. All I need is a wet cloth to wash away the blood."

She studied him for a moment, then nodded and stepped away. "Okay." Taking his hand, she followed the other immortals and Seconds who trailed after Seth into the dining room.

Admiring her profile, Zach saw her lips twitch. "What?"

She sent him a sly smile. "I knew you were faking. I just wanted to get you into bed."

Zach laughed.

As did those who had overheard her.

Releasing his hand, she detoured into the kitchen to fetch a warm, wet towel, then returned to him as everyone took his or her seat at the table.

Zach was pleased to see Ami sitting beside Marcus, their baby in her arms.

"So," Marcus said, "what did you see?"

Seth leaned back in his chair and swiftly filled them in.

Roland scowled. "Is this place going to implode? If the vampire mercenaries are attacking the human mercenaries . . ."

"No," Seth said, and Zach agreed. "Despite what I'm sure are other outbursts like the ones we saw, the higher-ups are managing to maintain enough control and order to continue to pursue their goal."

"Then we'll still strike?" Aidan asked, and damned if he didn't sound excited at the prospect.

"Yes, as soon as Chris has finished gathering his information and coordinating his Special Ops teams."

Chris rose. "I'll get started now."

Chapter Nineteen

Lisette tugged on the modified suit network employees had delivered to David's home the previous night. Her face twisted in a grimace. She had disliked it before. Now she hated it.

It fit like a diving suit. Tight, but stretchy enough to allow freedom of movement. The rubber had a rough, automobile tire–like texture. A bit smoother on the inside. But it still chafed.

Tug. Tug. Pull.

Was it thicker than before? It felt thicker than before.

Tug. Pull. She glanced at Zach and saw amusement twinkling in his dark brown eyes. "Laugh, and I'll kick your ass," she warned.

His straight white teeth flashed in a smile as he tucked throwing knives in the bandolier wrapped around his hips.

"Lucky bastard," she grumbled.

He *did* laugh then. He, Seth, and David (who, though not as old, could withstand several hours of sun exposure) were the only immortals who didn't have to don the special suits to fight today. The rest of them were stuck in this uncomfortable crap for however long the battle lasted.

The sound of Zach's laughter nevertheless lightened her

mood. "Just get over here and zip me up," she ordered with a smile and drew her long braid forward.

All she wore beneath was a bra and panties.

Circling around behind her, Zach drew a finger down her back, from her neck to the base of her spine.

A shiver rippled through her.

"How do you like the changes?" he asked as he drew the zipper up, careful not to scrape her skin.

"It feels bulkier," she complained.

When he walked around to stand in front of her, concern darkened his features. "Will it inhibit your movement?"

She rolled her shoulders, swiveled from side to side, raised and lowered her arms, did knee lifts, turned her head above the high collar. The Kevlar, or whatever the armor guys had added to protect them from tranquilizer darts, felt peculiar. "I don't know. Try me."

His wings tucked away, Zach swung at her with preternatural speed.

Lisette blocked the hit with her forearm and threw a punch of her own.

A flurry of hits and kicks ensued, all blocked.

"Halt," she called out.

Zach stilled, eyes glowing.

She grinned and shook her head. "You are so strange."

"Why?" he asked.

"You're turned on, aren't you?"

"Yes," he said, exhibiting no embarrassment, then shrugged. "Much like your brother, I admire strong women. Or rather I admire the strong woman standing before me. I don't really notice others."

"And now *I'm* turned on," she said dryly. A dozen supermodels could stand naked in front of Zach, and Lisette honestly didn't think he would pay them any attention.

Smiling, he leaned down to kiss her.

Her heart beat faster at the touch of his lips.

"You seem good in the suit," he murmured. "And I'll feel better knowing you'll have some protection from the darts."

"Me too," she admitted.

"I won't let you out of my sight, Lisette," he vowed.

"You aren't invincible, Zach," she said, leaning into him. "Don't lose your head, and I mean literally lose it, because you're distracted by whatever is going on with me. I need you."

"Don't worry about me. I'll be fine," he promised.

The assurance didn't dispel her fear.

Ten minutes, Seth spoke in her head.

Zach pressed his forehead to hers, his glowing golden eyes capturing her own. "I love you."

"I love you, too," she responded.

For some reason, the words sounded like a good-bye.

"Hooooooooly shit!" Ethan exclaimed.

My sentiments exactly, Lisette thought as she eyed the army of network Special Ops soldiers.

Chris had chosen the rendezvous point for Immortal Guardians, their Seconds, and the humans he commanded. They met several miles away from the mercenary compound, hidden by dense forest.

"What?" Chris asked as he spread a large map on the hood of one of many Humvees outfitted with a variety of mean-looking weapons.

"You think you have enough men?" Ethan asked, taking in the multitude of rough-hewn soldiers garbed in camouflage.

"This is just half of them," Chris responded absently. "The other half are already in place, observing the compound's perimeter."

Lisette looked to Seth. If even one man's presence had been detected, the mercenaries would know they were coming.

Seth must have read her thoughts. "None have been discovered," he said. "I monitored their approach myself."

"What the hell is that?" Sheldon asked, pointing at something atop the Humvee.

Chris followed his gaze. "A TOW missile."

Lisette's eyebrows rose. "And that?" she asked, pointing to a weapon atop another Humvee.

"Flame thrower."

Bastien stared up at it. "What's its range?"

"It can light up vampires two-hundred-fifty feet away," Chris said. "But, since it'll also light up immortals, we plan to use them primarily on the gate and on the grounds away from the main structures."

The automatic weapons mounted to the tops of the other vehicles, Lisette recognized from past clashes with mercenaries.

"Now," Chris said, pointing to an area on the map, "these are the training fields that will be active. Live ammo is used on the target ranges, so you'll face a lot of firepower there. The gates will be heavily guarded. Patrols walk the fence. There will be a changing of the guard in half an hour, so the soldiers on duty now will be tired and likely not as vigilant. Surveillance cameras are mounted on the fences here, here, and here, near the main structures and training fields. But they're sparse on the rest of the grounds. These red circles indicate where you'll find them.

"Once more, you'll find an ass-load of vampires in this building. The human mercenaries who work the night shift will be sleeping here in the building next to it. This over here is the armory. Anyone you let go in there will come out packing major weaponry. There's only the one door, and a hell of a lot of them are going to want to use it, so I suggest you park a couple of immortals in front of it."

"I'll do it," Yuri volunteered.

"Me too," Stanislav said.

Seth nodded his approval.

"Try not to blow up the building, guys," Chris said. "We could use the stuff that's in there."

Stanislav sighed. "You're forever spoiling our fun, Reordon."

Lisette smiled.

"The helos will have to be guarded. We don't want a repeat of what happened last time."

All eyes went to Krysta, who blushed a bright red. "I said I was sorry," she mumbled.

Grinning, Étienne wrapped an arm around her.

"That goes for the planes, too," Chris said. "We can't let *anyone* out, by land or by air."

"Richart, Jenna," Seth spoke, "you keep the planes and helicopters on the ground."

They nodded.

"Étienne, Krysta, and Sean, clear out the hangars," he continued.

More nods.

"Roland and Sarah, take out the vampires."

Chris shook his head. "That building is a hell of a lot bigger than the barracks Donald and Nelson housed their men in. I recommend you have two or three more immortals accompany them."

Aidan raised a hand and smiled. "Can I do it?"

Lisette thought it a little freaky that he seemed so entertained by all of this.

Seth nodded. "Aidan will do. He can teleport and is very powerful."

"Okay," Chris agreed. .

Marcus stepped forward. "I can take the building that houses the humans."

Chris shook his head. "No need. My guys can handle that. We'll also take out the humans on the grounds and those who remain on the training field. Lisette, if you'd like to give us a hand—"

"Lisette will be with me," Zach interrupted, his tone brooking no argument.

Chris raised his eyebrows. "And where will *you* be?"

"With Seth and David, killing everything that moves in the main building and torturing whomever I have to, to uncover the names of the immortals who betrayed us."

Silence.

Chris looked to Seth.

Seth shrugged. "I'm good with that. Marcus, why don't you join us in the main building? Edward, I want you, Bastien, Melanie, and Ethan to help Chris and his men clear out the training fields."

The five nodded.

"As for the main building," Chris said, pointing to it, "at first glance, it appears to be a flashy meet and greet. Lots of marble and granite. Nice foyer according to their Web site. But we couldn't get a clear infrared satellite image of what's inside, and a lot of bodies shuffle in and out of that place every day, so I think it's safe to say it's their hub. Their planning, experimenting, communications, and meetings likely all take place there."

"Not for long," David murmured.

Chris smiled. "On my mark, all cell phone reception will be disrupted and the landlines cut, but sat phones will still function, so keep your ears open and prevent *any* calls from going out. The electricity will also be cut, but there are backup generators here, here, here, and here. Seth, you and Zach have seen the place firsthand and can teleport pretty much anywhere on the compound, so I need one of you to use these"—he held up a cluster of grenades—"to take out the generators as soon as I make the call."

Zach crossed his arms over his chest. "I'm not leaving Lisette."

Seth took the grenades. "I'll do it."

"Walkies will still work," Chris said, "so some of the

mercenaries will have limited communication capability. But I've already identified the channel they use, so we'll know their every move and will swiftly locate and dispatch them. Seconds," Chris ordered, "park your asses behind the nearest bulletproof structure and guard your immortals. Shoot anyone with a tranquilizer gun. If your immortal is tranqed, use your walkie to call it in and cover them until we can get them out of harm's way."

"Should that happen," Richart said, "I can teleport the immortal to David's place."

"Good. The rest of the injured, mortal and immortal, should be taken to network headquarters. Our emergency medical team is standing by." Chris raked them all with a glance. "Any questions?"

Silence.

He nodded. "Seth, let me know when you and the other immortals are in place, ready to strike, and I'll make the call." He turned to his men. "Helmets on."

The network soldiers all donned helmets with chinstraps.

Seth eyed the immortals and arched a brow. "Well?"

Every movement broadcasting either reluctance or belligerence, the immortals dutifully donned the last piece of their protective suit: a head covering that resembled a ski mask and covered everything but their eyes. Even their mouths were covered, except for small breathing holes.

"Go ahead," Chris said. "Get it out of your system."

Grumbles and complaints erupted.

"I hate this thing."

"Feels like I'm suffocating."

"Is this damned thing thicker than it was before?"

"Yes, it is," Chris said as he rolled up his map. "Now suck it up and get moving."

Lisette smiled. Only Chris Reordon could get away with talking to immortals like that.

She raised her mask and started to pull it down over her hair.

Zach stopped her. Turning her toward him, he wrapped his arms around her and kissed her as if there were no tomorrow.

Lisette clung to him until someone jostled them walking past.

Zach raised his head.

Reaching up, she pressed a hand to his stubbled cheek. "I'll be all right," she told him again.

Nodding, he stepped back and watched silently as she drew the dark mask down over her face.

A peculiar feeling overcame Zach as he stood with the immortals and their Seconds in the shadows of the forest. Unseen by the guards, he and the others had an excellent view of the front gate.

As Zach studied the grounds beyond, his stomach felt odd. Not nausea. Something else. And tightness gripped his chest, his heart beating more rapidly than it should.

It's nerves, Seth spoke in his head.

Zach frowned. *I'm nervous? That's what this is?* He tried to recall if he had ever been nervous in the past and couldn't.

You're afraid for Lisette. Roland is the same way before every battle. He becomes even surlier than usual because he's terrified Sarah will be harmed.

Zach glanced at the antisocial immortal, but couldn't tell whether or not the scowl that often darkened his features had deepened.

Just breathe through it and stay sharp, Seth advised.

Zach took a deep breath and let it out slowly.

Lisette glanced up at him.

Seth was right. Zach *did* fear for her.

Okay, everyone, Seth told them mentally, *Chris is making the call. . . .*

Weapons slid silently from sheaths.

Seth vanished.

Wonk! Wonk! Wonk!

An alarm began to blare. The soldiers at the gate jumped and gripped their weapons tighter as they tried to look in every direction at once.

Boom!

Flames and debris seemed to fly from four different locations at once as Seth teleported from generator to generator with lightning speed and tossed the grenades. The alarm ceased. Mercenaries ran helter-skelter about the compound, trying to figure out what the hell was going on.

Zach saw two grenades skip across the ground toward the gate.

One of the guards caught the movement and looked down as the object came to rest at his feet. "Ah, shi—"

The explosion that followed hurt Zach's sensitive ears and left them ringing for a few seconds. Bodies and body parts flew. The gate blew open and broke apart.

Zach and the others ducked as pieces of metal embedded themselves like bullets in the trees around them. Then they raced forward, David in the lead, to confront their enemies.

From the corner of his eye, Zach saw Chris's network battalion surge forward in their armored vehicles.

Shouts rang out.

Mercenaries opened fire.

The front of the main building exploded into chucks of granite and glass.

David never slowed, just plowed right through it.

Zach followed, running in front of Lisette to take the brunt of the shrapnel as they dove inside.

More explosions rocked the building, sending dust and debris raining down upon them.

How the hell many grenades had Chris given Seth?

A quick survey revealed two main hallways off of which other, smaller hallways branched. Mercenaries poured into them all as Zach stopped to take stock, Lisette bumping into him.

Marcus joined them.

Wielding deadly katanas, David cut through the mercenaries on the right before they could get off more than a handful of shots. Marcus dove into the hallway on the left, his short swords Jackson-Pollocking the white walls with blood and gore.

Take the basement, Seth said in Zach's head.

Gunfire erupted directly behind him. Spinning around, Zach found Lisette peppering a dozen or so mercenariess outside the entrance with bullets from her Glock 18's.

Zach jerked as a mercenary bullet struck his arm.

Lisette did the same. *Okay,* she spoke in his head. *I'm liking the new suit better. It actually stopped that bullet.*

The mercenaries all fell. They must not have been wearing body armor while they trained. Either that or they hadn't been training and had only had time to grab their weapons.

To the basement, Zach told her.

Together they burst through a stairwell door and faced more mercenaries running up the stairs. Lisette's Glocks barked out bullets while Zach's daggers and throwing stars found purchase in soft throats. Bodies fell, cluttering the landing below them.

Zach heard more boots scaling the stairs. Grasping the railing, he leapt over it and plunged into a dozen or so men bearing automatic weapons, sweeping them down to the basement level and slamming them up against the door through which more tried to pour.

His blades flashed. Bodies piled up against the door.

Once all had been dispatched, he looked up in time to see Lisette jump over the railing.

Grinning, he caught her in his arms.

"Hi, handsome," she said from behind her mask, a smile in her voice.

The suits work, Étienne said in their heads. *At least the thicker parts do. I was just hit with a dart, but it couldn't penetrate the armor.*

"Good to know," Lisette said as Zach set her on her feet.

Bending down, he grasped the dead mercenaries by their shirts and tossed them up onto the stairs, away from the door.

The door burst open.

Bullets slammed into him.

Zach didn't even draw his knives. He just lunged forward and started snapping necks.

Mercenaries dropped like limp rag dolls. Others retreated down the hallway and into another, firing while they ducked out of sight.

Behind Zach, Lisette grunted.

He spun around, saw her sinking to the floor, and swiftly caught her up against him.

"Lisette?"

She moaned.

Panic threatened. *Not again!*

Kneeling, Zach searched for a dart and instead found a bullet hole in her mask just above her left eyebrow.

"Lisette!"

Jerking, Lisette opened her eyes. "What?" Pain streaked through her head. "Ahh!"

Zach batted her hand away when she tried to raise it. "Lie still." He pressed a large palm to her forehead. The pain eased, replaced by soothing heat.

She waited for him to withdraw his touch, but he didn't. "What—"

"Quiet," he ordered. "Brain damage is harder to heal."

Brain damage?

Oh. Right. One of the bullets had caught her in the head.

She saw a mercenary peek around the corner several yards away. Raising her Glock, she fired.

One less mercenary.

For good measure, she continued firing into the wall behind which he had hidden, a line of bullet holes opening in the Sheetrock as screams erupted in the unseen hallway.

She smiled grimly. *That's right, assholes. Bullets go through walls.*

Zach shook his head and removed his hand. *I take it you're all right?*

She nodded. *I'm good.*

He took her hand and kissed her gloved fingers. *Then let's go see what they're hiding down here.* Rising, he pulled her to her feet, then bent down and picked up one of the automatic weapons the dead soldiers had dropped. *How does this thing work?*

"What's happening?" a mercenary whispered.

"Shut up!" another hissed.

Hold it here and here, Lisette said, placing his hands in the correct position. *Then point it at your target and squeeze the trigger.*

He nodded.

"Why aren't they doing anything?" someone else whispered. "Do you think we got 'em? I can't hear—"

"Shut the fuck up!" the other hissed again.

Lisette had to admit, Zach looked good holding a gun.

A grenade flew out of the hallway, hit the wall, and bounced toward them.

In a flash, Zach teleported to the grenade and launched it back the way it had come.

"Fire in the hole! Fire in the—"

Flames and things Lisette didn't study too closely shot

out of the hallway. Acrid smoke followed, stinging her nose and making her cough.

She tugged off her mask.

"Leave it on," Zach ordered.

Shaking her head, she tucked the mask in an empty holster. "It makes it too hard to breathe with the smoke." She stepped into the hallway and took in the carnage.

"Hell," Zach said at her shoulder. "They must have all been clustered together, ready to rush us."

Every mercenary was down.

Beyond them, numerous closed doors lined either side of a long, narrow hallway. Each had an electronic key-code pad beside it like the vampire apartments down at network headquarters.

Zach waved a hand over one and opened the door.

Peering around his shoulder, Lisette saw a vampire manacled to the wall.

Arms stretched above his bowed head, he hung limply, knees not quite able to reach the floor. The bloodstains on the linoleum tile beneath him indicated he had been tortured. The limbs exposed by his dirty T-shirt and shorts were emaciated. The eyes that met hers, when he slowly raised his head, blazed with madness.

Zach silently ended the vampire's misery. They checked the next room and found the same. And the next. And the next. And the next.

Lisette didn't know how many they searched before they found something worse: a vampire manacled to a table with an IV in one arm, feeding him blood. A needle in the other drained him just as swiftly.

"Now we know where they're getting the virus," Zach said, the same disgust she felt evident in his voice.

"And how they've infected so many of their soldiers."

This vampire too had been stripped of all sanity. Torture and harsh living conditions tended to do that.

They found more of the same in the rest of the rooms and swiftly ended the vampires' suffering. When they finished, no heartbeats remained in the basement, so they returned to the ground floor.

Lisette's eyes widened as she glanced through the gaping hole in the front of the building.

Chris's men fired missiles at a tank the mercenaries had somehow managed to get moving. Another network Humvee spewed flames at vampires—willing to risk the sun in their attempts to escape Roland, Sarah, and Aidan—who stumbled out of the building that housed them.

A walkie-talkie on one of the mercenaries David had killed earlier squawked. Lisette holstered a Glock and picked it up.

"What are you doing?" Zach asked as they turned and strode down a bloody corridor, following screams and gunfire to the back of the building.

"Listening in." She tuned it to the channel Chris had designated as the network's, so she could hear the Seconds' and network Special Ops's chatter.

They stopped at the first hallway.

Empty. Or rather empty of anyone living. There were bodies aplenty.

They checked the next. And the next.

"David has been busy," Zach muttered.

"Where's Seth?" she wondered aloud.

Second floor, Seth answered.

"There's a second floor?" she asked. The stairwell from which she and Zach had just emerged had only gone from this floor to the basement.

Yes. There's a hidden stairwell at the end of the hallway on the right.

An explosion outside pierced her ears.

At the end of the hallway, they did indeed find what used to be a hidden stairwell. Seth had blown the secret. Literally.

"Can you understand any of that gibberish?" Zach asked, nodding at the walkie she had clipped to her belt.

"Yes. Chris isn't happy about how long it's taking to clear the grounds. And Richart and Jenna are having a hell of a time keeping the mercenaries out of the choppers."

She frowned. Who was backing them up?

Tracy? she called.

Yeah?

Where are you?

With Sheldon, backing up Richart and Jenna. Why? Do you need me?

No, just making sure you're okay.

Shit! . . . Yeah, I'm fine. These guys are really *determined! Are you okay?*

I'm good. Zach's with me.

I'm really starting to love that man. Shit!

Go fight. I won't distract you anymore. Just let me know if you need me.

Ditto.

The stairwell took them to a hallway much like the others. Seth stood in it, bodies all around him.

"There's something up here," he told them, looking around. "They seemed very determined to keep us from getting past this hallway."

"Us?" Zach asked.

David stepped out of a narrower hallway that branched off of this one. His face and form were splattered with blood, his clothing peppered with holes. Wiping his bloody katanas on his pants, he nodded to them.

"Shit!" Dmitry, Yuri's Second, shouted over the walkie. "Yuri's down! Yuri's down!" The *rat-a-tat-tat* of gunfire sounded. "I'm pinned down! I can't—"

"Noooooo!" Stanislav shouted in the background.

Seth staggered suddenly, as if the strength had left his legs. His face lost all color.

David dropped his weapons and lunged forward to grip Seth's arms and steady him. "Seth? What is it?"

Lisette's heart began to pound.

Seth looked . . . panicked. Stricken. *Something*.

"Seth?" David prodded.

Seth met David's eyes, his own wide. "He's dead. They killed him."

"Dmitry?"

Seth shook his head and swallowed hard. "Yuri. They took his head."

Stunned silence gripped them.

"Yuri!" They heard Stanislav bellow outside.

The building shook with a huge explosion. Sheetrock and dust fell from the ceiling.

More explosions followed, one after another.

Lisette threw her arms out to keep her balance.

"The armory's going! The armory's going!" someone shouted over the walkie amid static.

A final explosion that sounded like a damned A-bomb detonating, then . . .

Eerie quiet settled upon the compound.

Étienne! Lisette called frantically. *Richart!*

I'm fine, Richart said. *Jenna, Sheldon, and Tracy are, too.*

I'm okay, Étienne said at nearly the same moment. *But Yuri's gone. They decapitated him, Lisette, right before the armory lit up.*

Blinking back tears, she looked at Seth.

"Let go," he ordered David.

"You can't do anything for him now other than get the bastard who started all of this," David told him.

Lisette realized David was intentionally maintaining his hold on Seth to keep him from teleporting away and doing something rash.

The ground began to shake. Then the walls. The entire building.

She inched closer to Zach, who wrapped a protective arm around her.

"Seth," David said, demanding eye contact. "Seth, look at me. You can't lose control. Not now. Not when we're so close to ending this."

Cracks opened in the Sheetrock, crawling up the walls, splitting the ceiling.

A throat cleared.

Lisette's head snapped around.

Marcus stood at the opposite end of the hallway, face pale as he stared at Seth. "I think I've found what you're looking for," he said, and pointed to his right.

Lisette hadn't realized until then that the hallway was L-shaped.

The shaking stopped.

Features tight with fury, Seth shook off David's hold and strode toward Marcus.

Zach met David's gaze.

Both breathed a sigh of relief. That had been close.

David headed after Marcus and Seth.

Zach and Lisette brought up the rear.

Marcus stopped before a wall and motioned to two creases in it. "Another hidden door. I hear heartbeats behind it. A panic room, perhaps."

Seth waved a hand. A loud thunk, like large steel poles retreating, sounded. The door swung inward.

Zach stepped in front of Lisette.

A barrage of bullets emerged.

David waved a hand and telekinetically yanked the weapons from the hands of the eight men inside.

The leaders, oozing arrogance, weren't difficult to identify.

Four men dropped dead. Seth's work, Zach surmised.

And still the arrogance remained. A greedy glimmer even entered the eyes of one at Seth's exhibition of power.

Oh, yeah. These guys were definitely in it for the money.

"I wouldn't come any closer," one warned.

"I don't have to," Seth responded.

The man abruptly flew up, hit the ceiling hard, then fell to the floor in an unconscious heap.

One of the three left standing drew a tranquilizer gun and shot Seth with a dart.

Seth smiled. "You think it so easy to fell me?"

The mercenary frowned and shot him again.

"Oh, there's nothing wrong with the darts," Seth assured him. "They contain the right dosage. But no drug in your arsenal will affect me."

"Who are you?" the mercenary demanded.

"The last face you'll ever see."

Seth pounced, grabbing the mercenary by the throat and shoving him up against the wall.

The other two scrambled to get away and met Zach and David.

"Do what you will to them," Seth instructed, "but leave their memories intact."

David knocked his unconscious.

Zach was tempted to play with his a bit, but reluctantly did the same.

"You can't kill me," the mercenary Seth held gritted.

"Can't I?"

"I'm an international figure. Everyone knows me."

"I doubt they'll mourn you," Seth replied, no emotion in his voice. "Who told you about the virus? Who gave you the tranquilizer?"

The mercenary glanced at David, then Zach, and smiled.

He returned his attention to Seth. "I have information you need. As long as I don't tell you, you won't kill me."

"Oh, but I will. I only asked you as a courtesy."

The smug smile faded. The mercenary looked at Zach again. "What—?" His face contorted as Seth tore viciously through his mind and his memories. The man screamed, clawing his head in agony, pulling out clumps of hair. His feet kicked against the wall. Blood began to trail from his nose. His ears. His eyes.

Abruptly, his screams ceased, as did his heartbeat.

Seth dropped the mercenary's lifeless form to the floor.

Zach and David stepped back as Seth crossed to the two men they had incapacitated and knelt. He placed a hand on one's forehead.

Minutes ticked past.

He snapped the man's neck.

The man Zach had knocked out began to rouse.

Seth grabbed the man by the throat and lifted him up as he had the other. Pain tightened the man's features.

The golden glow in Seth's eyes faded. "David."

"Yes?"

"Take Lisette and Marcus and help Richart and Jenna keep the mercenaries away from the helicopters."

Zach wanted to protest. He didn't want Lisette out of his sight.

But just then, Seth dropped the mercenary and turned upon Zach a look he couldn't read. "Close the door behind you when you leave."

Zach glanced at Lisette. Brown eyes full of concern, she followed David and Marcus as they stepped out into the hallway and closed the heavy door.

The gunshots and explosions outside slowly diminished as the mercenaries' numbers decreased and the battle began to wind down.

The silence stretched as Seth studied Zach, his expression unreadable.

"Did you see who leads them?" Zach asked.

"Yes," Seth responded. "The mercenary leaders met with him shortly before we arrived."

Relief rushed through Zach. Finally! "Who is it?"

A pregnant pause ensued.

"You," Seth said.

Chapter Twenty

A sick feeling soured Zach's stomach. "What?"

"The man with whom these mercenaries met bore your face."

"That's bullshit," Zach snapped, his mind racing with the implications.

Seth held up a hand. "I know it is. Trust me. I've learned from recent mistakes."

"What do you mean?"

"I mean it was you, but it wasn't *you*. It was you the way you were before you met Lisette."

Zach stared at him, uncomprehending.

Seth shook his head. "You don't know how much you've changed since Lisette welcomed you into her home and her heart. And clearly whoever wants me to think you guilty doesn't either." He motioned to the unconscious man at his feet. "See for yourself."

Zach leaned down and pressed a hand to the man's forehead. As he did, a scent rose up to meet his nose. Shock shook him to his core. Fisting a hand in the man's shirt, Zach yanked him up and drew him close. He inhaled deeply. "Shit!"

"It's one of the Others," Seth stated, drawing the same conclusion Zach had.

"Yes." Zach straightened, the man still dangling from his hold.

"Do you know which one?"

"No." He thought furiously. "Get Ami."

Seth's scowl deepened. "I don't want her here. We don't know—"

"Do it, Seth. She may be our only hope."

Seth vanished.

Zach's mind raced, full of impossibilities that had somehow become probabilities.

Seth reappeared with Ami at his side.

"Ami," Zach said, "whose energy signature do you sense in this room?"

She cast a questioning glance up at Seth, then perused the room. She tilted her head to one side. "Yours. Seth's. Maybe David's."

"David was just here. Anyone else?"

Her brow furrowed. "I do sense . . . someone. Or the remnant of someone. But the signature is weak."

"Do you recognize it?"

"No."

"Is it strong enough for you to memorize? Strong enough that, should you ever encounter the individual again, you would know him?"

She closed her eyes. "I don't know," she said after a moment. "It's fading even as we speak."

"Memorize what you can."

She nodded. According to Ami, every living thing had its own unique energy signature. Once she was exposed to it, she could always identify it . . . which was how she had always known when Zach had visited David's home without Seth's knowledge.

Seth watched Zach in silence.

She opened her eyes. "All right."

"Thank you. Seth will take you home now."

"Can I see Marcus first?"

Seth shook his head. "I can't risk your being here if mercenary backup should arrive and engage us."

The two vanished.

Zach dropped the mercenary.

Seth reappeared. "In the past, Ami has had to be in close proximity to a person to learn his or her energy signature. How did you know she would be able to sense the Other even though he's no longer here?"

"I didn't know. I hoped." He motioned to the downed humans littering the floor. "Every time he comes here, the Other wipes the memory of his face from every mind here. With these few, he implanted the image of *my* face. That adds up to quite an expenditure of energy."

"And even when we focus our energy . . ."

"Tendrils of it escape and infuse the air around us. I hoped enough of that excess would linger for her to catch it."

"Good call. Have you figured out which of the Others it is?"

Zach shook his head, frustration beating at him. "I can smell him on the mercenary's clothes. He must have gripped the man's shirt in damned near the same place I did. But . . . we've occupied the same dwelling for millennia. Every room smells like every one of us."

Seth's face mirrored Zach's anger. "How is this even possible?"

Zach shook his head. "I would have sworn it wasn't. Not one of them has given even the *tiniest* inkling that he was losing faith in the path they tread, that he intended to defect. And a defection of *this* magnitude—"

"Is precisely what they all wish to avoid."

Zach still had trouble grasping it. "Straying as *we*—as you and I—did is one thing. We fell in love. We chose to *help* humanity. Protect them. Ensure they have the fighting chance they were meant to have before this virus came from who-the-hell-knows where and altered the playing field so dramatically. Straying as this Other has . . ."

"Is the complete opposite. Helping the mercenaries acquire the virus, helping them wage war with us and try to capture one of us to learn the secrets of our advanced DNA, helping them create an army of supersoldiers who can change the world—"

"Could do what the Others have feared *any* interaction with humans would do."

"Trigger an Apocalypse."

"And destroy us all."

Somber silence enshrouded them.

"Could that be his goal?" Seth murmured.

"To kick-start Armageddon?"

"I see no other end to his game."

Zach shook his head. "Seth, I'm telling you, none of the Others have ever evinced even a *hint* of discontent."

"None, including you," he pointed out.

"If I had succeeded in hiding my growing dissatisfaction with our way of life, they wouldn't have beaten me after I told you your phone was broken. They would have just assumed I had been there to warn you to keep your immortals in check."

Seth loosed a weary sigh. "Then this Other must be a better actor than you, because I just don't see an alternate explanation."

Zach's chaotic thoughts, which struggled to cling to denial, nearly drowned out the sounds his sensitive ears could hear outside.

Fire crackling. Boots trampling grass or crunching on gravel as the network began to clean up the mess and collect information.

Heavy vehicles rumbling across the grounds.

And weeping. Soft sobs. Jagged breaths.

Across the room, Seth's Adam's apple bobbed up and down as he swallowed hard.

"It wasn't your fault," Zach told him softly.

Seth held up a hand to stop him and turned away.

Zach watched as the powerful immortal leader bowed his head, dug the fingers of one hand into his eyes. There would be no consoling him. No easing the guilt that would eat away at him for not protecting Yuri. Seth loved each and every Immortal Guardian. He would take the loss hard.

"I've matters I must attend to," Seth uttered hoarsely.

Zach nodded. "If you need some time alone, I'll do anything you need me to."

"I appreciate the offer, but . . ." Seth turned his head just enough for Zach to glimpse his profile. "I'm glad you found your way to us, Zach."

Once more, Zach felt a growing kinship with him. "Thank you for showing me the way. Had you not, I never would have found Lisette."

Giving a slight nod, Seth opened the door with a thought and strode through it.

Zach followed him down the hallway, down the stairs, and through the hole in the front of the building.

Outside, the sun shone down on a dismal scene. Dozens and dozens of broken and bloody mercenary bodies littered the compound. A scorched foundation and scattered debris were all that remained of the armory. Black smoke clung to the ground like fog, burning eyes and stinging lungs.

Chris Reordon stood off to one side, issuing quiet orders to his men.

The Immortal Guardians, their masks removed, clustered together with their Seconds in the shade of some thick oak trees several yards distant. Husbands held wives. David consoled Yuri's weeping Second. Everyone, even the most stalwart and antisocial, bore tight jaws, red-rimmed eyes, and soot-stained cheeks marked by tears.

Clinging to Tracy, Lisette looked up as Zach and Seth approached. Both bore grim expressions.

"Go to him," Tracy whispered.

Lisette didn't argue. As soon as Zach stepped into the shade, she burrowed into the arms he opened to her.

The deaths of immortals during her existence had been exceedingly rare. And most had been faceless names to her. Warriors she had never met.

Yuri had been one of their family here in North Carolina. He had watched baseball games with her when Tanner and Ethan had refused. He had joined in their jests and defended them in battle.

That he had done so to the death today . . .

She still couldn't believe he was gone.

"Who did this?" Dmitry demanded. "Who started all of this? Did you find out?"

"Yes," Seth said. "Or at least we have a good idea."

"Who?" Roland asked.

"It was one of the Others."

Shocked, Lisette looked up at Zach, who nodded gravely.

"He planted memories in the mercenaries' minds to implicate Zach," Seth continued, "but I could tell they were false."

Sheldon stepped up to Tracy's side. "I thought you said the Others believed doing this kind of shit would trigger Armageddon."

"They do," Seth responded. "And it likely will, if he isn't stopped. I think it safe to assume that triggering Armageddon is his goal. The problem is . . . we don't know which of the Others it is."

"You've got to be fucking kidding me!" Ethan blurted, voicing the frustration Lisette felt.

Chris Reordon joined them. "Is there anything I can do to help you learn who it is?"

Seth shook his head. "I doubt it. These men have never been on the grid, and there has never been any record of their existence." He nodded to two network soldiers who walked past, carrying a heavy body bag between them. "How many of our men did we lose?"

Lisette had been so stricken by Yuri's loss that she hadn't even thought to ask about the network humans who had played such a crucial role in the battle.

"Seven dead. Nineteen wounded." Spoken unemotionally as Chris surveyed the damage. But Lisette saw the regret in his eyes. "Not bad, considering what we were up against, but still unacceptable." More lives lost that he would lay at his own feet.

"What should we do?" Marcus asked. He looked as disconsolate as the others.

A muscle leapt in Seth's jaw. "Go home. Regroup. Grieve. Tomorrow we'll—"

"Hey, guys?" a voice called hesitantly.

Lisette twisted slightly in Zach's arms to see Alexei, Stanislav's Second, limping toward them.

His face, pinched with worry, bore such a heavy coating of soot he almost looked as though he had smeared it with boot black. Speckles of blood dotted his neck and chin. More splattered his shirt and saturated his left pant leg.

All waited silently as he plodded toward them, half-dragging his leg behind him. He stopped a few feet away and regarded them all with what appeared to be fear. His throat moved in a swallow. Moisture welled in the eyes he turned on Seth. He started to speak, but couldn't seem to find his voice.

Seth reached out and rested a reassuring hand on his shoulder. "What is it, Alexei?"

Again he swallowed, and a tear spilled over his lashes. "I can't find Stan," he choked out.

Lisette tensed. She did a quick survey of the faces around her, only then realizing that Stanislav wasn't with them.

"I think . . ." Alexei rasped. "I think the explosion may have taken him."

Seth's hand tightened on Alexei's shoulder. Was he reading the Second's memories?

"He saw them. . . . He saw Yuri fall and took off toward him," Alexei said. "Then the building exploded, and all hell broke loose. I can't find him."

Releasing Alexei, Seth looked toward the remains of the armory, then turned his distressed gaze on the immortals. "Have any of you seen Stanislav since the explosion?"

Lisette held her breath, hoping someone would say that they had, that he had just needed some time alone.

But no one spoke.

Shaking his head, Seth stumbled back a pace.

This would kill him, she thought, losing two immortals in one day.

Swinging around, Seth strode through the smoke toward the armory.

Tears blurred her vision and obscured his form.

Dmitry crossed to Alexei and drew him into a rough embrace. Both men wept for the friends—the brothers—they had lost.

"Have your men help him search," Zach murmured to Chris over Lisette's head. "If the explosion killed Stanislav, there won't be anything left of the body." The virus would have seen to that.

Lisette's breath hitched in a sob.

Zach tightened his hold. "So look for his weapons," he

instructed. "Pieces of the Kevlar suit he wore. Anything that can give Seth the proof and closure he'll need."

Chris didn't just pass the orders along to his men. He went with them and helped them begin to comb through the still smoldering rubble surrounding the armory.

Thank you, Lisette told Zach, her throat too tight to speak.

Zach rested his cheek on her hair and rocked her gently from side to side. *I'm so sorry, sweetheart.*

Closing her eyes, Lisette let her tears fall.

Everyone bunked at David's place that night. All seemed to need to be near one another, though none knew what to say.

Lisette didn't think she had ever heard such painful silence in the large home. Even the baby seemed subdued, resting in Ami's arms and peering out at them with somber eyes until Ami and Marcus retired, taking her with them.

Lisette didn't sleep. (She wondered if *anyone* did.) She and Zach just held each other.

And when tears would occasionally slip quietly down her cheeks, Zach would cuddle her closer and make soothing sounds.

No one knew where Seth was. He had disappeared after Chris and his men had found a piece of Stanislav's mask and one of his swords, the blade having been broken in the blast.

While such had convinced the rest of them that Stanislav had perished in the explosion, Seth seemed steeped in denial. Buried by grief. Unable to accept two losses in one day.

Lisette didn't know how to help him.

David strode through dense trees and brush, letting the night sounds envelop him.

He couldn't seem to still his thoughts. Felt pulled in too many directions.

The immortals back home wandered aimlessly from room to room like lost children. For some, this was the first time they had had to cope with the death of an immortal friend.

Not so for David. He had lost many over the millennia.

It never got easier.

For Seth . . . David thought each loss was harder than the last, as if Seth believed he should have found some way by then to lend the Immortal Guardians true immortality.

Stepping out of the forest, David crossed a road and passed through what remained of a metal gate that creaked as the wind pushed it an inch this way and that on damaged hinges. The pungent scent of blood and death still hung in the air as though even the breeze could not usher it away.

David walked past decimated buildings and scorched earth.

Chris had already taken care of the cover-up. Large propane tanks had been moved in, the electric central heaters and stoves replaced with gas. Then the tanks had been ignited with grenades and incendiary rounds.

Disgruntled employees had been blamed for the death and destruction. Among the mercenaries' ranks, Chris had discovered nine men who had been facing criminal charges for actions taken overseas. All had repeatedly voiced their fury over Shadow River's distancing itself from them instead of defending them. So they had become the patsies.

Several of Chris's Special Ops men had posed as survivors who had *seen the whole thing.*

Since gunfire had been a norm on the isolated compound, explosions a little less so, authorities had not been alerted by those who had heard the battle, and Chris had had plenty of time to coordinate things. And little had remained for police and emergency crews to sort through.

David felt only mild relief upon sighting the tall figure

standing in the center of the slab of blackened cement that
marked the place where the armory had once stood.

Head bowed, Seth stared down at the charred foundation.
"Seth."

The eldest immortal didn't raise his head. "Why didn't I
feel it?" he whispered, the words filled with baffled despair.

David stared at him helplessly. Seth had *always* felt internally the death of an immortal, no matter how far away it
happened. "When Lisette, Richart, Étienne, and Bastien
were transformed, you couldn't feel Bastien's pain because
it was lost amongst that of the other three. Perhaps it was
the same with Stanislav's death. Perhaps it followed Yuri's
too closely for you to feel it separately."

Seth shook his head.

"Seth—"

He held up a hand. "Where's Zach?"

"My place."

"Where's Aidan?"

David sighed. "They're *all* at my place."

A full minute passed. "You know what I intend to do?"

"Yes."

"And you support me?"

"Always."

The word didn't seem to reassure him. "Send Aidan
to me."

David had known Seth long enough to recognize when he
needed to work something through on his own.

Nodding, David turned and headed back the way he
had come.

"She's beautiful," Lisette praised.

Smiling with motherly pride, Ami nodded. "Yes, she is."
Her gaze shifted to the large immortal sprawled beside
Lisette. "Thank you, Zach."

The three of them lounged on the cushioned floor of the training room while Marcus and Roland did their best to kick each other's asses. Both warriors grieved for their lost brethren. And, unlike Lisette, neither had felt comfortable expressing it through tears. So they worked their fury and hurt out as they always had: through battle.

"For what?" Zach asked, reaching over to tickle the baby's tiny feet.

"I know you helped Seth and David get me through childbirth and kept me from slipping away." She cast Marcus a worried glance. "I don't know what would have happened if you hadn't."

Marcus had already lost one woman he had loved. None of them believed he would recover if he were to lose Ami, too.

"I couldn't let you go," Zach replied with a smile. "You're the only one who gives me lollipops."

The women laughed.

"Have you chosen a name for her yet?" Lisette asked.

Ami nodded. "Adira."

"I like it," Zach said. "It suits her."

Ami's smile broadened. "Since she has both alien and *gifted one* DNA, we wanted a name that would represent both of her parents' worlds." She toyed with the baby's tiny toes. "On my planet, Adira is a shortened form of my mother's name: Adiransia. And, on *this* planet, Adira means strong, powerful."

Zach smiled as the baby grabbed his index finger and tugged. "She *is* that."

Lisette agreed. In more ways than one. Precognition was just *one* of the gifts they suspected little Adira possessed. "It's perfect."

Ami drew a hand over the baby's soft hair. "We thought so, too."

"Zach."

Lisette looked to the doorway and felt a rush of relief.

Seth.

None of them had seen him since the battle two days ago. "Yes?"

"A moment."

Zach gave the baby's foot one last stroke, then rose. "I'll be back."

Lisette nodded. "Take your time."

She thought David and Zach were probably the only ones who could reach Seth just then.

As soon as Zach drew even with him, Seth reached out, touched his shoulder, and teleported him away.

Lisette looked at Ami, who shrugged as Aidan strode through the empty doorway.

Zach contemplated his surroundings.

The earth around them curved upward on all sides into rolling hills as if he and Seth stood in the center of a large, grassy bowl. No trees rose from the ground to block the light beaming down upon them from a full moon. Not until one's gaze reached the tops of the hills. There, trees erupted into forest so dense that even Zach's sharp eyes couldn't penetrate it.

A light breeze combed through his hair. The knee-high grasses around them rippled like ocean waves, the swishing sounds they made reminiscent of the sounds water made as it lapped at the shore.

"Where are we?" he asked curiously.

"Neutral territory," Seth responded, eyeing the hills.

An odd choice of words. Why would they need neutral territory?

Then Zach felt it. First, a tingle. Then a genuine jolt of alarm as he detected the presence of the Others.

He looked at Seth in furious disbelief. "You sold me out?"

The last time Seth had taken him to an isolated place and

summoned the Others, Zach had been carted away and tortured. If they got their hands on him now . . .

He would never escape. Never see Lisette again.

Seth turned to him, his face inscrutable. "If I asked you to trust me, would you?"

Hell no, Zach wanted to say. This was too reminiscent of the last time. But, damn it, Zach had never been one to kick a man when he was down.

And Seth was about as far down as a man could go.

"Yes," he muttered, and was oddly pleased when the corners of Seth's lips twitched.

A flash of insight struck as Zach remembered something he had forgotten over the many years: He and Seth had once been friends. Long ago. Before Seth's defection.

"Hurt a little bit to say that, did it?" Seth prodded, the barest twinkle of amusement entering his dark eyes.

"Fuck you."

Seth shook his head.

One by one, the Others descended from the sky, tucking their wings in close as their feet touched the ground. Not all of them had come. According to Zach's quick count, they numbered only eight as they approached and took up what were supposed to be intimidating stances across from the two renegades.

When the breeze carried their individual scents to Zach, he did not find the scent he had detected on the mercenary.

Seth arched a brow. "Some of you appear to be missing."

"They elected not to come," Jared said. "They're too busy evaluating the shitstorm you and your little immortal superheroes just stirred up at the mercenary compound. Besides . . ." He cast Zach a sneering look. "We don't need them to bring him in."

"Are you sure?" Seth taunted. "He did escape you, after all, while under guard and being tortured."

The Others' eyes began to glow.

"It won't happen again."

"No," Seth said, "it won't. Because you won't be taking him with you when you leave."

The surprise and affront spawned by that comment was damned near comical.

Or would've been if Zach didn't fear this was going to end with him hanging in a dark cavern again . . . or worse. Seth was not in peak condition. Zach wasn't entirely confident he and Seth could keep these powerful men from taking him.

"What the hell are you talking about?" Jared demanded.

"I didn't summon you here to reclaim Zach and keep him in check. I summoned you here to inform you that one of your own is responsible for the shitstorm about which you just complained."

All eyes went to Zach.

"Not Zach," Seth corrected. "Someone else amongst your ranks."

"That's preposterous."

Seth's eyes flashed a brilliant gold as rage darkened his features. "No, what's preposterous is that, while you were getting your jollies off torturing Zach, one of you was a very busy little bee, buzzing in the ears of mercenaries, telling them all about vampires and immortals and the truckloads of money they could make if they followed in Donald's and Nelson's footsteps and used the virus to build an army of supersoldiers." Seth took a step forward. "One of you was stealing a sedative from my human network and handing it over to mercenaries along with detailed instructions on how to make it more effective, how to use it to successfully take down an Immortal Guardian."

"Bullshit."

"Whoever it was knew enough about the Others to try to make me believe it was Zach."

"It *was* Zach," Jared countered.

"He was in your custody, jackass, when the mercenaries miraculously gained their knowledge and began their quest!"

"Then you missed something the last time you fought mercenaries—"

Seth shot forward and gripped Jared by the throat.

When his brethren tensed, readying for a fight, Jared threw a hand out to halt them.

"I didn't miss shit," Seth informed him. "We killed *every-one*. *You* are the one who missed something. You were so busy sitting on your asses doing nothing that you didn't notice that one of you had lost his fucking mind and decided to do *something*. Something that could easily bring about all of the dire repercussions you fear so much."

"Zach—"

"It wasn't Zach!" Seth bellowed. Reaching into an inner pocket of his coat, he withdrew . . .

Zach frowned. What *was* that? A piece of cloth in a plastic bag?

Opening the bag with a thought, Seth shoved it in Jared's face.

Jared tried to jerk his head back, but couldn't with Seth's hand squeezing his throat. "What the hell are you—?"

"Smell it!" Seth ordered.

"What is it?"

"The shirt one of the mercenary leaders wore when he met with whoever has been feeding him information and egging him on."

Jared's struggles ceased. After a moment, he slowly poked his nose into the bag and drew in a breath. His gaze shot to Seth's.

"Smell familiar?" Seth asked.

"Yes."

Seth released him and stepped back. "Now smell Zach."

Jared looked at his brethren, then crossed to Zach. Leaning

in close, Jared drew in another deep breath. Frowned. Moved closer, his nose touching Zach's neck.

"I won't lie to you," Zach uttered. "This is making me a little uncomfortable." He really *wasn't* accustomed to being touched. Not by anyone other than Lisette.

Jared straightened.

Seth arched his brows.

"It isn't Zach," Jared announced, expression grim.

Mutters erupted among the Others.

"Do you know who it is?" Seth asked.

"None of us here."

"I already knew that," Seth retorted.

Jared shook his head. "The possibilities are few. We'll discover the malefactor's identity—"

"And nip this shit in the bud," Seth interrupted. "I lost two Immortal Guardians because of this asshole and nearly lost a third. I want him taken care of."

"We'll take care of him." Jared motioned to the bag. "Give it to the others. Let them get his scent."

Seth handed over the bag. "When you catch him," he said with a meaningful look as the bag was passed around, "do to him what was done in the past to those who transgressed similarly."

Zach looked at Jared.

He didn't seem happy about it, but must have agreed. "We will."

"I mean it," Seth said, deadly serious. "I want him buried so deep he'll never see the light of day again."

Jared nodded. "It'll be done." Reaching out, he grabbed Zach's arm and tried to start back toward the Others.

Zach didn't budge. No way in hell was he going to let them take him without a fight.

Seth held up a hand. "I was serious. Zach stays with me. He's one of *us* now."

Jared's face tightened. "We let you slide thousands of

years ago and have watched as the catastrophes you and your immortals foment continue to snowball. You just blew up a four-thousand-acre compound to cover up what happened when a second of our kind transgressed. Letting a third follow your example is unthinkable. Zach comes with us."

Seth took a step toward Jared, eyes still glowing gold. "No, he doesn't."

"I fail to see how you alone can stop us."

A slow smile curled Seth's lips. "Me alone? I don't know. I think I could give you a run for your money. But . . . I don't happen to be alone." He raised one arm and waved it in a circle.

The trees and foliage that formed a circle around them began to whisper with movement. Zach's mouth fell open as men and women with glowing amber eyes stepped from the shadows and moved forward to stand atop the hills. Hundreds of Immortal Guardians, hands curled around weapons that glinted in the moonlight. All of them ready to battle ancient immortals to the death, if necessary, so Zach could remain among them.

His heart began to pound with some unidentifiable emotion. His astonished gaze alighted upon Lisette.

The Others drew weapons and put their backs together.

"Really?" Seth asked. "Are you *that* stupid?"

"Why are you doing this?" Jared hissed.

"Because it's the right thing to do." Seth shook his head. "Don't you ever think about that? Any of you? Don't you *ever* stop thinking about what the *safe* thing to do is and consider what the *right* thing to do is?"

Of course, they didn't. The Others weren't going to ferret out the betrayer and take him out of the game because it was the right thing to do. They were going to do it to save their own asses, because they—like all intelligent people—feared what the Apocalypse might bring.

No. They feared what they *knew* it would bring.

The Others put away their weapons.

"And don't think you can grab him later," Seth added. "If you try to take Zach, everyone you see around you will be out for your blood . . . with me in the lead."

Movements stiff and radiating displeasure, the Others stretched their wings, leapt into the sky, and soon disappeared into the night.

As silence enfolded them, Zach stared at Seth. "How did you do it? How did you conceal their presence?" He motioned to their Immortal Guardian audience. "I didn't hear a single heartbeat. Didn't scent them on the breeze."

Seth offered him a weary smile that failed to reach his eyes. "Trade secret."

"One I hope you'll share someday."

"I may have to," Seth said wryly.

Lisette raced down the hill and joined them with a smile.

"How did you bring them all here?" he asked Seth as he wrapped an arm around her and drew her up against his side. Lisette had still been at David's house when he and Seth had left. As had Roland, Marcus, and several other immortals.

"Aidan, Richart, and the other teleporters helped me."

Some of whom had already begun to teleport immortals away.

"Welcome to the family, you lucky bastard!" someone yelled.

Seth actually laughed. "That would be Wulf. He was smitten with Lisette for a time."

Zach looked down at Lisette.

She shrugged. "I trained him."

"Did every immortal male you trained fall in love with you?"

"No," she said at the same time that Seth said, "Yes."

Laughing, Zach hugged her close.

Chapter Twenty-One

Alone in a room large enough to be a ballroom, Seth sat in darkness. No windows offered a moonlit reprieve. No carpets softened the cold stone floor beneath his butt. No furniture graced the room. The only ornamentation that prevented the cavernous room from being a large blank slate was an elaborate carving that whorled across the floor and up three of the four pale-gray marble walls. Hidden amongst the many shadows and crevices the massive engraving created were names, dates, and small notations made in an ancient language that would confound all but the one who had etched them. Only the wall encasing the door bore no markings.

Immortals and humans alike were forbidden to enter. Should any grow curious, they would discover—much to their frustration—that they couldn't open the door and peer within no matter how hard they tried. Though no visible lock could be found on the large oak door, any who sought to open it in Seth's absence would find the task impossible, even when force and power tools were applied.

This place . . . this room . . . was his alone.

Seth didn't know how long he sat there, staring at nothing.

Hunger and thirst were ever-present companions, but neither could distract him from his thoughts.

Self-recriminations and doubt pummeled him, grief urging them on. Beneath those, he heard the sounds of bare feet meeting stone and the faint rustle of clothing moving closer.

Déjà vu.

Through the open door his visitor came. Into the room. *His* room. The forbidden room. Unafraid of inciting his wrath. Padding toward him. Slowing. Hesitating.

From the corner of his eye, he saw small, pale toes curl against the cold stone. This time, instead of being nearly hidden by the frilly hem of a demure white nightgown, they peeked out from under black cargo pants.

Ami.

She touched his head, drew one of her small hands gently back over his hair.

Seth didn't look up. He couldn't.

She lowered herself to the floor beside him, her shoulder brushing his arm. Seated with her back to the wall, she stretched her legs out and crossed them at the ankles.

Quiet embraced them.

Long minutes passed.

"You should be with your family," he murmured. With her baby and her loving husband. Their immortal family in North Carolina. Not here in England, holding his hand.

"*You're* my family," she said. "And Adira's fine. She's downstairs with her daddy. She won't miss me for a while."

He hadn't even heard their arrival.

"David told us you haven't had any luck finding Stanislav."

Seth had spent weeks searching for him to no avail, striving to find some shred of hope that the blast hadn't killed him.

"Do you think, maybe, that he just . . . retreated somewhere to grieve? Alexei told us Stan and Yuri were as close as brothers."

Seth shook his head. "He would have told us, had that

been his intention. He wouldn't have wanted us to worry. And . . ." He fell silent.

"And?" she asked softly.

Seth swallowed past the lump in his throat. "I can't feel him anymore. Can't sense him when I reach out to him. There's just . . . a void."

Ami sandwiched one of his hands between hers.

Seth forced himself to continue. "Alexei must be right. Stanislav must have been killed, seconds after Yuri was, in the explosion. Otherwise I would have felt both deaths."

"I'm so sorry, Seth."

"I could've saved them. I could have prevented their being slain."

"No, you couldn't have."

"The Immortal Guardians know how powerful I am. I know some of them don't understand why I let the battles rage instead of merely killing our enemies with a thought and keeping the immortals safe."

Her shoulders moved in a slight shrug. "They're young."

He glanced at her from the corner of his eye. "Most of the immortals are hundreds of years older than you."

"But my *race* is ancient. As a people, we've seen more than even you and David could conceive," she said simply. "And we've learned from our mistakes. The immortals might not understand why you work so hard to maintain a balance, but I do. Their very lives depend upon it. As do the lives of humans."

"That doesn't make it any easier."

"I know."

Time ticked past.

"I'm so sorry for your loss, Seth," she whispered.

He nodded, eyes burning. Drawing her hand to his chest, he shifted until he lay on his side with his head in her lap.

Ami drew her free hand over his hair in long, soothing strokes, offering him silent solace.

Closing his eyes, Seth finally let himself weep for those he had lost.

"Before I'm Dead" sang through the kitchen.

"Ignore it," Zach implored, his mouth tempting Lisette's as no other's ever had.

She nipped his lower lip. "I can't. I promised Richart I'd always answer, remember?"

Groaning, he pressed his forehead to hers. His hands tightened on her hips, then relaxed as he took a resigned step backward.

Less than thrilled by the interruption herself, she took the call. *"Oui?"*

"Is this a bad time?"

She straightened, her eyes meeting Zach's as he, too, perked up a bit. "Seth. No, not at all. Hi." Ami had confessed to being worried about him. Even had she not, all knew Seth was taking the deaths of Stan and Yuri hard.

"Zach, is it a bad time?" Seth asked. "Lisette is too polite to say otherwise."

Zach laughed. "No. We were just about to have dinner. Would you care to join us?"

Lisette wouldn't have thought it possible to love Zach more, but—in that moment—she did.

"Actually that sounds good, if I wouldn't be imposing."

She smiled. "Our home is your home, remember? You could *never* impose."

Zach winked. "Well, I wouldn't go *that* far."

Seth chuckled. "I shall be there shortly."

Lisette set her phone on the counter and smiled at Zach. "That was kind of you."

Zach shrugged. "He's hurting."

Seth appeared in the kitchen and nodded to them both.

Lisette crossed to him and gave him a big hug.

Sliding his arms around her, Seth hugged her back. "What's this for?"

"For being you," she said. Releasing him, she winked and cast a sly glance at Zach. "And because they say jealousy makes the heart grow fonder."

Seth smiled, amusement brightening his haggard features. "I believe it's *absence* that makes the heart grow fonder."

She wrinkled her nose. "Oh. Really?"

Zach narrowed his eyes. "Don't even think about it."

"You know I can't stand being parted from you." She waved at Seth's coat and clothing. "Make yourself comfortable. I was just about to take the turkey out of the oven."

"Is that what smells so delicious?" Seth shrugged off his coat.

Lisette grabbed a couple of potholders and drew the enormous turkey from the oven. As she turned to set it on the stove, she caught Seth staring. "What?" she asked as she retrieved a carving knife from a nearby drawer.

"You cooked a whole turkey?"

"Yes."

Zach took Seth's coat and left to hang it on a hook near the door.

"Are you expecting guests?" Seth asked.

"No."

"I told you," Zach mumbled as he returned, "the woman is always hungry."

"I heard that," Lisette said.

"You were meant to."

Seth smiled, his shoulders relaxing.

Lisette motioned to him with the knife. "I'm serious. Make yourself comfortable. You can be yourself here."

He glanced at Zach.

"I think she has a thing for wings."

Grinning, Seth removed his shirt and draped it over a chair, then released his wings.

As soon as she filled all of their plates with warriors' portions, the three of them sat down to dinner: Lisette in the chair at the head of the table, the men seated across from each other on the bench seats.

She had to admit, it was heady to share a meal with two such incredibly handsome and powerful men, their dark, arresting wings cascading to the floor behind them.

They settled into easy, comfortable conversation, taking turns talking as they sated their hunger. During a lull, Seth removed a folded piece of paper from a back pocket and slid it across the table to her.

"What's this?" she asked, unfolding it to find it covered in tidy script.

"Exercises Aidan believes will strengthen your mental barriers."

Lisette's gaze skipped from Seth to Zach.

Zach studied Seth while he finished chewing. "Do you believe him?"

"It's how he says he made his own so impenetrable."

"How strong will her barriers become?"

"Aidan thinks they could potentially rival his own."

"Even though I'm so much younger than he is?" Lisette asked.

"Yes."

Her heart began to thump a bit faster. "So no one would be able to read my thoughts?"

Seth met her gaze. "Zach and I would always be able to if we forced it. But I'm hoping that performing those exercises according to Aidan's instructions would make it impossible for anyone else to read them."

"Even when I'm sleeping or don't have my guard up?"

"Again, that's what I'm hoping."

She looked at Zach. Would he then be free to share his secrets with her?

Zach clasped her hand.

"We will only be able to share our secrets with you if Aidan is correct," Seth warned.

"But you've given me hope," she said. "Thank you, Seth."

Zach nodded. "Thank you."

There was so much she wanted to know. She glanced at the paper. "Did he say how long it would take?"

Seth's look turned apologetic. "Years, I'm afraid, since you're so young."

Damn. "That's okay. I'll take it."

"Until then, it occurred to me that there is something you need to know now." He cast Zach a meaningful look. "But if I tell you, you will have to keep your guard up while you're around your brothers, Aidan, and any other telepaths who may visit the area."

"Okay."

"You can't slip, Lisette."

"I won't.

"And you can't sleep near any telepath who may venture into your mind before the walls you erect become permanent."

"I won't sleep at David's anymore and haven't spent the night at either of my brothers' homes since Zach and I started sleeping together."

"I'm sure they'll miss you, but this is important."

Zach began to stroke the back of Lisette's hand with his thumb.

Did he know what Seth intended to reveal?

"In light of Marcus and Ami's situation . . ." Seth began.

Lisette frowned. "You mean the baby?"

"Yes." Leaning forward, Seth braced his elbows on the table and laced his fingers together. "You need to know that Zach and I aren't infected with the virus."

She stared at him, uncomprehending. "What?"

Seth glanced at Zach. "We aren't infected."

She followed his gaze and met Zach's dark brown eyes. Dark brown eyes she had seen glow golden.

"But . . . your eyes glow like ours . . . and you have fangs."

"Actually, we don't," Zach corrected her. "If you think back on it, you'll recall that, even when Seth was at his most furious, you never saw fangs. Nor have you ever seen me sport them." And fangs, like glowing eyes, were involuntarily triggered by strong emotion in those who were infected.

"But you're so old."

Both men winced, but she couldn't worry about that right now.

"I mean you're both ancient. You're older than the damned pyramids!"

Zach continued to stroke her hand. "Yes."

"How is that . . . ? I don't understand how that could be possible if you aren't infected with the virus. What *are* you?"

Seth shifted, drawing her attention once more. "That we cannot tell you. Not until your mental barriers rival Aidan's."

"So . . ." She studied Zach. "You aren't infected."

He shook his head.

"That's why you wouldn't let me give you blood after you were tortured."

"Correct."

Seth sighed. "I fear we have a rough road ahead of us. The Others have successfully identified our enemy, but have been unable to locate him. I'm beginning to lose confidence that they can capture him and neutralize him. Zach and I may soon have to say to hell with them and take matters into our own hands. But, if he's strong enough to elude our detection and still bent on breeding chaos, things could get ugly."

"An understatement," Zach muttered.

Seth nodded. "I thought you needed to know that you shouldn't infuse Zach if he is ever wounded badly enough to lose consciousness."

"Oh."

"And, also . . ." Seth hesitated.

"What?" Lisette asked, wondering why Seth seemed uncomfortable all of a sudden.

"Ami is a mortal with incredible regenerative capabilities," he said at last. "Marcus is an Immortal Guardian. Together . . ."

Her heart gave a funny leap. "Are you saying I could get pregnant?"

"I believe it's possible, yes."

Lisette hadn't realized how much she wanted to have a child—*Zach's* child—until happiness at learning she actually *could* flooded her. She smiled at Zach and squeezed his hand. "We can have a baby," she whispered, awed by the possibility.

"No, we can't," he said, regarding her with a sad smile. "Because she's from another planet, Ami appears to have some resistance to the virus. A resistance that she passed on to the babe, protecting her. I don't have that."

Lisette's stomach plummeted. "You're saying the baby would be infected."

"Most likely, yes."

Fear struck. "Zach, we haven't been using condoms. What if I'm already pregnant?"

"You aren't. I can tell when you're ovulating and"—he glanced at Seth—"pursue other, ah, forms of pleasure—"

Seth grimaced and waved a hand. "She gets it. Spare me the details."

Lisette flushed.

The men laughed.

It was good to see Seth behaving a little more like himself again.

"Étienne is going to be a pain in the ass," Seth foretold.

"When is he not?" she quipped, earning another smile.

"He hates it when you keep secrets from him and will peek into your thoughts every chance he can get."

"Actually," Lisette said, "I think I've found a way around that. Marcus gave me the idea when he mentioned your poking around in his head a lot when he and Ami first got together."

"Don't tell me," Seth said, lips twitching.

"Any time I feel Étienne trying to nose around in my mind, I picture Zach naked."

Both men burst into laughter.

"He hasn't intruded in weeks," she crowed.

Their smiles lingering, they tucked into their meal once more.

"You know," Zach mentioned, "I remembered something the night we confronted the Others that I had forgotten for a time."

"What's that?" Seth asked.

"That we used to be friends."

Seth grunted. "*I* didn't forget. That's why I was more pissed than I normally would've been when I thought you had unburied Donald's and Nelson's memories and betrayed us." He chewed another forkful of turkey. "And it's why I'm here now." He winked at Lisette. "Aside from the beautiful woman at my side. I could never resist her company."

She blew him a kiss.

Skillet's "Monster" cut off whatever Zach intended to retort.

Reaching into a back pocket, Seth drew out his cell phone and checked the caller.

Zach smiled. "You changed your ringtone."

Offering him an insouciant salute, Seth took the call.

"Sì? . . . Dove? . . . Quanti sono? . . . Sono sui mio modo."
He pocketed the phone.

"Everything okay?" Lisette asked.

Nodding, Seth rose and drew on his shirt as his wings
vanished. "It's a bullshit call."

"What do you mean?"

"I've been getting a lot of emergency calls that aren't
emergencies lately from immortals who want to see if
I'm okay."

She watched him retrieve his coat and tug it on. *"Are* you
okay, Seth?" she asked softly.

"No," he replied, surprising her with his candor. "But I
will be." "Monster" rocked the kitchen once more. Sighing,
he took the call, then pocketed the phone. "This may take a
while." He vanished.

Zach twined his fingers through hers.

"Will he be okay?" she asked him, worried for her stalwart leader.

"Eventually." Pushing his bench back from the table,
Zach gave her hand a little tug. "Come here, love."

Lisette abandoned her chair and let him draw her onto
his lap. "Were you and Seth really friends once?"

"A long time ago."

"Do you think you can be friends again?"

"I think we're already on the path to it."

"No grudges?"

"No grudges. I'd rather spend that energy on more pos-
itive things." He pressed a tender kiss to her lips. "For
instance, have I told you lately that I love you?"

"Yes." Kissing him back, she looped her arms around his
neck. "But you're welcome to tell me again."

He kissed her longer, slower. "I love you, Lisette."

"I love you, Zach." Her pulse picked up as he slipped his
tongue past her lips to dance with hers. She tightened her
hold, her fingers encountering the silky soft feathers of his

wings. Drawing back, she met his smoldering golden gaze. "You aren't infected with the virus. You're immortal. And you have wings," she murmured, stroking one with light fingers. "You know what I want to ask you."

He nodded. "But you can't. Not until you've strengthened your mental barriers."

Seth had said it could take years. Lisette supposed years didn't seem so long when an eternity together stretched before them.

She rubbed noses with him. "I can wait."

"Until then," he said, urging her closer, "are there any other . . . curiosities . . . I can satisfy?"

She smiled. "Oh, I'm sure I can think of a few."